Shadowborn
Light and Shadow, Book I

By Moira Katson

Discover other books by Moira Katson:

The Light & Shadow Trilogy:
Book II: Shadowforged
Book III: Shadow's End

The Yeshuhain Chronicles:
Mahalia
Inheritance (*fall 2013*)
Origins (*fall 2013*)

Thank you to my friends and family,
whose support, encouragement, and feedback
have helped me to take this leap!

Cast of Characters

The Duke's Household

Catwin – servant to the Duke, Miriel's Shadow

Donnett – a member Palace Guard, who fought with the
Duke at the Battle of Voltur

Eral Celys – Duke of Voltur

Emmeline DeVere – younger sister of the Duke, Miriel's
mother

Miriel DeVere – niece of the Duke, daughter of
Emmeline and Roger DeVere

Temar – servant to the Duke, the Duke's Shadow

Roine – a healing woman, foster mother to Catwin

Members of the Royal Family: Heddred

Anne Warden Conradine – sister of Henry, aunt of
Garad; Duchess of Everry

Arman Dulgurokov – brother of Isra

Cintia Conradine – daughter of Anne and Gerald
Conradine

Elizabeth Warden de la Marque – cousin of Henry,
mother of Marie

Henry Warden– father of Garad (*deceased*)

Garad Warden – King of Heddred

Gerald Conradine – husband of Anne; Duke of Everry

Guy de la Marque – husband of Elizabeth Warden, father
of Marie; Royal Guardian to Garad

Isra Dulgurokov Warden – mother to Garad, widow of
Henry; the Dowager Queen

Marie de la Marque – daughter of Elizabeth and Guy

Wilhelm Conradine – son of Anne and Gerald; heir to the
throne

William Warden – Garad's uncle, Henry's older brother
(*deceased*)

MEMBERS OF THE ROYAL FAMILY: ISMIR

Dragan Kraal – brother of Dusan, father of Kasimir (*deceased*)

Dusan Kraal – King of Ismir

Jovana Vesely Kraal - Queen of Ismir

Kasimir Kraal – nephew to Dusan

Marjeta Kraal Jelinek – daughter of Dusan and Jovana

Vaclav Kraal – son of Dusan and Jovana, heir to the Ismiri throne

HEDDRIAN PEERAGE

Edward DeVere – courtier; Duke of Derrion

Efan of Lapland - courtier

Elias Nilson – son to Piter; betrothed to Evelyn DeVere

Elizabeth Cessor – daughter of Henry and Mary Cessor

Evelyn DeVere – daughter of Edward, betrothed to Elias Nilson

Henri Nilson – brother of Piter

Henry Cessor – courtier, father of Elizabeth

Henry DeVere – courtier, younger brother to Edward

Linnea Torstensson – a young maiden at Court; daughter of Nils

Maeve d'Orleans – a young maiden at Court

Piter Nilson – Earl of Mavol

Roger DeVere – father of Miriel DeVere (*deceased*)

OTHER

Anna – a maidservant in service to the Duke

The High Priest – head of the Church in Heddred; advisor to the Dowager Queen

Jacces – leader of a populist rebellion in the Norstrung Provinces

Chapter 1

I was an ice child, having the ill luck to be born early, in the deepest storms of the winter, when the drifts of snow can bury whole caravans without a trace, and the winds will cut a man open with slivers of ice. So they say, in any case, in the village in which I was born, the village huddled at the base of the mountain that houses the Winter Castle, the last outpost before the road winds west into Ismir.

And so, ill luck to me, and ill luck to my mother, for I came months early. The peasants who make their living in the unforgiving world of the mountains are notoriously superstitious, but it does not take superstition to make ill luck of a birth in a blizzard. With no way to call for a midwife, the birth nearly killed her, small as I was, and when it was over, she and I huddled together in the drafty little hovel, wrapped in the only blankets the family could afford. I, despite being undersized and weak, screamed to high heaven, and my mother, being half-dead of blood loss, slipped into a fever and spoke like a madwoman.

So it was that the sorceress Roine was called from the great castle itself, and she made her way down the steep steps, in the biting cold, to see me and cure my mother. Her poultices and teas—"Aye, and spells," the maids whispered knowingly—brought down the fever, and at last my mother's soul returned from its wandering in the lands of the dead, and came back to her body.

Roine begged my mother's leave to take me to the castle itself until I was stronger. The Lady had given birth not a month past, Roine told my mother. The wet nurse could take another child, and there was goat's milk as well, and Roine had all of her herbs. It would spell my mother, so she could recover as well. When I was healthy and strong, Roine would bring me back.

"And then what?" I begged to know when I first heard the story. I was six years old, and in the way of children, I had taken a liking to one of the maids, Anna, and had followed her on all of her chores, dogging her heels and clinging to her dress despite her sharp words to go sit by the fire. Finally, when she had told me that she had no time for a cuckoo's child, I had demanded to know what that meant. Anna, tired of my questions and eager to teach me a lesson, had been only too happy to tell me the story.

"And then," she said, leaning towards me, and smiling, eyes bright with malice, "your mother said not to bring you back. She didn't want you back at all, for she said you were a cursed child." I stared at her.

"So?" I asked. I had been raised by Roine, a woman I knew was not my mother. I knew that other people had mothers, but I had only the dimmest concept of what mothers actually were. In the self-centered way of children, I had never wondered much about them, and so I could not be entirely sure what to think about this new development—although I was somewhat offended, even at that young age, that someone had not wanted me around.

"Cursed," Anna repeated.

"Well, what does *that* mean?" It was my favorite question at the time. Anna did not think much of it, having been subjected to an entire morning of the query.

"Go ask Father Whitmere if you don't know," she said rudely, and I—not thinking highly of Father Whitmere—heaved a great sigh and went to go find Roine instead.

Roine sighed as well when she heard my question, and she set aside her spindle and lifted me onto her lap, where she ran her fingers through my fair hair as she talked. I leaned back and looked up into her beloved face, and I wondered, as I often did, why it was that Roine always looked sorrowful.

"Your mother did not say you were cursed," she said. "She told me that you were born to be betrayed."

"Well, what does *that* mean?" I demanded at once, and Roine considered.

"What do you think it means?" she asked, finally, and I shook my head so that my braid flopped about.

"I don't know."

"Neither do I." Roine kissed my forehead and set me down on the floor again. "Maybe it means nothing."

"I don't think so," I said stoutly. "How could it mean nothing?"

Roine had a peculiar look on her face. "One can always hope," she said.

"Did anyone ever say something like that about you?" I asked, for a moment she went quite pale.

—

7

"Not quite like that," she said. "Now run along, and keep out of the way. The Duke is coming, and there is much to prepare."

The Duke. The one terror of my childhood was the Duke, the Lady's brother. Her husband had died in the war, and the Lady had never remarried; she lived in this castle on the charity of the Duke, some said as a half-prisoner. I heard servants whisper that she wished to go back to the court, but he would not allow her—not after what had happened the last time. When they spoke of it, the servants would laugh in a way that I, as a child, could not quite understand, and once or twice it was murmured that Miriel was lucky she had her father's hair, her father's eyes.

The Lady might plead with the Duke—and, to be sure, there were always eavesdroppers to those conversations, and whispered accounts of her begging, and his cold refusals—but she would never defy him. No one defied the Duke. When he rode into the Winter Castle, it was with a great train of retainers and soldiers and priests, all wearing black and looking as grim as their lord. As if the soldiers were not terrifying enough, and the priests in their robes, like a flock of ravens, the Duke went nowhere but that he was accompanied by Temar, the man they called his shadow—and, some whispered, his assassin.

Worse, this grim man was the sole authority in my world. If the Lady could not make a decision, she would say, "I will write to the Duke." If someone would not obey, she said, "it is the Duke's order." If I misbehaved, from stealing a pastry to breaking a statue, the maids told me, "I'll tell the Duke on you," and I was told, in excruciating detail, just how the Duke had tortured a man to death once, or how he had put down a rebellion in the south, or just how he had won the Battle of Voltur, or how... until I ran away in tears.

Having a mortal terror of the Duke, who had most likely never noticed me at all, I had decided that the best way to avoid his wrath was to avoid being seen, and so I had become very good at that. I practiced by sneaking around after the maids on their chores, or the soldiers on their rounds. I knew where to stand so that the candlelight would not glint off of my hair as much, and I knew how shadows fell in doorways, and I knew how to move very quietly, and very quickly.

On his visit that day, the Duke took not the slightest notice of me. Nor did he see me the next time he came, or the next, or the time after that. For each visit, there were feasts in his honor, and Miriel, the Lady's daughter, was paraded out and shown off. Each time, he was said to test her, to make sure that she was perfect. Never mind that the little girl was as isolated from the world as a girl could be—she must still be able to dance, and sing, and dress as finely as any lady of the Court. The Duke expected perfection from her, it was said.

"So why does she not go to court?" I asked Roine, and she only pursed her lips and shook her head. "Is it the secret about the Lady?" I asked, thinking myself very clever. The servants laughed behind their hands sometimes at the Lady, and they talked amongst themselves, about something in her past—but no one would tell me.

"Don't gossip," Roine reprimanded. Her tone was harsh; Roine hated gossip. Other servants were fascinated by the Lady and the Duke, but Roine did not share their interest, nor did she approve of anyone who loved scandal.

After that, I was careful to hide my interest in the Lady's past, and the Duke's doings. I was fascinated by him—not seeking scandal, as Roine would think, but only observing, daring myself to see him and yet not be seen. The Duke did not care in the slightest about me, but each time he came to visit, I melted away into the background, and I later congratulated myself on my success at evading him. I saw no further than the next test, the next opportunity to—I thought—outwit this man and thus keep myself safe.

I had no thought that the Duke might have greater worries than the whereabouts of a serving girl, for I had not the slightest idea of what went on in the world beyond the castle walls. I knew that Heddred had been at war once, and knew that there had been a great battle near the castle itself, that the Duke had fought in very bravely; the guardsmen sang songs about it sometimes, very bloody indeed, and I was never allowed to sing them myself. I knew that some talked still of the war, and some of the guardsmen muttered darkly about Ismiri soldiers, but that was the way of things. Guardsmen muttered. It was to be expected.

But that was nothing to me. The life of the castle, now, was the only life I knew: I ran errands and helped Roine with her chores, made a nuisance of myself stealing pies from the kitchen, and learned to sneak as well as a growing child can. Years passed in the sheltered conclave of the mountains, and I grew from a dirty, disheveled child to an only marginally better-behaved young woman. Being wholly unmarriageable by birth, having no standing with any family in the village, and being no proper part of the Lady's retinue, I was given leave to wear britches, to run around as carefree as any young lad, and to get into scrapes with the servant boys.

I could laugh, now, to think on such a simple life: no intrigue beyond distracting the cook, no lies beyond covering up the grass stains on my tunic. But it was all I knew; we were isolated from the machinations of the Court, from news of the world. I lived my life as a peasant indeed, seeing no further than the next meal, or the next terrifying visit from the Duke. He was an organized man, was the Duke, arriving every three months, to the day, to inspect his lands, his keep, and his niece.

And then, late in my thirteenth year, the Duke came for an unexpected visit. That day, as every when Roine told me that the Duke would be arriving, I felt my stomach turn over. The Duke was coming to the Castle. He would arrive in a great clatter in the courtyard, and his retinue would follow after. First would come his hand-picked retainers: any fellow lords and his priest, his two guards—and the Shadow. Then would come the soldiers, horses lathered from the climb up the winding steps to the Castle.

The Duke would not dismount until he was surrounded by his men, and while he waited, his eyes would sweep from one side of the courtyard to the other, as if even here he was looking to scent out traitors to the crown, and every person there would look away to avoid meeting his eyes. No one was to be in the courtyard when the Duke appeared, save the Lady and her daughter, the hostlers, and the guards—and no one in their right mind disobeyed the Duke.

But that day, I wondered foolishly if I was so good at being unseen that I could stand in the courtyard and be invisible to the man. At the mere thought of it, I was gripped with excitement, such a mix of daring and fear that I felt my stomach twist as if I would be ill, but all the day long I could not keep from wondering: could I, little sneak that I was, creep into the courtyard where the Duke was waiting on his horse, and he would not see me?

As much as I could, I loitered in the courtyard. I took messages from the soldiers, and I brought them their lunch. I dawdled in the shadows by the steps up to the parapet, I snuck behind the barrels at the walls. I made a bet with myself, and with Tomas, the baker's boy, that I could creep from the stairs at the back of the courtyard, to the barrels at the front without any of the Duke's retinue ever seeing me.

In the end, that was easy enough. I thought I had timed my errands with care, but I was in the courtyard when the shout went up, and the soldiers pounded across the yard to lift the portcullis and let the Duke in. Like a frightened rabbit, I shot into the corner of the courtyard and huddled in the shadow of the stair. It was too soon, I was not ready; suddenly I was afraid that I had made a terrible mistake.

The Duke's big warhorse was the first into the yard, sweat glistening on its night-black flanks, and the Duke thundered almost to the great doors before he pulled up sharply. As I saw his head turn, I shrank further back, hoping against hope that the stone could swallow me whole and keep me hidden.

I was saved only by the great double doors swinging open. Forgetting my fear for a moment, I craned forward to look, for I knew the Lady would appear, and raised in the servants quarters as I had been, I had never seen her close to me before. Dinner without the Duke and his retinue was a quiet affair, and I would never have been chosen to serve.

Now I had the opportunity to watch her. I thought that she was the most beautiful woman I had ever seen; she was dressed in blue like the sky, with her shining pale hair piled below a tall headdress. She curtsied to the Duke so gracefully that I could scarcely believe she was human. She moved like a whisper, she moved like a dream, and trailing in her wake came a girl with hair the color of darkest night.

That was the first time I ever saw Miriel up close. She was my age—indeed, born a month to the day before me, sheltered from the blizzards by the thick walls of the castle—but there was a world of difference between the two of us. As soon as I had been weaned, I had been sent back to Roine's care, in a drafty tower far from Miriel's cozy nursery. Never would the Lady have allowed her precious daughter, born of a noble father, to be raised with a servant's child. The Lady might have been born a merchant girl, but she was proud of her noble marriage, and she considered herself and her daughter far above the companionship of servants. Miriel had been raised in almost total seclusion, given the company only of ladies' maids, while I had run wild around the castle since I was old enough to walk.

Now my skin was browned with grime and sun, and Miriel's skin was the same perfect ivory as her mother's. My hair had darkened from the white-blonde of childhood to the half-brown, half-blonde nothing color of the hill people, and Miriel's hair was a tumble of gleaming curls the color of ebony. My eyes were the same grey as the storm clouds that crept slowly over us in the winter, weighted down with their bellies full of snow, and Miriel's eyes—I could see even from this distance—were the same color as sapphires, a deep blue so beautiful I ached to stare into them. And where Miriel wore a version of her mother's gown, a fine blue silk with slashing on the sleeves, I wore boy's clothes, a shirt that was too large and pants held up with a frayed belt.

I disliked the girl on sight.

But there was no time to think: the moment had come to move: the Duke's retinue was assembled, and the men were dismounting, handing their horses off to the hostlers who moved amongst them. I felt a terror like I had never felt before in my life, and although I wanted nothing more than to curl into the corner and hope desperately that they would go away, I felt myself began to creep along the stone wall. I moved slowly, a shadow amongst the flickering shadows of the evening, careful of where I moved and where I stopped, and in what seemed both like an eternity and only a half a moment, I was crouched behind the barrels at the front of the courtyard.

That was where I erred. The bet had been too easy, I decided. Why, I could sneak anywhere. The guards said I moved like a little cat. Tomas would be impressed that I had made good on the dare, but I knew I could do better: I could steal the dagger from the soldier who had just walked over to stand at the edge of the formation.

Breathless, heart pounding, I eased forward in a half crouch, my leg muscles screaming. Closer I crept, and closer. The Lady and the Duke were speaking formalities, but I had a little time still. Closer...

I stretched out my fingers for the dagger—

And nearly screamed with the speed with which the soldier's hand clamped down on mine. When he twisted my wrist and brought me down in front of him, I did scream. My arm was on fire. I looked up into his black eyes and saw that I had chosen for my target not a soldier, not one of the rank and file of the Duke's guard, but instead Temar, the Duke's fabled assassin himself.

Chapter 2

There was a moment of horrified silence, and then I heard myself whimper in pain. Worse, I heard the clank of the Duke's boots on the cobblestones and in my terror, I felt tears seep out of my eyes. Still, everyone was silent. Everyone was horrified.

Everyone save Miriel, who let out a giggle—it could only have been her who laughed so beautifully. I tossed my head up to look at her, angrier than I could remember having been in my short life, and my chin was seized by the Duke himself, my face wrenched about so I could look him in the face. It was an honor I could have done without.

"What," he said, in a voice as chill as the winter air, "do you think you are doing?"

"She was trying to steal my dagger," the assassin offered dryly.

The Duke's hand closed around my throat. "Did you think to kill me, whores-get?" His fingers tightened, and stars burst across my vision. I tried to gasp a denial, but could not make out the words.

It was Temar who saved me. He laughed. "This child? An assassin?" No one else could have laughed at the Duke and lived, but Temar was different. He was the Duke's Shadow, and I would learn later that the Duke trusted Temar like he trusted no one else, even his own family.

Temar was still laughing. "No, my Lord, this is just a servant. But I did not see her until she was behind the barrels there, and I am certain she was not there when I came in. She moves very quietly." His voice dropped, so that the soldier next to him could not have heard it. Even I, pinioned between the two of them, could barely make out the words. "I would say she moves like a shadow. Wouldn't you, my Lord?"

They stared at each other for a moment, then the Duke looked down at me. He took his time to stare at me, and the moment stretched. I could not move, frozen by the pain in my shoulder and the Duke's grip on my throat. I stared at him like a snared beast.

His smile, when it broke across his face, was the single coldest thing I had ever seen in my life. I shivered convulsively.

"I would say that," the Duke agreed. "Like a shadow."

Within an hour, I was standing in the Lady's private receiving room, awed into sullen silence. I had been soaped and scrubbed and rinsed, dunked under the water until I thought I might drown. Anna had been the one to yank the tangles out of my wet hair with a comb, and braid it so tightly that I could scarcely move my face. As a last effort to make me seem more like a respectable servant and less like a grimy orphan, I had been dressed in an old gown found in a linen closet, free of stains but smelling musty.

"I don't like this," the Lady complained. "Why her?"

"Why me what?" I asked, my head coming up. She narrowed her eyes at me.

"You will speak when spoken to," she said coldly. I dropped my eyes back to the floor, biting my lip against a retort, and so I did not see her face as she said,

"She's practically a street urchin. She has no manners—she is no fit company for a Lord's daughter. Why not a noble girl?"

I could hear the Duke's impatience. "I will not explain this again."

"But—" He must have gestured to her, for she fell silent. I peeked out of the corner of my vision, and saw Temar watching me closely. I would have been afraid, but he gave a half-smile, a conspirator's smile, and I felt oddly cheered.

My cheer disappeared abruptly when the Duke said, "Look at me, girl."

My head jerked up. I stared at him. "What's your name?"

"Catwin."

"Who're your parents?"

"Dunno," I said sullenly. The Duke's eyes flashed.

"You will speak properly when spoken to by a noble." He sat back and waited until I muttered, "I don't know," and continued to wait until I added, "Sir."

"That's better." He considered. "Why do you not know?"

"Roine took me in when I was a baby. Sir." It seemed an unimportant piece of information to me, but the Duke's eyebrows shot up.

"Roine? The sorceress?"

"She's a healer," the Lady interjected. "I'd have no unnatural dealings in my household."

"Be quiet," the Duke said, absently. He had leaned back in his chair and was studying me, tapping one finger against his mouth. "What do you know of politics, girl?" I stared at him mutely. I did not even know what the word meant. "Do you know who your king is?" the Duke asked. I shook my head. All I knew of the King was that he was the Boy King, young and sick, and he lived far away in the East somewhere. "Do you know the family of your Lady?" Again, I shook my head. "Can you read, child?" the Duke was beginning to sound impatient. I shook my head, wide-eyed, and he sighed. "Ignorant as a pig-herder."

"She can be taught," Temar said pacifically. He looked at me. "Child, how many rooms are there in the Castle?"

"Four hands and three fingers. And the courtyard."

"How many guard towers?" I held up five fingers.

"And the one down the hill," I volunteered. "It's carved into the rock so you wouldn't see it, but you can hide there and there's a chain to ring the alarm bells at the castle."

"How do you know that?" Temar asked. He had leaned forward, resting his elbows on his knees, and he was staring at me.

"I went exploring one day and I found it through the tunnels."

"Interesting. If you needed to hide two people in the castle, where would you do it?"

I considered this question.

"There's a tunnel that goes down into the rock."

"What if someone found you?" Temar asked. "How would you escape them?"

I shook my head at him. "No one would find us. I'm the only one who knows my way down there."

"You can never assume that you are the only one with knowledge," Temar said seriously. His face was very grave. I stared at it, and found myself surprised by how young he was, his face smooth and unlined in contrast to the Duke's grizzled scowl. It was a color I had never seen as skin before, a warm brown like chestnuts, browner even than my skin had been from sun and dirt before my forced bath. "If some other person had explored those caverns, they could find you. And then you would have nowhere to run, would you?"

15

"No," I admitted grudgingly. I knew I had given the wrong answer, and for some reason I knew that I did not want to look stupid. Not in front of the Lady, whom I had found I hated; not in front of the Duke, who terrified me; most of all, not in front of Temar, whose eyes were so unexpectedly kind.

"There are two main things to consider when choosing a hiding place," Temar said. "First, you must choose a place that no one will think to look. Second, you must have a plan for escape if you are found." I looked up at him, and found him watching me steadily. "Can you remember that, Catwin?"

"Choose a place no one will think to look, and have a plan to escape," I repeated promptly. I wanted to make him proud, and I flushed when I saw him smile.

The Duke snorted; he was clearly tired of this interlude. "Listen, girl," he said, and the moment was broken. I looked over at him. "Temar thinks you can be taught. I have my doubts. So. You will stay here until my next visit. Lady Miriel's tutors will try to teach you the rudiments of a noble's education: that means reading, writing, geography, history—"

"Miriel's tutors?" the Lady interrupted. The Duke had only to look at her for her to close her mouth, but her eyes still blazed.

"You will learn all that you can—" his tone indicated that he did not think this would be much "—and when I return, I will be the one to test your knowledge. If I am impressed with your progress, you will study with Miriel for the next year, and accompany her when she leaves for Court. If not, you will go back to scrabbling in the mud. Is that clear?" His eyes bored into me. I wondered if this was a nightmare.

"Yes, sir." He smiled; I was rapidly coming to the conclusion that he smiled for the express purpose of terrifying people.

"I do not like to be disappointed, Catwin. Be warned."

So eager was I to be gone from his cold stare, and the Lady's anger, that I hardly spared a smile for Temar as I bobbed a bow and ran out of the room. I dragged the leather bindings out of my hair and combed it free as soon as I was gone, shaking my head around to feel the freedom of movement again. Anna pursed her lips when she saw me, but said no more, only helped me out of my borrowed gown and into a tunic and breeches once more.

They were new, the fabric soft to the touch and not a patch to be seen. There were boots of supple leather, to go over thick woolen socks. I had never had such finery in my life; my fingers traced the embroidery of the Duke's crest on my armband.

"Why do I get new clothes?" I asked Anna.

"Hush," she said shortly, and she braided my hair back, just as tightly.

"Ow!"

"Be still. Act like a young lady for once." She would say no more, and I left her to go find Roine, fear beating in my temples, making my pulse pound. It was sharp terror, the fear of looking into the Duke's eyes, and confusion, the fear of some new world to which I should be a part—and to which the Lady believed I should not belong. And it was something softer, the sense that the world was changing, and I could not know where it would settle.

Awkward in my new boots, I clomped up the stairs to Roine's tower, tugging at my braid with one hand. As I approached the door, I heard voices, and I stopped. After a moment's hesitation, I slipped off my boots and carried them, and I crept up the stairs to hover outside the door.

"But why?" It was a man's voice, smooth and persuasive.

"Because I am her guardian, and I say so!" It was Roine's voice. "Because I know her place is here, where she is safe."

There was a pause. "I think you know that she will be safe nowhere," the man said, and I recognized his voice; it was Temar. "Not one such as her. You have only to look at her to see it. And I hear there are rumors about her. Rumors about prophecies."

"Her mother cast her out," Roine explained wearily. "She said that Catwin was born to be betrayed." I frowned in the darkness. We had not spoken of the prophecy, she and I, since my childhood. I had forgotten it, the whole castle had forgotten it. Roine had not.

"Interesting," Temar said, and for all his city drawl, he seemed to mean it. Then he said, thoughtfully, "Do you know, I think you have only half the prophecy. Why, anyone could say they had been betrayed, if they lived long enough. Are you sure there was no more to it?"

"That's all there is," Roine said impatiently. "But do you not see why I would keep her here? Here, a betrayal is nothing—a young man's promise, perhaps. But at court...."

"Fate will pull her where it wills, regardless of your doings. And the fates do not take kindly to those who meddle. Mistress, you see it as well as I do. She is a fate-touched child, and you must know that she was born to more than this. You know she will seek it out one day. No, you cannot keep her safe by keeping her here."

"She will be safer here than at court! Nobles playing their games, and a rebellion against the crown—and you would have me send her to the center of it all! No. Perhaps there is no sheltering her, but I may at least try."

"You would not be prevented from doing so—the Duke would have you accompany us when we leave." There was a silence, and then Temar's voice dropped. I crept closer. "You could still look after her. And I would look out for her, and all of her tutors. You know that even the Duke would, in his way."

There was a pause, and then Temar said, his voice tinged with something I could not name, "You're very well informed for a healer at the edge of the Kingdom. The rebellion is letters and murmurs in taverns. It can never come to anything. Whoever told you of this rebellion, you should tell them that the Duke won a battle against the army of Ismir—and he will not hesitate to march south in the King's defense. But no matter." I could tell from his voice that he was smiling, but I did not think it was a nice smile. "Have Catwin prepared to leave in a year's time. I do not think she will fail at her lessons three months hence."

"You must tell your master…" Roine's defiance was weak, and Temar spoke over her.

"You know that you cannot prevent this." He raised his voice, "Come out of hiding, little one." I froze. He could not have heard me, could he?

"Catwin." Roine sounded weary. "Come out, child."

Shamefaced, I opened the door and stepped into the room. I knew that I should not have been listening, but I could not contain my curiosity.

"What were you talking about?"

"Your safety," Temar said. "Roine only wants to make sure you are safe, little one."

"And Temar has assured me that you will be," Roine said.

I looked from one to the other of them, and marveled at the strange world of grown-ups. They were telling a story, a story that fit with the words I had heard, and yet it was not the right story. Only a moment ago, they had been fighting; I was sure that what I had heard was a fight. Yet now there was no crack in their unity, not a flicker in their expressions to betray the lie.

Later, I would remember that moment, the concern on Roine's face and the easy smile on Temar's. I would remember that although their expressions fit with their story, their eyes were a blank as polished jet, and I would think that perhaps I should have known the tell-tales of betrayal hanging in the air.

But how could I have known? Here was the woman who stood in a mother's place for me, the woman who had fed and clothed and nurtured me all my life. Here was Temar, the young man who had singled me out and made something special of me and defended me to the Duke, the man for whom I had the easy adoration of a young child. How could I have suspected either of them—I, who knew nothing of betrayal and intrigue, who could not have dreamed the loyalties they held?

And so I, foolish child that I was, put it out of my head, especially when Temar bent forward to look into my eyes.

"Catwin, I have a task for you," he said, and he smiled. "A little test, just between the two of us."

"What is it?" I piped, as if it mattered. As if I would not have said yes to anything he asked of me. I took a moment to drink in the details of his face: he was clean-shaven, with a smooth line to his jaw, and dusky-skinned. His hair was cut short, and it fell fine and soft around his face, as dark a brown as hair could be without being black. His eyes were a true black, set above high cheekbones.

"I want you to follow the Duke's party every day that we are here," he said, and he smiled. "I want to you to learn as much as you can, and every night I will come and ask you what you have seen and what you have heard. You must not let anyone notice you as you do this." Roine drew a breath, as if she would speak, but when I looked to her she only smiled at me; it did not reach her eyes.

"But why?" I asked. "You know everything the Duke does, you go with him everywhere."

"Yes, that's true. But I want to see what you can learn. Try to make sure that even I do not notice you." I swallowed down a multitude of fearful questions, and nodded. Temar smiled at me. "Well, then, I will be back tomorrow. Good night, Catwin. Good night, Mistress." Roine nodded to him, and it seemed as if he was gone in a moment.

Temar always moved quickly.

"I'm glad you're coming with us to court," I said, cautiously, to Roine. It was no lie—even knowing that I might not go, were the Duke not sufficiently impressed with me, even knowing that our

19

departure would be over a year hence, I was grateful beyond words to know that Roine would come with me. But she came swiftly across the room to take my hands in hers.

"Neither of us are going," she said, her voice low and urgent. "I will not let them take you away. It is to put you in the gravest danger—the Duke can do as he wants with Miriel, but he shall not have you."

"But you said to Temar—" I protested, and she cut me off.

"I let him think what he would. But, Catwin, believe me when I say that the court is no good place to be."

"Well, what do I do, then?" I challenged her. I was angry— singled out by Temar one moment, and the next moment denied the opportunity to make him proud. "Do we just run away tonight? Do I go to my lessons with Miriel's tutors? Do I follow the Duke about?"

Roine chewed her lip, she was impervious to my anger. "Yes," she decided. "Do that for now. We don't need to run away tonight. We can find a way out of it before the Duke comes back next time."

Chapter 3

The Duke left two days later, having concluded his usual business of hearing petitions, settling disputes, and overseeing his holdings. He took his duties very seriously, I learned, and when he worked on the business of his estates, he applied himself wholly to it. When he listened to the disputes of the peasants, his eyes were fixed on the petitioners, his brow furrowed; his expression said that he would not take kindly to being troubled for a little matter, but I saw that he listened to each dispute fully, and decided fairly, even against his own soldiers and retainers.

He rode out with the builders himself to oversee the maintenance of the defenses—an important piece of our lives here, on the border of Ismir. The peace of my childhood had been hard-fought and hard-won by the Duke himself, but whatever memories he might have had, looking over the place where he had led his men to battle and glory and death, were hidden deep beneath his habitual scowl.

He would work through the dinner hour with the record-keepers, the stewards, the guard captains, leaving his chair empty in the great hall—though we served a dinner to it in any case, and the cooks made rich meals fit for a feast, to celebrate his presence there.

The Lady presided over these meals like a queen, calling for wine and music. She had done her hair very fine under her headdress, I noticed, and she wore gowns with gold embroidery and all her jewels. She had dressed the little Lady Miriel finely as well, although Miriel's hair was allowed to tumble over her shoulders. The girl was wearing velvets and silks, even little chains of gold and silver at her waist and pearls at her neck.

On the last night of the Duke's visit, I was serving wine to his soldiers, and so was standing by the little side hallway as he came into the hall. I knew, from creeping partway up the stairs to his tower chamber, that he had been discussing the increasing number of raids on our outlying villages, and I thought he looked tense. He looked up as he came into the hall, a figure in all black, hidden in the shadows at the edge of the room, and only I saw the look of contempt on his face as he observed the high table.

Later Temar would tell me, *sometimes one moment can give you the whole key to a person*. I did not know enough yet to have the whole key to the Duke, but this moment gave me one of many keys. It reminded me that he was a man, a man who could be spurred to anger like any other. For now, I saw that although the Duke publicly observed every pleasantry that a brother should, he loved the Lady not at all. More so, she was distasteful to him, worthy of no respect.

And I saw that the Duke's eyes flicked from the Lady, posturing and smiling, to Miriel, who sat quietly at her side. He watched his niece carefully, as if he would see everything about her from the curve of her cheek, as if he could learn everything about her from the set of her shoulders. He looked at her as he looked at his stone walls and his guard towers: something in the making, something to be perfected.

And then he looked over at me, and I shrank back against the wall.

"What are you doing here?"

"Wine?" I offered, and I held out my pitcher.

He stared at me for a moment. "Are you sure about her?" he asked, and I realized that Temar must be standing out of sight in the hallway. I craned my head to look.

"Very," Temar said, and he gave me a smile. "You should eat, milord."

"Yes." The Duke narrowed his eyes at me and strode away to the high table, and Temar shot me a wink before following. I smiled after him, and then went to refill the soldiers' cups, for they were shouting for more drink.

Later that night, as I shared the day's knowledge with Temar, I asked him, "Why am I to study with the Lady Miriel's tutors?"

"To see what you can learn," Temar said easily.

"But why?" I persisted. "No one tests the other servants. Why me?"

"That's a very good question," Temar said. "Keep thinking on it, little one."

"But *why*?" I asked. I felt my face warm when he smiled at me, when he called me by a nickname; but I had the sense that I did not want him to think of me as a child. He only laughed at my frustration, and I flushed.

"What if I were to lie to you?"

I was shocked. "You wouldn't."

He looked very serious, more serious than I had ever seen him before. "Wouldn't I?" His face softened. "You must learn to find things out without ever asking what you are after. I know you can do it, Catwin."

I was warmed by his praise, but still discontented. I looked down at my hands and nodded. Temar stood and stretched.

"Time for you to get some sleep. I will see you in three months' time."

"What?" I looked up, and Temar smiled his easy smile. "Don't worry. You will have much to learn while we are gone. Study well, make your tutors proud." Before I could move to hug him, or speak to beg him not to go, he was gone.

That night, I dreamed that I walked through driving snow, surrounded by the eerie whistle of a winter storm, engulfed in white. I knew this wasn't real; I had been out in enough blizzards, securing the flocks and battening down the shutters of the castle, to know the merciless bite of the wind on my skin, the slow seep of water into my old boots. No, instead I walked as if the wind could not touch me. I could feel nothing.

I craned to look about me, and could see only hovels, unlovely little shacks, battered and leaning. The path curved away and up, and I looked ahead: the castle, my home, rose into the sky at the peak of the mountain. It was half-lost in the swirling snow. White-out, I thought—a term I had heard the guardsmen shout to each other. No wonder no one was about. They were hunkering down, wondering if their supplies were lost on the trail. As soon as the snow cleared, they would venture out to see if any caravans needed help, and they would demand the goods in return for aid.

A cry caught my ear, the wail of a baby. It was coming from the shack near me, and after a moment's hesitation, I pushed open the door and went in. I knew that I was not truly here, but habit ran strong, and I closed the door carefully behind me, as Roine had taught me to do. In the little shack, a weak fire burned in the hearth, and a woman lay on an old cot, a man at her side with a baby in his arms.

"Just hold her," the man pleaded.

"No, no." The woman was wild-eyed. She looked so gaunt and so feverish that I wanted to draw the man and the infant back from her; there was death in those eyes. "I don't want her!"

"It's over, now," he assured her. "It's over, and we'll get the healer. I promise, you'll be well soon. Just hold her."

"No!" She pushed him away with her feverish strength, and fell back onto the pillows. The baby was screaming at the top of its lungs, wrapped awkwardly in a blanket. So small, I realized. Hardly any cause for the blood I saw on the blankets.

The woman was shaking her head; I could see her cracked lips still forming the words: *no, no, no,* over and over. Her eyes were half-open, and I saw that they were the same grey as the storm clouds of winter, an omen of the blizzard.

"Take her away," she said. "She's…"

"What is it?" The man held the baby close to him and leaned over to hear his wife more clearly. She whispered something and I could see his brow furrow.

"You don't know what you're saying," he said, but he looked worried. He looked down at the bundle in his arms, her little face still screwed up, yelling. "Please, rest. I'll go to the castle now, myself—" he cast a glance outside at the blizzard, and I saw his lips move in a silent prayer. It was foolhardy at best, and more likely it would be the death of him. Then he looked back at his wife, and his face twisted. He could not let her die. "Rest. Daniel will take care of you. I'll go now."

"Take her with you," the women rasped. "Take her, and leave her outside."

"What are you saying?" He recoiled, but she reached over to grab his arm.

"She'll be betrayed." The woman's voice had a sudden, awful clarity. "She was born to be betrayed." She had lifted off the pillows, but now she sank back. She was shaking her head again. *No.* "Kinder to let her die now. See how she cries…" She was slipping back into the fever haze. "Take her," she whispered.

With a start, I recognized the squalling little bundle as myself. Even knowing this for a dream, believing that this could not possibly be them, I took a step closer to look at my parents: my mother, with honey-colored hair and grey eyes, on the edge of death, and my father, with the strenuous leanness of the poor, holding my tiny self awkwardly in his big, work-roughened hands.

Was it possible that these were truly my parents?

The man laid my tiny self carefully in a cradle, out of reach of my mother, and he grabbed his hat and his cap and hurried out into the storm, quite oblivious to my silent presence. But when he was gone, I saw the woman's eyes focus on me.

"Are you an angel?" she asked, and after a moment, I shook my head. She was shivering, and as much as I knew it to be a dream, I walked over to the bed and pulled the covers more snuggly around her. Still, she shook with cold; she was far gone. Her head lolled towards me. "Please..." she whispered, and I leaned forward to her.

"What?"

"You need to take her away," she pleaded with me. "My daughter. She's cursed. She was born to be betrayed, and when it happens..." Her voice trailed off and I leaned closer still.

"What?" I asked urgently. "What will happen?"

"The balance...tips," the woman whispered. "Endings." She was fading away from me. "Promise me..." she whispered, and, with a start, I woke soaked in sweat, throwing the blankets from me and heaving for breath. Roine, already awake and at work, looked over at me curiously.

"Bad dream?"

"Strange dream." I sank my head into my hands. "I saw the day I was born." Roine put down her work and came over to me, kneeling beside my cot.

"What did you see?"

"It was only a dream," I said, irritable in the wake of my fear, but she shook her head.

"You dreamed of the prophecy," she guessed.

"I saw my mother. I thought." I shook my head. "I mean—I know I didn't." She only watched me, and I swallowed. "She said, I would be betrayed...and the balance would tip. It would end things." The words, so prophetic in my mother's feverish rasp, half-obscured by the howl of the blizzard, were ridiculous now. I shook my head again, to clear it. "It's nothing. It means nothing."

"She said the balance would *tip*?" Roine clarified, as I got up and began to move about the room. I cast an annoyed look at her over my shoulder.

"In the dream, she did."

"And end something..."

"Yes," I said impatiently. "It was just a dream." She did not respond, and I looked over at her. She was gazing at me, as sadly as I had ever seen her. Repentant, I ran over to give her a hug. "I'm sorry. I don't mean to be rude."

"I know," she said, into my hair. "Go get some breakfast. You'll need to go to your lessons, if you're to go to court."

"I thought you said we weren't going," I said, surprised. I felt a flush of joy at the thought of going after all, of seeing someplace new, of seeing Temar's smile again.

"Things change," Roine said simply. "Go now."

Chapter 4

The cane whistled through the air before it struck, and I tried to keep from wincing. I had learned to hate that moment, just before the pain. I had learned to hate the moment before it, too, when I saw the teacher's eyes narrow and his arm tense. Both of these were just as bad as the moment when the cane fell, and the pain blossomed out from it, stinging the skin, aching in the parts of me that were already bruised.

But each paled in comparison to the next thing that I knew would come: a breathless little giggle, only partly suppressed, from the Lady Miriel. Every time I was struck with the cane, for any mistake real or imagined, she would laugh: a little titter she could not entirely hold back. As I gritted my teeth against the pain, she bit her lip against a spiteful peal of laughter. Whatever it was that the Lady had told her about me, Miriel was my sworn enemy; she reveled in my failure.

And there could be nothing from me, no sign of anger or resentment. A harsh word to her had once earned me a cuff about the head and a lashing at the post in the courtyard—although Roine had pleaded for the use of a tawse, so as not to break my skin. I had learned from that, but I had found that a silent glare earned me another hit with the cane, and even the appearance of displeasure would make its way back to the Lady, who would have her revenge.

"My daughter's tutor tells me..." she would say, her fingers clutching at the arms of her chair, her back ramrod straight, and then would come the punishment: a beating, or no supper, extra duties in the kitchens at night so that I was yawning in the morning and beaten again for rudeness.

As often as not, the Lady watched these punishments, her eyes narrowed and the corners of her red-painted mouth curved in a smile. The first time she watched, I found myself seized by a desire not to show her my pain. I bit my lips against the whistle and crack of the rod, and I gripped the edge of the chair I was to hold, but in the end I heard my own whimper in the silence, and—even with tears blurring my vision—I could see the Lady's smile grow wider.

Thus began one of the first such struggles in my life: on the one hand, me, determined not to let the Lady see my pain; on the other hand, the Lady, determined to break me; neither of us would back away from it. And always, when she had won, she tempered it with regret—a disappointed sigh, a pretty frown. If only I were smarter, more good-tempered, more obedient, we would not need to go through this, would we?

I knew that she did not believe it. I looked past her pretty blue eyes and there was nothing behind them but spite. But, in the inevitable failure to outwit her, having lost once already—then, the thoughts slid under my skin. For a moment, I would believe her. And no matter how much I told myself that nothing I could do would free me from the Lady's spite, the pain ate away at my determination.

But I did not give up, I did not slink away to Roine's tower in defeat, and my stubbornness earned me the Lady's hatred. She had always been determined to see me fail, but she had not hated me, only my manners and my connection to her brother. My resistance changed that. It pitted us against each other, it spurred her to more cruelty—and she had a heart ready for cruelty. Whoever she had been once, perhaps a young girl with a pretty face and an unspoiled heart, time and disappointment and her forced exile to the Winter Castle had twisted her into something else entirely. In my dreams, she wore the face of a bird and twisted into a grotesque, half-human being, like one of the creatures from the old myths. Later, when I knew the word, I told myself that she was a succubus, who fed on despair; then, I only knew that I should let her have none of mine.

As the powerless will do, I dreamed of revenge. I resolved, with the strange all-encompassing anger of childhood, that someday I would have payback for what had been done to me, and on the worst days, I dropped into a strange dark place in my mind and I counted the lashes, so that I could reckon each back when at last the time was right.

If I failed at any task, I would be punished. I would get a cane across my palms for forgetting a noble's lineage, more arithmetic problems if I did one incorrectly, pages and pages of penmanship if the tutor did not approve of the shape of my letters. I could be sure that any further work would earn me a reprimand from the Lady.

"Wasting the tutor's time," she would say crisply. "Pages and pages of paper, wasted because of your abominable penmanship." If I failed, I whetted her appetite for her own victory over me; if I succeeded, I knew that I only stoked the anger that burned within her. When I won, I only ensured that every other failure, real or imagined, would be punished more harshly. There was no true victory in success...save for the true joy I found in the learning.

At the first, everything had been so new that I was nearly scared. Instead of the patterns of my fingers, the strange combinations of fingers and hands, I learned the higher numbers. I learned how to write them on the page, add them together and subtract them—although it was still easier for me to think about folding my fingers down. When I read, it was not only that I must puzzle out each word, but I must start by remembering each letter. In the first few days, I felt a wave of nausea when I saw a page full of letters and numbers.

And then it all changed. I had spent the first days counting the smallest victories and measuring them against the long list of my failures; slowly, the balance tipped. I did not even notice, until one day I realized that I had read an entire page without noticing the very words themselves. Then I noticed that arithmetic, so daunting to the Lady Miriel, was no more than a set of clever puzzles to me. I took a fierce joy in completing a set of problems first—though after her first tantrum, I learned to keep my paper to myself, and pretend to keep writing until after she had turned in her sheet with a triumphant toss of her night-black curls.

Maps and lineages came less easily, the old names softened by the years until one could deduce nothing of their pronunciation by sounding them out. Robbed of her opportunity to taunt me about how slowly I read, how poorly I reckoned numbers, Miriel took her joy in how little I knew about nobles. Every time I stumbled on a name, I could be sure that she would laugh at me. She had the perfect laugh, did Miriel: the cultured, throaty little giggle of a court lady. She knew just how to widen her eyes at me in disbelief: I had startled the laugh out of her, she had not meant to giggle, she was only surprised, you see—how could one not know of the de la Marque family, or the Torstenssons, of the Cessors?

And then there was philosophy, theology, trade: grand concepts about rights and honor, chivalry, the duties of men and women, the promises of the gods. My utter incompetence in

29

remembering the long list of names and philosophical schools was matched only by Miriel's instinctive brilliance in the subject. I might be able to count and remember dates better than she could, but where I stumbled through thuses and therefores, Miriel darted, lightning-quick, through schools of thought and dragged out historical events to prove abstract points. In those lessons, she was so frustrated with my slowness that she forgot even to insult me; she stamped her foot and pouted when she could not make me understand a point.

The first few weeks passed in a haze of misery. Miriel's fourteenth birthday came and went, with great celebrations and feasts, and a month later, my own birthday was celebrated only with a whispered congratulation by Roine, and a hug as I set off to the schoolroom. Most servants did not even know the date of their birth; I only knew because Roine could count the days on her star chart. I should feel lucky, I told myself. I should feel privileged. But I only felt miserable.

Every day, after the hours of lessons and humiliations, I ate my dinner as quickly as I could and climbed the steps to Roine's tower. There, I went to my little corner bed, hunched myself under the covers, and refused to answer any of her soft-voiced, worried questions. When I was certain she was asleep, I would muffle my tears into the little pillow. I cried like a child, I cried like an animal will cry, who cannot understand what is wrong, only that there is pain and there seems no end in sight.

But I had only so many tears to shed, and when my sobs eased, as they always did, I would lie awake and stare at the sloped ceiling of the tower. In the dark of those nights, I learned then that it was not enough for me to endure and wait. I must find a way out of this maze of misery.

That was a puzzle. For night after night, I could think of no way to escape. And then it came to me. There could be no retaliation against Miriel, and so I must fortify the one defense given to me: knowledge. If she laughed when I was wrong, well, then I would never be wrong. I would learn every name on the map, every obscure noble in the spidery lineages, I would remember the philosophers and their dry theories, and I would never need to hear her little titter of scorn. She had had schooling from the time she was old enough to sit and be fed; I had not. So, I must catch up.

I knew better than to try to sneak into the tutor's rooms, but I did know where other books could be found. The old library had been one of the first discoveries of my childhood, and although the contents of it were priceless, the room was ill-guarded and almost never used. Even I, when I first found it, had thought it boring and never gone back. Now I remembered it, and it was little enough trouble to sneak there after my dinner, and dart away with some books hidden under a pile of blankets I was bringing to Roine.

I studied by the light of a guard's lantern, somewhat I had begged from Aler, the chief guard. He was sweet to me, the little half-orphan, and when I could, I would go sit on the high, lonely walls, and listen to the wind with him. I was shy about my plan, and so I would only say that I wanted to study, and Aler looked at me, at the bruises on my arms and my face, at the furtive eyes and the determined chin, and gave me the lantern without a word—but, I thought later, with a little bit of pity in his eyes.

I began to read with the sole purpose of escaping Miriel's derision. I stared at the overwhelming numbers of books and felt the same sinking feeling from the first few days: that I was outmatched. Then I remembered that, hidden in these books, lay the key to my release, and my despair was coupled with a grim determination that, if I must suffer through days in Miriel's company, the days would not be any more miserable than they had to be.

When I opened the first book, sneezing from the dust, I saw only the relentless march of words, each to be painstakingly decoded, sounded out silently in the quiet of the night. I remember that I felt only exhaustion. The task was daunting. I struggled through that first book until I could stay awake no longer, and then I doused the lantern and stumbled to bed, barely making it to my little pallet and lacking the energy even to pull the covers over me.

Roine had to shake me awake, thrusting a piece of bread and a cup of goat's milk into my hand as I struggled to open my eyes, re-braiding my hair herself, and telling me the time so that I fairly flew down the stairs to the day's lessons.

I got a beating that day for arriving disheveled, with my clothes rumpled from sleep, and another for yawning—I waited until the teacher's back was turned, but Miriel had gleefully remarked upon it—but I barely cared. Behind the exhaustion was a new curiosity, a challenge such as I had never felt in my whole life.

I had learned to sneak and creep about so that I could avoid the Duke, for sure, but in all of my sneaking, I had discovered a love of exploring. It was quite a thing to follow an old passageway to the end and find where it led, or know all of the rooms of the castle, even the old unused ones with the shutters gone and the winter wind laying drifts of snow inside.

The books I had stolen—borrowed, I told myself—were as good as having a whole new castle to explore. I had only read a part of the first book, and already I had learned more things about the history of our country than I had ever suspected could exist. The old kings of the land had made their capitol not in Penekket, but in Delvard, in an icy castle much like our own and far to the east, only nearly unassailable. When, after generations of war, the kingdom of Heddred stretched all the way to the Voltur Mountains, my home, a peace was declared and the king moved his castle to Penekket, in the lowlands.

I, who had never known more than the confines of the castle, who had never dreamed of anything other than the bleak cold of the mountains, began to dream of other sights. On the nights that followed, I gulped down my dinner quickly, so that I might get to my books sooner. I saw the old maps, I learned of historic battles, and the names of kings and generals. I read of the Lady of the Mountains, whom some claimed was a woman and others claimed was an angel, who led the first Lord of Voltur to where this castle stood now, and told him to build the castle and guard Heddred against Ismir for all time. I read of the Prophesies of the Ancients, the old books still held in the libraries at Delvard, the books from which all priests told us of the times before, and the times yet to come.

I read other books, dull accounts of droughts and famines, trade routes and merchants. In every book, however, I lost myself completely, even the writings of the old philosophers themselves. There were bits of knowledge to be gleaned, whole worlds beyond this castle to be explored. I knew so much that I could barely contain it.

And this is where I made the error that nearly cost me my life.

It was a cold day, and I was sleepy. I had read an account of the Council of Lords, from its very founding, and although I had known that I should go to sleep, I had not been able to close the book until I had read to the very end. I had managed to stifle my yawns so that not even Miriel could see them, but my mind was very slow to work. I could barely make sense of the words the tutor was saying, until I caught a glaring error, and I raised my hand.

"Yes?" the tone boded ill, and many times in the hours and days that followed, I thought that I should have known better. It was true, what Roine said, that my pride would get the better of me one day.

"I beg your pardon, sir, but that's not correct," I said.

For a moment, he could not speak. Then he managed one word: "What?"

"You said that the battle was won by Arturus the Great. But it was Arturus II who won that battle. It's a common historical error because Arturus II was known as The Grateful by his followers, for he gave thanks after the battle to the priests who led him."

The cane came down on my hands, and Miriel stifled a laugh. "Incorrect," the teacher said. "Arturus the Great. You will write out, one hundred time times—"

"But, sir, Arturus the Great was born forty years *after* the end of the First Balic War."

All of a sudden, it dawned on him. He turned, slowly. "How do you know that?" he asked, softly. And then, "How *could* you know that?"

Nine days later, when even the hunger had fled and I had ceased to feel anything other than pain, I barely stirred when the door to my cell opened. I stared ahead of me, knowing that the guards had come to beat me again, knowing that I would cry and I could do nothing about it. I could not turn my head to the right anymore, to look at them, and the only defiance I had left was to pretend that I was not looking at them by my own choice.

"Get up," the guard said, roughly.

I said nothing. I could be as insolent as I liked. I had learned, and bitterly, that apologies and pleas got me nothing. But then he said the only words that could have moved me from exhaustion to terror. "I said get up. The Duke is here." Despite the pain, I turned my head as far as I could to look at the guard. He was smiling in anticipation. "He wants to see the thief."

Chapter 5

I was dragged from an icy cell and hauled up the stairs to the courtyard, to be flung in a heap at the feet of the Duke.

"What is this? This is the girl?" His voice was tinged with distaste. He did not even recognize me, but I heard a strangled exclamation that I thought was from Temar.

"This," the Lady said, with her voice like ice, "is the girl you would have had study with my Miriel. I told you that her low birth would show itself. She has been stealing from my libraries."

"My libraries," the Duke said. His tone was mild, but his words cutting. Then it was as if his mind caught up with him. "From the *libraries*?"

Few things in the world were more precious than books. I knew; I knew that Roine's collection of herb-lore was her most prized possession. I knew that the library at the castle was worth a small fortune. Books were so prized that I doubted anyone other than the mayor and the priest in the village had ever even seen one. To steal a book was a thousand times worse than to steal a goat, or even a piece of the fine china the Lady dined on.

The Duke crouched down beside me, his eyes narrowed, and I breathed, through broken and cracked lips, the words I had been repeating for days: "I put them back." I felt the tears start, trickling from behind eyelids that were almost swollen shut.

The Duke did not say a word; he stared at me, he looked directly into my eyes and I had neither the courage nor the will to look away. His gaze held me fast. He did not respond to my weak defense. I had learned that he kept his own council. Still, I feared his silence. What was he thinking? That my words were true, that nothing was missing? Or that I was lying, and that I should be given a thief's punishment: losing the thumb and first finger on my left hand?

Borne on fear and pain, I drifted; the stone under my cheek felt as soft as a cloud. I was lying almost on my back, and I could mostly open my left eye, so I saw that the Duke was staring at the Lady. I could not see her, but I knew from his expression that he had asked a question, and she had not answered well. Now he took a step forward, over my body, and I was one of the only ones who could have heard his hissed words.

"I told you that I wanted her taught. How much time has she missed because of this folly?"

"Folly!" The Lady's voice rang out before she dropped to a whisper, terrified of his anger and yet still defiant. "She is no scholar, she is a common girl. She stole from me—"

"From me." His voice was cool, impersonal. "And borrowed."

"She should be punished! And she must be removed from the schoolroom. She is no fit company for Miriel. For the Gods' sake, the girl wears britches and—"

"Go," he said, as if he would not even argue with her. Whatever was in his eyes, she did not argue; I could hear the swish of her gown as she fairly ran from the courtyard. The Duke raised his voice. "And someone take the girl to be tended to."

Temar was the one who took me to Roine. Roine, who was waiting in the shadow of the great doors. Roine, who pushed her way through the crowd of servants to Temar's side. She called my name, and I could only blink, whisper words. After all this time, it seemed all I could form my mouth to say was, "I put them back."

She shook her head and led Temar to her tower, where he laid me on her big wooden table and the two of them set to checking for broken bones. The wounds, thankfully, were minor. One shoulder had been dislocated, but the bone was back in its place now. There were the lingering effects of a concussion, but not severe. Whether my lack of broken bones was due to pure luck, or because the Lady had told her servants not to hurt me seriously, no one could say. My clothes were stripped away, the cuts cleaned, bandages applied, and then I was laid in my little pallet bed while Roine brewed tea with herbs to help the pain, and Temar went to find broth to restore my strength.

Roine would have had me rest for days, safe in her tower, away from nobles and their fights, but the Duke did not feel the same. The next morning, his guard came to the tower with orders to bring me to the Duke's study, and so Roine dressed me and made a sling for me, and did not say any of the protests that I saw in her face.

I did not say so, but I was glad enough to have something to do. During the day I had been allowed in bed, I kept my eyes trained on the wall and I repeated things to myself, bits of knowledge I had learned from the books, a list of rooms in the castle—anything to keep my mind from the thought of the beatings, and the sound of my own voice: "I put them back!" Walking provided more than enough distraction, if only I could keep myself from thinking about why I was in such pain.

The Duke was working when I arrived, his head bent over a stack of papers. There was only one lantern in the room, and no fire; the Duke was economical. He looked up as I came in, and his eyes measured me from looks to mind, in that way he had of looking almost through a person.

"What is the capital of Heddred?" he asked me, without preamble.

"Penekket. Delvard, once. Sir." I was fairly dizzy with the effort of walking.

"And Ismir?"

"Setnar, sir."

"What languages do the people of Mavlon speak?"

"Greater Common, High Common, and Mav, which they call Fet, which means common in their tongue."

"Why have the kings of Heddred never conquered Mavlon?"

I considered; this was a trick question. "Heddred has never conquered Mavlon, but does regard it as a principality, on the grounds that the two royal families intermarried and Mavlon no longer maintains a monarchy of its own. Mavlon calls itself a free nation, but has never raised arms against Heddred. Trade provides Heddred with iron and granite, and Mavlon with food. The borders are not secured."

After a moment, he nodded. "Adequate. Tell me what else you have covered in your studies." His eyes gleamed. "Including the books you read from my library."

I hesitated a moment, and decided that he did not want an apology. There was nothing in the set of his face to suggest that he was smiling, but I sensed that he might be, and in any case was not displeased. "Reading and writing. History, going back to the reign of Wulfric II, and forward to House Warden, but only through Arthur. Algebra. Geography and trade. Noble lineages. Sir."

"Why did you take the books?" he asked, suddenly, and I was too afraid to do anything other than tell him the truth.

"I didn't want Miriel to laugh at me anymore, sir. And then I liked reading them."

He nodded, and his mouth tightened slightly. "The tutor tells me that he was instructed to bring a list of your errors to the Lady each day, and that she had you beaten. Is this true?"

"Yes, sir." I trembled as the words came out of my mouth. I was terrified that this man could see right through me, but I thought perhaps I should have lied, and told him that his sister would not do such a thing.

I did not need to worry. He just nodded; he did not disbelieve me. "That will happen," he said flatly. "Expect it to happen. There are those who wish to see my plans thwarted; they will act against you, as my tool." His eyes bored into me, entirely devoid of sympathy. "I expect you still to do every task I set you, and do it well. As you did this time."

Praise. I could not believe my ears. "Thank you. Sir."

He was already pulling his papers back towards him, bending his head, as he said, "I will leave for Penekket in five days. You and Miriel will accompany me." He did not even look up again. "You may go." I stood, shocked, staring at him, but he did not acknowledge me and I did not have the courage to speak. I backed away slowly, and just as I was about to turn to the door, I saw Temar. He had been sitting at the side of the room, and he was looking down at the knife he twirled between his fingers. He would not look at me, either, and I thought that in that moment, he looked as sorrowful as Roine always did. I lingered, hoping that he would look up, but he did not—and I, still terrified of the Duke, left with a little backwards glance at the man who had changed my life completely.

It was late, and I was tired already, but I could not go back to Roine's tower. I knew she would ask questions, with her eyes if not her voice, and I did not know how to answer them. My mind was too much a muddle. Three months ago, I had been plucked from the life of a nobody and given the education of a noble; in the past days, I had wondered if I would die without ever again seeing sunlight. Now, in less than a week, I would leave the only home I had ever known, to travel to the Court. The world, which had seemed dizzyingly strange in the past weeks, rocked sideways once more. I could hardly understand it myself, let alone explain it to Roine.

So I went to the walls. The steps were a trial, and I could not put out my hand for balance. It was coming up on spring, but the nights were still deathly cold. The icy wind chilled me to the bone, and at that moment I was glad of it. This felt like home, up on the walls with cold that stiffened my fingers and ached in my throat as I breathed in. I had a sudden wash of homesickness, for the very place I was. I had learned about Penekket, about the eastern plains. I knew I was going someplace warm, green. This was one of the last nights I would have in the place I called home.

As I struggled to the top of the stairs, I heard a nearby clank and turned my head too quickly; the bones were still re-setting, and pain made me dizzy. The dark figure reached out a hand, and I recognized Aler, wrapped up warmly in a big cloak.

"Hello, little shadow." He held up his lantern. I didn't answer, and so he only moved to swing his cloak around me, warming me as he and I walked to the corner tower. It was slow progress with my limp, but he made no mention of it. In the scant warmth of the tower, more from lack of wind than from the small brazier, he pulled out a chair for me, and sat in one himself. I could see him looking me over, noting the bruises and the sling but saying nothing.

At length he took a swig from his flask, and passed it to me. I looked dubiously at it, and he said, "Drink up, little shadow. Puts warmth in you." I took a swallow, gasped, and choked—my throat was on fire. Aler laughed and took the flask back, and only smiled at my accusing stare. "Now, now, it's none so bad. You're warm now, aren't you?"

I laughed, a bit shakily, and tried to wipe my eyes with my hand, but found that my muscles were trembling. Laughing let out all of the emotion at once, in a rush, and I found that the tears from coughing were soon replaced with tears I could not control. Aler said nothing while I hiccupped and gasped over in my chair, just patted my hand when I put it on the table.

"Word is, the Lady gave you a bad time of it," he said quietly. I nodded, not trusting myself to speak. "They say that sometimes, when a thing like that happens, it's best to tell it to someone. Chases the ghosts away from it." His voice was neutral. He passed me the flask and after a hesitation, I sipped again, more carefully. Then I shook my head.

"I don't want to tell it," I said. "I don't want to remember it, ever."

He nodded, and I turned my head away so that he could not see my eyes. Since I had become so dubiously related to Miriel somehow, none of the other servants would speak to me, and Aler was the closest thing I had to a friend. I was afraid that if I told him the truth, I would lose him, too. How could I say that I did want to remember it, every moment of it, so that I could give the Lady her due when the time came for reckoning?

I had underestimated him. Aler might not have seen my face, but he knew, and he seemed to understand. He sipped from the flask again, then handed it over without looking at me; he was staring meditatively out into the night, along the wall.

"Some would say as there's no point in thinking on old scores," he said. I looked over at him silently, and he looked back. "Word is, lass, you and the Lady won't be staying here much longer. They say you'll be leaving with the Duke when he goes."

I nodded. My homesickness had come back in a rush and I bit my lip. Aler's face softened a bit, but his words were as cold as I had ever heard, even in his usual thoughtful tone.

"You want my advice, little shadow? Just leave the Lady where she is. Leave her to the cold. Let her rot here, knowing her daughter was sent away. That's poison enough."

I thought of the Lady, sitting in her tower rooms, staring out over the mountains, and I felt the most envy I had ever known. A life of leisure, the pristine beauty of the Voltur Mountains, a whole library at her disposal.

But then I thought of her face when she had stared down the Duke, and I remembered his words: *there are those who wish to see my plans thwarted.* I thought that maybe Aler was right, that what the Lady had been fighting for was to keep Miriel with her. I thought of the way her mouth twitched every time she walked out into the cold of the courtyard, how the braziers burned hot and close in her tower rooms, all the year round.

I took another sip from the flask, and this time I let the brandy roll in my mouth before swallowing it. Aler was right. Why keep the score, why even remember the Lady, when the cold and the loneliness would kill her for me?

Aler never knew it, for I never spoke to the man again, but he taught me as much about being a Shadow as Temar ever did.

Chapter 6

My lessons with Miriel's tutors were, mercifully, halted in the preparation for leave-taking, and for five blessed days I woke with the knowledge that I did not have to steel myself to the pain of a wooden rod, school my face to show no resentment, and face the unavoidable spite of the Lady. I saw some bruises deepen, and others fade, and I was glad enough to be allowed to spend my days with Roine, out of Miriel's company.

We were far from idle, for by the Duke's order, Roine would accompany us to Penekket, and that meant that the contents of her tower must be packed. I half-expected her to revive her protests against going, but she never again spoke of it to me. She only set to her work with her usual quiet efficiency, and I, my shoulder growing less sore by the day, helped her.

I owned nothing more than a change of clothes, and so there was nothing for me to pack, save Roine's possessions. She oversaw the preparations calmly, making sure that her books were strapped together and wrapped in oilcloth before being placed in iron-bound chests, her instruments placed carefully in crates filled with straw. I cleaned beakers and wrapped them, made sure that the books were organized by topic, and Roine checked my work with her usual sad-eyed smile.

When we had finally cleaned the room of Roine's belongings, we hauled the big table and her shelves into the center of the floor and I was given a big broom. I set to work sweeping the years' worth of dust from the edges of the circular room, digging the bristles into the cracks between boards, and dumping the dust out of the deep-silled windows. The windows were cleaned as well, and the sills rubbed with oil against the winter damp, Roine calling out panicked cautions as I scrambled up the sills, the windows beside me open to the steep drop down the castle walls, and I laughed and called back that I would never fall.

One of our last tasks was to prepare the room for the next healer. One would be sent from Penekket, the steward had said, but in the meantime the people of the castle would be quite without aid, and this offended Roine deeply. No one would have known it but me, for she only allowed herself a few choice words about poor planning, and the irresponsibility of nobles, and those were spoken quietly in the seclusion of her tower. Her outburst over as quickly as it had begun, she set to work creating an extensive kit that might be used to treat basic injuries until the new healer arrived.

At her direction I folded clean cloths and laid them beside a basin for hot water, rolled strips of linen for bandages, and wrote labels for jars of herbs and ointments that she was leaving behind. Scraps of paper were tied to each jar, detailing the uses and dangers of each herb, and I, who had been Roine's informal assistant with some patients, was inclined to ask a great deal of questions.

"Why aren't you leaving any valerian?" I asked, proud that I could read the labels and recognize the lack.

"Valerian is difficult to use," Roine said. "The new healer will collect their own, I am sure, but to leave valerian in the hands of the untrained would be to invite trouble."

"What would happen?"

She looked at me gravely. "The patient could die, Catwin."

"But valerian eases pain," I said, not comprehending.

"An herb may do many things," Roine said. "Valerian eases pain, but it also brings sleep. Too much, and the sleeper will never wake again."

I looked down at the small jar of herbs in my hand, and found that it was shaking slightly. I had watched Roine mix countless potions and bind countless wounds. Sometimes, when the wound was not urgent, she would let me measure out the herbs, counseling me to be careful. I could hear her familiar refrain in my head: *no more, no less.* But I had never known what that meant. I thought that a potion was like a puzzle: when the pieces fit, the potion worked, and when the pieces did not fit, well, no harm was done.

Roine smiled reassuringly, as if she knew my thoughts. "I will guide you when we work together, Catwin. I will not let you mistake the dose."

I bit my tongue and kept working. Roine knew more of the world than I, and if her assurances rang hollow to me, well, I had more important matters to think over, one in particular. The question had burned in my mind, all through the careful packing, through the loading of the carts and the cleaning, through the travel preparations with the guardsmen and the servants. It hovered on the tip of my tongue, threatening to spill out every time I spoke.

The question did not lie only in my heart. It planted itself in my head and then it spread, to everyone I touched, and to everyone each of them touched. It grew its spidery legs through the whole castle, until in everyone's eyes, I could see the same words hovering. They asked it of me without speaking, as if I were one to know the answer, as if I could tell them anything that they did not already know.

I never considered asking the Duke. He would tell me when it suited him, and so he either did not think that I should know, or he did not care—and either way, I knew better than to press him. I had thought I might ask it of Roine, but every time I tried to do so, I thought better of it at the last moment. Something in her eyes told me that the answer saddened her. Aler knew something of it, too, I thought, but whatever he knew, he kept well-hidden and disclaimed it loudly; I think now that he only guessed, and hoped that he was wrong.

With none of them to ask, I was left with three unpleasant options: first, to ask the woman who despised me above all others, the Lady. If I could weather the storm of her displeasure, I thought she might let slip some useful information. On the other hand, the bruises all over my body were vivid reminders of why I should keep my distance. I had a faint notion that the Lady was distressed by Miriel being taken from her, and that asking her might cause her some pain, but then I remembered Aler's words and resolved to leave her in peace—at least, as much peace as she could have.

The second option was to ask Temar. I yearned to talk to him, not only to know the answer to my question, but simply to be near him, to see his smile when he greeted me, to have him devote his attention to me for a moment. And yet, I shrank from him. I knew that Temar knew the Duke's plans, and that he was party to them; there was a strange, vague awareness that this was a game, and Temar was not on my side. I knew that Temar was watching me for the same qualities the Duke sought, and I wanted desperately to know what those were—and was also afraid to hear them spoken.

This left the most unpleasant option of asking Miriel herself. Whatever this strange journey, the bizarre experiment of teaching me reading and writing and history and arithmetic, whatever it meant that Roine was to come to Penekket with us and keep me safe, Miriel was somehow caught up in it. Indeed, I was not fool enough to believe that I was the cause. Miriel was the cause, she was the lynch-pin of all of this, and I was the one who was caught up in it.

The Duke would not have told Miriel his purpose, it would never have occurred to him to do so. She was my age, only fourteen years old, and the Duke did not trouble himself to ask our permission for whatever he intended to do, nor even explain in advance what that might be. But the Lady might have said something. She went around with her eyes red and swollen, snapping orders at the servants, quick to criticize the littlest thing, and there were tears behind her harsh words. That she did not want Miriel to go was plain enough. But might she have said something? Instructed the girl to disobey her uncle? Might she have let slip just what the Duke intended?

If we were caught up in this together, I reasoned, I might have a chance to speak to her. I hated the thought of going to her with a question, admitting that I knew nothing, but she was in this as much as I. She might answer.

I chose my time, and chose well, because I had taken Temar's latest lesson to heart. He had drawn me aside, as I was preparing to leave, and had said, "I have a task for you, Catwin."

I had smiled up at him, basking in the feeling of his gaze on me. "What is it?"

"You remember how I asked you to follow the Duke?"

I nodded. "Yes."

"This is more difficult," he had said with a smile.

"I can do it!"

He smiled at that. "I know you can, little one. I want you to follow the Lady Miriel this time." Across the room, I saw that Roine had gone very still. I looked at her, then back to Temar, who behaved as if he had not noticed.

"I can do that," I said scornfully.

"Here's the hard part," Temar said seriously. "The Lady will beat you if she finds out. You know this." My face must have changed, for Temar took hold of my shoulders. "So you must be very careful. You must know which servants report to the Lady, and you must not let them see you. You must watch Miriel without anyone realizing that you are doing it. Can you do that for me, Catwin? Will you be safe?"

When he asked, I stared at him wide-eyed, terrified into silence, and too proud to tell him that I wanted nothing to do with this new assignment. Watch Miriel? Here? Then, with foolish bravado, I had decided to do what I could. I would be away from the Lady soon enough. I would risk it. What I would not risk was Temar's disappointment.

"Yes," I said, and he smiled at me.

And so, I had watched Miriel carefully. It was there, in the flurry of our leaving, that I noticed the first strange thing about Miriel: she never truly smiled. She followed the Lady about with her beautiful face grave and composed, like a child playing dress up; she studied the Lady's expression, always, before she made one of her own, and when the Lady turned to see what her daughter was thinking, she always saw a little mirror of herself.

When the Lady scowled at a mention of a rival family at court, Miriel narrowed her eyes and set her little mouth in a miniature pout. When the Lady was pretending to look interested in something the Duke had to say, about trade or the paving of the highways, Miriel tilted her head and leaned her back in a tiny copy of the Lady's feigned emotion. When I saw Miriel nodding gravely as she listened to a discussion of the High Priest's new teachings on the Gods-given rights of Kings, I had to stifle my laugh into my hand, crouching as I was in the shadow of a curtain. Even the Duke would not have been amused at that.

Miriel was a consummate actress, clever and exact in her mimicry. But when the Lady smiled, startled into laughter by some story of exploits at court, Miriel's face could barely follow the motion. Her mouth stretched wide, and her eyelids crinkled, but her eyes were pools of black, falling away, a bottomless pit. Even if the Lady's laughter was cruel, or mocking, Miriel could hardly mimic it. And when she walked on her own, as she did more and more often while we prepared to leave, her face fell into a faraway look of sadness.

When I realized that she did not smile, I found myself thinking back on our lessons, on the times she had laughed, or so I thought. I thought of her perfect little giggle, and I realized that Miriel had never once truly laughed in my presence. She made the sound because she had learned to do so, because she had been taught, but there had been nothing behind her eyes. If I had not been distracted by my pain, then, I would have seen the strain behind the motion. I would have noticed the vague confusion whenever she smiled at her tutor, as if she had learned to mimic him but did not know what she was doing.

I could not think what this meant. I could not understand it. So I tucked it away, to think about, and I followed her, noting when she would slip away from her governess and her maids, fall back out of her mother's train and walk down side corridors. I waited until after dinner one night, and then shrank into the shadow of a doorway, waiting for her.

I heard the swish of her gown as she turned the hall, the quick patter of her feet that faded as she realized she was not being followed. Then I stepped into her path. I gave a little bow, as a servant should do, and Miriel stared at me with her eyes narrowed. Any surprise she might have felt was masked quickly enough with anger.

"I won't talk to you," she announced. I was far from surprised by the sentiment, but I felt irritation wash over me. We were the two singled out to go to Penekket. One would think that she would be as curious as I.

"You just did," I pointed out, petty, and she sniffed.

"Well, I won't anymore." I just looked at her, and she raised her little pointed chin. "Get out of my way." And, while she waited for me to move, she added, "And you're not to come to Penekket. I order you to stay here." She spoke the words like an apprentice magician—as if she had reason to think they might work, but no belief.

That was the key; I saw it in a flash. "Your orders don't matter at all," I said, easily. I stayed in her path, blocking her way down the corridor. "The Duke is the one who gives the orders. You just obey them, like me."

She bridled at that. "I do not!"

"You're going to Penekket, aren't you?" She stared at me in sullen silence, and I realized that I had backed myself into a corner. Now I could not ask her outright, for she would be only too happy to revel in her knowledge while I was ignorant. Cursing myself for my own stupidity, I went on the offensive. "And he won't even tell you why. You're just following his orders, too scared to wonder what it is you're doing."

"I know what I'm doing!" she shot back, her hands in fists. I crossed my arms and shot her a knowing grin, and she leaned forward as if she would scratch my eyes out. "I'm to go to Court."

"Everyone knows that," I pointed out, feigning boredom. I was surprised to see her draw herself up, her spine ramrod straight. I was even more surprised at the words that came out of her mouth.

"I'm for the King," she announced.

I blinked at her. "You're fourteen years old," I said blankly.

She rolled her eyes. "Not *now*," she said. "Later. When I'm old enough, I'm going to make him fall in love with me." She was glowing with her own importance, but as she tossed her head proudly, she realized what I had done. She stiffened, drew in a breath, and then could find nothing to say. Her glare was venomous.

"Never speak to me again," she hissed. Vengeful, she formed her mouth into a smile. "My mother will have you beaten for this."

"You'd never tell your mother you told me," I bluffed, genuinely scared. I had been the victim of my own pride once more. Would I never learn? "Telling the servants you're for the King."

She drew back from me. She could have told her mother any lie, but it had not occurred to her yet; I could only hope that it would not occur at all. She whirled and ran back down the hallway, never sparing me a glance, and I watched her go. I had learned more, but felt, somehow, as if I knew less than I had before. I knew very little of the world, but I was certain that if Miriel was betrothed to the King, someone would have mentioned that. It seemed important. My head buzzing with thoughts, I went off to find Roine and finish packing.

Chapter 7

Leave-taking was a curious thing, a strangely hollow thing. We left near dawn, so as to be at one of the garrisons by nightfall. I helped Roine haul the last of our furniture down to the servants' quarters, and then ran out into the courtyard to see the cavalcade of carriages. In the morning dark, the courtyard was lit by guttering torches, casting long shadows around the men who ran and yelled to each other, leading horses out and checking weapons.

I had to dodge amongst them, avoiding curses and horses hooves, to get to our cart. I stowed my pack in the cart where I was to ride, amongst Roine's books and herbs, and then stole away, heedless of Roine's call to stay close. I dashed across the flagstone floor of the great hall, cutting down the side hallways that would bring me quickest to our tower, and I pounded up the stairs to it, taking them two at a time.

The tower room where I had lived with Roine was now empty of everything I had known: the floor was swept bare, even the hay and strewing herbs gone. The tables and shelves were gone and stowed in the carts with Roine's books and herbs. My little cot had been moved down to the scullery for one of the maids, and even the rag carpet that Roine had placed on the floor between my bed and hers, so that we should not have to place our bare feet on the cold floor, had been packed away.

I cast a final glance around the room, but it no longer resembled the room in which I had been raised. It was as if every memory of cozy winter nights, bedtime stories, and Roine's healing had been swept away with the dust and cobwebs. The room might have been inhabited by my ghost, I thought; I could almost see myself, sitting at one of the tables, lying on my cot. I could see Roine, faintly, leaning over a mortar and pestle. But it was as if they were people far away from me, centuries removed; there was nothing to say that Catwin had been here only a week gone.

I shook my head to clear it, then went back down the winding steps without a backward glance. I did not look around me at the corridors I walked through, nor up at the shadowed rafters of the great hall. Even as I walked through it, the castle was fading from my memory.

The cold mountain air swirled around my feet and I shivered and hunched my shoulders as I came back into the entryway, back to the chaos of the preparations. I had been absorbed in my own thoughts, but when I reached the great doorway, I saw something that stopped me in my tracks. I slid into a doorway and lingered in the shadows.

Miriel and the Lady stood framed in the light from the courtyard, the torchlight gilding Miriel's black curls, making the Lady's hair gleam like liquid gold. The Lady bent down, her hands on Miriel's shoulders, and spoke urgently. What she said was for Miriel's ears alone, for there was no way to hear her over the clamor of the courtyard; I could only see the profile of Miriel's solemn face.

As they stood together in the center of the great doorway, the flow of servants back and forth from the caravan parted around them like a rock in a stream. It seemed almost as if no one saw them standing there at all.

I thought later that I was one of the only ones who saw them taken from each other. It was the Duke who broke through the stream of servants and took Miriel by the arm, issuing a curt order to her. She looked at him for a moment as if she would measure her will against his, but dropped her head back down and dropped into a curtsy to her mother, her back straight.

At the moment of leaving, I saw the Lady give a little gasp. She was speaking quickly, putting a hand out to touch his arm, but he was insistent, and Miriel gave a little half-hearted smile, a one-armed embrace before leaving as quietly as a mute. She looked like Old Clara, I thought, the maid whose mind had fled her, who stared at nothing and sometimes muttered to herself; Miriel's eyes were as blank, her manner as distracted. I did not think she heard the words her uncle was saying in her ear as he led her to a little pony.

She looked backwards only once, a long look over her shoulder at her mother, standing alone in the great doorway, even her slender height dwarfed, the bright blue of her gown muted in the torchlight. Miriel gazed into her mother's eyes, and what they shared, I could not know; I thought of what it would be like to leave Roine standing there as I began a journey, and my throat closed. I put my head down as I fought through the crowd, and did not answer Roine's question as to where I had been.

Our cart lurched forward, and I took a last look around me. On the wall, a lone figure in a black cloak raised his hand, and I pushed myself up on the crates, balancing precariously to wave back. I wondered if Aler was smiling, to think of what he would always say to me: "Get down, little cat, you'll break your neck!" I was smiling, but the smile did not come out quite right; I could feel tears running down my face as well. I ducked as we went under the archway, and as the cart rolled away down the hill, I sat back and looked up at the castle, like a little toy, candles flickering against the pre-dawn blue.

On a clear day, we could have seen the beauty of the mountains stretching away, and the plains, green and warm; in the dark, there was nothing to see at all, and so we wound down the mountainside without looking out, the mules stepping as daintily as they could, the carters cursing the thin mountain road.

The sky was growing pale as we reached the village, and the townsfolk stopped their chores and turned out to watch us as we rode through. They were neither friendly nor unfriendly, but watched us like we were the fae folk from the eastern fairy tales, not quite real, not quite of their world.

My blood chilled as I looked around at the place. Since Roine had carried my infant self back up to the castle, I had never returned to the village. And yet, I knew it perfectly. The dream I had had, all those months ago, was still so crystal clear that I could remember every moment of it. I could see the houses I had trudged past in the storm. I looked up and saw that the castle was the same in every detail: the placement of the towers, the curve of the road.

Only when I had looked at every other detail did I look to where I knew the hovel should be. And there I saw only an enclosure with a few hens. The shack was gone; so completely that it might never have been. Almost frantic at the sudden difference, I looked about me at the hill people.

They were looking for Miriel and the Duke, and while their eyes slid past me, I cast my gaze over them, searching for eyes like mine, hair like mine. I remembered my mother's broad cheekbones and my father's heavy brows. I saw nothing; they all looked alike, those townsfolk, and what differences there were, were obscured by years of grime. Still, I looked and I wondered for the first time which of these men might be my brothers, or my father, bowed now with age. I wondered if I would see my mother, if she had lived beyond my birth; I wondered if I would know her.

I could not say. I did not see the faces from my dream in the crowd of village folk. I do not know if I have brothers or sisters still living in the cold of the mountains. I do not even know my mother's name, and I have never been certain if she knew mine—or if she gave me away without even naming me herself. If I am honest with myself, I know that sometimes I doubt my parents ever existed. Sometimes, I think I was a child made of that swirling snow, borne of parents who faded into the mountains like ghosts after my birth, never to be seen again.

The Duke would later name me a Shadow, and after his naming, life itself wore me away to make his words true. I have been a Shadow for years upon years now. And yet, I think that if I were to trace back to the moment I started to fade away from the world, it would not be when I began my training, or when I first killed, or when I first spied upon my King. It would be the moment that I looked around myself, in that cold mountain village, and realized that I had no past, that I had come from nowhere. I might never have been born and no one would ever have missed me.

Chapter 8

Our first night on the road was desperately cold. There were not enough travelers for any decent inns to remain open on the mountain road, and so it would be two nights until we reached the shelter of a warm hearth and real beds. Most of us, even the Duke, were sleeping in tents, made of heavy canvas but still drafty, but Miriel had been made a little room in the back of one of the wagons, absurdly fashioned into a sort of house. It was built well, with its own little door and steps up to it, and the chamber was kept snug and warm with carpets and canvas draped across the sides of it.

The Duke called for me and bid me to see that Miriel was settled, and so I went at a run until I was out of his sight, and then continued to the wagon with dragging feet. I would never have dreamed of defying the Duke, but I did not want to be Miriel's servant any more than she wanted my service. I rapped on the door, only a formality with so many guards about, and slipped inside.

It was so warm in the wagon that I found myself sweating at once, but Miriel looked chilled to her very bones. She had always seemed at home in the palace, but outside its strong walls, she was no longer a child of the mountains; her father's southern blood had a strong hold on her. She was pale as death in her velvet-and-brocade dressing gown, very heavy and warm looking, and she had a blanket draped around her shoulders as well, but she looked desperately cold, and when she turned her head, I saw eyes that were shadowed with fatigue.

I felt, unexpectedly, a wave of pity for her. At least I had Roine to travel with, the closest thing to a mother I had ever had. Miriel was not close to her uncle, I could see that readily enough, and she did not even seem very close to her own mother. As we had left the castle, she had walled herself into her mind, and now she was all alone.

I forgot my pity when her face snapped into a glare. "What are you doing here?"

"Your uncle the Duke ordered me to see if you had everything you needed," I said, hating her once more, and hating the Duke, and hating that she could ask me anything right now and I would be bidden to do my utmost to get it for her. I saw that realization strike her as well, and for a moment, as her lips curved into her mother's smile, I wondered what she would say. In that moment, she was all malice, exquisite and poisonous.

Then her eyes roamed across the crowded interior of the carriage, she shivered in the cold, and the fight went out of her. Her cruelty bled away into the night, and she looked down at her hands where they were clasped in her lap.

"I don't need anything," she said, with an attempt at her mother's crisp tone. Instead of sharply, it came out of her quietly; there was resignation, there was the shadow of dignity. I blinked, unsure what to say, and she turned a face to me that was white as snow. "Get out," she said more clearly. "And never again enter my presence without my express permission."

I hesitated a moment, and then bowed and left the little room. It was an empty show, not for anyone's benefit other than her own. Miriel would be a fool to think I could do anything other than obey her uncle's wishes, and it came to me that I did not think that she was a fool. She was a little philosopher in the making, and she had not wanted to come to Penekket to be a pretty decoration at the court. But when forced, she had not stamped her foot and thrown a temper tantrum; she had locked her emotions away and now watched the world through narrowed eyes. I had the curious thought that she seemed to be biding her time.

It was uncharacteristic for the child I knew, so much the spoiled, favored child, so much the brat. I could not understand it. I went back to the tent Roine and I shared, and though I lay down to sleep on the hard ground, curled against Roine's warmth, I lay awake for a long time, staring out into the dark.

Just before I fell asleep, I suddenly remembered Temar's words to Roine, all those months ago: *Fate will pull her where it wills.* --I waited for the comfort that the priests had always said came from knowing one's place in life. Fate was guiding me, I thought sleepily.

It was not comforting in the slightest.

The journey passed in a blur, strangely, one part dazed wonder and one part growing unease. On the Duke's orders, I often rode close to Miriel. I was to train myself to follow her instinctively, so that I was always at her right shoulder, should she need me. I bit my tongue on the question of why Miriel should ever need me. I hated the Lady with all my heart, but had to admit that her questions had been justified. Why pluck a serving girl out of the dirt, train her to read and write, and then set her to be a maid for a young noblewoman on her way to the royal court? It was ridiculous.

And so my service was an empty gesture, with confusion on my part and disdain on Miriel's. I had never been a ladies' maid, and even if I had any knowledge of how to behave, there was not anything for me to fetch, or anyone to whom to send a message. There was little I could give in the way of service, and when Miriel did want for something, she would look around herself for her maidservant rather than ask for my help. She was unable to countermand the Duke's orders that I serve her, and so she did her best to pretend that she could not see me. She took every opportunity to demonstrate that her uncle could command my presence at her side, but he could not forge a bond between us like he had with Temar.

It gave me a childish pleasure to know that my presence annoyed her, but the journey was long, and the novelty of my spite wore off quickly. Worse, the Duke had ordered that I learn to ride, so that I could accompany Miriel when the court hunted, or when we traveled. I had to be close, always, not shut away in a cart like a servant. So I had been given a horse, one the guardsmen assured the Duke was docile, but with enough spirit to terrify me, who preferred to have my feet on the ground.

Riding was more exhausting than anything else I had ever done; I rode only a few hours a day, and yet I ached more and more as the days passed. The skin of my legs was raw, and sitting up straight was an agony. Worse, Miriel rode with the same easy grace with which she did everything else. She sat in the saddle like a princess, like an elfin huntress, and if she had not been pretending not to see me, she would gladly have mocked my incompetence. It was the schoolroom all over again, and I hated it.

I was glad for the times when I was able to rein my horse back and ride with Temar, for the Duke wanted me to waste no time in my training. He did not bother to explain this to me himself, leaving that task to Temar, who told me gravely and formally that he would teach me tumbling and fighting techniques when we reached the palace. I was left to puzzle out on my own why I should need to know that.

In the meantime, confined to horses, he taught me the things a good courtier should know: mainly, to be able to name every face I saw and not to trust anyone. There was a litany of names and lineages and secrets to learn, but I did not mind—I found that I missed learning, and Temar was as good as a library, an endless source of information on anything I could think of to ask. The afternoon sessions were structured, but he made a point to ride with me for an hour or so each morning before I was summoned to wait on Miriel, and answered my chattered questions with his easy grace.

Temar was strict as a governess—a thought that made me giggle to myself—in his insistence that I carry myself well, and speak clearly when I talked with him. He demanded absolutely that I take my learning seriously, and between my love of learning and my child's worship of him, it was an easy burden to do what he asked.

He used the journey to test my knowledge of the great families and the structure of power in the country. I had learned, and learned well, the knowledge held in the library at Voltur, but I learned that this was old information, a basis and nothing more. The more recent history I knew only vaguely, and Temar hastened to give me a more thorough grounding.

I learned that Henry, the Boy King's father, had never been intended for the throne. He had been thrust onto the throne when William died in battle, and he had been a poor ruler, with no head for intrigue. I learned that his Dowager Queen, Isra, had turned to faith in her grief, and went nowhere but that she had the Head Priest at her side. She was a competent ruler, and determined that her son should recover from his constant illness so that the throne should not fall into the hands of the Conradines once more, as the heir at present was Wilhelm, Conradine and Warden both.

I had known but little of the throne until a few months ago. I had not had any concept of rival houses, or warring factions. I knew that the throne passed by lineage, and so I had known that the ruling house had once been Conradine, and was now Warden, but had not known how this had come to be. When Temar described it, blandly, I knew better than to say that it did not sound righteous, but instead sneaky.

It was my first moment as a courtier, realizing that the truth of the thing was entirely unwelcome. I listened to the story of how Arthur had married his brother to the Kleist family and, with their support, swept westward across the plains to cut the Conradines down in their beautiful city. He had taken the throne for himself and claimed divine guidance, and if the gods had resented his use of their name, they had kept silent about it. The country—faced with only the women of the Conradine line left alive on the one hand, and a man commanding two armies on the other—had shifted its allegiance with scarcely a murmur of complaint.

Indeed, the constant power struggle of the court had continued unabated. The nobles who had positioned themselves the most aggressively for the favor of the Conradines now courted the favor of Arthur's family, House Warden. Marriages were made for new alliances, obscure houses who had been friends to Arthur's line grew to prominence: d'Orleans, de la Marque, Cessor, Staithe.

Now I knew the history behind the marriages I had memorized from the Duke's history books. It was dizzying; I had memorized the lineages well enough, but once Temar began to tell me the details about each player, and ask me to guess at their motivations and their actions, I could barely keep it all in my head. This, he would not tolerate.

"There is nothing more important, Catwin," he said to me seriously on the first day. "Believe me when I tell you this. It is well enough to protect Miriel from an assassin's blade when the blow falls, but better by far to know where trouble may lurk and avoid it from the start, and advise her on her own interests. You must know who those women are who were born to be her rivals, and warn her of them."

"She would never take my advice," I said, sulky, and Temar looked over at Miriel thoughtfully. He watched her almost as much as the Duke did; they both looked at Miriel as if they could wear away her very flesh with their thoughts, and see into her soul.

"Whether she wishes to take your advice or not, it is your duty to be there to give it," Temar said finally. "Whether she wishes to have you at your side to protect her, it is your duty to be there if she should need you. Do you understand?"

"No!" I burst out, surprising even myself. "I *don't* understand! Why me? What am I to do? No one will tell me why I am here, and anyway, why should I be with Miriel if she hates me, and I hate her?"

Temar did not try to argue with me. He rode with one hand on the reins, one hand on his hip, gazing out at the countryside while he waited for my outburst to die away. I had a moment before he looked back at me and I gazed at his profile, noticing that for all the ease he pretended, his jaw was tight and his left hand gripped the reins tightly.

"It is your duty," he said simply, when he looked back at me. "There is no escaping it, Catwin."

Why me? The question trembled on my lips, and I knew that Temar saw it, but I did not have the courage to voice it, and he did not answer it. Instead, almost without volition, he looked over at the Duke. Temar, the man who would later teach me to betray no emotion, to be impassive always, stared after the Duke with a look of such hatred that I was taken aback.

I could have pretended not to notice; Temar, absorbed in his emotions, would not have thought to look at me. I could have looked out at the fields and pretended... But I was curious, and so I stood and waited for him to turn and see me.

He did not startle when he saw me watching him; such reactions had been trained out of him long ago. He did not look concerned, or frustrated at what I had seen. He looked at me as if he would manage me. That was when I understood: none of us mattered that much to Temar. Only the Duke.

Temar only waited for me to speak.

"You hate him," I said finally, uncomprehending.

"Yes," Temar said simply. He did not even try to lie.

"Why stay?" I asked, going to the main point. "Why protect him? If you hate him? You could kill him in a moment and be gone before anyone knew."

"On the day you understand why," he said sadly, "you will become a Shadow."

I did not say anything. I could not think what he might mean. To understand his hatred was to become a Shadow—well, I had no reason to think that I would ever understand Temar. This was clearly one of the mysteries of grown-ups. I resolved to find some way to ask Roine about it.

"Now," he resumed, as if I had not spoken at all. "There are layers to history. Older events sink down, as if through running water to the bed of a river, moving little."

"They've already happened," I muttered, still sulky. "They don't move at all."

"Oh, you think you know everything now?" Temar raised an eyebrow, neither un-amused by my sulkiness, nor particularly charmed by it. "What if a noble were to die, a noble who might have

---

become the Lord Admiral of the northern fleets, and a decade later, a serving man confessed on his deathbed that the man died not of a fever, but of poison? What then?"

I only stared at him, struck by this idea, and he took the opportunity to resume.

"Other events move above them, changed and shifted by the groundwork. These are the rapids at the surface of the river itself, swirling and moving quickly, able to shift direction at a moment's notice. This is why you must know modern history as well as ancient history: the older events lie deep, shaping the course of the river, but a river may be disturbed and shift its course quickly, the currents may change without warning to the unwary." He looked at me for a moment, as I thought about this, and cleared his throat so that I would remember to sit up straight and keep my eyes forward on the road. He watched, and he waited for my eyes to fix on something ahead.

"Tell me about the Conradines," he said at random, when he knew my attention had been caught by a flock of birds. Temar liked to do this, startle me and see if I could remember my knowledge.

"The bloodline of the Wulfrics," I said promptly. This was a gentle question, however, a way to pay homage to the older history I had studied, and I smiled at him to thank him for the kindness. "Their line continues in Wilhelm, who is Gerald's son by Anne, and she is the king's aunt. Gerald was the sole surviving male heir of the Conradine line, but by Wulfric III's younger brother Wilfred, so he would not be of the main line. Arthur had all of them killed." I tried to think of anything else I might know about their more recent history. "They were taken from their family seat after the war," I volunteered. "They all live in the city now."

Temar nodded, he knew I had no further knowledge. "Gerald is the Duke of Everry now," he said. "Everry is a new title. You knew that? No? Everry has no history, it has no land. The Conradine line remains loyal, but it has no tenants to arm, no rents with which to pay mercenaries, no keeps in which to wait out a siege. King Arthur was superstitious, but he was clever. He dared not end a royal line entirely, but he bound it to his own and he stripped it of the ability to make war. Now Anne and her son are noble, but they have little to call their own."

"I heard she was an enemy of her cousin Elizabeth," I said. "One of the Duke's men said something about it."

"Anne has said that she should have lands that are Elizabeth's, because she descends from Arthur and Elizabeth descends from Charles."

"Is that right?" I asked uncertainly, and Temar shrugged.

"Anne has a higher claim in royal lineage, but the lands Elizabeth holds once belonged to the Heimarre family, who turned out to fight for the Conradines. Elizabeth and her husband have no true claim, but better she has them than a Conradine."

"Better for whom?" I asked, and I was rewarded by the dark gleam of his smile.

"An excellent question," he said. "Think about it tonight and tell me what you think in the morning." And he spurred his horse up to ride with the Duke, who was having a very serious discussion with his stewards about the uprising in the southeast.

This left me to my thoughts, and my grudging service of Miriel. The girl was an enigma to me, unexpectedly out of place in a landscape that grew increasingly warm and lush. The countryside suited her looks perfectly, and I expected the girl who had been so cold and so miserable on the early part of our journey to be glad of the heat, but instead Miriel seemed to grow paler and more miserable.

I wondered what she saw waiting for her at the end of this road. She was to be in the lap of luxury, very far from the drafty castle in which she had been raised. She would be attended to by servants with better manners than her companions had ever had. She would have the companionship of the richest and most well-bred women in the whole of Heddred. The thought did not seem to please her, and I could not think why—nor could I ask. Her resolute indifference to me was as much a barrier as the difference in our statuses, and any pity I had was prone to ebb when I saw her look of dislike at my presence.

And so I spent the journey caught between curiosity and determined ignorance, pity and anger. I would look at her sad profile and I would spur my horse forward to speak to her, smile at her; catching her glare, I would feel anger flare in my blood. Every time she would order me away from her, I tried to put a name to why I felt so driven to protect her. It was as if, when I looked at her, I saw someone else. I thought she was someone who would laugh at my jokes and be a friend as Aler had been my friend.

Why I thought so, I could not say—the first time we had seen each other was when she had laughed at my pain in the courtyard, and our later encounters had not been any more promising. We were worlds apart, there was no reason that we should ever have been close. Yet, every time I saw her, in the moment before I remembered that she hated me, and I her, I thought of her as a friend. And that made her studied indifference all the worse.

When puzzling out Miriel's character wore on me, I watched others. I studied laughter, having noticed that she never laughed; now I had begun to watch for it in others. In any case, Temar had told me that I was to learn to observe people, and so I had, most especially Roine and the Duke; Roine, because I rode with her and loved her and wished I knew what went on in her mind, and the Duke, because his word was my law. I did not dare watch Temar, for fear that he would notice and laugh at my efforts to be covert.

I watched them, and I noticed that their faces sank into reverie sometimes, as if they forgot that they might be being watched. Roine was inclined to look tired and sad, and the Duke weathered and grim; when startled from such a mood, though, their faces were a wonder to behold. One day, as we rode, a flock of birds leapt from the field alongside us and sprang into the air, their plumage brilliant, their calls beautiful. I watched as the Duke stared at them, the grimness worn away to contentment by this strange, natural phenomenon. Roine was startled to laughter; she smiled spontaneously and clapped her hands at the sight, then looked at me with genuine pleasure. I forgot to smile for a moment, and only looked at her to memorize her face; even with all that came later, it is one of my happiest memories: the sun on her face, the smile on her lips.

But when I looked over to Her, to my liege lady, I saw her staring after the birds almost sadly. Still, even in this beautiful, lush land: Miriel never smiled. She never laughed. Oh, she made the motions of it, but never once did I see her caught unawares, never once did she look up at her uncle and smile, or chatter amiably with her companions. Hers was not the face of a girl who is amazed by the world she beholds. When startled, she would falter, but never smile.

I thought back to her giggles when I had been reprimanded by her tutor. They were note perfect, but now I remembered the flatness of her eyes as she smiled. She had not been amused, or even cruel as her mother would be. Malice depended on the amusement at one's own cruelty; Miriel had no amusement and no joy. She was only fourteen years old, and unable to find a smile for a rainbow, or a fawn and its mother, or the chorus of birds at dawn. I wondered when the last time was that Miriel had been happy. I wondered if the truth was that she had forgotten to smile truly, or that never known how.

So it was that the first kind emotion I felt for the girl was pity. It was the emotion that would turn her most strongly against me out of furious pride, but it was the only thing that could have softened my heart to her.

Chapter 9

"Seven gods and seven hells," I whispered in awe.

"Don't swear by the gods," Roine said sharply. She had been un-amused with the language I had learned from the guardsmen that rode with us. I nipped my lip and offered up a whispered apology, but I could not stop staring at the vista before me.

A gentle swell in the land gave us the most beautiful view I thought I had ever seen. I, who had grown up in the spare beauty of the mountains, had thought there was nothing more striking. Even the rippling fields of green and gold, while pretty, did not move me. But Penekket was something else entirely.

The capital was a strange city, not so much a sprawl of buildings as two, bleeding one into another. At the north end was the city itself: teeming with life, spanning the river Ves. Further south, along the river, the palace itself and the houses of the nobles, clustered to the east of the fast-flowing water. Between them, bleeding from the palace into the city, were the academies, the courthouses, the more prosperous banks, and bleeding from the city to the palace were the guildhalls, the docks, and the brothels.

Between them, Penekket Fortress rose like something out of a fable. It was built of a white stone from the quarries in the south so that it shone like a beacon, visible for leagues. It was a thing of true beauty, extravagantly fashioned, built in the brief peace of Evan III as a twisted reminder of the wars Heddred had endured; within three years of Evan III's death, Penekket had been attacked once more, and the royal family became accustomed to withdrawing to the fortress in times of war.

I stared transfixed as we approached it. I knew from my reading that the Fortress was as deadly as it was beautiful, the walls built smooth to keep away grappling hooks, the arrow slits so cunningly hidden with gorgeous carvings that one might never even see from whence the arrow came. Penekket Fortress had withstood three attacks, all well funded, all perpetrated by exceedingly ruthless men. All three generals had failed, and had watched their men drop like flies in the rain of arrows, reaching the walls only to be felled by burning oil poured from ornamental spouts. All the while, the Fortress had sat in serene beauty, built so strongly that even catapults had not dimmed its elegance.

King Arthur, the Boy King's grandfather, had known the power of the Fortress, and had respected it. His rebellion was unexpected, quick, and ruthless. He did not fight on the open plain and battle his way to the heart of the city. He never made a single challenge to the Conradines; he cut them down in their beds, as they slept. He succeeded in taking the throne, most said, only because he had caught the royal family before they could seek sanctuary.

He had been a cunning man, Temar told me, never one to meet a foe in outright battle if it could be avoided, and his son William had inherited his ruthless strategy and adaptable conscience. William would have ended the war with Ismir in months, I was told, if he had not been felled by camp fever. The reign of his brother Henry, the Boy King's father, had been marred by Henry's stubborn insistence on meeting foes in the open. The war with Ismir had nearly been lost time and again, and peace had only been won again at Voltur with the cruel tactics of the Duke.

Now, Heddred was at peace again. Freed, faithful men said, from the warlords. Waiting, others said cautiously—or worse, hopefully—for the warlords to return. For sure, their Fortress sat either as a beautiful, immovable reminder, or as a beacon. I, who had never questioned the stability of the King's rule before speaking to Temar, was struck by how ominous the beautiful tower seemed. I fancied that I could hear it calling for its long-gone masters, and I shivered.

Beside the fortress, even the gold-domed roofs of the cathedrals and palace buildings seemed unimpressive. They looked as if they might be easily crushed by some vengeful giant, wiped away like a child's play house made of sticks. I had the thought that, were the city to be felled by a plague, the buildings would crumble and be overtaken by the land, but Penekket tower would rise serenely over the landscape for millennia to come, unchanged, unbowed.

As we drew closer to the palace, a swathe of green caught my eye. Beyond the palace to the south lay a strange thing: a forest, but somehow orderly and neat, bounded by fences of iron and stone. The fence itself was well wrought but formidable—I thought that if I were to stand on a tall man's shoulders, I would still not nearly be high enough to climb over.

"What's that?" I asked Roine, and her mouth tightened.

"That is the forest where the King hunts," she said shortly. She braced herself as the wagon jolted over the paving stones.

"It looks..." I could not find the word.

"Unnatural," she supplied. Her face was grim.

"How d'you mean?"

"Speak clearly," she reprimanded. The idea that I should behave like a noble was one of the few things she and Temar agreed upon. In other matters, she would defer to him—she never argued—but with the air of a cat that has its claws out and its back arched. But on the matters of manners and speech, Roine has always insisted that I behave as a girl of good birth, instead of the orphan bastard child that I was.

"How do you mean," I said clearly, and she gave a little nod at my diction.

"I mean that the forest did not grow there on its own. It was built by the kings before. It is not a true forest."

"I think it's pretty," I said. In truth, I did not care much either way, but I wanted to see why she disliked it. I was not disappointed. Her eyes flashed.

"It is a pointless extravagance," she said flatly. "The gold it took to build that forest, and stock it, and tend it, and fence it in, could feed all the poor in Heddred for years."

One of the guardsmen looked over at us, askance, and Roine glared back stubbornly.

"I don't think you're supposed to say things like that," I whispered, worried without understanding why. For a moment, neither of them backed down, they both ignored me. Then Roine gave a small sigh and let the tension flow out of her shoulders. She smiled at the guardsman, then down at me.

"Out of the mouths of babes," she said clearly, her voice carrying. "The King is wise and just, Catwin. It is not for us to question him. Say you agree, child," she added.

"I agree," I said obediently, and I was rewarded with her smile. But I thought that deep down, behind her smiling mouth and her pleasant demeanor, she looked just like Miriel—biding her time.

As our party moved quickly over the last few miles, the palace gained in grandeur, and my own fear grew. Our journey had been like an enchanted time, when I was servant neither to the Lady nor to her daughter. I had flown free of my former life, and for a few days it had seemed almost that I would be free all my life, but now the city loomed up out of the plains and I knew that I was soon to be caged inside it.

And this was no little place like the Winter Castle at Voltur. Now I could see the sheer magnitude of it—I gazed up at the fortress and almost shuddered at the size of that—and I found myself scared. I had been raised in a palace...I thought. It was the former seat of Ismir's royal line, and I had thought it grand.

It was nothing to this. Even the road that led to the palace was beautiful, made of paving stones interlocked together. It was kept neat; someone kept the weeds from it and replaced the stones when it cracked. I thought it must take a small army of servants, and wondered what Roine thought of that, but knew better than to ask.

We approached Penekket from the west, with the setting sun at our backs, and when the road branched like a river delta—something I had seen in one of the maps Temar showed me—we followed it south, always south. This was the road that would lead us to the heart of the palace, and it grew finer every time we branched away, lined with beautiful hedgerows and well-built walls. Guards patrolled these stretches, standing deferentially to the side and saluting as our party went past.

We had to cross a great and deadly bridge to gain access to the palace, as beautiful as a bridge could be, but built by the best engineers of the ages. It could kill a man in a dozen ways, and hold back an army; twice, it had done just that. It had been a good defense when the kings of Heddred feared invasion from the Ismiri, driven back only four generations ago now and still hungry for our rich farmland and our great lodes of gold and iron ores. Less useful, the clever bridge had been, when Arthur marched with an army from Dalvbard, sweeping from the east and catching the Conradines unawares.

Still, useless as it was, I shivered when its shadow fell over me. Penekket was a city of unutterable beauty, but the buildings rose from the streets like the bones of a predator. I knew myself for a fool, but I thought that I could feel it breathing, I thought that it knew itself to be lying in wait. It was like a great mountain cat, full of claws and teeth as traps for the unwary; a glimmer of eyes on a dark winter's night, a flash of teeth, a growl. It was a city for peace, but shaped unquestionably by war.

No one else seemed to notice, or care. The guardsmen were happy to be back near the city, laughing and jesting with each other about the inns they would visit, a few of them calling out their whores by name. Roine shot them furious glares, mindful of my young ears, but I did not mind. They reminded me of Aler, and when I listened to their conversation I found that I relaxed, and did not think of what lay ahead.

Slowly, however, the palace turned from a pretty child's toy, far away, into a great jumble of buildings. In the dusk, I saw the lamps being lit, the pretty carvings at the windows standing out against the golden light inside. When we passed through the gates, the guardsmen called out to their friends on the walls, and those men lifted their pikes in a salute to the Duke. The Duke was still a legend, and those who rode under his standard were welcome here, we had allies in the king's guard and the army. That made me feel better.

It took some time to ride from the gates to our courtyard, for the palace was not, in truth, a palace at all. At the center of it all was a building that one might call a palace, with pleasure gardens and marble floors and carvings on the walls; the king lived there, and a few select members of the Council, from old families that had been close to the throne back when the palace was new-built. The business of the realm was conducted in that building, itself many times the size of the castle I had grown up in, which had once been the royal castle of Ismir.

But generations of nobility and royalty had come and gone, each leaving their mark with a new wing or an elaborate chapel. Even as the royalty became more ensconced, the nature of royalty changed. Wulfric's line had once been content with mead and smoky halls, caring little for anything save their raids and their battles. That had changed with Evan I, who had been known as the peacemaker; he had built great libraries while his kinsmen were off waging their wars. As the royalty proceeded into war and peace, at turns, the palaces had become places of leisure, with great kitchens and dancing halls, and then fortresses, with menacing walls. It was like the rings in a tree, I thought.

I was bone-weary when we all dismounted, and I could hardly fathom the thought of unpacking our goods and setting our rooms to rights. I wanted to be home, asleep on my little cot, and I could have cried when I remembered that I had no home now. We had stripped the tower room bare and another maid slept in my cot, another healer would take their place in the apothecary's rooms. There was no home to go back to.

We tumbled from the wagon, and I stood close at Roine's side, frightened by this noisy courtyard, still a jumble of activity even in the night. Even though it was only the courtyard for one of the buildings that lay about the castle, it was easily three times as large as the courtyard in Voltur, at the Winter Castle.

I was grabbing a crate of our things when one of the guardsmen came to find me. He was one of the Duke's personal guard, a great tall man stinking of horse and the road, and he had no sympathy to spare for a servant of the Lady's daughter, who would rather share a room with her adopted mother.

"You're to go with the little Lady," he said, jerking his thumb to where Miriel stood, accompanied by her maidservant and surrounded by liveried guards, unloading the endless trunks of her things.

"Surely there's no work to be done for the Lady Miriel tonight," Roine said, drawing me in to her side with an arm around my shoulders. I looked up at her, praying with all my heart that she could save me from this man. "I'll send Catwin to the Lady Miriel's rooms in the morning. She has unpacking to do for me tonight."

"She's t'come now," the man said, unimpressed. "Duke's orders. She'll sleep in the lady's rooms." His large hand rested idly at his waist, by the hilt of his dagger, and that decided matters quickly enough. He was not threatening us; he had likely never needed to threaten anyone since he had pinned the Duke's sigil on his cloak. Everything about this man showed the Duke's power.

"Go, then," Roine said, in my ear. She embraced me quickly, then took my shoulders and pushed me away before I could bury my face in her shoulder and cry. "It's not so bad as that," she said, forcedly cheerful. "I'm to give you lessons. I'll see you soon."

"I can't leave you," I whispered, but the man's hand closed around my arm and cut off the goodbye.

"Remember what you are," she whispered to me fiercely, and then I was dragged through the crowd, hating him and hating the Duke, hating Miriel for being a girl I needed to serve and— absurdly—hating Roine, in the very moment after I had clung to her for comfort, for not being able to save me from it all.

The Duke wasted no words in greeting me. His eyes flicked over me like I was a horse in his stables. He took the measure of my failings.

"You'll sleep in the Lady Miriel's rooms," he said shortly. "In her chamber, to guard her." I saw Miriel's eyes flare at this, but she did not say anything. "In the morning, you will go with Temar to get fitted for clothing. I will not have my niece accompanied by a girl who looks like a street urchin."

"She is a street urchin," Miriel said, sulkily.

"She is a royal servant," the Duke corrected her, irritated.

"She's a whore's bastard."

"Watch your tongue." The Duke did not flare up, as she had done. He did not even get angry. He went at once cold, deadly. "*You* will behave like a Lady." His quiet words were more frightening than anger would have been; Miriel dropped her eyes to the ground and said nothing until he looked away, then cast a quick glare at me. Sure it would annoy her, I shrugged back at her and grinned cheekily, and she clenched her teeth and looked away.

Temar stepped around the Duke to come to my side. "I will come to fetch you in the morning," he said quietly, and I looked up at him. He smiled. "Be brave, Catwin. The palace is not so big as it seems right now."

At this unexpected kindness, I looked down, blinking away tears. I wanted to ask why I was to sleep in Miriel's room, and what the Duke expected me to be able to do to protect her. That, and a dozen more questions swirled in my head, but Temar's hand rested lightly on my back as he pushed me forward, following the small train of Miriel's servants. At the doorway, I looked back over my shoulder, and saw Roine through the crowd. I raised my hand in a little wave, suddenly gripped by dread, and after a moment she raised her hand to me as well. She seemed to be trying not to cry.

I clenched my nails into my palm so hard they bit into the skin, trying not to cry myself, and then I turned and ran to follow Miriel and her servants.

Chapter 10

As good as his word, Temar came to find me the next day. He raised his eyebrows to find me curled in an armchair, still wearing the same clothes as the night before.

"Why are you not in Miriel's room?"

"She locked the door on me," I said. I winced as I stood, and stretched carefully.

"Well, then we'll have to get you lock picks," he said, unimpressed. I raised my eyebrows, but he was serious. "You would have needed them anyway. But Miriel must not command you away from her side."

"Was it like this for you?" I asked curiously, shoving my feet into my boots. "When you first were chosen to serve the Duke?" I thought he would laugh and tell me that yes, it had been this way, but it had gotten better. Instead, his face went as blank as I had ever seen it.

"No," he said shortly. "It was not." I remembered seeing his face when he had looked at the Duke, during our journey, and I decided to ask no more. He held open the door for me to precede him, and then led the way through the corridors so quickly that I had to half run to keep up with him.

We had been in a building near the heart of the palace, and Temar led me across the courtyard at the center, through the corridors at the other side, and out into the sunshine, where, instead of joining the steady stream of people moving about in the paths between buildings, he led us on a route that made use of the tiny alleyways. We squeezed around water barrels and hopped over crates, and a few times Temar nudged a sleeping drunk with the toe of his boot to wake them.

At last, we arrived at the Arena, a place I would learn later was halfway around the palace center from the building where we lived. Here were housed the fighting animals, the great lions and bears, and also the wrestlers, the acrobats, the king's small army of entertainers. The building had dozens of courtyards and gymnasia, and each was filled with performers, practicing their craft. I wanted to stay and watch, but Temar kept moving at a punishing pace, and more than once I was left scrambling to catch up, peering down corridors to see the flick of his black-booted feet moving out of sight.

In a large building, connected to this one by a makeshift corridor, the Quartermaster held court. On its other side were the barracks, so that the Quartermaster could serve the royal servants, and all the army as well. Indeed, there seemed to be a jumble of surly men waiting their turns to be fitted. Temar took my hand and dragged me through the crowd to an old woman at the side of the room.

"Clothes for the Duke of Voltur's new page," he said curtly. The lady nodded, having seen the sigil embroidered black-on-black on Temar's chest, and eyed me critically.

"Come with me," she said over her shoulder as she disappeared into a storage room, and Temar pushed me after her.

The woman thrust a tunic and pants at me, and some linen. "Try these on."

"Here?" I looked around me at the servants who moved through the rows of shelves, but the woman glared.

"Don't waste my time. Here."

Shivering, self conscious, I pulled off my own tunic and then my linen, pulling the new over my head as quickly as I could. No one looked over at me, no one cared about a skinny child; still, I felt horribly ill at ease. I blushed as I stripped off my pants and pulled on the new. Everything was black, like Temar's clothing, and too large for me. I felt like a crow with too-big feathers.

The woman looked me over once and nodded, then pulled my arms and legs about to check the length of everything. She called orders over her shoulder, and a servant disappeared to find more clothing.

"Three sets of pants and shirts," she said to Temar. "One tunic. One change of linen. Your own seamstress'll put on the patches." She marked something down in the great book in front of her, and waited until the servant came back with the stack of clothing, all tied together with twine.

"Where are we going now?" I asked Temar, as we set off still deeper into the building. He shot a glance at me.

"To get you some food."

"Thank you," I said, mindful of my accent. "That is kind." Temar smiled, as I had known he would.

"Very prettily done," he said, and he sat me in the corner of the mess hall and went off to find food for both of us, while I looked around me, wide-eyed, at the soldiers.

"Are we allowed to eat here?" I asked Temar, when he came back. He smiled as he set out the bread, and bowls of some sort of porridge. When the food was arranged, he tapped the sigil on his chest.

"We're Voltur's people. They like us here."

"Because the Duke won the war for King Henry?" I asked, and Temar nodded.

"He's well-regarded." He dropped his voice lower. "He was ennobled after that. You know that? Yes. So, he was a commoner before. He stayed a commander after the war, until he was made part of the King's Council, and the men say he was still good to them, he still listened to their counsel and treated them well. And that battle is army legend," he added, shrugging. Then he blinked. "Done already?"

I nodded and flushed. I had shoveled the food into my mouth as fast as I could, and wiped the bowl with my bread.

"I had forgotten how much children eat," Temar said, scratching his head. "Here, have the rest of mine."

"I can't eat your food," I protested, and he grinned and tapped me on the nose, his ill-humor from earlier quite forgotten.

"*I* can find the mess hall on my own. If I leave you, you might wander off and starve before you could find another meal." He drummed his spoon on the table. "And don't gulp your food like that."

"Why not?" I asked, with my mouth full, and he raised his eyebrow. I swallowed, hastily, wiped my mouth on my napkin, and said again, "Why not?"

"Appearances," he said. "The Duke doesn't starve his servants; we should act as if we have enough to eat. And it's not well-behaved to gulp your food." I nodded, glumly, and tried to eat more slowly, thinking that there were an awful lot of rules for behaving well.

"Now," Temar said, as I ate. He leaned forward to me. "I'm to explain to you why you're here." My head jerked up. "Do you want to know why I chose you for this, Catwin?"

"Yes." *Oh, yes.*

"You're brave," Temar said, seriously. "You were foolhardy to try to steal my dagger, but brave as well. You proved you would

---

70

walk towards danger if there were a reason. When we first called you to speak to the Duke, I saw that you were clever. You had found a way to count all the rooms of the Winter Castle without knowing higher numbers. You explored, and I saw, also, how much you saw in others.

"But there's more to it than that. Be honest with me, Catwin, you've always been good at manipulating others, haven't you?" I frowned. I did not know the word, and I was desperate to know where this was going. He answered only my confusion. "You know what to say to get your way. You know how to say things—your voice, your words, your face—to make people think one thing when maybe the truth is another way.

"Don't look so worried. I am not upset. Catwin, that is a gift. You can see into people's hearts from the words they do not say, and you know what to say to conceal your own heart from them. You may never have had to use it for anything more than—oh, let me guess—stealing pastries? Yes. But you will need both in the years to come."

"Oh."

"And I saw that you could move quietly and quickly, and I had heard from the servants that you could climb well and that you were quiet, you did not speak of gossip with them. I had asked them to keep an eye out for one such as you. And they told me another thing as well: they told me of the prophecies made at your birth."

"Oh?" This did not make the slightest sense to me.

"Those whom fate has touched...well, let us say that they are drawn to one another." Temar's face went still, he was very grave now. "Catwin, do you know what I am to the Duke?"

"You're his...shadow." Suddenly, confronted with Temar's unsmiling face, I was afraid to say the word *assassin*. Temar had no such compunctions.

"His bodyguard. His spy. And his assassin," he said. "Those at the Winter Castle suspect it. Some here, too. But no one dares speak of it outright, and so people pretend that they do not think it. In fact, because it is so obvious, they tell themselves that it is a foolish thought and then they disbelieve it. Do you understand how that would work?"

I did, and I did not want to. Suddenly, having Temar single me out did not seem good. I did not want to be a person who understood these things. I did not want to be the girl whose fate had been foretold. I looked around us, but no one seemed to be paying us any attention. Soldiers were laughing and shouting, eating noisily. None of them spared time for us, save to give Temar a respectful nod.

"Do you know how many other nobles have someone like me in their train?" Temar asked me, and I shook my head. "None," he said simply. "None, other than the royal family themselves." His voice took on a touch of smugness. "Even their bodyguards are not nearly so well-trained. A few nobles have bodyguards. Many pay servants for information on their enemies—one of your tasks will be to identify those servants in Miriel's rooms. A very few have paid mercenaries and assassins to make their enemies, or even members of their own families, die as if by accident. Yes, that happens," he said, when he saw disbelief on my face. "But no one other than the Duke has someone like me. I am every one of those things, and more. I am known as the Duke's messenger, I am his clerk. I take notes for him in meetings of the King's Council, and I make sure I notice who mislikes him or speaks against him."

I nodded. I did not know what to say, I did not know what I could say—for now I realized what a fool I had been all of this time. I had spent the journey to Penekket wondering why I had been singled out, I had searched for answers, and only now did I realize that I had not been able to find an answer because I had closed my eyes to the only answer there could be. The Duke and Temar had even told me, the very first time they saw me, and I had closed away the memory and pretended not to know.

"Catwin, you are no fool. You know that the Duke has great plans for Miriel. When those plans come to fruition—that means, when it all works out, Catwin—Miriel will be one of the greatest figures of the Court. Do you know what that means?" Silently, I shook my head. I did not want to think about it. I did not want to know where this was going.

"It means that Miriel will be in danger every day," Temar said simply. "Anyone who rises at court has enemies. The Duke rose fast, and made many enemies that way. Miriel will have all of his, and she will have her own as well. And they will act against her."

Carefully, I laid my spoon down on the table and folded my napkin. The room was pressing in on me, the sound of the men eating was beating at my ears and I thought I might be sick. I wondered if it would be possible to get up and leave, to turn around and run as fast as I could for the door, run fast enough that Temar

---

could not catch me, and far enough that the Duke could not reach me.

"Do you understand what I am telling you?" Temar asked me. I shook my head. I would not say it. I did not want to say it, superstitiously believing that if I could keep from saying it, it would not become real.

"You will be all of these things and more for Miriel," Temar said. He did not spare me: "You will be her shadow, shaped to her as I am to the Duke. You will be her bodyguard when she needs one, you will take note of those who mislike her or speak against her so that she will know her enemies. You will collect information on the enemies of Voltur—of Miriel, of the Duke—and if necessary, you will eliminate them. You are to be loyal to the Duke, to him above all. Above even the King."

There was a long pause. I would not meet his eyes.

"Off to the baths, then," he said easily. He was terribly calm, as if he had not just told me that I was to become a spy, a mercenary, an assassin, a murderer. He seemed to know that he had overwhelmed me. "Bring your bowl," he added. I picked up the bundle of clothing, and my bowl and spoon, hopelessly awkward, and followed him through the bustle of the mess hall.

In the baths, bundled off to the women's rooms, I dunked myself under the water and tried to stay there until the air left my lungs. Each time I came up spluttering, my body not obeying my wishes, and finally I went over to the hottest pool of water and scrubbed my skin until it was nearly raw. Then I sat, staring into the mist, trying to accept what I had heard, and not know it, all at the same time.

That night, I lay on a cot in Miriel's room and stared, sleepless, into the dark. I did not cry—even if Miriel had not been only a few feet from me, sharp eyed and eager to see me in distress, I would not have cried. I was not a baby, to cry at misfortune—and in any case, this was far beyond tears.

And what had I to complain of? Of everyone I had ever known, I would be one of the first to wear a new suit of clothes, to own my own pair of boots. I was sleeping on my own bed, snug and warm in the royal palace at Penekket. I lived in rooms with a lock on the door now. I had had two meals today, as much as I wanted to eat. People had gladly killed for less than that, and my peasant self, my hungry self, the self that had woken in the winter dark to do chores, track down herd animals that had wandered off in the biting cold—that self told me not to be a fool. That self told me to stay where I would be fed, where I would be warm.

More, it did not matter if I liked this life better than my old one. I faced, with calm certainty, the fact that there was nowhere for me to go. I was a girl with no prospects for the future, an orphan with no trade to learn, an unmarriageable girl who had never learned to how to keep a house or raise livestock, who had steadfastly refused to learn to spin or sew. I had been granted a place at the castle in Voltur only because Roine had taken me in. There was only one noblewoman there now, the Lady; the castle was hardly short-staffed.

With a start, I realized that all of this meant that I would never again face the Lady, and for a moment, I considered what it must be like for her now that we had gone. Miriel's rooms would be quiet, scrubbed clean and closed up. At dinner in the great hall, the Lady would sit alone, her husband's chair empty beside her, as it had been for over a decade, her daughter's chair newly empty at her other side. She would stare out on a table half-empty, no nobly-born ladies to entertain her, few enough servants to guard her. She would travel the hallways like a ghost, her beauty fading with each long, cold winter. She would know every day that her daughter was far from her, being ordered by the brother she mistrusted.

Careful not to make a sound, I turned my head to look towards Miriel. I could hear the wheezy snores from her maidservant, who shared a bed with her, but Miriel breathed quietly; her chest rose and fell so little that she might be dead. I thought she might be awake, too, and I wondered what she was thinking.

I turned my head away and sighed, as quietly as I could in case Miriel was indeed awake and listening to me. It was a sigh of acceptance, an acceptance that I could feel ebbing and flowing, coming on more strongly now in my exhaustion.

Even if I could escape the Duke—unlikely, and the idea of his anger made me shudder—there was nowhere for me to go. An orphan had no prospects, and an orphan girl had even less. If I went onto the streets, I knew where I would end up. In the taverns on the road, I had seen girls only a little older than me, and some who might be twenty but looked older than Roine. I had seen the deadness in their eyes.

But—my mind went round and round—how was I to be an assassin? I had only ever held a knife to cut ropes or brambles. I had never learned to fight with a sword, my archery—learned only to scare the mountain cats away from our flocks—was passable at best. I did not know anything about making poisons, only that certain herbs should not be eaten. I knew how to walk quietly, and hide in the shadows, but it occurred to me that I had only ever done so in a drafty old castle where I was an unwanted child. Now I was in a castle full of curious stares, with the Duke's own sigil embroidered on my shirt and my tunic.

I scrunched my eyes shut and berated myself. If I had been smarter, or simply less willfully stupid, I could have foreseen that this was why they wanted me. Now that I knew, I could see that Temar had told me—twice. I could have failed in my lessons and they would have found another girl to accompany Miriel. I would be at home with Roine, and everything would be as it had been, as it should be. That could have been mine if only I had had the good sense to appear as stupid as the Duke expected me to be.

But how could I have known, until it was too late? I comforted myself with that thought. What little girl had a bodyguard? What danger could she possibly be in, to merit such a precaution? The Duke was not stupid, he never did anything without careful thought, and so...he must know something I did not. I shuddered. Still, I shook my head at the notion. How could I have believed, even if I had guessed, that I would be a spy before I was fourteen years of age? It was beyond belief, it was ridiculous.

And—my heart gave an unexpected twist—if I had pretended to be stupid, I would never have learned to read. I would have been stuck in the Winter Castle all my life, with no idea of books, or trade, or history. I would never have learned mathematics, either, although I thought that I might not miss accounting so much. I realized now that I could not go back, I could not bear to go back.

I sighed again and squared my shoulders at the ceiling, set my jaw, crossed my arms. I was here, for now. I was stuck with a girl who hated me, for now. I could not see any way out. But that was now, and not four months past, I had been a girl who was a nobody. Now I was a girl the Duke of Voltur knew by name. Who could say what could happen in the future?

Chapter 11

When I was very little, Roine swore I was an impossibly practical child. She said I had no sense of the fantastical, no appreciation for the lore of life. She despaired of ever telling me bedtime stories without me interrupting, for I insisted on asking why—*why* did the prince go into the dragon's lair, *why* did the woodcutter go into the enchanted wood?

Roine told me that the prince was a brave warrior, that the woodcutter needed to feed his family, that it made the story better—and finally, exasperated, that no one could know why and that children who asked too many questions attracted the notice of mountain sprites. That shut me up, but I thought privately to myself that with so many omens and prophecies to warn them off, heroes were really awfully stupid to go wandering into dark caves.

By my second morning in the palace, I no longer wondered why the heroes in stories disregarded warnings. I wondered, instead, if they felt the same way I did: that the world had gone horribly, completely wrong and the only way open to them was to keep walking forwards. As if it was a dream and my mind was crying out for me to stop walking, but my body kept moving of its own volition—reaching out to the forbidden door, wandering down into the crypts.

The world was so topsy-turvy that there was nothing I could point to and say to myself, *this. This is wrong.* It had begun when Temar had told me of my purpose, and with every passing moment, my life seemed stranger and stranger. I was reminded of the serving girl who had been plucked out of her life and given a beautiful gown to go to the ball; I wondered if she felt as out of place as I did.

So I did what no self-respecting hero would do: I ran away.

"Did he say why?" Roine asked me. She was kneeling on the floor of her new set of rooms, surrounded by crates of jars and packets of oilcloth. She was not to be one of the palace healers, for there were many of those already, but the Duke had ruled that she would put her talents to work as our own healer.

I had thought that was odd, but Temar had explained to me—before I ran away—that it was quite normal for a noble family to have its own healer. Every faction had its enemies, he explained, rich enemies who could easily bribe a healer to slip something extra into a tincture, or who could be paid to do nothing more than look the other way and pretend to help while someone died of a curable disease.

Nothing of the sort had ever been known to happen, he assured me, but no one could ever be sure. There was always the chance. I believed him—more, I knew from his carefully casual tone that I was certain that such a thing *had* happened, and that I was fairly sure it had been Temar who had done it. And that I, too, might be expected to do such a thing someday.

I shivered at the thought and pulled my knees up to my chest. He would be looking for me now, for my lessons with him. I should be in Miriel's rooms, only I had crept away to see Roine. As an act of defiance, I thought that it was fairly safe: I could always claim that I had gotten mixed up and thought I should be studying with Roine today, and anyway, it would not be difficult for Temar to find me here.

But in the meantime, I would not have to look into his smiling face and know him for a killer. I would not have to wonder what magic trick he would do, like the evil sorcerers in fairy stories, to turn me into an assassin. I had never even been able to slaughter the animals at home. I had been good at scaring off the mountain cats who stalked our meager herds, but I had never hit one with an arrow; I had never wanted to. I had been raised by a *healer*, I thought desperately to myself—I could not kill anyone.

I realized that Roine was staring at me, waiting for an answer.

"No. He didn't say," I said tonelessly. The Duke had declared, mysteriously, that Miriel was to have her own rooms. She was not to sleep in the maidens' chambers, as any girl of the great families could do, and she was not to have a small privy chamber in the Duke's spacious apartments. She was to have her own set of rooms, to herself, with a maidservant. No other family kept their daughter in such fine estate, not even Guy de la Marque, the guardian of the King. Miriel's seclusion was not improper, nor was it in violation of any of the unspoken rules that governed the Court—still, no one had ever done such a thing before, save the Princess Anne, in her childhood.

"Maybe he didn't want anyone to know about me," I ventured.

Roine snorted. "A man like the Duke knows better than to try to keep secrets like that in the palace," she said drily. "No, this is something everyone can see, but no one could guess. There's more to this than a whim—the Duke never does anything without a reason." She lined up a set of jars on a shelf, turning each one carefully so that the label faced outwards. "So. What has you looking so peculiar?"

Still thinking about Miriel and the Duke's plans, I was going to shrug my shoulders and make some excuse. Then Roine's question set off a set of realizations, and a wave of anger.

"You tell me," I said, leaning forward to her. At last I understood her arguments with Temar. "You knew, didn't you?"

Roine did not pretend to misunderstand me. She tilted her head to the side. "Not exactly," she said. "But I knew it was no business I'd want you involved in. No one serves the Duke without getting shit on their hands." I widened my eyes at her words. Roine had never used foul language in my presence. But Roine had been strange since she learned that we would be coming to the palace. Now she shrugged. Her voice was not angry; it was as if bitterness had been worn away by time.

My own bitterness was still fresh. "He uses us to do his dirty work, then."

To my surprise, Roine was startled into laughter—she gave a great crow of it and shook her head at my sullen face. "Oh, no," she said, amused. "He's not afraid to do his own. He's done a great deal of dirty work in service to the crown. How do you think he got his title? But there are places he can't go, jobs he can't do. That's why he has me, and Temar. That's why he chose you." She raised her eyebrows at me. "And I still don't know exactly what it is you're to do, so you might as well tell me."

I bit my lip. "I'm to be like Temar," I said. "I'll be a spy and a guard like him. And…" the word *assassin* stuck in my throat, but Roine knew what I meant. I guessed from her stillness that she had known, she had guessed. She had only been waiting to hear it, and hoping all the while that she was wrong.

"Will you?" she asked me, and I felt tears come to my eyes at once. It was the worst question she could have asked, for it laid bare how powerless I was now. I had liked it better, I thought, when I was the orphan girl no one noticed, and no one cared about. Aler had been right when he said it was best to escape the notice of nobles.

"I don't have any choice," I said. "You know that."

She shook her head. "The Duke's not the only powerful man in the world," she advised me. "You always have a choice in your allies."

A knock sounded at the door and I jumped, terrified to be listening to such words when anyone could be listening. What if the Duke heard of this? I looked, wide-eyed, to the door as it opened and Temar slid into the room.

"Ah, here you are, Catwin," he said easily. "The Duke has summoned you and Miriel." He held open the door with a smile, as if he had not just caught me out at trying to avoid him, as if he was not the most dangerous person that I knew, and I slid down from my perch on one of the big tables and followed him from the room, with only a glance over my shoulder at Roine. I did not beg her to say she needed me, and that I must stay—I no longer expected Roine to be able to shield me from the Duke.

Roine, for her part, nodded to Temar and gave a little wave to me. She sat amongst her herbs and her bandages, and she smiled blandly, as if she had not just been telling me to defy the most powerful man I knew. I wondered if Temar knew of these thoughts Roine had. It did not occur to me to wonder, yet, what thoughts she had that *I* did not know.

Temar said nothing as we trotted through the hallways, back to Miriel's rooms. He pretended that nothing had occurred, and I, for my part, trotted along in increasingly distraught silence, until I could stand it no longer.

"I don't want to do my lessons," I blurted out. As soon as the words were out of my mouth, I would have had them back. If I had never said them, I thought, I would have been able to deny those thoughts later. But Temar only nodded, and stopped at a crossing point in the corridors.

"Which way?" he asked me, testing my knowledge. He did not care in the least what I had said. My wishes were as trivial to him as the color of Miriel's gown, and he would train me whether I wished it or not. I expected to feel the wave of panic that had accompanied my realization that I was stuck here. All I felt was sadness.

"That way," I said, pointing to my left, and he nodded. We fell into the flow of people, moving towards Miriel's rooms, and he looked over at me.

"You know," he said, his tone still easy and conversational, "there's an awful lot to learn. Have you ever heard about the royal library, Catwin?" He laughed when he saw that he had my full attention. "They say there are books there that exist nowhere else in the world. There are histories of countries that no longer exist. You could learn anything you wished. Of course, you'd be killed if you set foot in there yourself," he added, as if it were an afterthought, and I gave a pout at the ploy he had used. He smiled, equally amused that it had worked, and pleased that I had seen it.

He let me walk in silence. As much as I tried to think about my reasons for wanting to run away, about knives and sneaking about spying, my thoughts kept drifting back to the Royal Library. Why had I not thought of this before? I had a feeling that it would make the small room of books at the Winter Castle seem like nothing, just as the palace dwarfed the place where I had grown up. There would be more books here than I could hope to read in a lifetime, and Temar knew without having to ask that I wanted nothing more than to dash off to the library this moment.

Sensing that I was off my guard, Temar spoke quietly.

"There's more to this than the part you fear, Catwin. I cannot shield you from it forever, but it will not be the whole of your life, I promise you that. I can promise you, also, that if you learn all that I teach you, you will live a life less violent than you think." In front of Miriel's door, he turned to face me, seriously. "Be careful," he advised me. "Your fate is bound with Miriel's now, and you cannot hope to escape that. You have no idea what defiance could cost you."

Roine's words had filled me with frustration. Foolishly, I thought that she could not possibly understand what it was to be singled out by the Duke. Also foolishly, I did not think to question why Temar might disagree with her. I did not wonder why he whispered to me so gravely that I should avoid the Duke's enmity. His words echoed my own fears so closely that they dropped into my mind without disturbing the peace. I only looked down and nodded, and went into the room ahead of him.

Miriel was still being settled into her rooms, and it was a chaos of color and scent and glittering things. Trunks of clothing lay open, petticoats frothing out of one trunk, underskirts gleaming in another, and yet more trunks filled with gowns of brocades and velvets and silks. Colors abounded, and the air was heady with the smell of lavender sachets. At the center of it all, in her element, was Miriel.

She shone. The spiteful brat I had first known had been replaced by the girl who rode in silent misery through the countryside, and that girl in turn had been eclipsed entirely by this other Miriel. This one sparkled. Her gown of deep pink accentuated her creamy skin, her maid had brushed her hair until each curl gleamed.

Miriel stood in the middle of the room, hands clasped together excitedly as she directed the women to put some gowns here, others in another room. Some of unspeakable worth she waved away as if bored. She had a smile on her full lips, she was reveling in this.

She scowled when she turned and saw us.

"Ah, the crows," she said disdainfully, and I remembered that I was dressed all in black. I had caught a glimpse of myself in her mirror earlier that day, and I had thought myself striking. My skin was pale against the black linen and leather, and my hair—freshly washed, I had never been so clean in my life—was the color of dark honey. But I was nothing to her.

Temar bowed, and a sideways glance at me prompted me to echo his gesture; I had been pleased to learn that, although I was to wear my hair long and braided like a girl, I would not be confined to skirts, and would not be expected to behave like a young lady. Temar had given me a brief overview of bows, and I saw that he watched mine out of the corner of his eye. His face was impassive as he said,

"My Lady, his grace the Duke requests your presence." I saw her consider a refusal. Whatever her mother had told her, Miriel was not keen to obey the Duke. I saw, in the brief flicker of her lashes, that Miriel was considering how her refusal would go.

"Of course," she said, inclining her head as regally as if she had been born and bred a princess, and not brought up alone in the country, far from the graces of the Palace. She moved across the room as if she was floating, and when she smiled at me, she was as sweet as poison. "You will stay here and help the ladies unpack," she said.

"My Lady, forgive me." Temar's voice was soft, but unyielding. "His Grace requested Catwin's presence as well."

Miriel bit her lip against a retort and swept past me, her gown brushing against me so that I must step back. I met Temar's eyes and he only gave a distant half-smile. His words echoed in my ears: *It is your duty to be at her side, whether she wishes it or not.*

We walked in stony silence, Miriel pretending that I was not there, Temar acting the part of a respectful servant. I concentrated on memorizing the corridors. They were low and dark in this part of the building, the rooms set back from the hallway proper; I thought it would be a good place to hide.

The Duke had good rooms, on the side of the building closest to the Palace proper. His was one of the oldest titles, but he was common-born; he was not given leave to live in the same building as the king himself. Still, he was well-guarded and well-housed. The guards uncrossed their pikes and swung open the doors at the sight of Temar and Miriel, and the three of us were ushered into rooms larger and airier even than Miriel's. A fire roared in the grate, fine carpets were piled on the floors, and the curtains were rich brocade.

We continued through the outer chamber, and the Duke looked up as we entered his study. It was a cheerless room; the Duke hated luxury. He kept up appearances in his receiving rooms, but in his private world, there were no rich carpets and no ornaments. He was economical even in his words, was the Duke: he wasted no time on greetings, not even for Miriel.

"Temar says he told you why you are here," he said to me. "I will explain again, so that there can be no mistake. Pay attention, girl."

"Yes, my Lord."

"You, Catwin, no longer exist. You no longer have a fate of your own, a will of your own, or indeed a soul of your own. Henceforth, you and Miriel are to be as one: she the light, and you the dark. You are to cease thinking of yourself as other from my niece—you are to be her shadow, as Temar is mine. You will go where she goes, you will watch instead of being watched, you will hear instead of being heard. Do you understand me?"

"Yes, my Lord." I did not. I did not understand in the slightest. I did not like the uncharacteristic, lyrical tilt to the Duke's words. I did not like that, over on the side of the room, Temar had gone so still that he might have been carved from stone.

"Swear it," the Duke said. There was no refusing.

"I swear." My voice was barely audible, but he nodded.

"You will both take instruction from me as to how to behave, what to say and what not to say, and how to remain safe. There is no safety for those alone in court, but you will be under my protection.

"You, Catwin, are to take lessons with Roine, Temar, and one of the guardsmen. Temar will tell you where to go." He said no more, not that he expected me to do well, not that he would be displeased by failure. Either it did not occur to him that I would do poorly, or he considered me frightened enough to do his bidding without further instruction.

He turned his face to Miriel. "Your governess will continue your lessons as usual. You will also study with other tutors. They will teach you how to dance, how to play instruments, how to sing, and most importantly, they will teach you how to behave at court."

He stood and came around the desk, and I admired Miriel for not flinching as her uncle looked her over. He looked at her as an engineer might measure the strength of a bridge. He did not look at her as if he would see into her soul, he cared only that she might fail him. Miriel looked back at him so blankly that I wondered for a moment if she might be slow in wits, if I simply had not realized it until now.

I would realize only later that Miriel's beautiful face could be as formless as water when she wanted it to be. She gave the Duke nothing upon which to comment. Miriel was learning to play his game; she said nothing, and waited.

"You are to dress with care," he said at length. "Your dresses are to be of the finest cloth, in colors and cuts that suit you. If you must create a new style in order to be flattered, do so; but wear nothing scandalous. Your dresses should be simple in cut, and your jewelry should be sparing, but you are to be elegant. *That*—" he pointed to Miriel's beautiful gown "—is of an old fashion, and you will dispose of it. You are to dress as a princess, not a merchant's daughter."

I thought, irrelevantly, of the piles of gowns in Miriel's rooms now, of the gold that had been spent on the rich fabrics, the exquisite workmanship. All of it would be tossed away without a thought.

Miriel had been looking at the floor. Now, the Duke paused until she looked up at him. Then he continued, staring into her eyes.

"You will behave in a charming manner. I expect you to be the finest of the ladies in the court in everything that you do. You will be the most elegant dancer, you will learn to sing and compose music, carry a harmony, and play cards. If you require instruction in anything, no matter how small, you will tell me of it and I will make sure that you have the training you need. You are to be perfect.

"You are to learn, most importantly of all, how to enchant a man. You will learn when to talk and when to be silent. You will learn when to compete with men, and when to let them win. You will learn to lose without seeming to do so a-purpose. You will learn how to hold yourself to stir a man's desire without ever appearing to flirt."

I stared at the Duke, frankly shocked by his cold discussion of the topic. Miriel might be of age to be betrothed, but she was only fourteen years old, like me. She was not a lady of the court, to be lacing herself tightly into a gown or flirting with a fan, she was a child. She should not be learning to enchant men.

The Duke appeared to have no such reservations. His voice was impassive, wintry. "You are to learn to arouse a man with nothing more than a smile, but I expect you to be as chaste as a temple virgin, Miriel. Whatever your mother may have told you about how to attract a man, you are to forget it at once, and you are never to use what she taught you. There will be no bawdy language or overt suggestion, no provocative gowns, no knowing glances. You are not, in short, to use a whore's tricks. You will be untouchable, and I expect you to behave with such propriety that there is never the chance for a rumor about your honor.

"If ever I hear that you have done something shameful, you will be beaten to within an inch of your life, *after* which you will be given a chance to explain why such a rumor was given fodder to spread. If the answer is to my liking, you will be taken from court or not as I see fit, so as to give no grist to the gossips, and brought back when the time is right. If the answer is not to my liking, I will banish you back to the mountains, or a nunnery, or kill you. As I see fit.

"Do you understand me?"

I wondered again at the fact that the Duke never asked me such things. Was it because he could not fathom that I might fail him, or was he attempting to use etiquette to impress his point upon his niece? I wondered, also, why he had waited until she was here to tell her this. It would have been simpler to teach her this before she arrived. Then I remembered her mother's protests, and realized that the Duke had not trusted his sister to train Miriel

---

84

properly. *Whatever your mother may have told you...* Interesting. Interesting, indeed. I wondered if I could ask Temar about it.

Miriel was undaunted by his cold words. She stood with such an easy bearing that they might have been discussing the weather. She did not seem the slightest bit frightened. "I understand," she said, easily.

Too easily. The unspoken hung in the air, both of them daring the other to say it.

"And?" the Duke prompted. From the look in his eye, I thought that Miriel would pay for making him speak first. Miriel knew it, too.

"I will," she said sulkily.

The Duke settled into his chair and picked up a quill, dipped it in ink and wiped it, began to write.

"You can go," he said carelessly.

She looked over at me for the first time since we had left her rooms, just looked, and I had a sense of seeing down through shifting layers. I had seen her masks, the part she played with her mother, the quiet mask she had worn on her journey, the gay, sparkling mask she had worn just moments before. Now I saw a part of Miriel that was truly her own. Miriel had learned her mother's mannerisms, she had learned to react and be as changeable as water, as malleable as a winter sky. But today I saw down to the core of her, stripped bare by the Duke's win.

Miriel hated to lose.

Chapter 12

"Up," Temar said mercilessly, and I tried to push myself to my feet. I could not draw in a breath, and everything ached. I was reminded of the time, once, when I was small, that I had tried to climb onto the high shelves in the kitchen to get at the honeyed dates. I had lost my footing and fallen flat on my back, and had lain for a time on the floor, gasping and trying to pull air into my lungs. I thought bitterly, now, that no one had expected me to get up and try that fall again.

When Temar had told me that I was going to learn to fall correctly, I had laughed. I was regretting that now. It turned out, to my immense surprise, that there was indeed a correct way to fall. I did not know it, and I did not seem to be getting any better at it as the morning wore on. We had tried this same fall 57 times—I was learning to count, and Temar was using this for practice. He found the whole thing much more amusing than I did.

"You know," he said, from where he was lounging against the wall, "it hurts less if you do it correctly." I gave him a look, and he grinned. "Cheer up, little shadow, that's all for today. Time for your lessons with Donnett."

"The guardsman?" I asked, recalling the Duke's words. Temar nodded, pleased that I had remembered.

"You should learn about him," he said. "I expect you to know, within the week, everything about the man. Whether he's married, if he has children, if he has brothers or sisters. Any loyalties he holds, any of his particular friends. I want you to learn his mannerisms. Use his speech to figure out where he's from, and learn to mimic the accent. You never know when an accent will be useful."

It was a dizzying amount of information. I frowned. "Why?"

"You should know that much and more about everyone in your life," was the reply. "You will learn the same about Miriel's ladies: if they have a fancy to any man, a rivalry with any woman. You will learn what foods they like. You must know everything, and this is practice."

I nodded, retying my braid with shaking hands. I was exhausted. Every moment, it seemed, there was something new. I had seen more, since coming to the palace, than I had ever dreamed existed. I felt every bit the provincial nobody. It was a wonder, really, that Miriel was not as overwhelmed as I was.

My hands paused on my hair. I thought back on the past day, on her never-ending smiles, her boundless energy, the proud set of her shoulders. She was pretty and charming without stopping, always ready with one of her beautiful false smiles—or, if she was talking to me, a sharp and witty comment. She was light on her feet, always ready with one of her perfect ripples of laughter; every day, watching the courtiers for inspiration, she got better at mimicking mirth. It was a wonder she was not dead on her feet with exhaustion, crippled with anxiety; she, who was in the forefront. At least no one paid attention to me.

No, there must be more to this. I resolved to watch Miriel tonight. She must be tired, she must be scared. I was driven to know where the cracks lay in that beautiful façade. When I looked up, Temar was watching me. I gave him a smile as bland as the one he showed to nobles, and rotated my right arm gingerly in its socket.

"I'm ready," I said. "Let's go."

As we walked together through the bustle, I asked him, "What happens if I never learn to fall?"

He shrugged. "Nothing much."

"What?" I was incredulous. "Nothing?"

"Nothing *much*," he repeated.

"You're joking with me," I said, uneasily.

"Oh, no, I'm quite serious. You'll get in a fight, and you'll go down wrong."

"And then?" I did not quite like the gleam in his eyes.

"Well, you'll be injured. That's difficult to come back from."

"Well, what if I don't come back from it, then?"

He looked at me as if he did not care at all. "You'll probably die."

I shut up.

Donnett was housed in the barracks. When, after only one or two wrong turns, I had managed to navigate the two of us to the building itself, Temar took the lead and guided me through the hallways, down a flight of stairs, and to a storage room in the cellar.

The guardsman was already waiting for us, and not looking particularly pleased at his new assignment. I was dismayed when

Temar bowed courteously, minded me to return to Miriel's rooms after this lesson, and left at once, taking the stairs two at a time. I stared after him, wanting to call him back but not daring to do so.

When I looked back, I saw that Donnett was giving me a once over. He was not impressed with what he saw, and for a moment I saw myself through his eyes: a girl short for her age, still round-cheeked, with the wide face of the mountain people and her straw-colored hair drawn back in a braid. Her clothes were too big, and she looked scared of everything she could see.

"Jes' like a noble, innit," Donnett said, sighing. When I frowned, he jerked his head to the stairs. "Bringing me someone's all tired out. Expectin' me to teach ye. Seven gods, this was a short straw. Do it for the Duke, he said. And then ye, yer what he brings me, and all bruised already."

I opened my mouth to reply, and he waved a hand at me to keep me silent. "It doesn't matter," he said. "Yer never going to make a fighter. Ye, now, *ye* need to learn how to *run*."

It was strange, I thought later. All that morning, I had wanted nothing more than to run away. I had not wanted to learn what Temar had wanted to teach me in the first place, and my complete failure to learn the very first thing had given me a strange kind of hope. I was a failure, I reasoned. If I wanted to run away, the Duke would not care very much. Better than sticking around to face his anger when I kept failing at my lessons.

Something in Donnett's tone, though, made my chin come up. Even having Temar watch me fail had not pricked my pride like this. I flushed, and my eyes narrowed.

"I'll show you," I said, in my best proper accent. My voice was quiet, but cold. He raised his eyebrows. It was not what he had expected from a weakling—he had thought I would cry and run away—but he did not believe my words yet.

"Right, then. Hit me."

I looked at him suspiciously. That was all? Hit him? But he did not seem to be joking. I readied myself, as still as I could be, and prepared for a burst of blinding speed, the sort which had always won me fights with the other servant children. I was very fast, I thought smugly.

I opened my eyes to a view of the ceiling, and Donnett's grin.

"Care to try again?" he asked, and I did not bother to respond. Making use of what little dignity I had left, I climbed to my feet and readied myself again. And again, I ended up on the floor. After a moment of self-pity, my curiosity got the better of me.

"How did you do that?" Wondering how was better than feeling sorry for myself, anyway.

"Yer like a pit bull," he said, snorting. "Anyone could see yer attack coming leagues away. Did that fancy lad teach ye nothing?"

I turned my head and spat out some blood. "Today was my first day." At that admission, I could feel tears stinging in my eyes, and I sat up and ducked my head to hide them. When I had blinked them away, I pushed myself up. To my surprise, Donnett clasped one of his big hands around my arm and hauled me to my feet.

"First rule," he said gruffly, ignoring my tears, "is to set 'em off guard." I looked up, and saw that he was not playing. I nodded, and waited for more. "That means, either ye get 'em first, or ye take the hit and make 'em think it's not a fight anymore. Then ye hit 'em when they let their guard down."

My fist shot out, and he blocked it away from himself easily. I froze, trapped by his hand around my wrist, but he laughed, and I saw that he was not upset at my sneakiness.

"Not bad," he said. "But I was sneakin' up behind Ismiri scouts and stabbing 'em in the back before ye were even born. So let's go again, and see if ye can hit me." Wearily, I spat out the rest of the blood and turned back to face him. I had the thought that it was going to be a very long morning. This filled me with such exhaustion that I tried something Temar had told me at the beginning of his lesson: I tried to clear my mind, and see only the next few moments.

One hit, I told myself. That was all I needed.

When I pushed open the doors to Miriel's rooms, a few hours later, I heard all talk cease at once. Miriel turned in a swirl of silk, and instead of crowing with laughter, as I had thought she would, she merely lifted one eyebrow and shaped her mouth into her mother's cruel smile, as if this were the most delightful costume.

"Good gracious," she remarked sweetly. "Whatever happened to *you*?"

"It's nothing," I said. I moved my mouth as little as possible, but I could feel my lower lip split open nonetheless. My right arm, so tender after Temar's lesson, was now in a sling. My nose had finally stopped bleeding, but I knew that my right eye had been blackened, and I knew also that there were at least a dozen more bruises covered by my clothing.

Miriel did laugh at that, her delightful little peal of laughter. Even studying the flat incomprehension behind her eyes did not soften the sting of her mockery. "Nothing? You look half-dead." She tilted her head to the side. "You can't possibly accompany me about like that, you know."

I made no response. Temar had been very specific about my duties, and they did not include arguing with Miriel. More, I knew enough to be sure that the Duke would learn of any spat between me and Miriel, and that he would not be pleased by it. So I merely bowed.

"My Lady, is there anything I can do for you before I go to my next lesson?" Head down, I waited for the jest I knew was coming. Some jab at me, some witty turn of phrase.

"Well, perhaps you could help my uncle's servant hang the curtains in my privy chamber," Miriel suggested.

I closed my eyes briefly at the thought of taking my arm out of the sling, but kept my head ducked so that she could not see it. One part of me said that there was no point in being brave. There was no point in pretending not to care, for Miriel had known that this task would cause me pain. What was there to be gained when she would see every little wince and know it for the truth?

But another part asked, what was left for me beyond pride? If I let Miriel crush me now, that would be no victory. I would endure her spite either way. And if I gave way, I might as well have let the Lady break me, I might as well tell Temar that I had given up entirely. I was to be shaped perfectly to Miriel, but I could not serve her if I were to crumple under her cruelty.

So I bowed, and went to help the man with the curtains, ducking my head out of the makeshift sling as I walked. Miriel's ladies gathered around her, twittering, and it was only Miriel herself who spoke up to call me back.

"Oh, don't," she said. "My uncle would be displeased if I broke you so soon after he'd given you to me." If I could have, I would have turned the words on her, reminded her of her own status, no better than mine; she was as much the Duke's tool as I was. But the words stuck in my throat, and she landed the next blow as well: "Shall you take notes for me, and act as my clerk?" she asked innocently.

"If my Lady wishes," I said, through gritted teeth.

"No." Miriel laughed. "With your penmanship, we should never remember what I had dictated!" There was a ripple of laughter, nervous, from her maids. I bowed again and waited.

"Or perhaps you could dress my hair for tonight's banquet?" Miriel tossed her beautiful curls. "You've been trained in that, yes? ...no? Oh, how curious. Well, at the least, you could advise me on my dress."

There was no longer any point in replying. I bowed, and Miriel glided towards me across the room, stopping when we stood face to face.

"You see?" she said quietly. "You're of no use to anyone." No one could have heard her words but me, and no one, seeing the sweet smile on her face, would have guessed what she had said. "Run along to your lessons," she said, her voice carrying, and dismissed me with a wave of her hand.

I bowed again and left to see Roine. I had survived the encounter, and I had not hit Miriel. Or cried. That was something.

"These bruises will be worse tomorrow," Roine warned me, and I shrugged. I was so glad to be sitting down, and that I was not being punched, that I cared about nothing. That day's lessons took place after another thorough bath, and focused on mild pain remedies, the proper bandaging of joints, and what herbs could be used in compresses over a bruise. "Are you alright?" Roine asked, worried.

"I just have to survive this," I said with a laugh. "If I can last through these lessons..."

Neither of us finished the sentence. Neither of us wanted to contemplate the thought of what my training would lead me to do. I wrapped my good arm around myself and leaned forward to study the herbs on the table, and Roine cleared her throat and began her lecture once more.

Chapter 13

I do not remember those first few weeks clearly. I remember that I was often in much pain, and that each night I took a thorough accounting of my aches and my bruises, which grew gradually less varied as I grew stronger. I would have thought it best to ignore them, but Temar had made a lesson of it.

"The way you protect yourself is a tell," he said. "So. Each day, you will protect your injuries, and you will do so in a way that keeps me from noticing what they are." I did not feel as if I made any progress in those bouts, but near the end of the third week, I managed to score a solid hit on Temar, and as he doubled over and tried to catch his breath, he asked where my injury had been.

I could not help but laugh, a gurgle of self-satisfied laughter. "It's the arm I hit you with."

"That didn't hurt?"

"Oh, it did."

"You're learning," was all Temar said, but I knew he was proud.

From Donnett, I learned all there was to know about army watch patterns and the way the Palace was protected by the guard. The Royal Guard had their own patterns, he told me, known only to them, but he was able to tell me where they drilled and when, and once or twice I managed to sneak into the courtyard before them and hide, watching closely as they sparred and marched in formation.

The guardsman taught me the use of dagger and short sword, laughing at the thought of someone my size using a properly sized blade. He gave me a shield for a few practice sessions, but warned me against use of it. All of our practice sessions with a shield were devoted to footwork.

"Little fellow like you can't afford to take hits," he said, conveniently forgetting my gender. Donnett was unnerved at the thought of teaching a young girl how to use blades, and liked to pretend that I was a boy. "Any hit you're blocking with a shield is a hit you should have avoided."

More than hits and blocks, Donnett seemed to know something about everyone. He was a guard, housed with soldiers from every corner of Heddred, and when I asked him about a piece of gossip I did not understand, or why a certain lady had snubbed another, he always had an explanation. Intriguingly, Donnett even seemed to know somewhat of Temar, although he refused to tell me much.

"Temar taught me to speak like a northman today," I piped, one morning, and Donnett only shook his head and snorted.

"He was always strange, that one—even from a boy."

"You knew him when he was young?" I asked, surprised, and Donnett nodded.

"Aye, after a fashion, though I doubt he remembers me. I saw him before the Battle of Voltur. He was just a lad then, waiting on the Duke. Well, *he* wasn't the Duke, then, either. We all thought the Duke had a taste..." His face colored, and he coughed. "Well, never you mind," he said gruffly. "It's not fit for young ears. But the lad's still around, anyway." No matter how I pleaded, he would not tell me more. But, he said, if I would only shut up and listen, he would teach me to find out everything I could ever want to know.

And so, slyly, he taught me to watch both servants and nobles. Nobles could watch each other as closely as they wanted, he told me, but they would never see what a servant saw. The courtiers spent all day pretending to be one thing, and that wore on them—it was the servants who knew the true self of each courtier. A lord could tell things to his groom that he would never tell his wife; a lady might tell her seamstress or her hairdresser any number of court secrets, gleaned from watching her husband. And so, the servants were the ones who knew every little scrap of information, and traded the best pieces to the highest bidder.

Donnett even taught me to sit in the corners of the kitchens and watch, for the more cunning of the nobles knew to duck through the kitchens to travel from one place to another. It was as if they could not perceive the gaze of the servants upon them, marking the sigils on their clothing and where it was that they went. There was much to learn about which way the wind blew, for a sharp-eyed girl, hidden in the shadows, might see a powerful lord walk with his shoulders slumped, and all the telltales of a downward slide about him.

I had very little time to sit and watch, however. No matter what other duties I might have, my studies were the most important thing. I trained and I learned every day. Every hour that I was awake had a purpose: waiting on Miriel, or training, or studying. My head was a whirl of thoughts from the moment I woke up until my head touched the pillow at night, and although I was so tired that I fell asleep as soon as my head touched the pillow, I even dreamed of my training. I practiced falling and sneaking, making potions, binding wounds, swinging maces.

Gradually, I began to notice the changes in my body. When I looked at my body in Miriel's mirror, taking my account of my injuries, I could see the lines of muscles under the skin. I had more stamina as well. I had come to the palace with the energy of a child, but had been exhausted by my drills with Temar and Donnett. Now, the weeks of dogged perseverance through pain and exhaustion had given me the ability to keep going longer, to push harder, and I began to notice that I was able to move more quickly, that I was more balanced on my feet, that I could block a blow.

If I had hoped for praise, I was to be disappointed. I might be getting better—cleaner with my forms, quicker in my strikes, quieter as I walked—but the closest Donnett ever came to praise was an approving grunt, and Temar's praise came in the form of, "Again." If I mastered a technique, my reward was to start learning another, and another after that, with endless repetitions of the basics to perform every night.

Temar in particular wasted no time. For all his easy humor, his lessons were tinged with urgency. Temar alone knew how much I had to learn, and he also knew what was at stake if we failed. This training was not an idle exercise: moving quietly was essential, and striking quickly and effectively could mean the difference between the life and death of both myself and Miriel.

At Temar's insistence, I now listened to the gossip of the servants and the nobles, and so I knew that his worries were becoming more and more specific. The rumors—always abundant—were massing, and becoming more pointed: of war with Ismir, tensions with Mavlon, whispers of rebellion all across the south from the Norstrung Provinces to the southern Bone Wastes. Servants whispered the name *Jacces*, and quieted hastily when nobles came into earshot.

I knew that I did not know everything, for I had only the rumors of the minor nobles and the servants. Donnett's words on secrets and servants rang true almost always, but the state secrets, the most important secrets, were kept in the minds of the tight-lipped Council members. Temar was the one who attended late night council sessions with the Duke, and so he knew the best information. He came to train me in the morning with his eyes shadowed by fatigue, and somewhat more. He did not speak to me of his fears, or of the Council meetings; I had to guess if I wanted to know what troubled him.

Slowly, over the weeks of listening at dinner and creeping down dark corridors after drunken Council members, I built up my theory. Voltur was the first line of defense against Ismir, and so the war itself would be a problem for the Duke to attend to, if it came to that. The Duke's own lands would be in danger first and foremost. But for Temar, the thing to fear was the rapid shifts in favor that a war engendered. It was the way that the court could turn on a man in a moment, when they saw the opportunity to snatch what was his.

The Duke had risen to nobility from his work in the last war. He had been granted an old title and new territories, the spoils of war, and with success he had made enemies—not of those who fought with him, for any man who had fought at the Duke's side was loyal to a fault, but instead of the nobles whose names were older, and whose purses were lighter. Those men whispered in corners that Eral Celys, that merchant's son, should never have been made a Duke. He had risen higher than he should. In war, anything could happen. Men died, and no one thought on it. Perhaps it was time for the Duke of Voltur to have an accident, so that his lands could be given to another.

I knew some of their names: Henry Cessor, Guy de la Marque, Arman Dulgurokov. All were fellow members of the King's Council, who sought power and prestige and wealth, and feared the influence of the Duke, who had risen from nothing to snatch one of the choicest duchies out of their waiting fingers. When I had asked Temar about them, he had looked at me askance, and then assured me that all of them were ruthless men, men who could kill and not think twice about it, and that I should never trust any one of them.

A threat to the Duke's safety, that alone Temar would not fear. It was to be expected. It was the very reason for Temar's presence at court, and I knew that he could win a fight against any single combatant. Likely, he could win against multiple assailants— and the Duke was hardly helpless, himself. But the Duke was not the only one in danger. It would not be enough for the Duke to die, for if he fell in the King's service, who was to say that the King might not gift all of Voltur and more to the Duke's heirs? And the

Duke, having no children of his own, had only one heir before his line was ended.

Miriel.

And so Temar trained me with single-minded, desperate intensity. He trained me over and over on the quick draw of my weapons. I knew not only how to strike and stab, how to fight with short and long blades, but also the way to flip a knife to throw it, and then switch my grip back to the haft. I learned how to adjust my throw to the balance of the knife, so that I could use any weapon that came to hand. I was quickly becoming lethal with the razor-sharp set of daggers the Duke had ordered made for me, but now I could be almost as deadly with a use-blunted, battered old blade.

I learned to shut my mouth when he taught me a skill that seemed ridiculous, knowing that he was teaching me for a reason. One day, Temar brought a basket full of strange objects. I peered through the box, wondering what sort of lesson this could be. I saw decorations, china ornaments, earthenware mugs and wine goblets, plates, even a clock. Temar would place one just out of reach, spin me around until I staggered, and then I must pick up the object and throw it at a target. I had been amused at the exercise, but the grim look on Temar's face suggested that he found it no laughing matter, and from that I knew that either he had won a fight this way, or it had been used against him.

Gradually, the piece of my training that I feared came into play. It had started subtly; after tumbling, I had learned to drop from ten feet, fifteen feet, and land quietly. When I had learned to draw my weapons quickly, without looking at them, Temar taught me to draw them without even a whisper of sound. When he saw how well I could sneak, he taught me to wrap black cloth over my hair so that it would not gleam in the shadows.

Neither of us mentioned it. Temar's own silence was a dare to me, I knew, and I did not have the words or the courage to take it. And so, by the time Temar undertook to teach me garroting, or the use of poisons, the training had gone too far for me to plead a delicate conscience. I swallowed my protests and set to work, quietly ignoring the feeling that the makeup of my own self, my very morals, was shifting while I was not watching.

To my own disquiet, I was good at mixing poisons. It was not a complete surprise, for I had learned the rudiments of herb lore from Roine and her books. I knew already how to steep leaves to release the oils inside, how to grind leaves and shred roots, how to mix a powder and a liquid evenly. I possessed the innate sense for proportions, and Temar only nodded at each of my creations. He taught me his own uses of Roine's knowledge, how to dip a blade or a dart in poison, and how to handle it once it had been coated in the stuff.

We practiced throwing knives that had been dipped in a poison that would slow my muscles but not—at this dose—cause me harm. I shredded the spike-edged leaves myself, then marveled at the dreamy feeling that came over me when I nicked my finger on the blade.

When Temar gave a yell and attacked me, driving his shoulder into my solar plexus, I felt only the vague sense that I should be feeling alarm, or surprise.

"*Fight*, Catwin!" he yelled, his voice echoing strangely in my head.

Oh, I thought dreamily. *Another lesson.* Vaguely, I knew that he had hit me in the face; I knew that I should care. I wanted to care, but even the wanting seemed very far away.

"Catwin!" Another hit. Realization: I did not have to care, I only had to win. It was another hit while that realization worked its way from my mind to my muscles, and then, as Temar dropped towards me, I managed to bring up my fist. My aim was off, but training held my wrist straight. With a muffled curse, Temar staggered away.

"I win," I said softly, and I rolled my head to look at him, where he was on all fours trying to catch his breath. I thought it funny, the drug still working in my blood, but he did not.

"You got in one strike," he said, and his tone conveyed that one strike was not good enough. I was still cushioned by the drug, too relaxed to be offended, and in any case, a thought pierced through the haze: he was afraid, not angry. He was expecting an attack, and he was deeply worried that I would fail.

"There must be a part of you that nothing touches," he said, as he helped me to Roine's rooms. "Not hits, not pain, not drugs."

"That's not...how drugs work." In the wake of this one, I felt sick. The lights were too bright, and I was dizzy.

"Listen to me." He swung me around so that I could lean against the wall and look up into his face. I tried not to be sick. The corridor was deserted, but still he leaned close to speak to me. "When you realized you were drugged, you let go and you gave up. But it's like drunkards at a feast—they *want* to be drunk. You have to fight to keep your head clear. If you don't, when there is an attempt—and there will be—Miriel will die."

I went to my lesson with Roine with Temar's words ringing in my ears, and later, that night, I dreamed again of the day of my birth. I stood in the drafty little hovel and listened to my own wailing, and I watched my mother and my father argue, him holding my little self out to her, her pushing me away. Watching the conversation again, identical in every detail, I wondered if it was truly a dream. I wondered if this was how it had happened; I wondered why my mother had been so determined to have me killed. Had she known that the betrayal that was coming was worse than death? Or had she known, I wondered now, that I might become a Shadow? I woke in the darkness, with tears streaming down my cheeks, and wondered if she had wanted me killed, because she knew how many I would one day kill. If she had thought that the world would be better without me in it.

Chapter 14

"You took that herb hard," Roine remarked, a few days later. At Temar's insistence, she was teaching me the use of other poisonous plants, feeding them to me in small doses, so I might know the effects. Her voice was carefully neutral; only when Roine was absolutely sure we were alone did she show that she disliked my training. She pointed to a set of tools and jars on the table. "Come here, I'll show you how to make the antidote."

Roine always asked which poisons I had learned to make with Temar, and she taught me the antidote whenever she could. From the Duke's largesse, Roine's storeroom was stocked with herbs she had never been able to procure before. Many a time at the Winter Castle, confronted with an illness she could not treat, she had said, "If only I had..." and she had frowned, because Roine hated, above all else, being unable to cure a patient.

She wanted for nothing now. She had every herb she had ever spoken of; I was sure that she had every herb that was named in her beautiful books. Her shelves held bandages of good cloth, her stores of herbs were fresh and abundant. She had access to new books, and she worked and read by the light of good candles.

In fact, the only thing Roine lacked was patients to treat. Aside from my constant accumulation of bruises and scrapes, Roine had little to do—officially, that was. I knew that Roine had become a healer for the women of the palace. Rarely did we have a lesson, that we were not interrupted by one young woman or another, huge-eyed and hesitant. Roine spoke to each kindly, pressed packets of herbs into their hands with specific instructions, and sometimes gave them the doses herself. The servants, she was careful to call by name; the nobles, she was careful to pretend not to recognize.

As I ground the herbs carefully, Roine asked, "And Miriel?"

"The same." Roine was one of the few to whom I could speak of Miriel, as herself, as a person. To the Duke, Miriel was a commodity; he did not care in the slightest how alone or terrified she might be as long as her smile was constant and her manner charming. To Donnett, Miriel was a noble, and Donnett thought all nobles were the same—excepting the Duke, who had been born a commoner. To Temar, Miriel was a puzzle for me to solve; I was to learn her patterns, so that I might learn to anticipate her wishes. Roine, alone, seemed to care how Miriel fared.

I scowled into the concoction. Roine cared so much that it was difficult to tell her how I felt about my strange companion. With Roine asking after Miriel's health and happiness, mentioning how difficult it must be to be a noblewoman not raised at court, commenting on Miriel's precarious place in the world, I began to think that Roine was taking Miriel's side.

"She has a hard road to walk," Roine said now. It was something she said often. I shrugged and said nothing. Miriel's life was new dresses and dancing lessons; it did not seem difficult to me. Miriel had never in her life been punched in the stomach, thrown down a flight of stairs, and then expected to win a fight. While I was learning to defend her, she was learning to flirt with her fan. While I learned the antidotes to save her, she was having her hair dressed with strands of pearls for a banquet. Even when we lived at the Winter Castle, Miriel might never have felt the cold; she had stayed inside, away from the wind, but she had worn fur-lined robes and velvet all the same, while I shivered in homespun.

"You think I am wrong?" Roine lifted an eyebrow. "Now, don't mash that. You only need to bruise the leaves. Here." Her hands steadied my own. I tried to let the tension out of my shoulders, and she craned around to look into my face. "I don't mean to be hard on you Catwin, but you of all people should know that new clothes to wear and food in your belly does not make an easy life."

"It's different," I said, my pride pricked.

"You should ask yourself why the Duke has her here," Roine said sternly. "You told me she's for the King. Do you think that was true?"

I paused, then nodded. It fit with everything I had seen: Miriel's absence from court in her youth and her strange seclusion from the other girls now, the Duke's insistence that she be perfect in every way, how he had instructed her to be irresistible and yet untouchable. The Duke wanted to make Miriel into the perfect woman by the time the King came of age, a woman untouched by the court's spite, a woman no other man could have.

"Ask yourself why he intends that," Roine said. "You can bet money on the fact that it's not for her benefit."

"It's for him," I said, without thinking. That fit as well—even in the few weeks since I had come to court, I had noticed that his title gave him wealth, but little else. Servants whispered about "the upstart," nobles sneered at him, and ladies of the court steered their daughters away from Miriel. The Duke had done a great service for Heddred, and had been ennobled, but still he was reviled for his common blood, his advice disregarded. This was revenge, of a sort.

"What I wish I knew..." I bit my lip, then pillowed my chin on my arms. "Why has *he* never married?"

"What?" Roine frowned at me.

"His sister failed him, and so he decided to use Miriel to gain power. But he could use his own heir, if only he married. And he could marry, there are nobles who'd marry their daughters to him. He could have a dozen heirs of his own by now." Roine had paused, her brow furrowed.

"You're right," she said slowly. "I had never..." Her voice trailed off. Then she shook her head, shrugged her shoulders. "Well, no matter. This is all for him, anyway, you were right. So you watch Miriel," Roine advised. "You'll see the strain."

"I do nothing *but* watch her." My voice was sharp. I had decided that it was nothing to me if the Duke intended for Miriel to catch the King's eye. Every noble had the same plan. I should have known better, but I was too exhausted by my training to think properly. Roine did know better, but she did not say so, she only shrugged.

"At least you have me to talk to. Who does Miriel have?"

One of Temar's first pieces of training had been to be quiet about watching people. No use noticing another assassin, he had said, if you gave yourself away. Then you lost your advantage. So I forced my hands to keep moving slowly, bruising the leaves as Roine had instructed. I kept my tone light, and somewhat bitter. For sure, Roine was no assassin, but I assumed that the basic principle would hold.

"Worried that Miriel is lonely?"

I got nothing for my subtlety. "No," Roine said. "But you should be. A lonely person is drawn to others like a moth to flame. Miriel will attach herself to the first person she finds who pays attention to her."

I put down the pestle and stared at her. "And so?"

"You had better be that person," Roine advised. "Who else can you trust?"

Roine's words alarmed me, and in the weeks that followed I tried to become, if not a friend, less Miriel's outright enemy. I had no wish to be nicer to a girl who belittled me at every turn, but the words, *at least you have me to talk to,* rang out like a warning.

When I was exhausted, angry, despairing—then, I ran to Roine. I spoke to her in complete trust, as a fellow servant of the Duke. I knew that when I spoke to her, my words went no farther. My disloyal sentiments would not be used against me, and I could speak freely of my role, no need to hide behind the usual disclaimers that I was only the Lady Miriel's servant, nothing more—a girl, of course, as the Lady was so very proper, very like the Dowager Queen.

But where did Miriel run when she was angry, when she was afraid?

For I was sure, now, that Miriel was afraid. Everyone was afraid now; the word "war" hovered unspoken in every conversation, the men of the council were missing at dinners, and the whole court had been called. Courtiers who were more wont to be with their families in the country were here in great numbers; the great hall was packed full each night, the minor nobles turned away from dinner. Instead of the few children who might usually be at court, Miriel was surrounded by the children of each high noble and minor noble who held any stake in Heddred.

Reports came in daily, some whispered as rumor: raids on the border villages in the mountains, the ascendency of Duke Kasimir, the second heir to Ismir behind Prince Vaclav. Worse were the reports from the heart of Ismir itself, from the spies placed as servants to Ismir's council. When those messengers came, they were taken to the council room at once, and what they said, no one knew. Were there traitors here? the court wondered. How else could Ismir hope to fight back over the mountains? Everyone watched the Council members, and they walked as if they scented betrayal and intrigue in the air.

A show of unity would have put the court at ease, but the tensions within the council itself had worsened with the onset of war talk. Each council member had his own faction to advance, but there were only three seasoned generals in the council: Guy de la Marque, husband to Elizabeth Warden; Gerald Conradine, husband to Anne Warden; and the Duke.

It was hardly a contest. The majority of the men had massed behind Guy de la Marque. A general, of course. Married to House

Warden, of course. The man the Dowager Queen herself had chosen to be the Boy King's guardian. Of course. Better than Gerald Conradine, for sure, for who would trust a Conradine with House Warden's army?

And better than a merchant's son, however high his title. Guy de la Marque had few true adherents, that was clear, but the council was eager to blunt the influence of the Duke. Never mind that Isra, the Dowager Queen, paid scant heed to the Duke. Never mind that Henry's passing had all but halted the Duke's rise. Never mind that the present King was hardly in a position to grant favors. The Duke had a dukedom—he, a commoner born. It was not to be tolerated. Henry's mistakes must be unmade.

"Fools," Temar murmured under his breath, as we passed by a pack of noblemen singing Guy de la Marque's praise.

"Why specifically?"

Temar waited until we were well clear of the men. "Better de la Marque than a Conradine, they say. Nonsense."

"Because he married Elizabeth?"

"Just so." Temar nodded. "He has the Kleist men to rally to his standard." I nodded, not needing him to explain any further. Guy de la Marque could command the soldiers of House Kleist, by dint of Elizabeth. And here was the piece that no one other than the Duke's faction seemed to consider: Guy de la Marque had more soldiers now than House Warden could command as the Royal Army, and House Warden had no true commander.

And what was then to stop de la Marque, the man with the full trust of the Dowager Queen, from doing the same thing that Arthur Warden had done only two generations past? It had been an unwinnable coup but for House Kleist's support, and what was now to keep the dog from turning on its master?

None of the nobles asked themselves this. Whatever heroics Gerald Conradine had performed in the Bone Wastes, stemming the tide of Ismir's influence, they would be wiped away for the taint of his name. Regardless of the fact that the Duke had won the single decisive battle of the war, his actions could be countered with his low birth—so who was left? Clearly, only de la Marque; the other two now had the council ranged against them.

Into this pit of poisonous sentiment, the Duke placed Miriel. Each day, she was forced to walk into a room of people who despised her. She started from nothing, from less than nothing; only Cintia, Gerald's daughter, could claim a social status so strange.

Miriel was provincial, she was only a half-blooded noble, and yet the Duke had told her that with only her wits and her beauty, she must become the finest of courtiers. Even knowing that Heddred itself might fall, starting with her homeland of Voltur, she must focus only on being witty and charming.

Somehow, she managed it, the impossible task. She put on a good show. As her uncle had ordered her to be, Miriel was a charming courtier. She was unendingly pleasant, with a practiced half-smile on her lips. When she was out amongst the courtiers, it always seemed that she was delighted with her surroundings, and could not think of a finer place to be.

The opportunities for her to excel publicly were few enough, for children did not dance after dinner, nor flirt with fans, nor—generally—get asked their thoughts on military history, or the populist uprising in Mavlon. Only those of us who served Miriel, or taught her, knew that she could ride with consummate skill, could perform pairs dances with the same light grace she brought to the children's jigs and reels, and could speak seriously and insightfully on theology, history, or politics while simultaneously steering the conversation away from unpleasant topics. And she could sing, as well, in a smoky alto that put me in mind of brandy on a cold winter's night.

But no one knew this, and so the balance of Miriel's talents lay in reserve. For now, she was being polished and honed like a beautiful weapon, and the Duke required constant reports from her tutors, each one hand-picked, loyal, able to tell the Duke which other young ladies would be Miriel's rivals.

What we did not know was how Miriel would behave if she were to be at the center of the court. We could only wait to learn that. In the meantime, Miriel displayed her first stroke of genius: she refused absolutely to pursue the friendship of the well-bred, favored daughters of the court.

On her father's side, Miriel's blood was equal to any of theirs: her father had been the second son of the DeVere family, older even than the Conradines. But the Lady was a Celys, a merchant lifted on the tide of her brother's heroics and her pretty face, and every one of the young ladies knew it.

From Temar's relentless drilling, I knew their names: Alexandra Dulgurokov, the queen's niece, Anna and Linnea Torstensson, Evelyn DeVere, Elizabeth Cessor, Maeve of Orleans, Marie de la Marque—and others, a flock of girls with everything to play for. All pretty, all well-taught, all of good birth. I had seen them laugh and dance together when the maidens withdrew to their chamber each night after dinner.

The Dowager Queen kept a strict court, sending the gentlemen away to the King's Rooms on one side of the great banquet hall, while she and her ladies retired to her own rooms, on the other side of the building. The gentlemen might beg leave to dance, or sing, or watch an entertainment, but it was only the Queen's acquiescence that gave them license to mingle with the ladies.

The older maidens, those who must now navigate the difficult waters of courtship, were allowed to the Dowager Queen's rooms as well. They were able to catch the eye of the Queen, as the rising nobility, so that she could watch them and learn of them, and they were also sheltered by her fierce scrutiny: courtship could take place with a strange freedom, the young women protected from rumors of scandal by the Queen's presence.

The younger maidens were deemed unfit even for the strictly controlled world of the Dowager Queen's rooms. They were to withdraw to the maidens' rooms, under the watchful eye of the Queen's servants, where they might practice their music or dancing, or listen to sermons from the Queen's chosen priests. They were to be separate from the gossip and scandal of the court, kept pure.

In truth, they gossiped as much as any of the courtiers. Without the long years of practice in sifting truth from lies, they spread spiteful, wild stories about each other. And of all of them, Marie de la Marque was the most spiteful, the most eager to remind Miriel of her place. She was the daughter of Guy de la Marque and Elizabeth Warden, quick to remind others of her royal blood. She had thick golden hair and blue eyes, the very picture of female beauty, and her father was besieged with requests for her hand in marriage.

It seemed that every night at dinner, Marie managed to remind everyone that Miriel was not simply the heir of any commoner, she was the heir of The Commoner, the enemy of the Council. Every girl who waited on the Dowager Queen knew that Miriel was not favored by those who held power. Marie was the ringleader, and she had spoken: given a chance, each and every one of the best-bred young ladies—and a few who thought they were better bred than they were—would gleefully have excluded Miriel.

They did not get a chance. Miriel was as sweet and courteous as the most placid of girls. She was deferential; she never intimated, by word or deed or gesture, that she resented them or noticed their sneers. If paired for a dance, Miriel would do her part with her usual perfection. If asked to sing in the maids' rooms, she would change her voice to fit against her partner's. When the girls went in to dinner at their table, she never jockeyed for position as the other girls did, each trying to be closest to the King's table on the off chance that the poor, sick boy would look over at them.

Instead, Miriel spoke courteously and engagingly to those who chose to sit with her. She sparkled just as brightly as if she had been trying to charm the King himself. She did not longingly watch the ones who thought themselves her betters, and she did not behave for a moment as if she would rather be elsewhere. She toasted her companions and laughed merrily at their jokes, inquired about their health and offered opinions on their gowns, if they asked her—Miriel was fast becoming an object of envy for her beautiful wardrobe.

"Oh, but it sets off your eyes!" I might hear her exclaim, as I waited on their table at dinner. "No, you mustn't give it away. Trim it with new ribbon and it will be lovely."

The girls were too young to see it, but I thought it was like watching the currents in a river. Slowly, Miriel was becoming the focus. Those around her were happy in her presence and glad to see her; gradually, as I watched, more and more heads turned at her approach, more voices offered her greetings, a seat on a bench, a partner for a dance. Miriel was rising through the court, as her uncle had told her to do, and against my will, I began to wonder where all of this would lead.

Chapter 15

To those who watched her when she was at dinner, or speaking with the other children after the meal, Miriel was a perfect girl, without flaw. None of them knew that when Miriel retired to her rooms at night, she did not put on her nightgown and robe and retire. Each night, she practiced something, be it the turn of her head to greet a newcomer, the delicate sweep of a curtsy, or her now-envied smile, a spontaneous burst of light across her face, as if she were overcome with joy. While I studied manuscripts or sharpened my daggers, Miriel practiced walking, talking, eating, and breathing.

"What are you looking at?" she snapped at me one night. I had been given leave to return early to my rooms, as Temar had told the Duke that I needed time for my studies. The Duke had warned me that I would be given such liberties only until I was fully trained and I, secure in the knowledge that I was endlessly outmatched by my studies in weaponry, had reveled in the chance to be away from Miriel and the courtiers for a few hours.

But Miriel had returned early, and she was—as was becoming usual—annoyed by my very presence. Miriel was scrupulously kind to her maidservant, to the pageboys who brought her messages, to the maids who lit her fire and cleaned her rooms. The same courtesy was not extended to me.

That night, I only shrugged in response to her sharp-tongued question. I was reading a history book, and even I, who adored books, had to admit that this one was a particularly dull account of Wulfric II's reign. Miriel was practicing running, and the tap-tap-tap of her heels on the floor made it all the more difficult to study. But the past few weeks had been an exercise in not voicing criticisms, and I did not wish to break my pattern now. Someday, I told myself, Miriel would stop regarding me as her enemy.

Not now, however. Tonight, my avoidance gained me nothing.

"Am I *disturbing* you?" Miriel asked dangerously. "Is my practice disturbing your studies?" Mutely, I shook my head, but her temper had sparked and there was no returning to quiet. She wrenched the book out of my hands and threw it at the wall, then whirled back to stare at me, fists clenched, breath coming short.

"Do I ever complain of your studies?" she demanded. "Do I ever order *you* to be quiet? No! I never do. But you see fit to criticize *me*, when I have the harder task by far—"

It was the last untruth I could tolerate in silence. "No, you don't!" I jumped down from my seat on the table and matched her, face to face. "All *you* have to do is wear fancy clothes and go to parties! *I'm* the one who has to guard you, *I'm* the one who has to learn poisons and spying—and I'm the one who's going to get beaten if that book is ruined!"

Miriel was staring at me, open-mouthed. She never expected me to talk back. Adults, she ceded too—her tutors, who knew things she did not, her mother, who she loved, her uncle, who she feared. They were older and more powerful. I think I was the first person her own age who had dared to counter her.

"And you criticize everything I do, anyway," I added. I was warming to the theme. For weeks, I had been respectful, I had bitten my tongue on retorts and bowed my head against barbed insults. A dozen times or more, I had bowed when I would gladly have slapped her face instead. Now, every retort spilled out.

"You think I *want* to be here? You think I follow you around because I like you? I would rather be at home, out of your way, away from you nagging at me and out of this whole stupid place. You think I wanted to learn to kill people? I didn't, and I never wanted to be your whipping girl, either!"

At this, Miriel laughed. Shockingly, she threw back her head and laughed, the first genuine laugh I had ever seen from her. She was wild-eyed.

"My whipping girl!" she exclaimed. "Oh, my whipping girl? I would like that! Can I order you to be that, then?" Savagely, she ripped at her gown, tearing at the laces, ripping the delicate fabric. She dragged at it until she stood completely naked in front of me, and I shrank away.

Until her shift was off, I had thought her quite unhinged. Now I was horrified: from her ribs to her knees, Miriel's skin was mottled with bruises, some in stripes from a cane, some from fists. I knew the way knuckles left a mark. I stared at her, unable to look away, trying not to be sick.

"Last week," Miriel said, now unnervingly calm, "I made a joke that my uncle thought was unladylike." She pointed to one of the bruises, a thick stripe along the side of her ribcage. "The week before, he saw that I had missed a step in a dance." She pointed to another bruise on her thigh. "Shall I name all of these for you?"

I shook my head.

"When *you're* in pain, you're allowed to wince," Miriel said precisely. "This one is from when he saw me slouching at dinner. He has a guardsman beat me," she added, irrelevantly.

I stared, and found myself shaking. Until now, I had not quite believed that any of this was real. Being an assassin had still felt like a jest to me, as if it were too dark to be true. And now Miriel had showed me her own flesh, covered in bruises as bad as my own, and the whole world felt a little bit darker, a little less like a jest, even a dark one. I had the sense of being dragged down to the bottom of a river, caught in currents too strong for me.

"Lace me up, please," Miriel said, still calm. Her hysteria had disappeared. She had pulled her shift back over her head, and stepped into her gown. I moved towards her as in a dream.

"Don't you want to sleep?" I asked her, as I took the laces in my hands and began to pull them tightly. If I watched very closely—and now I did—I could see her wince as I tied up the gown.

She turned a look on me that was haunted. It was not the look of a child. It said that she did want to sleep, she wanted to sleep and never wake up. Her voice was eerie.

"I still have to practice," she said. Finally, with the same courtesy she showed to the daughters of minor nobles, to the palace servants who cleaned her rooms—but she had never before shown me—she said, "But you can go to bed if you like."

"Miriel..." It was the first time I had said her name out loud. She did not look at me. "You should have someone see to those."

"I've been to see Roine," Miriel said simply. "She gave me a salve for it. Thank you for your concern." She had shown me her naked body, she had shown me the very cause of her perfection, and yet it was as if she was farther from me than she had ever been. I did not know what to say; I stepped away from her and let her return to her practice.

So Roine had known. Roine had seen, and not told me, she had waited for me to learn it on my own. I wondered if she knew every noblewoman's secrets, and filed the thought away for later. Someday, a cold, remote part of my mind said, I would need to know which of those beautiful young ladies had been to see Roine, looking for herbs and potions.

"Miriel..." I said again. This time, she looked right into my eyes.

"When I catch the King's eye," she said softly, "and I have his heart—then I will be free of my uncle."

I pretended that I had never heard her words; close to treason in the tiny enclave of the Duke's faction. Miriel and I never again spoke of Miriel's tasks, or my own. Our resentment of each other now had a form: Miriel could not forgive me for seeing her practice each piece of perfection, for having seen her bruises, for being a piece of her uncle's plans for her; I could not forgive her for being the reason I was here, learning skills no child should know, witnessing darkness that should not be a piece of the world.

In the days that followed, a gulf grew between us, an enormity of horrors we knew together and yet could not speak of. Both of us were consumed with surviving, and each of us hated the thought that the other might escape—as if there were only so much survival and luck to go around.

Watching Miriel was painful now, and I watched her even more closely than I had before. When I saw her duck through the arch of arms during a dance in the maids' chamber, when I saw her embrace a friend, I knew how much pain lay behind her joyful smile. Miriel hid her bruises as carefully as she ever had and continued to be the charming new favorite of the children. For the first time, I came to admire her strained charm as much as I was ever weary of it.

Now when Miriel snapped at me—for after the kindness of that one night, we returned to our hostility—I remembered how I had felt on the first night of our journey, when I looked into her deep blue eyes and saw a girl who knew already how to wait. I remembered realizing how formless she was, how easily she shaped herself to her audience. I had the disquieting thought that I might live with her every day and never really know her.

And now I helped her. She played cards well, but resented the element of luck, and so I had Donnett teach me ways to cheat, that I might pass on to her. To my shock, she possessed an uncanny knack for it, pulling off the dirtiest tricks without batting an eye. We developed a trick, she and I, where I would watch for the Duke; when he appeared in the room, I would offer wine to one of Miriel's companions, and she would know to abandon her cheater's plays before he saw.

Miriel's tutors reported to the Duke that she read well, wrote with beautiful penmanship, could do passable mathematics, and had a good understanding of history and politics. Her dancing instructors assured the Duke that no young lady was as graceful as his niece; when he asked me, summoning me for my own report on her, I could assure him that their words were true. At rest, Miriel was only a skinny—if beautiful—child, but in motion she was a wonder to behold; and she was always in motion.

She might be a child, but the Duke was careful to ask me, at every report, if there was any whisper of impropriety. Every time, I shook my head and responded, "No, my Lord," with absolute confidence. Other girls of the maids' rooms flirted with boys, the immature flirting of children who are to be betrothed, the pretty girls always ready to hope that a man might overlook their low birth, the well-bred girls driven not to be outdone. There were none of the sideways glances and secret smiles one could see in the court proper, but there was always a childish flirtation or two going on between the young ladies and the young gentlemen.

Miriel was never involved in these. When a boy would arrive to sit with the ladies, Miriel alone did not swivel to stare at him. She would include him in the conversation, polite to a fault, splitting her attention equally between each of her companions. She would include him in her toasts and laugh at his jokes. But never did she look into a boy's eyes with anything other than polite interest. Other girls might make cows eyes at a boy, or stare wide-eyed at the young man on the throne, but Miriel had a frank, disarming way about her when boys were present, as if posturing for marriage were the last thing in her head.

The Duke's suspicions were not entirely unfounded, however. Four times—for I, increasingly nervous, had counted—Miriel had been drawn into discussion with Wilhelm Conradine, the King's heir. Wilhelm was a fine-built young man, handsome, with clear blue eyes and sandy hair that fell softly across his forehead; if he had not been such a strange figure at the court, the King's heir and yet an outcast, utterly mistrusted for his father's blood, all of the best born young ladies would have swooned over him as the minor nobles' daughters did. Miriel did not seem to see his high cheekbones and full mouth, her eyes did not linger on him as the other maidens' eyes did—even Marie de la Marque would steal glances at him. But Miriel would speak with him, on philosophy or theology or politics, and their conversation was so quick that I could hardly understand the words.

Only once had she forgotten herself enough to look for him. She had craned her head up and over to the young men's table to see him. Then she had remembered herself, and turned her head to see if I watched her; I had looked away, as quickly as I could, but she still suspected that I had seen her indiscretion. She was not willing to ask outright, and she would never have thought to ask if I might keep her secret; it would never have occurred to her. So she watched herself. Now when he came to sit at the maidens' table, she was cool and impersonal, she would turn away from him to speak to the other girls; and yet I could see that she was always aware of him when he was near her.

For reasons I could not have explained, I kept her secret. I had never told the Duke of this, not by word and not by a flicker of my expression. I had taken the time to puzzle out, while I walked to a meeting with him, that I did not trust him and I did not like him. And so I learned to prevaricate: he asked me only what she did? Well, she did not do anything wrong. And until he thought to ask me the secrets of Miriel's heart, I would say confidently that she had shown no favor to any young man. I could not say why I did not open my mouth and let the words spill out; he had called me into service for just this purpose, to look at people and see their hearts and minds. But it was the first secret I kept, and I kept it for Her.

In the meantime, as I watched her, I wondered—and I knew the Duke wondered, too—how she would manage when she came of age to be married. Then, there would be no childish innocence to hide behind. But for now, she did brilliantly. She was indeed a perfect courtier, and her achievements were surpassed only by her seeming modesty.

Unlike the Duke, I began to wonder something else: how long Miriel could keep going as she was now. Only I and Anna, her maidservant, knew how draining this was. When Miriel fell into bed each night, she was asleep as soon as her head touched the pillow; she had to be shaken awake each morning. Despite her exhaustion, she would not stop to rest. But how long could that continue? She drove herself near to collapse, and she did so, I now realized, out of fear.

Unlike the Duke, who seemed to believe that Miriel was some sort of porcelain doll, I knew enough to see that she could never continue this charade forever. How long would it be until

Miriel was so exhausted, so angry, that she no longer cared what punishment she might receive? What would happen when she no longer cared enough to play along with the Duke's plans? What if she took the reckless notion into her head to follow her own desires? How long until she decided that even the King's protection was not worth as much as a smile from a boy she might truly love?

I watched her warily, but she had never, since those first few days, wavered in her focus. When I had brought back the card tricks to her, she had insisted on playing until she had each play and trick and wile down perfectly, until she could fool even me. We stayed up, that night, until well past midnight. Miriel's maidservant had fallen asleep by the time Miriel felt ready to go to bed, and so she had me help her undress.

A Shadow might be called upon for any task, Temar had told me—from spying and assassination to being a personal servant or a clerk. But Miriel had never called upon me at all, and women's gowns were utterly foreign to me. The castoff clothes Roine had been able to procure for me had always been boys' clothes. I had been an androgynous child, easy enough to pass off as a serving lad if I wore my hat down over my ears, and Roine considered it safer for me to play the part of a boy in any case. When I was forced to wear dresses, they were simple things: a shapeless sack like the serving women wore, that tied at the waist and at the neck.

"Just unlace it," Miriel said, frustration evident in her voice. "It isn't difficult."

"Maybe for you, it isn't." The laces were done up in ornamental knots, a fashion introduced by Isra Dulgurokov, and by halfway through the task of unlacing the gown, I was feeling strongly that the fashion should be replaced by something simpler. When at last Miriel stepped out of it, I held it out to her, and she shook her head at me.

"Hang it up."

"Where?" Miriel had whole wardrobes full of clothes. I only had a little shelf with my spare uniform folded on it.

"With the other green gowns." Miriel seemed halfway between amused and scornful. "And fetch me my nightgown. And my robe; I'm cold." I shot her a look and went off to find the correct clothing. "Not that nightgown," Miriel called. "It's dowdy."

"Then why do you have it?" Miriel only shrugged elegantly. My patience was fraying fast, but that hardly mattered to her.

Indeed, when at last she was attired and I made to go to my little bed, Miriel stopped me once more.

"Brush my hair," she said. I cast a glance, annoyed, at the maidservant who was fast asleep on the bed, and began to brush at Miriel's curls. As I brushed, careful not to split the curls, Miriel studied herself in the mirror.

"It should be enough," she said. She said it as if to herself, but I knew it was for my benefit; Miriel kept her thoughts locked inside her head when she did not want to voice them.

"What should be?" I asked, curious despite myself. Miriel met my eyes in the mirror, but she pretended not to hear me, turning her head this way and that to look at the sweep of her eyelashes, the pout of her lips, the elegant lines of her cheekbones. Finally, I snapped, "Who are you hoping to impress, then? You see no one except the maids and your tutors, so who is it, the Duke? Your own uncle?"

She shot me a look, anger quickly turning into derision, veiled under those thick lashes. "There's always someone to impress," she said. "That's why I'm me, and you're you. I never stop thinking for one moment about enchanting men." She smiled her most dazzling of smiles. "I could enchant anyone. Maybe I'll enchant Temar."

I swallowed; my hands curled briefly into fists—it was enough. She smiled again, this time in triumph, and I cursed myself for a fool that she had already seen that weakness. I narrowed my eyes.

"What about Wilhelm Conradine?" There was a leap of joy in her eyes, and her lips parted. Then she looked down and her expression went blank.

"I don't know who you mean," she said. It was a weak excuse; Miriel knew every lineage there was to know; she had known Wilhelm's name before she had come to court. I struggled between my anger at her jab, and the sense of guilt at the sadness in her eyes.

"You're only a child anyway," I said. "No one looks at you like that."

"They all do," Miriel said, quite unmoved by my spite. "And you should know what I meant." I sighed and paused to think. *It should be enough.* All of a sudden, I remembered the first conversation we had had, in the dark hallway at the Winter Castle. And the sadness in her eyes now made sense.

"For the king," I said. Miriel only inclined her head with a little half-smile; the curious, blank smile I remembered from the Winter Castle. She knew the correct mannerism, but her eyes were completely blank. Then I frowned. For the first time, I truly thought about the Duke's plans.

"The King would never marry you," I said. Miriel's smile disappeared abruptly.

"You don't know what you're talking about."

"He wouldn't," I insisted. "He has to marry for advantage, bind in families who are discontented. Even if you could make him love you, it's not a matter of choice for him."

I had shaken her confidence, and I had remembered too late what happened to Miriel when she failed the Duke. She had blanched, but she took refuge in her pride. She stood up, turned, and pulled me close by the collar of my tunic.

"I *can* make him love me," she said. On the face of it, her confidence was ridiculous—she had never met him, and I could count on one hand the number of times we had even laid eyes on him—but this was no false bravado. Miriel was serious, and when I stared into those beautiful blue eyes, I could believe her. She shook me, small hands wrapped in the fabric of my shirt. "He's the King, he can do whatever he wants. And I can make him want to marry me. You wait. You'll see. And you'll help me." She shoved me away from her abruptly. "And never say Wilhelm's name to me again."

Chapter 16

"What? No."

"Just give it here!" Miriel made a grab for my spare uniform and I pulled it out of her reach. For a moment, she shoved against me, but I did not yield, and she knew better than to try to win a fight with me. Her uncle and his retribution were not here—and in any case, she would have had to explain why we were fighting in the first place.

She drew herself up to her full height. "Give it to me," she said in her best noble voice, and she held out her hand, palm up.

"Not until you tell me why you want it."

"You're my servant!" Miriel looked ready to stamp her foot, or make a lunge for the uniform. I held the uniform behind my back, and said a silent thank you to Temar for teaching me to play keep-away with an object.

"I'm not giving it to you," I said wearily, "until you tell me what this is about."

We stared at each other in silence, and to my surprise, she yielded first. "I want to see the palace like you do."

At once I saw what she meant. I gripped my fingers around the clothes. "No. Oh, no."

"I won't get caught," Miriel assured me. "Promise. You could teach me to sneak like you do, I thought, and—"

"You *will* get caught, and you'll be punished." A thought struck me. "And so will I."

"So we both agree that it's important for me not to get caught," Miriel said, far too reasonably. I looked at her suspiciously, and she spread her hands out, palm up, and showed me her winning smile. In spite of myself, I was impressed. I had seen Miriel turn her charm on others, but never had she used it on me. I was surprised at how trustworthy she looked now. Still smiling, she lowered her voice a little. "And I'm sure I wouldn't get caught," she said persuasively, "if I only had help. I've watched you, you're very good at moving quietly. I bet you could find the best path through any building, and not get seen."

For a moment, I flushed with pride. I had been training on just that. Temar had given me a sword one night—forbidden for servants—and had me sneak my way through one of the buildings close to the Palace proper. I was good at finding paths, and I was very good at not being seen. I was happy that Miriel acknowledged my skill...and then my sense of misgiving returned. I did not like the sound of this.

"You can't do this," I said flatly. "It's too risky." I had only been allowed to try after months of training. Miriel, no matter how sneaky she was, should not attempt this.

"No, it isn't," Miriel stepped forward and laid her hand on my arm. Her eyes were enormous, luminous in the faint light of the bedroom. "All I want is to go into the great hall at dinner."

I choked. "All! Is that all? Everyone there knows your face!"

"You said yourself that no one looks past a servant's clothes." I sighed. It was true that no one looked at my face. But my face was not one of the most beautiful and most recognizable faces in the kingdom. I decided that I did not feel like saying this aloud, and being reminded of my own plain looks.

"It's too risky," I repeated.

"I want to see them when I'm not there," Miriel said. "That's important, you know it is. I need to be able to know if they speak of me behind my back. I need to know what to look for, and I can't do that properly if I'm trying to entertain all of them."

"I watch them for you," I said. It was true. I knew which way the factions could splinter: I saw which of the well-bred girls genuinely enjoyed Miriel's company, and would not have snubbed her, and which of the minor nobles resented her and would speak against her.

"You won't always be there," Miriel said. "I need to know, too." A lie mixed with truth was always best, Temar told me. I saw that a persuasion mixed with truth was best as well. It was too risky, and yet...

"Your uncle will hear that you were late to dinner," I said weakly.

That made sense to her. She tilted her head to the side. "Sometime near the end of the meal, I'll say I've broken my heel," she said. "Then I can run and change, and see the hall, and say when I came back, they had already left for the maids' chamber, and that's why I was gone so long."

"What if they stay late over dinner?"

She shrugged. "I'll say I went to the maids' chamber first, thinking they would already be there." Again, I was impressed. Temar was attempting to teach me how to lie, but I was woefully bad at it. I admired Miriel's quickness of thought, and consoled myself with a stab of moral superiority: at least I was honest. Then caution came crashing in once more, and I bit my lip.

"I really don't think we should," I said, as firmly as I could. I saw something in her eyes, and she looked down.

"You won't tell my uncle I asked you to do this for me?" she asked, and I swallowed.

"Of course not." I knew what trouble she would be in. I did not even want to think what the Duke would do if he thought she wanted to sneak about. Without realizing it, I had walked into a trap. Miriel's eyes flashed upwards at me, and in a moment she had shifted again, no longer persuasive.

"You know I will do this, with or without your help," she said. "Some day when you are at lessons, I will sneak away from my own, and if my uncle catches me, I will tell him that you had known I meant to do this and you did not tell him." I only stared at her. I could not find any words, I was so angry. Of all the reckless, stupid—so like a noble…

"Fine," I spat at her. "I'll help you. But you do what I say. You listen to me." I stared at her, at her triumphant face. "Promise." She considered.

"I'll do what you say. I promise."

"And you're going to go dressed as a maid," I said, staring at her mouth, the delicate point of her chin, her long lashes. "You'll never pass for a boy."

So it was that two nights later, I lurked in the shadows of a side corridor, and thought that I might be sick with nerves. This was a bad, bad plan, I told myself. I thought that my heart was about to beat out of my chest. It had taken all my skill to get us here without being seen: counting seconds after the guards passed a corridor, calling up the layouts of every building we went through, slipping along side corridors and teaching Miriel to walk purposefully, like a servant. And now we were here.

I looked around the hall, and felt, instead of the familiar contempt at the obliviousness of nobles, a terrible fear that tonight would be the night one of them looked, actually *looked*, at a servant. One of them would recognize Miriel, and word would get to her uncle, and he would make good on his promise to kill her—and, likely, me.

"Can I come out of the hallway?" Her voice was tight with excitement. I tilted my head down to pitch my voice to her.

"Quiet." I scanned along the row of tables once more. I had insisted that we stay here, at the head of the hall. There were more people who might recognize us, but I could not take the chance of a soldier or a petty nobleman seeing Miriel. At the thought of a drunkard seeing those eyes, that skin—

I knew how serving women were treated, and the thought made me sick. I was sure I could help her before they knew what was happening, and I was sure I could help her escape. But I was not sure I could do it without killing someone, and I knew that could not be done without questions being asked later. Questions that would lead the Duke, inevitably, back to us.

And so, only slightly less dangerous than waiting on the men: waiting on the noble ladies and their daughters. Isra, the Dowager Queen, was pious and strict, and so the ladies and the gentlemen did not sit together at dinner. Her ladies in waiting had their own tables, just below the royal table. These were the mothers of the girls with whom Miriel associated, the women who would tell their daughters whether or not to speak to the Duke's niece.

Below their tables, the marriageable young noblewomen. At fifteen, sixteen—a few desperate at seventeen, and one or two who had been given leave to sit there at fourteen—these ladies were decked out in the most extravagant jewels their parents could afford, dressed in the finest silks and velvets. Their hair was dressed with ribbons and, if they were lucky, with strands of pearls or jewels. Each had the strained look of a woman on show, a woman who knows that everything depends on her ability to catch a man's eye. They spoke to each other with studied indifference, as if every male eye in the great hall was not trained on them: the young men, hoping to make a love match, and the older men, searching for a woman who would be an advantageous match for their sons.

The women never looked towards the tables on the other side of the room. They knew that the Dowager Queen watched them, as well, on watch for immodest behavior. And so they coquetted, laughed elegantly, turned their heads to show off the length of their necks, or tossed their hair to show the gleam of it, leaned forwards to each other across their table; it was the most dishonest thing I had ever seen, and one of the most fascinating.

I spared a moment to look at Cintia Conradine. She was one of the most careful, the most reserved. Once, she cast a look over at the noblemen's table, but only to smile at her brother Wilhelm. Cintia's success in finding a husband would rely on the unpredictable currents of court favor, and to be sure, she did not have favor now. The Dowager Queen's eyes rested on Cintia more than on any of her companions, as if Isra would catch her out at something. As if, from Cintia's demeanor, Isra could determine the family's loyalty.

Isra herself sat in state, to the right of her son's empty chair. Her throne might be set lower, but there was no doubt in anyone's mind that the ruler of Heddred overlooked tonight's feast. Isra wore a gown of purple, so heavily-embroidered that it might have been cloth-of-gold, and if her golden circlet was plain, she was adorned so heavily with rings and bracelets that it was wonder she could hold up her arms.

As always, the Head Priest sat at Isra's side. He ate and drank little; he had the hollow face of a true ascetic. It was said that Isra consulted his advice in every matter, seeking her guidance from the words of the scriptures. He was a fanatic for the early church, Temar had said, determined that the church and the country should return to its early purity of spirit. He wanted the priests, whom Roine so disdained, to give up their jeweled robes and priceless works of art, and devote themselves to the care of the people. The High Priest was not a favorite amongst his followers, but he was the head of the church, and he had the favor of the Dowager Queen; they could not dislodge him. He led the church with single-minded, almost fanatic intensity.

It was said, also, that his advice bordered on the mystical, and that he sought his own guidance from ancient prophecies and visions. I could hardly believe that, knowing how deeply pious the Dowager Queen was, but still, I spared a moment to watch him carefully, in the ways that Temar and Donnett had taught me. This man had the ear of the Queen, and she had control of the kingdom. It would be worth knowing who he was, and who he had been before he entered the church. It would be worth knowing what he, who sat at the right hand of a woman dripping in gold, thought was purity of spirit.

If I had not been so terrified of what Miriel was getting up to, I would have been watching everything and everyone—a task that seemed, to me, entirely at odds with the bladework and grappling I was learning, and yet was something that Temar absolutely insisted I learn. He was trying to teach me to watch without expectation, let my mind be carried on the currents of what I saw.

It was one thing to learn sparring in dark cellars, Temar had said—but another thing entirely to learn to be a Shadow in the court, watching the undercurrents and coming to outright combat only rarely. As a Shadow, I was trained to strike quickly and kill quietly, but that should be only the smallest piece of what I did. The majority of my task was watching and giving advice, and then, only rarely, acting as the unseen force of Miriel's will.

I turned my gaze back to the young women, younger than the marriageable girls: dressed in simpler clothing, gazing around themselves as if to drink in every glimpse of the court. Children, nine or ten and younger, were never allowed to court at all, and the young women Miriel's age were only allowed to be a part of the court at dinnertime. Isra had decreed that they were there to learn proper manners, not to be shown off as potential brides. In reality, they were there to remind the court of the Lords who had daughters, and a great deal of marital bartering went on at the Lords' table.

On any given night, Miriel would be sitting one or two tables down from the older girls, depending upon the mood of the other maids; the seats closest to the throne were highly coveted. Tonight, after a council meeting in which the Duke had been accused of trying to subvert Guy de la Marque's influence, Miriel was in disfavor. Her seat had not been kept open for her, but instead another girl had moved up to take her place.

I looked over at Miriel and saw her draw her gaze back from Wilhelm Conradine; purposefully, she retrained her gaze on the maidens' table. Unconsciously, she was fidgeting with her sleeves and shrugging her shoulders; the rough fabric of the serving girl's gown I had found for her was irritating her skin. She was nearly unrecognizable, dirt smeared on her face and her neck so that the lily whiteness of the skin would not give her away. She had tucked her curls up inside a cap, and instead of her own boots, she was wearing a pair of mine.

"We should go," I said to her.

"Just a moment." She was watching another of the girls intently; I recognized Elizabeth de la Marque's daughter, Marie. She was a beauty, with pale skin and hair of a rich gold, shining like

121

sunlight, like honey. The baby of the family, I had heard, the apple of her father's eye. I had heard the servants whisper about what de la Marque might be planning for his lovely daughter, and I found that I wondered, myself. Then I remembered where I was, and who was at my side.

"Dinner is almost over," I whispered to Miriel. "You need to leave before they get up." And before the Duke returned from a dinner meeting of the council. Please, Gods, before then. Before he noticed her chair was empty and before Temar was there to scan the hall. When Miriel did not move, I said desperately, "You promised."

She shot me a look, but stepped back reluctantly, into the little side hallway. I was scanning the hall for Council members. They did not like to sit long at their meetings and miss their dinner, but neither did they like the King to undertake his decisions without him. I could only hope that their meeting dragged on, and the Duke was not here to find us out. If anyone would pick out our faces in the shadows, it would be him. When I heard Miriel exclaim in surprise, I felt my heart seize. We had been found out.

I whirled and ran into the hallway, skidding to a halt as I found Miriel laughing quietly, being helped up from the floor by a young man in the plain clothes of a clerk. He was pale, and strenuously thin, but he helped Miriel up with a firm grip under her elbow. She was trembling with relief, and smiling the radiant smile she showed to servants.

"Oh, no, miss," the boy said. "I assure you, it was entirely my fault. Here." He reached down and picked up her shawl, handing it to her with a courtly bow, an exquisite bow. I looked more closely, and when he looked around at me, he had light brown hair and grey eyes. I saw the set of the cheekbones, the thin mouth—

I stared at him in complete horror. I could not find any words, not even when he flashed me a smile, clearly enjoying my shock. His eyes took in the crest embroidered on my clothes, and then slid back to Miriel.

"But perhaps not a servant?" He inquired smoothly. "For surely, no serving girl was ever so fair, except perhaps the poor girl in the tale, who was given a dress to go to the ball." Miriel swallowed. Now she knew that something was not quite right.

"My Lord—sir—" I stumbled over the titles. He could not know, he *must* not know who it was who was skulking around in disguise. But it was too late. He waved a hand to keep me away, and I, not knowing what to do, felt my hands drop, leaden, to my sides.

"May I assume that I have the pleasure of speaking to the Lady Miriel DeVere?" he inquired. She was frozen with fear, but his smile was as warm as dawn breaking, and mischievous. Miriel smiled back, in spite of herself. "Don't worry," he said, and he held a finger up to his lips. "No one will hear it from me. It will be our secret." He shot a glance at me.

"Thank you," Miriel murmured. She had recovered, she sank into a beautiful curtsy.

"Now, I must go." The man bowed again. "My Lady, a pleasure to meet you." He gave a nod to me, and went out into the hall itself, walking close to the wall and watching the nobles as they ate.

"He was nice," Miriel said, looking after him.

"We're going." I grabbed her hand, heedless of protocol, and yanked her after me down the hallway.

"Catwin. Slow down!" I did not listen. I half ran, tightening my hand around hers so that she could not wriggle away. I ran until the sound of the banquet was a faint roar, I ran out through one of the little-used alleys, Miriel's breath beginning to come short. I ran, determinedly thinking of nothing, and cursing myself all the while. I should never have agreed to this.

All was not lost, it was not, it was not—

"What's wrong?" Miriel demanded. "Why are you upset? Did you see—"

I kicked open the door of her room and shoved her inside, then slammed the door behind us and slid the deadbolt before grabbing her hand again and pulling her through the receiving room and the privy chamber to her bedroom. When I saw that it was empty, that Temar was not waiting for us, only then did I admit to myself what had happened. I doubled over and shook.

I was terrified, and, I found—to my surprise—I was furious. Of all the women in the world to serve, I was certain that my luck had led me to the very worst. She was willful, uncaring, heedless of danger, and worst of all, she was the favored tool of the most terrifying man I knew. Any misstep she made would be the end of both of us, if the news made it to the Duke.

"Catwin, you will tell me what that was about." Miriel was trying to be dignified. She did not expect me to reach up and grab her by the collar of the dress, dragging her close.

"You idiot," I said through clenched teeth. "You didn't recognize him, did you?"

"Who?" Miriel pushed me away.

"Miriel..." I could feel a hysterical laugh welling up in my chest. "That was the *King*."

Chapter 17

I waited for the summons for two days, sick to my stomach with fear. I said nothing to Temar, I said nothing to Donnett—who had asked angrily why I was wool-gathering during my lessons—and I said nothing even to Roine. There was no one that I could trust with this. I did not even say another word to Miriel, and neither did she say anything to me. Whatever camaraderie we might have gained from our escapade had been lost in our determined silence.

Finally, I knew what Temar had meant when he said that a Shadow must know more than hand-to-hand combat. Here was a problem that could not be solved with a quick, quiet strike. Only with logic, with a careful play by Miriel, could this situation be brought round to our favor. And we were truly on our own. I could not ask Temar's help, for admitting that we had defied the Duke would be as good as asking to be killed.

It would have been terrifying enough if I had been sure that we had ruined everything, but what made things so much more confusing was my growing belief that perhaps all was not lost. Every time I thought that, I disbelieved it. I turned the information over and over in my head in the way that Temar had taught me, trying first to name and discard each of my preconceptions about the situation, and then remembering each facet of Miriel's discussion with the King in as much detail as I could. Each time, I came once more to the same baffling conclusion.

In fact, when I let my mind wander through the problem, I wondered if perhaps the meeting had been a stroke of luck. For one thing, we alone now knew that the King might ever be watching, dressed as a servant. That was a piece of information that any number of spies would have paid highly for. Miriel alone knew to watch her tongue at the maidens' table as if the King himself was listening.

And anyone could have seen that the King had seemed quite charmed by Miriel. He had found her trick delightful—not least of all, I thought, because he was employing the same trick himself. Of all the charming, beautiful women of the court, Miriel would now stand out, for her beauty shone even through rags and dirt. Miriel did not need jewels in order to glitter.

He knew now that she was kind, for he was shrewd enough to know that while I had recognized him, she had not. She had not belittled him, whom she thought a servant, she had apologized for her own clumsiness and smiled at him. For a man who was used to sycophantic service, that could be a powerful draw.

I thought of how she might have played him at their first meeting if she had been forewarned, and I thought it lucky that she had not known. She would have been reserved and dignified, as she was with everyone who thought themselves her betters. She certainly would not have turned that dazzling smile on him. For sure, Miriel had shown herself to be adept at navigating the court, but I thought that this meeting had been better even than she could have engineered.

And, for the first time, I could stop worrying over her liking for Wilhelm; she had seemed charmed by the King, just as he had been charmed by her. She had thought that flirting with him would be a chore, but if she had taken a true liking to him, perhaps she would never have the urge to go against her uncle's will. When they worked in concert, they could be formidable indeed—and I would be spared the Duke's angry questions as to why she was mooning after another boy.

Further, what other young lady could claim to have had a private audience with the King? Not simply a few moments of his attention—although most would have gambled anything for a chance even at that—but a conversation completely in private, without the watchful eyes of his mother and his guardian. It was likely that Miriel had secured a place in his heart that, if she was careful, would not be lost to another woman. It was, strangely, an auspicious beginning.

I did not think, even for a moment, that the Duke would see things the same way. The Duke had his own plans for Miriel and the King, he would have calculated what he thought was the best way to introduce the two of them. He had lost control of his sister, and had vowed not to make the same mistake with Miriel; he played a more refined game, for greater stakes, and he chose every move deliberately. His choice to bring Miriel to court now had been deliberate, his choice to keep her in her own rooms had been deliberate, and from her continued avoidance of the favored girls, I knew that he approved of that tactic.

He played a long game, and he had planned every step of it; he would not appreciate improvisation, even were it to be successful. The Duke had his own plans to make Miriel a focus, irresistible, of unimpeachable reputation, practically unattainable. When I thought on what he might do to the two of us if he found out what had happened, I had nearly been sick with fear. I walked now like a girl who knew that she was marked for death.

He would summon me to explain her absence from dinner, I knew that, and it would be imperative that I did not betray that anything—*anything*—had happened beyond the broken heel and the changing of her gown. My expression could not flicker, and my posture must be easy. There must be no tremor in my voice. Where the Duke went, sharp-eyed and sharp-eared, there was also Temar, and he had taught me everything I knew about deception.

The one saving grace, I thought, was that the Duke had absolutely no reason to suspect that Miriel might have met the King. He might suspect that she had gone to meet another man, he might suspect that she had wearied of this endless game she played, but there was no reason that the thought of her running into the king, dressed in a servant's clothes, should ever occur to him. Even if I slipped, they might never suspect the truth.

I spent so much of my days waiting that, when the summons arrived at last, all I could wonder was why it had taken so long, and why I had been called alone. I tormented myself with hope on the too-short walk to the Duke's rooms. Perhaps the Duke did not find a broken heel to be sufficient reason for concern. He had much on his mind, after all. He might not care in the slightest. Perhaps something else entirely had happened, something that boded ill for Miriel. Was I at last to learn of a true threat on her life? Or—I gulped—Donnett or Temar had complained about how distracted I had been during my lessons, and the Duke was going to yell at me to remember my duty. I left Miriel with her governess and hurried along the hallways, slipping down side corridors and padding up back staircases, trying to tell myself that the summons had nothing at all to do with our dinner excursion.

Temar met me at the door, his eyes full of worry, but his face as impassive as I had ever seen it. I realized, when I stepped into that silent room, that it was not Miriel's enemies who were the problem for her, and it was not my own inattentiveness that was the problem for me. I slowed, not wanting to face the Duke, but Temar ushered me forward with a hand in the small of my back. He was not going to let me slip away, no matter what I was in for. He nodded for me to open the door to the Duke's study, and followed me inside.

The room was dark but for one candle on the Duke's desk. His work had been pushed aside, and the Duke had gone to the window and pushed the heavy winter drapes aside. He was standing, silhouetted faintly against the night sky, and looking out at the plains to the west. I wondered if he was homesick. Then he turned to me, his eyes glittering black in the darkness, and I forgot such irrelevant thoughts.

"My niece has taken strange ideas into her head," he said carefully. His nostrils were flared, his voice measured in the way it was only when he was upset, when he was holding back the anger that would burn away anything in its path. He looked to me for an answer, and so, despite my feeling that any answer was a trap for me, I was bidden to speak.

"Yes, my Lord?" His eyes narrowed, and I suppressed a sigh of irritation. Why did he bid me speak, if he would only be upset?

"Do not think to play the innocent with me," he warned.

"I do not, my Lord," I answered honestly. "I know not of what you speak." Indeed, I did not. Strange ideas? I knew that I looked confused, and this should have soothed him. But, for the first time I could remember, he did not look at me as though I were his vassal, a girl he could terrify into the truth. He looked at me as if I were a woman grown, a person who might hold her own secrets, a person who might lie to him for her own gain. Under his gaze, I found myself unsure which was the truth. I started to turn my head to look for Temar, for comfort, and then checked myself before I gave the Duke that key to me.

And, I thought with a pang, I could not consider myself on the same side as Temar if there were secrets between us. I had hidden something from him, and Gods willing, it would never come to light. That it was my choice to hide all this did not make it easier to bear.

"My niece has become…unbiddable." The Duke's mouth curled in distaste. All at once, I saw the resemblance between him and the Lady, my one-time mistress. I had thought it strange, all these years, that she should look so soft and beautiful and he look so hard and weathered. But when his face twisted in anger, the anger of one whose plans have been thwarted unexpectedly, I saw the kinship. They had the same thin mouth, and the same hard blue eyes. Life had not been easy for the Celys family.

Again, the Duke waited for me to speak, but I said nothing. I did not know the rules of this game, and I was not going to speak until I could see where the traps might lie. And, I reasoned with a flash of humor, if I was a woman with secrets, then I should behave like one. There was a long pause while the Duke stared at me, and I stared back. Between us, Temar watched this defiance with an expression that said I had gone mad.

"You understand, do you not, that a child is bound to obey her legal guardian?" The Duke was unamused. He drummed his fingers on the table as he waited for me to speak.

"I do, my Lord."

"And I am Miriel's legal guardian."

"Yes, my Lord."

"Did Miriel tell you what transpired yesterday?"

"No, my Lord." I forced the words out from between cold lips. Miriel had been quiet last night, studying a religious text instead of dancing or singing. I had known that something was wrong, but when I had asked—her maid being out of the room—she had only looked at me coldly and said that she was well, as if I was a presumptuous fool to ask.

"I heard a tale that my niece was missing at dinner two nights ago," the Duke said. I opened my mouth, unsure if I should speak, but he did not want a response. "When I asked her why she had been gone...she lied to me."

In those last words, I finally understood. The Duke had always considered Miriel suspect; she was his sister's daughter. Even if I did not understand why the Duke hated his sister, even if I did not know what it was she had done to lose his trust and inspire his disdain, I knew the vague shape of what had transpired; he mistrusted anyone associated with her. The Duke had separated her from her mother at a vulnerable time, knowing that Miriel would be unsure of herself as she approached marriage. He had thought that he might find her, if not reliable, at the very least biddable. He had thought that he could frighten her into disregarding her own whims.

It had never occurred to him that she would purposefully betray him: stray, and then have the will to lie to him about it. He had never thought that she would be clever enough, strong-willed enough, to make her own plans. She was not a flawed, weak-willed girl who followed her desires without a thought—it turned out that Miriel was a girl with her own ends. In the Duke's anger, there was the hint of some softer emotion, as if the Duke had reached for his sword in battle and found it broken. He was vulnerable; he was unarmed, he was betrayed. But Miriel was not an object, to be re-forged, she was a human who now had a streak of disloyalty, and a streak of independence. And the Duke knew how very difficult those would be to eradicate.

This could be my only chance to persuade the Duke that he had been mistaken. I barely had time to think before I launched into one of the stories I had practiced. I could only hope that I had learned what Temar had taught me, well enough to fool even him. I shook my head and shrugged my shoulders.

"I don't know why she would lie to you, my Lord." The Duke had been looking down at his desk; now he looked up and I had to fight to keep my face in its same puzzled expression. "Her heel broke on the way to dinner." Simplicity. Breathe slowly. Ignore the narrowing eyes. Don't think of Temar watching. "When we were there, one of the girls said they should dance after. So Miriel had me accompany her back to change her clothes. We missed them going to the maids' rooms, but we met up with them there." I shrugged again. "I know you would not want her to miss dinner, my Lord. Perhaps she was worried that you would be upset? She took a very long time to choose a new gown."

"Why a new gown?" The question was sharp, he hoped to catch me unawares.

"She said her old gown did not match the new slippers, my Lord," I said limpidly. We stared at each other, and I saw that he was doubting himself at last. I struggled to keep my expression clear: free of evasion, free of triumph.

"Catwin." Temar's voice was unexpected. I looked over to him. "You want to protect Miriel, don't you?"

"I do." It was the only answer I could make. The unexpected question had brought the truth bubbling up. How could I possibly explain that when she tossed her head at me and told me I was nothing, when she looked at me as if I were a willing participant in the Duke's plans, when she made no thanks for my service, I wanted nothing more than to leave her to her own life and let her protect herself?

But I would not see her dead. How could I let that happen? And so: *I do*. And worry about where Temar would take this. I had not practiced for his questions.

"We can only protect her if we know where she is," Temar said. "You're sure you're not lying, Catwin? The Duke would not be upset, he would be glad to know that Miriel had been safe. You're sure it happened just as you said?"

All I was sure of was that the Duke had no idea what had happened. I clung to that.

"I'm sure." I shook my head as if at a loss. "Why...? Why are you worried? I was with her the whole time, she listens when you say to be safe, she would never have gone back unescorted. Sir, I really am doing very well at my lessons—"

"Do you have any idea how many would gladly see my heir with her throat slit?" the Duke demanded harshly. I felt my eyes widen. "Do you?"

"I know—" I broke off. "I know that your family has enemies, my Lord."

"Don't be dense." He stared at me. "If ever she wants to leave the hall again, she is to wait until she can inform me of her attentions, and I will see to it that she is guarded." I stared at him, not sure what to say. He was having me trained as her bodyguard, I was to wait on her at dinner. If he truly thought that I would be useless against an attacker, he would have us accompanied by guards. He would, certainly, not be trusting me with the protection of her life. So he must know that I would take this new order either as a lack of confidence in my ability, or as an indication that he did not trust me or his niece.

I was not quite stupid enough to voice those thoughts. I bowed.

"I will tell her so, my Lord."

"I have no use for an heir who will not do as she is told," he told me, his eyes glittering. "Tell her that, too. You can go."

I left, almost giddy with relief, and walked back to my rooms with the sense that I had only barely escaped the fall of the axe. There, at her curious look, I dutifully told Miriel of the Duke's words. I had wanted to blunt them somehow, but at her cold-eyed demand as to why I had run off when she might have needed me, I only repeated them word for word. She might have been carved from marble for all she reacted; she hardly seemed to hear the words.

131

"You can go," she said, and she turned her attention back to her book.

I stared for a moment at her beautiful profile and tried to find the words to tell her that I had not gladly been the bearer of this message. I wanted to tell her that I had lied for her and the Duke was at least less sure of her rebellion; she was no longer his outright enemy. I had meant to tell her that I did not think she had done poorly with the king.

It was a small thing, a few words to give a girl who was terribly alone a small piece of comfort. I warred with myself. She was being cold because she was in pain, and she did not know that I had protected her from the Duke.

She looked up again. "Why are you still here?" she asked coldly. "I told you to go. Do I need to be even clearer? Are you a complete simpleton?"

I sketched the shallowest of bows, and then I turned and left her to her studies.

The next morning, Temar sent a scrawled message that he would see me after lunch. I was to study with Donnett in the morning, instead. I made my way out of the building and into the faint chill of a fall morning, hunching my shoulders and squinting up at the morning light. I thought that the warren of buildings was a cruelty. In a proper building, I would travel from place to place inside, but in this palace, every place was separate: our sleeping quarters, the palace proper, the armory. Every time, I stared up at the sky and wished that I could grow wings and fly away.

To my surprise, the Armory did not have the usual sullen quiet of a morning—soldiers battling hangovers, men coming in from their watch. There were so many soldiers moving through the place that it took me fully ten minutes to make my way from the door to the staircase into the cellars.

"Yer late," Donnett grunted.

"It's chaos up there." I pointed. "What's going on?"

"Ye haven't heard? With that fancy lad training ye, and him working fer the Duke?"

"Donnett. What is it?"

But before he had a chance to answer, I turned and dashed back up the stairs, poking my head around the door and watching the crush of men as they funneled into the armory to be outfitted.

There on armbands, on boots, on tunics, was my answer. If I had not been so determined to get to the cellar, I would have seen it at once.

"Just so," Donnett said, when I went back down the stairs and he saw my incredulous face. "Guy de la Marque says it'll be war within a year, and he's brought his wife's men to start drilling. Marched 'em in without telling anybody, and here they are. A whole army of his own—so what d'you make of that, lad?"

Chapter 18

We waited, all of us, for the axe to fall. In the Duke's household, the fear of de la Marque was overlaid with the echoes of Miriel's struggle with the Duke. I practiced my sparring and waited in silent misery, torn between my liege lord and my sullen mistress. She practiced her dancing and waited in icy silence. Donnett grumbled, and Roine said nothing. The Duke went around with a face like thunder, Temar trailing worriedly behind him.

The court was terrified into silence. Even de la Marque's supporters on the council had been unnerved to wake one morning and find an army camped outside the city walls. What could such a display of power mean, from a man who was already the power behind the throne?

Those who still supported de la Marque pointed out, reasonably, that if the man had wished to overthrow the king, he could easily have done so before now. And it was a poor time to make such a move unless he truly believed it to be necessary— the unrest in the Norstrung Provinces meant that, by rights, de la Marque should have left his men where they were, in the event that the rebellion spread; that would be protecting his interests. Surely, it was said, de la Marque spoke honestly when he said that he had brought his forces to defend the realm. Perhaps he knew of a threat that none else did.

Others asked, just as reasonably, if the King had commanded this. It was always possible, of course: new to council meetings after his illness, and fearing war, the Boy King had ordered his forces displayed, as a young boy might build a wall on a little pretend fort. He was still before his majority, but perhaps he might have commanded it, and de la Marque acceded.

I thought of the young man with the grey eyes and the quick mind, and guessed that he was smarter than to do such a thing. But even those who asked the question suspected that the answer was no—why would the King order such a thing, knowing that it was to provoke the Ismiri? If he did, why would the council not block it? They would be justified. And if he had done so, why did no one else on the council know of it?

No, the only answer was that this was Guy de la Marque, acting in concert with his wife. And then the question was, was this a political misstep, or was it a public warning to House Conradine, or was it something more—was it the groundwork for a coup? The man had overstepped the bounds of a good courtier, but why?

No one knew, and the fear of power that swirls in every court took hold. No one would question openly whether the protector of the throne, the King's guardian himself, was a traitor. There was a conspiracy of silence, where all thought it and none said it, and people began to convince themselves that they did not speak up, not because they were cowards, but because it was too ridiculous a thought to voice.

Those who did not think so could only wait. The Duke and Gerald Conradine scrupulously avoided meeting each other's eyes in public, for it was clear that their stars were rising in opposition to de la Marque's, and equally clear that the man with the large army would not take kindly to that fact. In spite of his own worry, Temar took me aside one day and told me to watch the court carefully, and learn from de la Marque's techniques; for the Duke's Shadow, even this was a learning opportunity.

And then the truth came out: the rebellion had grown violent. Henri Nilson, brother to the Earl of Mavol, had been ambushed, kidnapped, and hung in the Earl's own cathedral. At the Earl's plea, a detachment of de la Marque's men had been sent to the Norstrung Provinces at once. The rest had been sent to the city, to join with the King's forces and then march south. Too risky, de la Marque claimed, to march any significant portion of the Royal Army south, and leave Penekket unprotected. It invited trouble from the Ismiri.

All true. Every fact, every rationale, could be checked and picked over. And yet, one could not help but notice that Guy de la Marque had acted not only without consulting the King, but also without consulting the Council. One could not help but notice that it would have been simpler to leave his men where they were, and march them due south if a summons was sent by the King; to march troops west was to provoke the Ismiri. Most of all, one could not help but notice that Guy de la Marque was the only noble with a strong army at his command. It was an open show of power, calculated to remind the Council that Guy de la Marque was the power behind the throne not only by right of law, but by right of strength.

Guy de la Marque and his royal-bred wife, however, had failed to consider the King's intelligence, and his growing stubbornness. They had neglected to consider that the King might have his own opinions on de la Marque's display of power, and on the future of Heddred itself. And so the King seized the opportunity to teach his Council a lesson. I learned of the incident through a puzzle that Temar had set me.

"You're going to tell me about the war," he said one day, when I arrived for my lessons. He pointed to a chair in the center of the room.

"Which war?" I asked, as I sat.

"The war that's coming."

"It might not be war," I said, watching him for the gleam of knowledge. Instead, he was thoughtful. This was a strange test of my knowledge, if he did not know the answers.

"Oh, I don't think there's any avoiding it now," Temar said, shaking his head. He paced around me. "Too much unresolved. Bad feeling and betrayal in Ismir. In Heddred, a land of plenty and a sickly young King. The only one between him and the end of the Warden line is a man with Conradine blood, and the man with the largest army in the kingdom stands to lose his power when the King comes of age. So what do you think of that, my little shadow in training?"

"The King is getting better," I said.

He looked at me sharply. "That's not what they say in the halls."

I narrowly stopped myself from swallowing, one of the signs of deception. Temar was right. They said in the halls that this was just like all the other times, the declarations of the King's health and then the inevitable decline back into illness. But the man I had seen in the hallway was recovering, sprightly and energetic. Death did not hang over him. I tried the first lie that came to mind.

"I thought he had stayed well longer this time." I shrugged. Temar gave me a look that said he did not believe me, but returned to his query. He stabbed his finger in the air.

"Tell me what happens with the war. Tell me who's involved, how it begins—how it ends." I sat in silence for a few moments, turning the problem over in my head. Temar was one of the few people who would sit quietly while I thought. He liked me to take my time and answer carefully.

"It all hinges on what de la Marque wants," I said finally. "And what he can persuade the King to do."

"The King is fourteen," Temar reminded me. He was watching me closely, and the conversation was veering close to secrets. I worked to make myself shrug.

"Doesn't that just mean he thinks he knows everything?" Temar chuckled, and I tried not to look too relieved. I pressed on, before the silence could grow. "Look, the King has been sitting in on Council meetings. He would have to be blind not to notice that the court fears de la Marque now. Don't you think?"

"I might," Temar said silkily. "You tell me."

Lessons, always lessons. I rolled my eyes and tried to think, drawing from Donnett's angry words over the past weeks, from my own training, from what I knew of the King, and of Guy de la Marque.

He was, it was said, formidably intelligent. He had a mind for war. And yet, any potential of his had been blunted by his upbringing as the baby of his family, accustomed to be pampered. He had not reclaimed it, he had not honed himself into a weapon. All of his life, things had been given to him: a priceless education, a wife of royal blood. Circumstance had given him his brother's birthright, and the guardianship of the king. Life had been easy for Guy de la Marque, and that made him impatient, and vicious.

"Guy de la Marque does not withdraw the troops," I said. "He brought them here for a reason. He wants something, and he does not want the Council to speak against him while he tries to get it, so he's trying to scare them. Or distract them."

"What does he want?" Temar asked softly.

"Power."

"Too simple. Tell me more. Does he want the crown?"

"No," I said, after a pause. "The country would never stand for it. He must know that." It was true, even if de la Marque could force the King to abdicate, he would never be able to control the Council. They would turn on him in a moment—he had an army of his own, his wife's men, but they owed him no strong allegiance, and the Royal Army would splinter into factions. So what could de la Marque be after?

"He wants something that only the King can promise him," I said, "Something the Council can't deny once it's done. He's using the troops to scare everyone else, but he'll try to play it as a good thing for the King—say he's brought the troops in to help, and then ask a favor in return. Is that it?"

Temar only watched me, his usual sardonic smile on his face. I sighed.

"Okay, so he'll try to use that as leverage. He will try to look like he's not delaying, but won't send the rest of the troops to crush the rebellion until he gets what he wants. Then Ismir readies for war, because they hear that we have troops at the ready and they think we want to invade. Then one of two things happens. First, nothing. Guy de la Marque gets what he wants and marches the troops off to the south—Ismir realizes there's no war, things return to normal. Or, second, it takes too long and someone finds a reason to go to war."

"The word is 'pretext,'" Temar informed me. "But what of the King? What of the King, in his sickness—or health?" Neither of us mentioned that speaking of the king's health so casually was near treason. We were in the Duke's rooms. We only lowered our voices.

"I don't know, I can't see." I shook my head. Thoughts were gathering, but I could not voice them until Temar said,

"You're thinking of him like a King. Think of him like a man, like de la Marque. He's only a boy, really."

The thoughts fell into place. "He's been ill, he will want to prove that he is well. He will want de la Marque to heed him. He will want to assert himself."

"And de la Marque?" Temar's voice was soft; I hardly heard him.

"He will resent that." Anyone could, no man wished to be beholden to a boy. No battle-hardened veteran would wish to accede to the ideas of a boy who had not even been born when the last war was fought. It would rankle, it would chafe even a sensible, loyal man; and if my instincts were correct, de la Marque was neither.

I frowned. "He will try to keep power," I said. "That's what I cannot think—what is he playing for? How will he keep power? Killing the King would do no good—then the throne would pass to Wilhelm." A thought struck me. "Unless..."

"Unless?"

"Unless the King were to marry de la Marque's daughter..." I tried to remember her name. "Marie! And have a son by her. Oh, but she's his cousin."

"Second cousin. Royalty do that, you know."

"Really?" Now that I thought on the lineages I had read, I realized that he was correct. "Oh. Well, then, Marie. But there still might not be a war."

Temar was actually smiling. "Oh, very good," he said. "Now, be truthful, did you know?"

"Know what?" I basked in the praise. For a moment, I could pretend that this was weeks ago—before the fight between Miriel and the Duke, and the question I still saw lingering in Temar's eyes. He was proud of me now, and I tried to let that moment wash away the others. I shrugged with the obligatory modesty of the highly praised. "I might be wrong. We'll have to wait and see."

"Ah, but we won't." Temar was still smiling. "You really didn't know, then? Remarkable. Just this morning, there was a fight between de la Marque and the King."

"In public?" I knew my eyes were round.

"In a Council meeting. Much the same. Everyone will know by this evening."

"What happened?"

"The King told de la Marque that he had endangered the country by displaying the army so openly. He said that Heddred and Ismir needed peace and friendship, not to re-open old wounds."

"What did de la Marque do?" I was breathless. Things were happening, finally, after all the waiting and wondering.

"Made flowery apologies," Temar said grimly. "He said he only wanted what was best for Heddred, and had wished to provide the crown with loyal soldiers and generals."

"He never meant the Duke would be disloyal."

"He could have meant anyone. So no one could say a word against it. And the King is..." Temar's face twisted. "Soft. He did not press. He did not want to make a scene."

"So is de la Marque in favor with the King again?" It would be the worst thing for us. I remembered, belatedly, that it would be wrong, also, for Heddred. I believed it, truly, and yet when I remembered that the two things were not the same, I felt the hairs on the back of my neck stand up. I prayed that this was not a premonition.

"No one knows. The King keeps his own counsel, it turns out. Strange in a boy of his age. Not one of the nobles or their spies knows what the King is thinking." I saw him watching me, but this time I had nothing to hide.

"And how do you know that?"

"How do you think?"

"You know what I mean. How do you make those contacts? How do you build a web like that?"

"Why should you need one?" His face was impassive. "We have one already."

"You said you would teach me everything," I said.

"I said I would teach you what you needed to know to protect Miriel. And you don't need to know this."

"But someday we might not be in the same place—"

"Enough, Catwin!" His hand slammed down on the table, and I jumped. "You are a child. There are things that you do not need to know, and this is one of them."

There were so many retorts that I could not pick one. *But I can learn to kill*? I wanted to cry. *I'm to learn to spy and poison, but I can't learn this?* But the look on his face stopped me from saying more. I had never seen him angry before; I was frozen, as much as I was angry.

"I'm sorry." I knew I had to say the words; they would unlock his sympathy. I hated saying it, and despised him for the smile he gave me. He looked at me as if everything was wiped away, as if—like a child—I would forget what had happened.

He should know better. Someday, I thought coldly, he would realize that.

"But what we do know," he continued. "What we do know—sit up straight, Catwin—is that de la Marque met later with the Dowager Queen, and they discussed the marriage of the King, and de la Marque left smiling. As you said."

"The Queen agrees with him?" My anger over our disagreement was pushed to the back of my mind. This latest news was disastrous for us.

"Why should she not?" Temar asked silkily. "With her son well at last, should he not be married? And Marie is of royal blood. De la Marque did his work well: all the court knows Marie to be very pious, very ladylike. He will have assured Isra that Marie would be biddable.

"Catwin, think—do you think that Isra wished to be queen only for a handful of years, and then spend the rest of her time on the throne waiting for her son to supplant her? How does she keep power when her son marries, save by choosing a girl she can order?"

Temar rose up from his own chair and began to pace around the room. His pleasure in my lesson had been forgotten, as had his anger at me. He was as grim as I had ever seen him. He turned to look at me, his eyes narrowed.

"So, here's a different test. Now de la Marque's plot seems to have worked, he has an army camped outside the walls, and his daughter is the favorite for the throne. And where does that leave us? How do we fix that, Catwin?"

Chapter 19

The Duke called us to his chambers barely a day later, and Miriel walked confidently ahead of me through the bustle of the crowd. She had been watching Marie de la Marque carefully, marking the way the girl seemed nervous, ill at ease in the tense court.

"There's the lesson," Miriel said to me, as she dressed. Since our escape, and her beating, she no longer spoke to me unless she wanted to tell me how clever she was. "She's waiting for the court to give her father power."

"So?" I preferred my lessons in politics mixed with dagger strikes and armies; I could barely follow Miriel's stories about who had snubbed whom with a careful flutter of a fan, or who had flirted by swishing her skirt.

"So, the lesson is, when she looks uncertain, the other girls do not behave as if she's in power." Miriel waited for me to nod in understanding, and then rolled her eyes when I did not. "Behave as if you already have power," she said slowly, as if speaking to a simpleton, "and they will treat you as if it is yours. They will give it to you."

"It can't be that simple."

"It is," she had said confidently, and since then she had been walking about as if she were a princess herself. She never turned her nose up at others, nor gave orders—but, in everything she did, Miriel looked confident. She walked always with her head up and her shoulders back, as if she were a woman grown, with power of her own.

She was confident in every moment, save when she met with the Duke. Then, Miriel stood like a girl. She looked down at the ground and she spoke only when spoken to. Both of us were wary, after our defiance and near-capture. When we entered the Duke's study and saw that he was smiling, both of us gave tiny sighs of relief. I saw some small amount of tension melt out of Miriel's shoulders.

"The King has given me command of Guy de la Marque's army," the Duke said, without preamble. He saw my wide, startled eyes. "Not for good. Simply for the duration of the rebellion." He smiled his predatory smile. "This Jacces will soon be dead, and the rebellion finished. If anyone asks you, you are to say—"

"Excuse me, my Lord Uncle..."

"What?" The Duke did not like to be interrupted. Miriel saw that she had made a misstep, and curtsied.

"My apologies, my Lord Uncle. I was wondering, how did Guy de la Marque lose control of the Kleist army?"

"The King decided that de la Marque's ideas were sound. To leave troops here, and yet march on the rebellion as well. However..." the Duke smiled. "Guy de la Marque provoked the Ismiri, and the young King wishes to make it clear to them that he does not approve of de la Marque's behavior. Why are you smiling, Catwin?"

I jumped, as I always did when he said my name.

"I'm very sorry, my Lord. I just thought...well, it's clever of the King."

"Oh? Why do you think so?"

I tried to find a way to flatter the Duke. "Well, he's doing this to show the Ismiri that he won't use the troops for a war, so he's pushing Guy de la Marque aside. But you won the Battle of Voltur, my Lord—so it's a warning to them, too."

The Duke actually smiled.

"You may have been right," he told Temar. "She's learning. You are correct, Catwin. This is a warning to many people. It is a warning to Guy de la Marque, it is a warning to the Ismiri, and it is a warning to this Jacces. Now. Preparations. Miriel."

"Yes, my Lord Uncle?"

"We know from our spies that Guy de la Marque has secured the Dowager Queen's support for a marriage between the King and Marie de la Marque," the Duke said. Miriel's head jerked up, and I felt sorry for her. Miriel might have suspected Marie as her rival, but she had not known how favored Marie was. Now she stared, uncomprehending, at her uncle. He smiled.

"You have a role to play in upsetting de la Marque's plans," he told her. He scowled at the thought of the marriage. "He cannot be allowed to gain that sort of power."

"What is my role, my Lord Uncle?" Miriel queried. I could see her fairly quivering with excitement. She had thought that it would be years before she was able to catch the King's eye. Now, she hoped that her uncle would give her a chance to do so soon— and escape his power earlier than she had expected.

143

I did not speak, but I thought I knew the Duke's plan. Miriel could make herself irresistible from the start: the forbidden woman. Garad's mother wanted to choose his wife, and we knew now how keen he was to assert his independence, how poorly he had taken de la Marque's meddling. A word here, a smile there, and Garad would never be able to forget Miriel.

"I just think it would be best if the King were to have his own reasons for opposing the marriage to Marie," the Duke said smoothly. "It is an advantageous match. Certainly, she is of good birth. She brings an army with her, and de la Marque is rich. But advantage means nothing to a young man, when he is pursuing another woman."

Miriel knew better than to speak. She stood quietly, but with the air of a hunting hound that is only waiting for a command.

"The King is shortly to learn that his guardians have been making plans without consulting him." The Duke's mouth twisted in a smile. "The Council, also, will learn this. It will complete de la Marque's fall from grace—and the matter of the King's marriage will be opened to the court. They will need to make a show of choosing a good bride for the King. All of the unmarried women of the court will be shown off, paraded under his nose." His eyes narrowed.

"You are to enchant him," he said abruptly. "You will turn his head from Marie. Your task—the only thing you should focus on, from now until I tell you otherwise—is to make the King fall in love with you. I will gain a chance for you to have a private audience, but until then, you must be the most charming, the most fascinating, the best of all the young ladies at court. Your tutors tell me that you would be ready for such a test," he said. She did not waver under his gaze, and without warning, he turned his head to me.

"Catwin. Will she be ready?" I nearly laughed, so ridiculous was the question. Miriel enchanted everyone she saw. She was only waiting to step into the spotlight of the court.

"Yes, my Lord," I said.

"Ah." The Duke seemed pleased with my response. "Well, then. I will tell you how to dress, and how to behave, for any events that are planned. You may go now."

As we withdrew, Temar followed us into the antechamber. "The guards will escort you back to your room, my Lady," he said politely to Miriel. When she was gone, he frowned at me. "Will

Miriel be ready so soon?" he asked. "Tell me truly, Catwin." I laughed at that, and his frown deepened.

"I'm sorry," I said. Another giggle escaped me. "But, really, you should know—she's perfect." I sobered for a moment, remembering the beatings she received if she was not perfect.

"We can trust her to behave properly?" Temar asked, and I saw an opening. I had not been able to convince him of Miriel's trustworthiness, but this would be a good moment to sow doubt.

"You doubt her, too!" I said, my brow furrowed. "Just like the Duke." And then, temptingly, I saw another chance. I was still curious about the Lady. "Why does he doubt her? Is it because of her mother?"

"An interesting question. But, then—yes, you and she have a history, don't you? Do you want to know about her?"

"Yes." He had told me never to ask directly for what I wanted to know, but there might never be another chance to learn this.

"She came to the court after the Duke won the battle at Voltur, and was ennobled. She was married to Roger DeVere. You knew as much, yes? She was...self-seeking. Even when she was newly married, she was setting herself forward, she would look at any man of higher rank.

"She shamed herself—and she shamed the Duke, and she shamed her husband. When they found she was pregnant, she was sent away to the Winter Castle before anyone knew. They were not certain, the Duke and DeVere, that Miriel was DeVere's child. Well, that was clear enough in the end, she's the very image of him, but the Duke would never have brought her back. Even when DeVere died, the Lady stayed in Voltur.

"This is not," Temar said diplomatically, "a court that tolerates commoners. She was making trouble for the Duke. He uses Miriel because she is his heir, and she has qualities that make her...useful. But he watches her. Who know what trysts she might be arranging? And, Gods know, her mother had no head for intrigue. She chased any smile."

"She might have, but Miriel is fourteen years old," I said, annoyed. It was always me reminding them of this. "She doesn't think of trysts, she is a child. She does think of marriage—and girl at court does. But she obeys the Duke." I did not add, *so far.*

When I had said my goodbyes and was walking back to Miriel's rooms, I found myself thinking that if the Duke were not so blinded by his dislike for his sister, he would see that Miriel was just as self-seeking, but far cleverer. And instead of being flighty, she was growing into a woman who knew how to hold a grudge. Where the Duke might have made a powerful ally, he had seen only a flawed tool. He was so blinded that he had blinded even Temar—but the assassin, clearer-headed, knew something was amiss.

He was right to be suspicious, and I had nearly told him so. It would have wiped away my guilt. Gods knew, I had no reason to give my loyalty to a girl who hated me, who would have seen me beaten for her prank without batting an eye. The Duke cared nothing for me, either, but he at least was powerful enough to reward loyalty. Common sense dictated that I ally myself with the Duke, and with his servant.

And Temar was the first one who had ever seen me for more than a nobody, except, perhaps, Roine. When I had first met him at the Winter Castle, his smile had warmed me through—that, and the way he looked at me, as if I were someone special, not just another servant, not just another peasant child. I had thought that he would make me something more than I had been.

It had all gone wrong, I thought miserably. Temar was not making me something more. For all of his talk of my education, for all that I could read and write and tumble and heal, I sometimes thought that I was lower now than I had been born. Temar and the Duke, between them, were twisting me into something dark. Sometimes, in the deepest hours of the night, I thought that I might not be quite human anymore.

Temar, for himself, I would have followed to the ends of the earth, but as the Duke's servant, I no longer had any trust in my heart for him. There was only the longing to trust him. We were on different sides now, and even though it was me who had lied, I thought that he should have known. And the Duke should have known. They had built me from nothing; they should see my deceit in an instant.

With a shiver that I *knew* for a premonition—even if I believed in none of that—I thought that the Duke had made a very big mistake when he had given me to Miriel. He had not really wanted someone to be for her what Temar was for him. Away from Temar's anger, in the clear light of day, I could see now that Temar had been ordered to make sure that I would always be less than he was. The Duke had thought that he would be able to control Miriel through me, and me through Temar.

I did not think that was going to work out well for him.

Chapter 20

As news of the Duke's ascendancy raced through the court, he made an outward show of preparing for his march south. He spent hours upon hours in the Armory, overseeing the selection of gear, watching the men drill, and exercising his formidable memory for names and faces. He remembered each of the men who had served with him, and they in turn were glad to sing his praises to the other troops.

His long hours in Council meetings, and his abundance of preparations for the war effort, did not mean that he was too busy to oversee Miriel's preparations for her debut. He went to her lessons to watch her dance, he ordered a new wardrobe for her in beautiful fabrics, and he drilled her endlessly on her curtsies, pleasantries, and planned phrases on any topic. He was determined that Miriel should be able to turn any topic away from overly political waters with ease, subtly stressing the Duke's military career and her family's loyalty before bringing the conversation around to a lighter topic.

"As if I could not do so on my own!" she exclaimed. "As if I were not the best dancer, the best at everything—everything!"

"It's not for long," I soothed her.

"What does that mean?" she snapped back. I tried not to rise to her.

"Just that…what you said." I paused as the maidservant came through the room and curtsied to Miriel. She left the room, carrying a sack of dirty linen to the laundry, and I resumed. "As soon as you have the King—"

"I don't know what you mean," Miriel said shortly. "I think you are misremembering." I blinked, confused. Miriel's uncle watched her closely, but even he could not hear our words here. The rooms were empty now. I was opening my mouth to tell her that I always checked the rooms for intruders, and would have caught any spies her uncle had set on us, when I realized what she really feared.

"You think it's *me*," I said. I was shocked. "You think…you think I'm reporting on you to the Duke."

"I know you are," Miriel said coldly. "He calls you to his rooms alone, and he asks you about me." I stared blankly at her. She could not think...

"You don't trust me," I said, testing her. She looked at me as if I were an idiot.

"Of course not."

"But you know I've kept secrets," I said. I could feel my pulse beginning to pound. "You know I have." I could not even find words to tell her how angry I was. I had never told her uncle about Wilhelm, I had never told him that she had plans to escape him, and I had never told him about Miriel's impromptu meeting with the King. She looked at me, and she never even wavered.

"I don't trust anyone," she said. "Everyone has a price. If you haven't given up my secrets yet, it's only because he hasn't offered you enough. And someday, he will."

"I wouldn't do that!" To my shame, I felt tears coming to my eyes. I blinked them away and dug my nails into my palm, trying to use the pain to distract myself. "You trusted me enough to help you with disguising—"

"That was a mistake," Miriel said coldly. She drew breath, but I did not want to hear what she would say next. I walked away from her without even bowing, hoping she had not seen my tears. I paced around her privy chamber, trying to think. It had been a mistake to believe that she might trust me, that she might ever appreciate the things I had hidden from her. I had not only hidden her indiscretions, I had lied to Temar about them—and all I had gotten was mistrust and spite.

Confused, far from home, and feeling at once terribly angry and terribly hurt, I did the only thing a child thinks to do: I went to go find my mother. I went not knowing why, not even knowing I was upset, and so when Roine opened the door to her chambers, I surprised both of us by hurling myself into her arms and bursting into tears.

"Catwin—child—are you well?" I was sobbing too hard to speak, I could only shake my head. Everything had been so far from normal, for so long, that I had not shed tears over it. I had not cried on the nights when Temar taught me a new killing strike and I awoke from dreams of using it. I had not cried at any of Miriel's taunts, or the Duke's threats. It turned out that the tears had only been waiting. Now that I started to cry, I could not stop.

It was fully half an hour before I had calmed down enough to speak. Roine, having held me in her arms and made shushing noises, finally wrapped me in a blanket and went to make tea. When she returned with the pot, she carefully brushed my hair back from my face and re-braided it. She gave me a cloth soaked in cool water for me to wash away the signs of tears, and then pressed an earthenware mug of tea into my hands, wrapping my fingers around it.

"Now," she said. "Tell me what's wrong."

I felt the tears start once more, and only by clenching my teeth did I manage to hold them back. I swallowed painfully, and ducked my head to take a sip of tea.

"I hate this place," I said finally. "I wish we'd never come."

"Why?"

"Did you know it would be like this?" I asked, and I sniffed. "Is that why you wanted to stay in Voltur?"

She tilted her head to the side, and her eyes were faraway. She wore her usual sad smile, and yet for once, she looked hopeful. "No, that's not why. I thought..." She sighed, and pursed her lips, and I saw her for the first time as a person.

It was a horrible thought, to realize that I had never thought of her in that way before. When she had said to me, *I thought*, I realized then that I had never wondered the *why* of her. I did not know where she had been born, or why she had never married. I did not know why her slanted brown eyes were always sad, or where she had learned to read and write, why she had become a healer. Roine disliked being beholden to the Duke, she spoke of the irresponsibility of nobles and healed servant women without ever asking payment—I had seen all of these things and never thought more about them.

"I saw that Penekket would be a place of turmoil," she said finally, and from the faraway tone in her voice, I knew that she did not mean just for herself and for me. "I saw events unfolding that would cost hundreds, perhaps thousands, of lives, and I wanted to keep you from that."

"What's going to happen?" I asked. "What do you know?"

"Know—as the Duke knows things? Which man is loyal, and which can be bought?" Roine's voice was scornful. "I know a great deal of that, as it happens. But if you ask what I know, as me, then: I know that fate lies heavy on this place." She paused, and tried to close her mouth on the words; it was as if they were dragged from her. "And it lies heavy on you." Her eyes squeezed shut for a moment.

"Fate—Gods, you and Temar both!"

"What?" Her eyes had snapped open.

"You and your talk of—" I clenched my hands around the mug, shook my head. "...of fate! Of prophecies, of curses. It doesn't make any sense. And you were never one for that, anyway." Temar lost no opportunity to remind me of the prophecy at my birth, and that it had led him to pick me. He was determined that I acknowledge the prophecy as truth, and I was determined that he should stop talking about it, stubbornly unwilling even to consider the possibility that it was more than fever madness. I could not bear for Roine to tell me the same thing.

She looked at me strangely. "I'm not one for the priests and their church, no. Not generally. But I am faithful to the teachings of the Gods. Catwin—there's more to this world than we can understand. There are forces at work that are beyond us. Yes, there are," she insisted, when I shook my head. "And it does not take a sorcerer to scent change on the wind."

"What kind of change?" I rubbed at my nose.

"The nobles fight amongst themselves, they bring us all to war. The King is weak, he cannot control his dog pack even when he throws dukedoms and lands to them. A fight in the south, a fight in the west. How long can Heddred stand as it is?"

"A fight in the south?" I frowned. "Oh, the uprising. It's..." I tried to remember the word Temar had taught me.

"Populist," Roine supplied, and I raised my eyebrows at her. Roine could read, but her knowledge was that of a healer, not a court advisor. She shrugged. "The servants speak of it—you would know as much if you were not always watching the nobles."

I bit my lip at the implied reproach. "The servants are not a danger to Miriel," I said. "Nobles are."

"She will die if you think that way," Roine advised me. "You may be blind to it, but she knows better. She courts the servants— quick with praise and smiles, sparing in her demands. She knows to be wary of those who cook her food, set fires in her rooms: they hold her life in their hands." I stared at Roine, horrified, and she only smiled. "Every day, you think of which nobles might kill Miriel. Is it so strange to think that servants might have their reasons for doing so as well?"

"Has someone spoken of this?" I demanded fiercely. Roine shook her head, no longer amused.

"No. No one would—I tell you, Miriel is beloved of the servants. But you don't *hear* me. I tell you there's change on the wind, that the people are rising up to claim a voice in their world, and you look still to the nobles. There are larger forces at work than their squabbles, larger even than the war with Ismir—although that could be quite a catalyst. If you want to think of Miriel's safety, you had best think of the world beyond the court."

"I hardly have time to keep her safe *at* court," I said bitterly. "You don't understand. She and her uncle work to the same ends, only he can't see it, and so she has all of his enemies and none of his goodwill. And those enemies are more powerful than the uprising, and they're *here*, not in the south.

"And how could you not tell me about the beatings?" I demanded. "You knew I was to know everything about her."

"You were to know it because you found it out for yourself," Roine said sharply. "You spent all day in her company and you could not even see that she was in pain! It was to teach you a lesson. You had better wonder what she does when she's not in your company, if you want to protect her."

At least you have me to talk to. I had failed entirely at my mission of being the one in whom Miriel could confide. She had trusted me once, to help her with her plan to sneak about, and she thought now that I had failed her. She did not know that I had lied for her, not only to the Duke but to Temar. She would not trust me again.

"What is it?" Roine asked. She was studying my face.

I sighed and sank my head into my hands. I could have cried again.

"It's all wrong," I said. I was shaking.

"Something has happened?" she guessed, and I shook my head.

"Well, yes. But I can't tell you."

"Catwin." Roine was smiling. "You can tell me. What is it you fear?"

"The Duke." I looked at her. "He'd hurt you, too, if he knew that you knew, and you hadn't told him. I..." I felt tears come, and sniffed them back. "I have to keep him from knowing. And that's impossible."

"Catwin, it can't be as bad as that. Is this why you were crying earlier? What have you done, then?"

"It wasn't *me*!" I said, fired into truth. "It was Miriel! I just..." She waited, and I brushed tears from my eyes angry swipes of my hand. "She said she wanted to see the castle like I did," I said, in a desperate whisper. Even at the hearth, far from the door, I could not believe that Temar might not be waiting, that there might not be a spy who could take my words and twist them. "She said if I didn't help her, she'd do it on her own. She was going to take my uniform."

"So, you helped her." I nodded. "And you say the Duke doesn't know." I shook my head. Roine pursed her lips. "I wondered...what was the horrible beating she got a few weeks back, then? She would not say."

"He knew she was hiding something, but he didn't know what. He had her beaten for lying to him."

"Ah. And so, then you lied for her as well, would that be correct?"

"Yes," I whispered. "But I don't think she knows that."

"Tell her," Roine said simply. "She needs an ally. She's more fragile than you think."

"You don't like nobles," I said, resentfully. "You never do. Why *her*?"

"She's only a young woman," Roine said. "Who knows what she might grow up to be?" For some reason, the thought seemed painful to her. "Anyone would pity her the life she has been given." She reached out to take my hands. "I know it's difficult, Catwin, love—but try to be kind to her." She squeezed my hands. "Now, see, that wasn't so horrible a secret, was it? No harm done. And I won't ever tell the Duke."

"There's more," I admitted.

"Oh?"

I hesitated, my hands trapped in hers, her eyes on my face, and then the words came out of me in a rush: "When we were out in the castle, we met the King." I gave a quick look at Roine. Her eyes were wide, her lips parted. "It was okay," I assured her. "Nothing bad happened. I think...I think he *likes* her. And you see, that's what the Duke *wants*. But he'd be so angry."

"You met the *King*?" Roine asked, as if she still could not believe it.

"Yes, yes—" I waved my hand at her. "But the point is—"

"How?"

I sighed, not wanting to say that the King had been sneaking about, too. "We just did. He recognized Miriel. He said he'd keep her secret. He was quite nice, actually," I added, remembering Miriel's own words.

"My." Roine chewed her lip.

"The Duke can't know," I said, suddenly afraid that she would tell him.

"He won't learn it from me," Roine assured me. "I would not tell him. Do you think the King..."

"Yes." I nodded. "He did, I'm sure of it. And she can use it to her advantage—and she will, she's good at that. You know that. But the Duke would never see that. He'll have planned out some way for them to meet."

"Hmm." Roine took a sip of tea. "Well, if you want my advice..." I nodded, and Roine took a sip of tea, considering her words. "Tell Miriel that you lied for her. She has to know that she has a friend. And let her play this her way. You're right, she has a talent for it. Your task will be to be her shield against the Duke."

I felt a sick sense of fear. "Keep lying for her?"

"You've done it once. Catwin, you fear the Duke, not respect him. But I think you do respect Miriel. She may be ambitious, but she has a kinder heart than he does. Unless you want to serve yourself, you will need to serve one of them, and you would do best to choose someone you believe is good at heart."

I looked away. She was right that I feared the Duke, but she was wrong—I did respect him. I knew that he had won the war with unspeakably brutal tactics, that he was ruthless with those who defied him. I did not believe him for a moment to be above murdering a rival.

But I had seen how he treated his tenants, how he listened to them and fortified their walls and made sure that the guardsmen protected them against border raids. He was not an easy liege lord to serve, but he was fair, and I knew now from watching the other great landowners at court that the Duke spent more time ensuring his people's safety than did any other great lord of the land. A good heart, a kind heart? Perhaps not. But fair.

Conventional wisdom told that men were warped by power. I could see that in de la Marque, and in many men of the council. I turned the thought over in my mind, weighing the Duke's character. Common-born and revered, then ennobled and hated. He did not seem to be as greedy as the other lords, hungry for money and lands, but his plans for Miriel showed that he had some aim at the throne. Had power warped him? If not, what was his aim?

It was worth thinking on.

And I did not know how power might change Miriel. She was kind to servants now, but who could say what might happen if she were to be queen? For certain, she was not kind to me, nor had she ever been. She was ambitious, not as one who wants power or money for its own sake, but as one who has been told she deserves neither, and so sets out to gain by her wits what others have gained by their birth. She had much to prove, did Miriel.

I recognized even then that such ambition was a hollow thing. I had seen into Miriel's eyes and I knew her to be lonely. She was waiting for something, and I doubted that even she knew what that might be. In the meantime, she honed her wits and her beauty, and she learned to keep score, so that one day she could reckon back her wrongs.

Roine was right: Miriel needed a friend. For if she was left to her ambition and her intelligence…

I shuddered.

"I won't ask," Roine said, sounding amused for the first time in days. "Are you ready for your lesson? They don't stop just because you've had a hard day, you know."

Chapter 21

It took only two weeks for the Duke to prepare the troops. They were armed and drilling even as the Council prepared a sharply-worded letter to be distributed in all the towns of the Norstrung Provinces. The violence was to cease immediately, the letter said. Jacces was to turn himself in for trial in the murder of Henri Nilson. If he did not, he—and any found harboring him—would be sought out by the King's forces. There would be two thousand men marching south, joining the three thousand already in the command of the Earl of Mavol, and these new troops would be commanded by one of the most notoriously ruthless commanders in recent history.

The court was delightedly scandalized. Their King, their weak, sick, Boy King was willing to send his army to keep the peace. He had taken his guardian's advice, but not to the advantage of his guardian. He would now be as ruthless with the rebels as Guy de la Marque would have been. He would let the Duke be as ruthless as he had ever been in the last war with Ismir.

And then we discovered that Jacces could be ruthless as well.

I was in Miriel's privy chamber, studying apart from her, as close to rudeness as I dared. For months, we had conducted our studies together, at the large table in the public room. But our fight was not over; I could not forgive her words, and she clearly still suspected me of being her uncle's spy. When there was a knock at the door, I did not move to answer it. If she wanted to receive guests, let her answer her own door. When the knock sounded once more, I heard her cross to the door and open it.

"Lady Miriel DeVere?" It was a man's voice, and one I did not recognize.

"Yes," Miriel said. "What are you—" The door slammed suddenly, and I heard a thud and a choked-off cry of pain.

I was moving before I realized what was happening, running for the door into the public rooms, skidding around to see the man holding Miriel pinned, her arm twisted behind her back, his other hand trying to force her jaw open. I could see a bottle in his palm, he was trying to tip the liquid into her mouth. He swung around as I came into the room, and I saw shock cross his face. He had thought her alone in her rooms. He did not know who I was.

It was over in an instant. I hardly felt myself move, but he was falling away from her, Miriel gasping and crying, wiping her mouth on her sleeve, and then giving a scream as she turned and saw him with my dagger embedded in one of his eyes. I was frozen where I stood, my arm raised, my fingers held fixed, just as they had been when I had released the knife to throw it. His legs twitched once, and then he was still.

For a moment, neither Miriel nor I moved.

"Are you okay?" I demanded, and she nodded. "Did you swallow any of the poison?" She shook her head. She did not seem to be able to speak. Her eyes were growing wider and wider.

As if in a dream, I crossed to the door and bolted it, and then cautiously, reluctantly, approached the body. I knew what to do. Temar had taught me what to do. But I did not want to touch him. I was half-sure he was still alive, and he would kill me as soon as I was within reach; I realized that I almost wanted him to be alive. Even as I knelt at his side, feeling blood seep into the cloth of my pants, I half hoped that I had not killed him, but I knew as soon as I touched him that he was dead. His skin was warm, but there was no life in him. I scrambled away, and was promptly sick on the floor.

"Catwin?" Miriel's voice. She was still frozen, staring at the man, staring at me. Her voice was high and thin.

"I killed him." My stomach twisted again and I knelt on the wooden planks and stared down at my own vomit. "Oh, Gods. Oh, Gods. I..."

"He was trying to kill me," Miriel said, and I drew a deep breath and nodded. Yes. The man had been trying to kill her. She was correct. He had been trying to kill her, that was the thing to remember. He would have killed her, and he might have killed me, too. I had not simply taken a life, I had also saved one—maybe two.

"He was trying to kill me," Miriel said again, and I heard the first notes of hysteria in her voice. She had gone so white that she looked like she might faint at any moment, and I pushed myself to my feet and went to her, unsteadily.

When the knock came at the door, both of us jumped, and I shoved Miriel back, away from the door. She clapped both hands over her mouth and I saw her bite down on the side of her hand; she was trying not to scream.

"Catwin—Catwin!" It was Temar's voice, and I let out a shuddering breath.

I unbolted the door and it fairly slammed open as Temar rushed past me, the Duke following with his guards. When they saw the body on the floor, every one of them turned to stare at me. I tried to find words, and then, to my shame, I felt my stomach twist once more. I dropped down to my knees and retched. The Duke snorted, but Temar knelt at my side and smoothed my hair back from my face.

"Can you tell me what happened?" he asked. "Have you moved him at all?" I shook my head to his second question.

"He tried to get Miriel to drink poison."

"Did she?" the Duke demanded.

"No," Miriel whispered. "Catwin came in and—" She pressed her lips together and I saw her fighting back tears. "No, I didn't drink any."

The Duke's shoulders slumped.

"What's going on?" I asked suddenly. "How did you know to come?"

"The Duke received a note," Temar said, helping me to my feet. "It came with food from the kitchens, and it said only that Miriel had been given a poison, and that if he wanted the antidote…"

"That's enough," the Duke said. Temar protested; he was the only one who would have dared.

"My Lord, I think it best that Catwin knows who might move against Miriel." The Duke considered this, and waved a hand for Temar to continue. "It was an agent of Jacces," Temar told me.

"The leader of the rebellion?"

"Just so." It fell into place at once.

"The note said that, to get the antidote, the Duke must promise not to crush the rebellion," I guessed, and Temar nodded.

"Exactly." He placed his hands on my shoulders and peered into my eyes. "Are you feeling better?" He must know that I was not; the realization that I had killed a man kept reappearing in my mind; each time, I felt as if my blood had turned to ice. I was shuddering. But I knew that the Duke would not be sympathetic.

"I won't be sick again, if that's what you mean," I said, and Temar squeezed my arms gently.

"Then check the body," he instructed.

They watched me, all of them, as I edged towards it. I knew I must show no weakness in front of the Duke and his men. Temar would be watching to make sure that I remembered what he had taught me, but the rest would be watching, judging whether or not I was suited to my task as a bodyguard.

I patted the man's arms and legs gently, checking for hidden weapons or pockets, anything that might stick out into my hands. Then I carefully untied his cloak and pried it away, undid his belt and lifted his blank tabard away so that I could see his shirt. I searched through his pockets, laying the objects I found on the floor next to the body. One item, a scroll, I passed to Temar to look over. I stripped the man down to his breeches, and we could all see the tattoo on his chest: a circle in black ink.

"So," the Duke said grimly. "That's the symbol of the rebellion, then." He stood. "You two, stay here," he ordered two of the guards. Then he looked to Temar. "Search the rooms again, take Catwin with you. Make sure there is no one else here, and no way of entering the rooms other than the door."

We set off into the bedroom, and before Temar started checking the room, he took a moment to look into my eyes again.

"How are you?" he asked me. I only shook my head. I had no words for him. My skin felt hot and cold all at once, I thought I might be sick but I had nothing in my stomach, and I was shaking like a leaf. Temar nodded, as if I had told him outright.

"They say it's always like that, the first time."

"I killed him," I whispered, and Temar nodded again.

"You did, and thank the Gods for it. You did your job, and the Duke is pleased." I managed to keep my mouth shut on the sentiment that I did not particularly care if the Duke was pleased. I would rather he keep wondering. Temar gave a little smile. "And don't worry, Catwin, no one other than those here now will ever know of it."

Panic stabbed through me. "What do you mean?"

"Catwin…killing a man is a hanging offense."

"But," I was stammering, I was so upset. "But he was trying to kill Miriel, they could never hang me for—"

"Who knows what a jury might decide?" Temar asked me. "But you have the Duke's protection, Catwin. It will be as if this never happened. And now, put it out of your mind. If you must talk of it, come speak to me. But try not to think about it. Trust me, it's the better choice. All you need to remember of tonight is that someone tried to hurt Miriel, and you kept them from doing so. Can you do that?"

"Yes." *No.*

"Good. Now, show me how you search this room."

Chapter 22

"I'm afraid," I said to him the next day. The words tumbled out of my mouth as I arrived for my lesson. I had tried to sleep, but had not been able to, torn between the memories in my waking mind, and the nightmares in my sleeping mind. I had walked from Miriel's rooms to my lessons, now more aware than ever of the whispers about Voltur and de la Marque, passionate arguments about which viper a man might trust. I felt that every person who looked at me was one of the soldiers of the rebellion; I was sure that anyone looking at me could see from my face that I had killed a man.

"As well you should be." Temar did not try to blunt his words. He looked up from where he was studying a map. "But about what, specifically?"

"I used to have nightmares that someone would try to hurt Miriel, and I wouldn't be able to stop them."

"Now you know that you can." Despite himself, he looked pleased.

"Now it's worse!" I cried. He raised his eyebrows. "I used to wake up, afraid I'd heard someone in the room, someone coming to kill Miriel. But I told myself it wasn't true. She's fourteen, she shouldn't have any enemies. I thought...I had time. But people are already coming to kill her."

"And you're scared of that." He was testing me, but I did not know the correct answer. I nodded, having decided to tell the truth.

"And yet..." Temar looked at me. "You and Miriel barely speak." I sat for a moment and digested, as he had meant me to do, the fact that he knew what went on in Miriel's rooms. I had the disloyal feeling that I had not been fair to her yesterday; she was correct that she was watched, always. Why should she trust me?

I jerked my thoughts back to the present.

"I wouldn't want her to die," I said finally. "That would be awful. I just..." He looked up and stared at me, steadily, until I said, "I just don't like her very much." That was woefully inadequate. Miriel could be charming, she could smile at me so that I forgot an insult she had made only a moment ago. Her spite was matched by strange gestures of kindness: she would hold the door for me, or save a sweetmeat for me from her lunch meal. And yet, she never stopped with her taunts, and I could not forget that she had told me to my face that she would never trust me.

I did not think that Temar could ever understand.

"So you don't like her," he said, and I nodded. "But you say you wake afraid of someone coming to kill her."

"I would have to kill someone." I swallowed. "Again." I did not add, *and that was more horrible than I had even feared*, but I knew from the flash of sympathy in Temar's eyes that he understood. Then the wall came down once more behind his eyes.

"You know how to hide," he suggested. "You could hide and let them kill her, and they would never know you were there. You would never have to kill again."

I was shocked. "I couldn't do that!"

"Why not?"

I nearly stood up and left. My mind was running, faster and faster. If the Duke knew of this conversation, he would have me horsewhipped for admitting that I did not care for Miriel—but Temar was asking, and so this must be a test—but what if it was not a test? Temar knew that I had killed, when forced to it, so why ask me this, now?

Temar tilted his head to the side. "You don't know why," he observed. I sat frozen, trying to figure out what he wanted to hear. "I can tell you, if you want, but you won't like the answer."

"Tell me," I said without hesitation. I could hear Roine's advice, *it's always better to know than not*, and Donnett's, *let them talk, the more they talk, the more you know, and the more openings you get.*

"You understand now that your fate is linked with hers," Temar said simply.

I blinked at him. "That's ridiculous." The words sounded tired; I was too preoccupied by fear even to feel my usual rush of anger at his endless talk of fate.

"Is it?" Temar frowned. "You swore it was true yourself. And your own mother pronounced you cursed at your birth, that's hardly less strange. She swore you were born to be betrayed. But..." He frowned. "I have wondered, Catwin, was there more to her prophecy than that?"

"That's superstitious talk, it means nothing." I did not want Temar to speak of my mother. I did not want him to know the rest of the prophecy, to look back at my life and find a story in it. And I did not want him, or anyone to know that every night, without fail, I dreamed of my birth. I would walk through the snow and the wind, and I could choose to go into the house or not. I would push open the door and go in, and witness the same conversation acted out: my father's desperation, my mother's fear. I grew bolder in my invisibility: I would walk close to peer up into my father's face. He never noticed me, but if I stayed long enough, my mother would.

The first time it had happened, it had been only a dream—easy enough to shrug away in the light of day. Now, over time, I came to wonder if she truly had seen me that night, and the thought was so unnerving that some nights, I did not go into the hut at all. I chose to walk through the village, or sit outside in the drifting snow, trying to ignore the wails of my newborn self. I curled up on the ground with my arms around my knees and I tried to think that this was only a dream. It still took me a very long time to wake up.

Temar was not dissuaded by my abrupt tone.

"Think, Catwin. You were a child born to a peasant, you were to live and die as one of them, never knowing anything more than cold and hunger. Yet, you are here, a girl risen far beyond her station, more educated than some Kings. Such a divergence does not happen by accident. Something has chosen you. At every branch, your life has led you here."

"The Duke chose me." He sighed at the look on my face.

"Laugh at it if you want," he said. "But one day you will wake and know that it is true. You will look back and see a pattern. You will see that you are tied, irrevocably, to Miriel—as I..."

His voice broke, and he covered it with a cough.

Realizations are strange things. They are composed outside of the conscious self, they are the ends of paths we cannot tread in our waking minds, and for this reason, the most shocking realizations may stab across one's mind, and yet be gone in an instant, fleeting, known-and-unknown. Roine told me once that in the old religions, seers breathed in the smoke of strange plants to bring on the visions of their sleeping minds, and that their words were recorded so that the dreams would not be forgotten.

I had no such luxury, and so in the years to come, I realized and forgot the most important truth about Temar more times than I could count, the truth I had first seen on a Summer's day on the ride to Penekket:

Above all things in his life, Temar hated the Duke.

In an instant after the realization, the thought was gone, and all I could remember was a vague sense that I should know more than I did.

"Now you are bound to Miriel by blood," he told me. "You can mock it, you can tell me that it is nothing, but it is true. Once you have killed to save another, the two of you are bound to each other. It is nothing new. Your fates have been intertwined since you were born, and it is only now that it is becoming clear." He sighed. "You should go early to your lesson with Donnett. I must run an errand for the Duke. I wished only to see if you were well."

He waved me away, but I lingered. I watched his eyes stray back to the map he had laid out on the table, and thoughts clustered together in my head. *You were born a peasant—those whom fate has touched...well, let us say that they are drawn to one another.* I looked at Temar's smooth brown skin, at his dark eyes.

"Where were you born?" I asked him, and he grimaced. Temar hated questions about himself. If I had thought he might answer me today, I was wrong.

"Figure it out for yourself," he said lightly. "And while you're figuring, go to your lessons. There's no time for rest. Not anymore."

I did not go to see Donnett. Feet dragging, I walked to Roine's rooms. It was as if I was walking in a dream; I could not stop my legs from carrying me forward, even as I shrank from seeing her. Roine was the closest thing I had ever had to a mother. How could I hide this from her? And yet, she was the woman who had raised me, a healer by trade, the woman who had taught me right from wrong. How could I ever tell her what I had done? I had not gone to my lesson yesterday, I had hidden in Miriel's rooms with my arms around my knees, curled into a little silent ball near Miriel, who sat as if she was carved from stone, the terror still showing in her eyes.

I pushed open the door to Roine's room and it was clear at once that she already knew what had happened. When she looked up from her worktable, I saw that her face was white and her eyes were red-rimmed from crying. I looked over to the corner where she prayed, and saw the little altar disturbed: the low table was out of place, and the candle lay on its side on the floor. Before I had time to fear that she could never forgive me for what I had done, she ran to me and enfolded me in her arms. At her tears, I began to cry myself.

"Please don't hate me," I whispered, and I felt her shake her head.

"Never, never. I could never hate you for what you did," she whispered. "Not even..." She shook her head again. "Not ever," she promised me. She took my shoulders in her hands and held me away from her, looking into my eyes. I waited for words of comfort—Roine was always ready with wisdom—but she was determined, not comforting. Her jaw was set.

"You have to go," she told me.

"What?" I felt my stomach drop. Even now, I feared that she had changed her mind. She truly thought me a monster, and she wanted me gone from the palace.

"You have to leave," she said earnestly. "You cannot stay here."

"The Duke is hiding it," I said uncertainly. "I don't have to go. Temar said no one would ever know." A shadow of distaste crossed her face, but she shook her head.

"Not because of that," she said impatiently. "You're in danger, Catwin." I shook my head, but she gripped my arms. "*Listen* to me, Catwin. The Duke is the greatest enemy of the rebellion, he is their target, and they will not hesitate to hurt Miriel. And now they know that someone is protecting her—that will lead them to you."

I could not breathe; I felt a rush of fear. I had woken up time after time last night, my dreams one endless nightmare of the man's surprised face, his legs twitching, Miriel's scream. I had been so consumed with guilt that I had not been afraid. I had not once stopped to think, but Roine had. She was afraid, and she was right to be afraid. The rebellion had sent an assassin, and he had been killed. They would want to know who had killed him, and how. If they were willing to kill Miriel, they would not hesitate to kill me.

For a moment, I was ready to run. Roine would help me, she could help me and we would run away. This life at the palace had been a terrible dream, but we could still get away. I knew enough that I could escape Temar. Roine and I would go where we could be safe.

Then I remembered what Roine clearly had not:

"But if I leave, who will protect Miriel?" I was frowning. How could Roine have forgotten this? Sometimes it seemed that she was the only one who cared for Miriel's welfare. But Roine shook her head so impatiently that I realized this was no oversight.

"You have to think of yourself," she said earnestly. "No one would think less of you for protecting your own life."

"You said yourself they'll come for her again," I protested. I spread my hands out. "If I left, she would have no one. They'd kill her."

"Miriel makes her own choice to stay or go," Roine said fiercely. "I only care about keeping you safe. I thought when we came here that I could do that, but I cannot, and I cannot live everyday knowing that you are in danger." Once, such an admission would have pleased me—I had sought such an affirmation from her for months. But now I felt my frown deepen. There was a sense of wrongness.

"You can't think it would be right to leave her defenseless," I protested. "Not you—*you* taught me right and wrong. You know I can defend myself. Roine, I can't go, not knowing that she would be in danger with no one to protect her." Roine wavered, and I pressed on. "It would be like not healing her if she were injured."

"It's not the same," Roine protested. "Last time, you surprised them. Next time, they'll be prepared." She shook her head. "Miriel is no friend of yours," she reminded me.

I swallowed. I knew that Miriel was not my friend. I knew it very well. I remembered her speech about trust, word for word, and I still felt raw inside when I thought of it. I also knew my answer: the same answer I had given Temar.

"I would never want her dead."

"Catwin, *please.*" Roine's voice was tight. "For me." I hesitated, but shook my head. There was a shape to the wrongness now. If I left, it would eat away at my heart as long as I lived that a young woman had died because I would not help to protect her.

"I know you want to keep me safe, but I can't just leave her to die. It doesn't matter…" I shook my head. "I could never forgive myself if something happened to her." It was true, I could feel it right down to my bones. "Please tell me you understand," I pleaded. Roine enfolded me in a hug.

"I do," she said quietly. "And I'm proud of you. I want you to know that. And I love you." I smiled.

"I love you, too. And you taught me to be this way. It's because of you that I'm staying." I tried to crane my neck to smile up at her, but she would not let me from her embrace.

"I know," she said, her voice choked. "I just wish I could know you would not suffer for it."

Chapter 23

In the cold weeks approaching winter, the Duke's household had sunk into waiting, once more, for the axe to fall. The disappearance of his assassin must have unsettled Jacces. The Duke had sent a note back, stating only that his obligation was to root out violence in the King's realm. If Jacces would not end the rebellion, the Duke would march southwards. The violence, such as it was, seemed to disappear overnight; the rebellion was once more composed of murmurs.

No one, from the Councilors to the scullery maids, believed that the peace would hold, but the King was determined he would not send his army to put down a rebellion that no one could find, and that had sunk once more into waiting. However his Councilors pleaded, he put the march south on hold indefinitely, instead sending spies to the Norstrung Provinces to root out the identity of Jacces.

And then the King made a bold move: he sent an invitation to the court of Ismir, asking for a representative to be sent, that the courts might work together in peace for the future. He wanted, he said, to begin a golden age for Heddred and Ismir. Together, with their differences set aside, the two nations might find peace and prosperity beyond all dreams.

I was at my lessons with Roine when I found out. We had finished with the earlier lessons, naming and identifying different plants, and making specific poisons and antidotes. Her latest task for me had been to create antidotes for a series of four liquids she gave to me. I was to determine, however I could, their composition and strength, and determine the precise counter to each, and we would have no more lessons until I could do so.

The liquids sat in little stoppered vials at the back of her workroom, and each day for the past week, I had come to sit for hours and decipher clues. We worked in silence when we could, disturbed by the steady stream of servants coming to ask Roine's aid; more than once, she had asked me to interrupt my work to splint a broken bone, or bind an open wound. In a palace nearly as large as the city itself, there was always someone to heal, and Roine had become known for her abilities. What I did not understand was why I was being drawn into it.

"Injuries don't wait," she said sharply, when I asked why I must interrupt my lessons. "And you need this practice."

I knew that there was no reason to complain. She had given me a little table of my own to work at, a luxury by any reckoning. Luxurious, too, were the candles I burned when I worked late into the night, and the paper and ink I used to keep notes. Just because this luxury was paid for by the Duke did not mean that Roine permitted me to squander it: my notes were to be neat and my writing small, and I was not allowed to burn candles unless I worked after my dinner.

I was working on the second of the four liquids when Temar arrived, and I had unstopped the bottle to sniff cautiously at it. The potion was thick, but the fragrance was so faint that I could barely make it out. If I closed my eyes and blocked out the world when I smelled it, I could imagine a clear mountain day, with sunlight glinting off snow. But I could not put a name to the scent. I was close to thumping my head onto the desk with frustration when I felt a hand on my shoulder.

"The Duke called for you," Temar said without preamble, and my stomach gave the weird drop it always did when I knew I had been summoned. I steadied myself by nodding, very dignified, and then restopped the bottle, dried my quill carefully, and made sure the notes for each potion were laid out by the bottles.

"She'll be back when she can be," Temar said to Roine, and she nodded without looking up from her own work. Roine and Temar barely spoke, although I had noted that they were scrupulously polite to each other when they did. They existed in a state of quiet enmity, both tolerating the other out of convenience, and Temar seemed to find this more amusing than Roine did.

Out in the hallways, there was the steady buzz of conversation, and at once I picked out the undercurrent of energy that accompanied new information. It was in the pitch of the murmur, in the way people inclined their heads to listen, in the way nobles and servants lingered to speak to each other.

"What is it?" I asked, dreading the answer. Why would the Duke care enough about a rumor to summon me? What could Miriel possibly have done to engender this type of talk?

"The King has made a formal declaration of friendship with Ismir," Temar said. He did not bother lowering his voice. All of the servants and minor nobles in our path were chattering excitedly about the same news.

I allowed myself only a moment for a sigh of relief. Not Miriel, then. But if I was summoned, it could only mean that this was a surprise to the Duke. Else, he would have coached all of us on how to behave when the news became public. Often, Temar would stop by my lessons with a brief message: "If anyone asks you about..." he would say.

We always worked to a single purpose, all of the Duke's household: everyone had their own stories to tell, rumors to spread. He had instructed me to run errands to one guild or another, place orders in the Duke's name, carry messages—all with the purpose of confusing the Duke's adversaries on the council. I was not Miriel, the figurehead, the golden girl, but the Duke knew that any of us might be watched.

"A surprise to the Duke," was all I said, and he nodded, and then unexpectedly, he grinned.

"No one else knew, either," he said, as if it were a great joke, and I knew he was thinking of de la Marque, and of all the adversaries who had thought themselves ahead of the Duke—only to find themselves outside the circle of power.

"The Dowager Queen?" I asked.

"Good question." He switched to the dialect of the mountains, shocking me; I would have thought there would be little use for him to know such an obscure accent. I found myself smiling to hear it again, and to know that I could reply freely. Now that I spoke with a carefully-cultivated city accent, I knew how difficult it would be for bystanders to understand it.

"I couldn't say yes or no to that yet," Temar said, "but I know what my guess would be. It's just as you said, Catwin. The little lion cub has claws after all." There was a laugh hiding behind his voice.

For a moment, I considered asking him if the Duke did not think better now of his plan to be the King's chief advisor. The boy had made a fool of de la Marque, and the man could do nothing about it. He could be as capricious as he liked, could Garad, and no one could gainsay him. It did not sound like a master I would choose.

"So you agree," I said, and he looked over at me. "It's good. For us."

He raised his eyebrows. "Ambition, little one? But yes, it could be. If we play it right."

At Temar's amusement, I wondered if the Duke had not been waiting for something like this. For sure, he was no favorite of the Dowager Queen. He was working to make Miriel irresistible to the King—he would welcome a show of independence from the boy. As unexpected as this was, I rather thought the Duke might be ready to play it for all it was worth.

But was it unexpected to him? That was an interesting thought, and an unsettling one. These past months, fading into the background as Guy de la Marque belittled him at every turn. Had he gambled that eventually, with no one to check him, de la Marque would make a misstep? And then, relatively unscathed, the Duke could rise. Having been honored by command of the troops, he could now play his hand, knowing exactly what the young King disliked in an advisor. If that was so, he had played Guy de la Marque masterfully. I thought, as we pushed our way through the hallways, that I found the idea of the Duke lying in wait even more unsettling than the thought of Miriel lying in wait.

Miriel and the Duke were waiting for us when we arrived in the Duke's rooms, and the Duke spared me a glare for a greeting; he was not, then, wholly pleased. He was pacing back and forth by the window, Miriel standing quietly in front of his desk. She did not look over at me as I arrived; Miriel had lately taken to ignoring me, as she had first done.

"The King has offered a formal vow of peace and friendship with Ismir," the Duke said without preamble. "He has invited an envoy to our courts, against the advice of the Council. The man will arrive near midwinter." There was the faintest curl to his lip, and I realized now that I had thought only of the machinations of the court, and not of the heart of the news Temar had brought me. The Duke had fought against the Ismiri, and regardless of his silence in council meetings, I knew him not to trust the tenuous peace of the last decade.

"We will support the King," the Duke said abruptly. There it was: he was bad-tempered because this had been the chance he sought, and it came at the expense of his own common sense. "Catwin, if you are asked, you shall say that I am in favor of the King's efforts for peace. If necessary, remind them that my brother died in battle in the last war."

"Yes, sir." I knew, also, to pass along the names of all who asked. He always wanted to know that.

"Miriel." The Duke turned his cold gaze on her. "If asked, you are to say that you think the King brave for leading the country to peace. Not a word against the Dowager Queen, or Guy de la Marque, and if pressed to it, you will say that the King has wise counsel, and you are sure that he acted with their guidance."

Miriel swept a curtsy, her head down. From the faint twitch of her mouth, I could see that she had had much the same plan. I was glad to see her irritation; it marked a return to the Miriel that I knew. She had passed the last weeks in silent fear, and even as I understood it, I worried at it. Anyone would have felt a twinge of sadness to see a young woman dart looks into dark corners, now rightfully expecting assassins to be waiting for her.

The Duke had noticed neither her fear nor her irritation. He nodded and settled into his desk chair. He was looking at Miriel intently, and I knew that he had put the matter of the envoy behind him.

"On the matter of the King's marriage..." he said idly, and Miriel's head came up at once. I saw the Duke smile. I shot a quick glance at Temar and saw him watching Miriel intently. I pursed my lips, but there was no way to warn her. In any case, she should know that she was watched always. If she had any sense, she would keep her face straight for the Duke.

"I hear you have developed a reputation for being intelligent," the Duke said to Miriel, and she gazed back at him, unsure how to respond. She excelled in her lessons in part because of his insistence that she must, and yet his tone was not pleased. "Be careful. You make yourself known already to Isra. Therefore..." He drummed his fingers. "When asked about the King's marriage, and whom he will choose, you will say that it is for the Council to recommend brides for the King, and that you are sure that he will choose for his political advantage.

"If you hear Marie de la Marque's name mentioned, you will be surprised, but you will not disparage her. Sing her praises. You are her greatest supporter. If asked about Cintia Conradine, you will say the same, and yet make sure others know she is a risky choice. And too old." Miriel gave the faintest of frowns. She curtsied respectfully, but I knew that her mind was working furiously. The Duke studied her for a moment, and then looked over at me.

"They will be presented at the ball to honor the envoy," he said, and I took *they* to mean the young ladies of the court. "At the Midwinter Festival. Your lessons will be suspended. You are to be at Miriel's side always. I want to know who looks at her, I want to know who speaks her name in the servant's halls, who greets her and who does not. If any of the servants who come to her rooms change, you are to let me know at once, and you are not to permit them into her bedchamber under any circumstances. Do you understand?" I nodded, and he looked back to Miriel.

"Eat no food and drink that Marie de la Marque has not eaten first," he said. "If you are hungry, send for food from my rooms after dinner. I will take no chances now."

I saw a flash of worry in his face. This was earlier than he had planned. He was not ready. I did not know how that could help Miriel, but I knew that I should tell her.

"Behave no differently than you have," he said finally. "Do not set yourself forward, under any circumstances. You have done well," he added grudgingly. As Miriel smiled slightly, he added, "Your whereabouts are to be accounted for at all times. Do you understand me?"

His voice was like ice, and her smile disappeared at once. I knew without looking that Temar would be watching me, and I fought to keep my expression attentive and my shoulders relaxed. We had come too far for them to learn the secret now; I was determined that they should not learn of it through my actions.

"I understand, my Lord." Her voice was clear and light, her curtsy precise.

I was silent as I accompanied her back to her rooms. I knew that the Duke's men who trailed us through the building were indeed bodyguards, but I knew also that they would report to the Duke what we had spoken of. I thought briefly of asking about trivial things, to make it seem as if I was not at all concerned by what the Duke had said to us, and then decided to say nothing at all. Miriel and I would walk in icy silence, as we always did, and the guards could report that we were still not friends; I had rather that the Duke saw no connection between the two of us.

"I have to talk to you," I said, when at last we were in her privy chamber, her maid readying a gown for dinner in the bedchamber.

"Why, are you leaving me?" She asked me. "Are you running away at last?" I had been half-expecting the question for so long that I forgot what I had been intending to say. I had known that someone would ask, but I had not thought that it would be Miriel herself.

"What?" I asked, and she turned her head to look at me. She had been practicing that, turning only her head to look at someone. I had seen her posing in front of her mirror the night before. She swayed her torso to make an elegant line as she looked, and more importantly, she knew how to smile dazzlingly and yet leave the focus of her gaze feeling as if they did not have her full attention. I had never been the focus of it before, and I found it fascinating.

"Are you going to run off and leave me here?" she asked. Her tone was so neutral that I could sense no hint of reproach. That was unusual. I looked into her eyes, but could not understand what I saw there.

"I couldn't do that," I said honestly. It was true, even if I could not understand why.

"You're the only one who thinks so," she said, with a hint of her usual sharpness. She looked back to the mirror, pretending to study her face. I saw that although her lips were parted attractively, her jaw was tight.

"I *would* never leave you," I said. She did not look over to me, but she had gone very still. "That wasn't what I wanted to speak to you about." I cast a look over my shoulder; faintly, I could hear the rattle of the jewel box. Satisfied that her maidservant was not listening at the door, I lowered my voice to a whisper.

"I wanted you to know that the Duke doesn't suspect...anything." I still could not bring myself to say what had transpired that one night. "I was able to speak to Temar about it, and ask him why the Duke was suspicious. I made it seem like it was unfair, like there was nothing to hide. They aren't sure anymore, now they think they could have been wrong that you lied to them." There was a silence. "Anyway, I wanted you to know," I said awkwardly.

"Oh." Miriel tilted her head in the mirror to study the line of her cheek. She took a hairpin from her hair and tucked one curl down more firmly, and after a moment of waiting, I bit my lip in silent frustration.

It had been just as foolish to expect thanks or trust, I thought bitterly. I knew Miriel well enough, I knew that she would

---

173

not quickly forget a slight. It had been foolish to expect that she would believe me when I explained what had happened—after all, I now knew that she expected me to run away, she thought me faithless. For some reason, that hurt more than her refusal to acknowledge my words. I went to the main room, pushing the door open as roughly as I dared, and sat down to study. It was a text on the religious practices of the Bone Wastes, and I did not have much heart to read it.

"Catwin." Miriel's voice was not sharp, nor was it worried. I sighed in frustration, marked my place in the book, and took a moment to compose my face before returning to her privy chamber. Miriel was in the doorway of her bedchamber, looking over her shoulder. "You're to be at my side at all times," she said, with no hint of mockery in her voice. "It's time to dress for dinner now."

Bemused, I trailed after her and sat on my little cot as she selected her dress from the ones laid out by her maid, and then looked over the contents of her jewel box. When she had been laced into her gown, a deep blue that offset her eyes, she looked over at me critically.

"Change into your other suit, it's cleaner. If you're to accompany everywhere now, you'll need new clothes. Not what you wear to fight." I refrained from pointing out that I might need to fight at any time, and watched as she selected small drop earrings of a golden stone, and a thin chain of gold for her waist. She was careful to wear jewelry, as every girl did, and yet she wore very little. Anyone who watched Miriel knew that she possessed many fine jewels, and chose not to wear all of them.

"I will ask my uncle to have a new suit made for you," Miriel said simply. Her voice was still neutral, and her face expressionless.

It was a poor gesture, as peace offerings went, but I was not in any position to dictate the terms of this exchange. I was confused; I always went to things head on, telling Miriel exactly what had transpired, going to the heart of it all. Donnett had been right, I was like a pit bull. But Miriel always came at things sideways, sliding things in under my guard, talking in puzzles. I could not understand it, and I could not understand her.

That night, as I watched Miriel eat and drink, talk and laugh, I thought that the puzzle of her was her ability to distract those on whom she had turned her attention. When she was alone with someone, she could turn their attention whichever way she wanted. But when she was at a banquet, or when she was dancing, she sparkled, she shone brightly so that she could dazzle any thought out of the minds of those who watched her. I did not think that even Guy de la Marque could have watched her without forgetting for a moment that he watched the heir of his enemy.

Chapter 24

Miriel thawed towards me once more, bit by bit. She and I still did not speak often, but she acknowledged my presence now. She showed it in little ways: nodding at me when she came into a room and found me there, taking care to ask for two mugs when we studied late into the night and she sent for tea. And, only a few nights after I told her that I had lied on her behalf, Miriel asked me to get a book for her.

"From the royal library," I specified.

"Yes."

"I'm not allowed in the royal library."

"I know that," she said simply. I rolled my eyes in irritation and looked from the scrap of paper in my hand, to her serene smile. She did not seem to be making a joke; in fact, behind the smile, I could see her curiosity. But it seemed too strange to be true.

"This book," I said, still unable to believe it.

"Yes," she said, simply.

"You're sure," I said, again, testing. The small flashes of irritation I saw in her had not led to a return of the Miriel I knew. Her frozen fear after the attack, the way she had of looking around a room, starting at small noises, walking always as if she feared a knife between the ribs, had given way to an eerie calm. Miriel was thoughtful these days. She had given no indication that she trusted me more, knowing I had lied for her, knowing I could protect her; neither had she snapped at me, insulted me, or been cold to me. She had been so withdrawn that it was nearly a relief to see anger in her eyes.

"Yes," she said again, her voice emphatic. "Is there some problem?"

"I suppose you know it's death to steal any of the King's books," I said drily. I was certain that she had thought nothing of the danger to me, but the delighted gleam of her smile surprised me, and I found that I could not help but smile back. Her grin was not malicious, it was the smile between two conspirators.

"Oh, I know," she said.

"You just want to see if I can," I said, torn between amusement and wounded pride, and she laughed, but shook her head as well.

"No, I also want the book. So. Get it for me." And she swept out of the room, leaving me staring after her and wondering a great many things.

As I lay in bed, still dressed, I tried to let my mind go blank, as Temar had taught me, and seek the answer from the information I had. Why would Miriel wish to read the writings of a populist sympathizer, a long-dead priest? Her tutor had only ever glossed over the writings of the priest, a man martyred five centuries before as he stood between the royal army and the common people of a small village. His sentiments would most certainly be considered treasonous, and even the church did not espouse his writings. How had Miriel remembered the brief mention of him from our history lessons? And why would she ever want to read his work?

I did not have long to think. Anna, Miriel's maidservant, slipped off to sleep quickly, and when she had been snoring for a few minutes, I eased myself up out of my cot, took a small linen sack, and crept out of the room, down the corridors, across a few frigid alleyways, and into the Palace proper.

It was almost too easy. The Palace Guard, who patrolled the ragtag group of buildings around the palace proper, wore leather plates of armor and carried swords, or spears, or daggers. The Royal Guard, who had control of the main building, fairly dripped with weapons, and so wherever they went, there was the steady clank of their boots, the shifting of ringmail, and the scrape of metal.

I was able to hide, not even a yard from them, as they patrolled past me, looking serious and noticing nothing. Each hallway was lined with ornamental columns, statues, pedestals with sculptures, all casting strange shadows and accounting for a gleam in the darkness. It was a spy's dream, so easy for a girl who had grown up as a sneak that I nearly gave myself away by giggling out loud.

It did not take overlong to make my way to the library, and I found that it was shockingly poorly guarded. There were not even guardsmen at the doors. Presumably, I thought after a moment, they had decided that no one would break into the palace in order to sneak, light-footed, past the sleeping King, and then wander through hallways lined with priceless works of art, only to borrow a book. I smiled to myself and opened the door a crack to slip through.

I closed the door softly behind me and when I turned around and saw the library itself, I gasped, and my knees nearly buckled. Terrified that someone would have heard me, I scampered over to the shadow of a shelf and crouched there, hardly breathing—but there was no one there, no one to hear me. This was not a court hungry for knowledge; I thought of the libraries at the academies in the city, and wondered what the philosophers would make of all these books sitting untouched.

I stayed there for a moment, staggered by the thought that any one of the dozens of books within my reach would be worth more than the house I had been born in. I had wandered past oil paintings that would have cost enough to feed a village for a year, I had seen Miriel curl her lip at a priceless diamond bracelet; for reasons I could not name, it was the books that impressed upon me how much my life had changed.

At last, with the echoes of my gasp dying away, I forced my trembling legs into action and stood. I leaned against the shelf for a moment, then peeked out at the room. It was just as incredible this time, and, greatly daring, I wandered into the very center of the library and turned, looking around myself in awe.

It was a column of many levels, so many rows of books that there were spiral staircases leading to balconies that lined the walls. At the center were huge tables, for spreading out maps or the old, huge books. A great skylight would have let light in during the day; now, I could see the stars glimmering through it, so fine was the glass, and a great chandelier hung, twinkling, beautiful oil lamps suspended and burning, burning priceless scented oil to light a room no one used.

I had to keep moving. What if a guard thought to poke his head into the library? I shook my head to clear it and set off. Miriel's book would be filed with philosophy and theology, and so I trotted round the perimeter of the room until I found the section. I scanned through the books quickly, my fingers pausing occasionally over titles I had seen referenced, but never been able to read, and eventually I found the volume she sought.

Strangely, it was not covered with a layer of dust. Someone else had read this volume recently. I frowned and plucked it from the shelf, then rearranged the other books to that one might not see a gap. Then I tucked the book into a bag that lay flat against my back, and took one last look around me—now that I knew how easy it was to sneak in here, I knew that I would be back.

But first, there were other puzzles to attend to. The next morning, I waited until the maid had bustled off with the laundry, and then I presented Miriel with the book. I saw her smile of genuine delight; she fairly snatched it from me and she ran her fingers over the cover.

"There," I said. "Now what did you want it for?"

"I should think it would be obvious," she said lightly. It was not an insult. She was serious.

"Not to me," I said, feeling self-conscious at my apparent stupidity. I hopped up to sit on the table and watch her. To my surprise, Miriel pursed her lips and took the time to find words.

"They tried to kill me," she said. I waited for tears, for the undercurrent of tension in her voice, but there was nothing. She paused, clearly searching for a way to convey her thoughts. "And I thought—who kills a child?"

I nodded, feeling an upswell of anger. She was right to be furious, I thought—and better furious than afraid. But then I realized that she only looked contemplative.

"I thought..." She looked down. "What's worth killing for? What's worth dying for?"

"Protecting others," I said promptly, and she shook her head at me, too lost in thought to be impatient.

"No...not like that. I mean, that man. He knew that if my uncle did not give in, I would die. He would have that on his hands, and he would be damned forever. But he believed that the rebellion was worth it." I could not put a name to what I saw in her face.

"You admire him," I said slowly, shaping my mouth around words that made no sense to me. Miriel nodded, eagerly. "But he tried to kill you," I said, not understanding. "You should hate him. He tried to kill you." She shook her head again; her black curls flew.

"At first I was just scared. And then I was angry for a bit. But I'm not anymore. Can't you understand?"

"No," I said flatly. "I can't. Not at all." She frowned.

"Aren't you curious? Don't you wonder why he did it?" I paused, considering. She would wonder that, I thought. I had not. I knew why he had tried to kill her, he had done it for the rebellion, and it was not a good enough reason to me. I would have thought that she would be even angrier than I had been; but trust a noble to be this backwards.

179

"I wondered why," Miriel said finally. She looked at me directly, her beauty not animated with her sparkling smile or her usual temper; she was in repose. "It's not as simple as him trying to kill me, Catwin." She leaned forward, earnestly. "You should read the book, too," she said. "I could give it to you. You'd have to hide it, though, you know my uncle wouldn't approve."

"That's only another reason that we shouldn't—" I stopped, confused. This was wrong, all wrong. I was a commoner, I was not crazy enough to walk into danger for nothing. But Miriel was nobly born; she said nothing, she was only waiting, with a half smile.

"He's a philosopher," she coaxed.

"The kind of philosophy that gets people hanged," I said flatly.

"No! No. Not with Garad on the throne," she predicted confidently. "You'll see. I heard the other night that he's speaking of this as a Golden Age, free of war and strife. I hear he has many new thoughts, enlightened thoughts."

With a little more thought, I could have seen that she was, for the first time, happy about her uncle's plans for her. Miriel thought of the kind young man in the hallway, and she thought of her own success at the court, and for the first time, her own goals were aligned with her uncle's. She imagined the King to be a man as smart as she was, with a mind as quick as hers in politics and philosophy. Miriel was prepared to believe that Garad, enlightened, would be exactly what he wanted to be: the harbinger of a Golden Age, the knight on a white horse that could save Miriel from her uncle's machinations.

I should have seen that and been kinder, gentler. I should have tried to sway her away from it—Seven Gods, what could have been avoided later if I had managed to caution her then? But I was oblivious, too afraid by the drift of the conversation to see the shining happiness in her eyes. I was not gentle.

"He doesn't want this kind of change," I predicted.

"Oh, what do you know?" she snapped, my warnings turning her good mood quickly. I shut up, but glared back.

"You be careful," I said finally.

"*You* be careful," she said right back. "And don't you tell."

"I won't tell on you." But she and I knew that she was asking more than my silence. As I bowed and went off to gather my own study materials, I found that I was already practicing wide-eyed lies in my head, and hoping that I would be clever enough to deceive Temar when the truth came out.

I bit my lip and looked back at her, where she was already poring over the book. I shivered. Miriel might be confident, but I had my doubts. I had seen the Boy King's gentle smile as well as she had, but I thought that I knew the limits of his kindness. I had heard that he was sponsoring the Academies, asking the philosophers to go out into the markets and hold their lectures there, that the people of Penekket might participate as they had in the old days.

I thought he would be less understanding of this self-named philosopher, who denounced the very notion of a monarchy, who said that all humans were created equal, and separated by nothing more divine than gold. These letters claimed that no man was given a divine right to rule, only that some men were allowed to do so by the complacency of their people. That, the Boy king would not be able to stomach—I would stake my own meager pay on it.

But Miriel never spoke of the book again, beyond leaving it below my spare uniform so that I would know to return it. The next night, she made another peace offering: she asked me to watch Cintia Conradine at dinner. She threw the request over her shoulder while she dressed for dinner, as if it was nothing. I gave a murmured assent as I tied on my new belt. As if by magic, after my success in finding her the book, new clothes had appeared for me: a shirt and tunic of fine soft wool, a belt of black leather, and a pair of new boots with sheaths for my daggers.

I had said thank you, somehow ashamed to be so pleased by the gift. I had the fear that her offerings might mean very little to her, who had jewels worth a fortune at her fingers and her ears, and that my happiness would show me as the commoner I was. I had bit my lip and did not speak much to her for the rest of the night, but thought—or hoped—that I saw a pleased gleam in her eye that I liked her gift.

"Why Cintia?" I asked now, and Miriel smiled at her reflection.

"She's the only other one who has what I have," she said, and I nodded. Cintia Conradine was no beauty, though pretty enough, but she had the same allure as Miriel: courting her would unsettle the Council, most particularly Guy de la Marque. Other matches might be of no advantage, too low for the king—but none could object on other grounds unless Garad chose the daughter of the Commoner, or the daughter of the former ruling house. And

Miriel was right, if Garad was making what was, to all accounts, an ill-advised peace with Ismir, might he not also make an ill-advised match with a Conradine, to bind the country back together?

Rumors of the king's marriage had broken through the court like a boar through bracken. The boy king had been ill for so long that the court had not dared hope he would live. Offering marriage to a sickly boy would have been uncouth; no one had dared, and Isra had not sought allies in that way. Now, still pale and thin—but stronger every day, the servants whispered, not like the other times—the King returned to his throne in triumph, and every man with a daughter began to see a path to rise at court.

The Duke chose this moment to reveal his knowledge about de la Marque's planned marriage between his daughter and the King, and the news raced through the court. The men of the council shouted at de la Marque that he had taken too much power upon himself, each of them swearing that his own interest was the interest of the kingdom, no one mentioning their own daughters, their own nieces.

But they did not shout for very long. Their quarry was out in the open now, and the hunt was on. Every girl, no matter how poor, had new gowns. Together, they were dazzling: each bedecked in silks, dripping with as many jewels as they afford, or borrow. Some of the elder girls laced themselves tightly in the new fashions, with wide-necked gowns that came close to showing their shoulders. Others chose demure gowns and fashionable veils over their hair, playing for the Queen's favor.

Miriel alone behaved as if nothing had changed. When she left her rooms to go to dinner, it was as if the truth of her near-murder faded away. She seemed to have no care in the world. She danced and sang as well as she had ever done, opened conversations with thought-provoking questions on any topic except the King's marriage, and continued to dress modestly in her priceless gowns.

She treated the young men of the court with her same sweet courtesy, and they, now completely overlooked, flocked to her like bees to honey. Still, she never spoke to them more than would be proper, she never smiled on them as warmly as she did her female companions. Determinedly, she would greet Wilhelm Conradine with a pleasant nod, and then ignore him completely, choosing to smile at any of the other young men. She let them single her out as the most desirable, and then she played on her modesty.

It was not only Wilhelm that she ignored; Miriel never even glanced up at the royal dais, save when protocol demanded it. She seemed quite unaware of the King's comings and goings; she alone did not preen and posture when the King was at dinner. I watched her and wondered at her reticence, and I was not disappointed—a few nights later, Miriel made her move.

Chapter 25

Miriel had planned to catch the King's eye, and she chose her time carefully: it was the end of dinner one night, when the children of the court left to return to their own chambers for simpler, more suitable entertainments. Each night, the boys would stand up and bow to the throne, and then leave, and then the girls would step forward and curtsy, and leave as well.

It had always been an empty gesture, at most a chance for the Dowager Queen to see the children and notice who might be missing. With the King's return, however, the once-empty ritual had become the focus of the night. Girls fussed with their hair, smoothed their gowns, fiddled with their necklaces. They blushed as they all curtsied, and each had her own flourish to add: the flick of a skirt, the curve of a shoulder. All save Miriel, of course, who managed to curtsey as solemnly as if she was directing the gesture solely to the Head Priest at Isra's side.

Then, one night, as the girls turned from their curtsies to leave, Miriel caught her heel in the rushes and stumbled. When she righted herself, she was blushing, and she cast such an anguished glance up at the Queen's throne that for a moment even I believe it to have been a mistake. I thought of the thrashing she would get for this, and my throat tightened.

Everyone else who had seen, however, found it deeply amusing. The Queen was watching Miriel with the faintest hint of a smile playing around her lips; she was no supporter of the Duke, it was in her interest to see Miriel falter. Miriel, seeing it, ducked her head, and then cast another frightened look up—just the quickest glance—at the King's throne.

I saw her eyes widen when she saw him, it was the most beautiful look of surprise I had ever seen. She looked as if she had not the slightest idea of what to do to enchant him, she stared at him as if she had quite forgotten herself for a moment, then she swept another curtsy and ran after her companions, head down, the Dowager Queen's low laugh following her.

It had been masterfully done, and it was over in a single moment, from stumble to curtsy. I doubted that anyone had even noticed, aside from the Dowager Queen and the King. She was smiling, she had not seen the moment of apparent surprise, and she could not have understood it if she had. The King had the good sense to share a smile with his mother, as if he, too, were amused by Miriel's clumsiness. As if I had not seen his fingers go white where he gripped the arms of his chair, when she turned to look at him.

I wondered what it must cost him not to gaze after her as she hurried away. When she had looked at him, I saw that he had been waiting, every night, for her to look up. He wondered if she knew whom she had met that night in the hallway. Now he believed—the fool—that I had not told her, and that she had not known. He believed, from her downcast gaze and her startlement, that she had not looked up before because she had never imagined that she could catch the King's eye. He believed from her blush that she was embarrassed to learn it had been him she met that night.

Unexpectedly, I felt a wave of melancholy strike me. The young man we met in the hallway had helped her to her feet before he saw her face, and he had not betrayed her secret. He was as kind as he believed her to be, and he was intelligent, and now that he had survived he was thrown into a pit of vipers. He had not been prepared for this, everyone had deemed him a dead man. It seemed incredibly sad to me that he should lose his heart to a girl who was not real, only a puppet for ambition.

Then I stole a glance ahead at Miriel, and one back towards the young men's table, where Wilhelm sat, pretending that he had seen nothing. I felt my first wave of distaste for power itself. If Miriel's uncle had not had such ambitions, she would have been able to talk and laugh with Wilhelm as much as she wished; they might have been married, if they were a good match still in a few years' time. He would not look so sad, and she would not be so determined.

Then I shook my head. It was ridiculous that I should find this sad. Seducing the King had always been Miriel's purpose. Even she had never lost sight of it. She was choosing her own path, and the King was far from helpless. He could have any woman he chose. And yet: there was something heartbreaking about watching her tactics find their mark. My gaze, jaded by even this few months in the court, was not yet so jaded as that.

Before I left the hall, I craned to see Temar and the Duke. Both were grim, troubled. It had been well-played and subtle, but I knew the Duke worried. *She was always setting herself forward.*

Miriel would be called before her uncle to explain herself, I thought, and I needed to warn her of that.

"I saw an opening and I took it," she said, later that night. Her voice was clear and unapologetic. Only I, standing at her right shoulder, could see that her hands were clenched behind her back and shaking with fear. "It was a way to inspire his pity and demonstrate modesty. He must know that 'I do not set myself ahead of the other girls. Now he believes that I think myself unworthy."

The Duke watched her, narrow-eyed.

"I do not like surprises." As always, his voice made me shiver.

"I am very sorry, my Lord Uncle," Miriel said. She looked truly scared, as I knew her to be. Either she could not mask her fear, or she did not do so a-purpose—I could no longer see for certain, when I looked at her, what was practiced and what was real. I thought that just now she stood to gain from appearing vulnerable. She knew it, too, I thought—only it was not my pride that suffered when she apologized to him, but hers.

She pushed down her pride every day when she stepped aside to let the other maidens go ahead of her, and when she did not answer back to their taunts. It was a wonder she did not choke on the indignity of it every day she spent in court, let alone now, in the face of her uncle's arrogance. I offered up a silent prayer to gods I did not believe in that she would not undo her progress with angry words.

"Go," the Duke said at length. "But Miriel—"

"Yes, my Lord Uncle?"

"Remember my promise to you. If ever I hear a rumor against your chastity, you will wish that you had never been born. And remember that, were it not for my protection, you would have died, not a month past." She did not reply to that, for there was nothing to say. She curtsied, and then we went from the Duke's rooms together, with me padding along silently behind her.

We did not speak of it again, although I yearned to ask her if she had truly seized an opportunity, or if she had planned it out. We had more urgent things to prepare for: preparations for the envoy's arrival were in full swing, and as she studied her curtsies and her court manners endlessly, I asked Miriel's permission to go inspect the building where the man would be housed. I asked her, also, for a few pieces of silver, and she looked at me suspiciously.

"Ask my uncle if you want more pay," she said. "And what do you want it for, anyway?"

"You'll see," I said. "I can't ask him." I did not want to tell her my plan, in case it should fail, and I knew how strong Miriel's curiosity was. "I want to try something," I told her. "And if it doesn't work, it'll be best for you to be able to tell him truthfully that you didn't know what I was about."

"And if it does work?"

"I still wouldn't tell him," I said promptly, "but I will tell you." I was rewarded with the gleam of her amusement.

"Well, it had better not be gambling you want to try," she said, but she drew a few coins from her purse and dropped them into my hand.

I stripped off my tunic, with the Duke's insignia, took off my armband, and tucked my hair up under a cap, and then trotted over to the small building where the envoys were housed. I whistled as I walked, happy to be out in the sunshine and away from the relentless scheming of the Duke and Miriel. There was a chill in the air, and I thought that winter was coming late, and fast.

The envoy would be quartered in one of the smaller buildings, lying to the southwest of the castle proper. It had fallen into disrepair over the years, used less and less as Heddred and Ismir absorbed neighboring nations. First, the plains princelings had asked the aid of the Conradines to fight the Ismiri, and they in turn had banded with their own western lords to fight our forces.

Few envoys enjoyed the King's hospitality anymore—there were few enough nations now. Not many still remembered that our nobles were the remnants of the duchies that had been scattered across Heddred once. They were both lords and envoys now, expected to keep their lands prosperous and their tenants loyal to the crown.

The only countries that remained now to send envoys were Aphra, to the far southwest, stubbornly clinging to their independence on the rocky shores, and the scattered tribes of the Bone Wastes, whose land was too harsh and too poor to be worth conquering. Mavlon, to the southeast, claimed its independence, but did not even take up arms. In the north, the Shifting Isles kept to themselves, some said—and others said that only a fool believed that the Shifting Isles existed at all.

It had been a very long time since the diplomatic building had been full, and as fewer and fewer of the rooms were used, the place had gradually been shuttered. Now, however, it was a bustle of servants, dusting and airing a large set of rooms that faced towards the King's forest. The envoy would have a pleasant view, but no sense of the city.

I held a door open for a group of men carrying a carved table, smiled at their grunts of thanks, and followed them into the rooms. As I had expected, no one paid me the slightest attention, and I was able to walk through each room, peering up at the ceilings and into corners. I looked out each of the windows and marked their place on the walls, and tried to memorize the layout of the apartments.

At last I found what I was looking for: the bedchamber, with a lone serving girl airing the wardrobes out and clearing them of spiders. I rapped on the door of the chamber and she startled, gasping in fear and then—as she recognized me for a girl—staring at me suspiciously.

"What d'you want?" she asked me.

"You're to do laundry for his lordship, then?" I asked, pitching my voice into the strongest city accent I could manage. "Start fires for him, clean his rooms?" Her face was closed.

"Aye. What's it to you?"

A piece of silver appeared in my fingers. "I want to know anything interesting that you see," I said easily. "Ladies in his rooms, visitors late at night, any scraps of paper you find in his clothes."

"And if I do?" It was a poor bluff, given how hungrily she stared at the coin.

"More." I turned the coin so that it glinted in the light, and then tossed it to her. "A piece for each bit of information. A piece to know who else asks you, and a chance to match what they offer." I held out my hand, palm up. "Give it back, then, if you won't do it."

"I will!" She snatched her hand back against her torso. "How do I find you?"

"You know Roine?" She nodded. "You can find me in her rooms, often enough, and if not, tell her where I can find you." She nodded again. "And there's another piece of silver in it for you if you can find out the names of others who serve him," I said. "Hostlers, cooks. But you must be discreet."

"I will be." She said it almost scornfully, and I realized that it must be no new thing for a royal servant to be bribed for information.

"I'll leave you to your work, then." I swept a bow and left, heading for the chapels.

When I returned, a few silver pieces lighter, Miriel was already dressing for dinner. Lately, she had been dressing in pale greens and muted reds, the only pale colors that suited her complexion, and every day she was especially careful with her appearance.

"What are you planning for?" I asked, suspicious.

"He's going to seek me out," Miriel said, as if it were the most self-evident thing in the world. "I must be prepared."

"Seek you out how?" I was nervous.

"Not like that. But he's going to make some excuse to come find me, and propriety dictates that he could only ever do that in public. When else could it be, but at dinner or after?" I nodded at her logic, and began to change into my more formal clothing.

"What were you doing with my money, then?" Miriel asked, as soon as her maidservant was out of the room. Neither of us ever spoke of the matter, but we both knew that the woman was in the pay of the Duke. She was kind and considerate to Miriel, but how could such a woman ever keep a secret when faced with his wrath? And so, Miriel and I never burdened her with knowledge she would rather not have torn out of her.

"Making a spy's web," I said softly. "We have a serving girl in the envoy's chambers now, who will report to us of his doings, and we have a chorister in the Queen's chapel."

Miriel turned from her preparations to look at me. "Why did you do that?"

"Temar has one, but he wouldn't teach me how to make one myself. You know your uncle doesn't tell us everything. But we could learn it ourselves." I tried to tailor it to her own interests; I could not admit to forming a spy network out of contrariness. But I saw the habitual flash of irritation in her eyes.

"Yes. But it's a bad plan." She pointed a hairpin at me. "Temar's going to catch you," she predicted.

"He's not going to catch me," I said, with more certainty than I felt.

"Then you'll tell him," she suggested, with a sideways glance. There was both taunt and bitterness in her look.

"Why would I ever do that?"

"You don't need to play games with me," she said coldly. "I know you would choose him over me in a moment."

She was still angry that I had not agreed with her about the rebellion, that I had not accepted her peace offering of a secret between us: the book, the discussion of philosophy, the clandestine trips to the library. I could have acknowledged that, or turned away. It would have been better to do so, and I meant to tell her just that.

I wanted to say, *I would not betray you to Temar.* I could have said, *Haven't I already lied to him for you?* I might have tried to explain how little I trusted him, how horrified I was at the things he taught me. I could have told her that even as I believed him to have a good heart, I saw that there was something that was twisted in him.

But what I said was, "Have you ever given me a reason to be loyal to you?"

Any growing trust between us was severed in a moment. What I had said was true, she could hear it in my voice. What she could not know, as she went pale at my words, was that I was loyal. Without any cause greater than pity and shared torment, and a few moments of dark humor, I was loyal to her before the Duke, before Temar, before Roine. I would have been loyal to Miriel before the King.

I wished immediately that I could take the words back, but there was no doing so. She turned back to her mirror, and I saw the face that her enemies would see: pitiless, cold. There was no crack in the mask. Miriel had retreated from me completely.

Chapter 26

A few nights later, Miriel's predictions came true. The maidens had withdrawn after dinner, and someone had called for music. The girls had gathered around, and one pair circled each other: Miriel, and Marie de la Marque. They curtsied and began the dance, their smiles perfectly sweet, Miriel as deferential as always to the golden girl, the girl who was still the tenuous favorite of the maidens' chambers. Both girls danced prettily, their feet moving faster than thought.

I watched from my post near the door. Each night I came to the room a few moments after the maidens had arrived and stood at the wall, silent, for the remainder of the evening. There were a few stairs down into the room itself, and from here I could watch all of the girls without having to circle the room.

I had thought the Duke's plan for me insane, thinking that to give Miriel a bodyguard would be so noteworthy as to be ridiculous, and so I had been surprised that no one seemed to pay me the slightest attention. There were always servants about, and the girls were accustomed to being watched. Only a few of them had noticed me at all, in all the time I had spent in the maidens' rooms, and once they saw that I was a girl, they disregarded my presence entirely. No one came close enough to pick out the black-on-black insignia I wore, and Miriel never looked over at me.

After the months of training, it had been dizzying to watch the room not only by my own instincts, but also with Temar's training. As I watched the smiles, the veiled insults, the few genuine peals of laughter, I saw present and future: the directions of the young ladies' parents and their own little groups and friendships. The next generation of nobility, with all of their squabbles over land and trade rights, were growing up here. It was a strange thought, to think that someday the bitterest rivalries I saw before me could be settled with soldiers and arrests.

Tonight, just as the music was rising in speed, the two girls matching each other exactly, there was a stir at the door. My hand dropped to my side, open, ready to pull the dagger from my boot, but the men who entered were the Royal Guard, and with them came the King and the Dowager queen.

There were muted exclamations from the young women, and the musicians clattered to a halt, rising to bow hastily. The girls were sinking into their curtsies, and in the sudden absence of conversation, there was only the rustling of a dozen dresses. Marie de la Marque looked up at the King and the Dowager Queen with a confident smile, and at her side, Miriel looked, resolutely, down at her feet.

"You may rise." The King's voice was at once amused and awed. He could see the currents of behavior, the yearning of each girl to catch his attention, and yet he was unnerved by the stir he had created. He was, I thought, more like a woman than a man—afraid of the power he held over the opposite sex.

"Good evening, maidens." The Queen's voice was commanding, and I thought that she was trying to awe the girls. It must be galling, I thought, to see girls so young and know that one day, one of them would take her place on the throne.

"Good evening, your Grace," came the chorus, girls stumbling over their words. A few exchanged covert glances.

"Pray, do not let us disturb you," the King said. "Please. Go on." Deliberately, he looked away from the two girls standing at the center of the circle, to say something to his mother, and she clapped to the musicians to begin playing once more. Even then, as Miriel and Marie de la Marque began their dance again, he did not look back. He bowed over the hand of Elizabeth Cessor, a tiny girl with hair so fair it was almost white, and he spoke a few words to her, and then he circled around the edge of the crowd, his mother at his side.

I watched them carefully, conscious of his guards at my side. They would not take kindly to me circling the room near him, I thought, and so I might not be able to hear his whispered comments. I must glean as much as I could from his expression, and hers.

I saw that his mother was watching where he looked. She would take notice of which girls he singled out, I thought, and what he said to each of them. I wondered if she would think to notice where he did not look, for there was only one place in the room that his gaze never touched. He looked briefly at Marie, as she danced away from the center of the room, but his gaze slid away as she moved back towards Miriel.

Did he know that his mother would disapprove of Miriel, I wondered, or did he only suspect as much? For certain, she looked around her as though she wished every one of the pretty, youthful faces would disappear. I did not think that any woman the King chose would be beloved of the Dowager Queen.

At last the dance ended, and at the shouted congratulations, he turned and smiled absently, clapping. As was customary, he stepped forward to offer his own compliments, and I stiffened at his ready smile for Marie de la Marque.

"Very pretty, my Lady," he said, and he bowed over her hand; I noted the familiar smile between cousins. Marie was radiating satisfaction, smug in her triumph at being singled out. Her smile died as Garad turned to Miriel; at his side, smiling coolly, Isra went still.

"Ah, Lady Miriel." He bowed over her hand as well, and though he stepped back at once to his mother's side, I saw his eyes meet Miriel's for one moment. "Shall we return to the banquet?" he asked his mother, and she nodded.

"I bid you good night," he said to the assembled maidens, and they curtsied as one. As he left the room, however, he saw me. I saw him recognize me, and take note of my face, and he gave the faintest nod of his head to me. I dared do nothing more than bow my head in return, afraid of attracting his mother's attention, but she swept past me without a word, her face mask-like. It took no training to see her displeasure—her son had spoken to all of the high-born ladies, yes, and then he had shown familiarity for the Celys girl, the niece of the upstart Duke of Voltur.

Garad might think highly of his subtlety—indeed, he had said only three words, spent barely a moment focused on Miriel—but it had been enough to alert his mother, and indeed, enough to alert the maidens. In the center of the room, the whispers were rising. How did the King know Miriel's name? She had been at court only a year, he had barely seen her. But he knew her. He had looked at her. The girls crowded around Miriel, and I saw the self-conscious turn of her head, heard the falsely uncertain laugh. At the center of the crowd, I saw Marie de la Marque watching this, and I knew that her father would know of the King's words by the end of the night.

"He recognized me," I said later that night. The maidens had been commanded to retire early, and so Miriel had gone back to her rooms to practice her smiles and dancing and then, when her maidservant left on an errand, to take out the book I had gotten her and keep reading it. She was nearly all of the way through it, and I did not like the enraptured look on her face when she read it. If I had hoped she would disagree with the writings of the rebels, and that would be the end of her interest, I had been wrong. I was trying to distract her, but I saw now that my efforts had been in vain.

"So?" Her tone was light and impersonal. For the past days, Miriel had behaved as if I were a guest in her rooms, a temporary visitor to be treated courteously, neither friend nor foe.

Her question was easily enough answered by her own intelligence, so I did not respond to it. I only stripped down to my linen and pulled on a pair of loose pants. At Temar's insistence, I wore pants and a shirt to sleep in, not a nightshirt, as others did. Too difficult to move in, he said, and he had also insisted that all of Miriel's nightgowns be cut with wide hems, so that she could run in them if necessary.

"Do you'll think he'll try to contact you?" I asked curiously. I thought the King would not be satisfied for long with a glimpse of her face and a few moments in her company.

She behaved as if I had not said anything, and I cursed myself again for my foolish words in our argument. Now openly doubting my loyalty to her, Miriel shared no secret glances with me at remarks we heard in the halls, she did not make confident predictions of the course of events, she did not even practice at night in the same room as I did. If I studied in the main room, she would go to her bedchamber. I no longer saw her practice a head tilt or a smile. She might have been learning to throw my daggers, for all I knew.

"I heard from the serving girl today," I said, making another attempt to bridge the chasm between us. It felt like using silk thread to build a bridge for an army. "She said they've been told to expect the envoy a day before the winter festival."

"I see." The news might have been nothing at all to do with her, instead of the largest political event of the decade. I thought for a moment, and then tried another tactic.

"I wonder if they'll use Voltur pass," I said. "I should think they'd be in the mountains now, if they're to arrive in two weeks' time."

Just for a moment, she was caught off guard. The walls came down behind her eyes quickly enough, but I had seen a longing for home, a wish to be far away from the court where she was so successful and so favored. Even now, when Miriel had the King himself ensnared, I thought that she would give it all up to see the mountains again, and have an embrace from her mother.

It was the first reason she had ever given me to be loyal to her, and I could not find the words to tell her so. And so we went to sleep in the same silence that filled all of our nights now, and I lay awake for a very long time, staring at the ceiling and wishing I could find a way to make things right once more.

The next day, Temar told me that the envoy's party would arrive just before the winter festival, and I nodded as if this was new information. We were practicing in the early morning dark, not in our abandoned cellar room but instead outside, in one of the practice courts the soldiers used. Temar was insistent that I be able to fight in the cold, in the heat, in the dark, on uneven ground.

"You knew how to compensate for this," he would say sharply, as he knocked me to the ground or laid the fake knife to my throat. "And yet you focused on it instead of on the fight. Now, you're dead, and Miriel is dead." He always ended his admonishments with that phrase, and I was learning to hate it.

"Again," he said now, seeing that I was still stretching my left leg. He had thrown me from the ground, and my hip was sore. "We need to finish this. The Duke wishes to meet with us before the Council meeting."

I duly launched myself from the ground, driving my shoulder into his thighs. I heard his grunt as he hit the ground and then I was on top of him, scrabbling for his neck while he held me away from him easily, his longer arms pushing me back. I leaned back out of the reach of his fingers, and he took the opportunity to roll forwards and pin me.

"Are they presenting the ladies at the banquet?" I asked, my face squished into the ground. I wiggled my fingers to signal a yield, and sighed with relief when he released my arm.

"Yes." I had rolled to my feet, and he used the same throw to take me down again. I rolled so that my right leg was free for a kick, and he nodded approvingly. "Good. Again."

"How is Miriel?" he asked a few moments later, as we toweled off. "Her lessons are going well?"

I nodded. It was easy to be honest with Temar when things were going so poorly with Miriel. It was a bitter irony to me that I had once worked to pretend that there was no friendship between myself and Miriel, so as not to give the Duke cause for alarm. Now, gods knew, there was no need to pretend.

195

"She is as she always is," I said wearily. "Best at everything. She speaks of the King's marriage only when others bring it up. She dresses modestly, very few jewels—nothing cheap," I added, at Temar's raised eyebrow. "No especial friends, although there are those who seek her out. Elizabeth Cessor, Katherine Norcross, Linnea Torstensson. It does not please Marie de la Marque, but Miriel does not encourage it."

Temar nodded. It had been a delicate business, courting the favor of the maidens without disturbing the balance of power within the group, and no one could have managed it forever. The trick in any group, Temar had explained, was to get as close as possible to one's target before anyone noticed your aim. For better or worse, Marie de la Marque now knew Miriel to be a rival, at least for the friendship of the girls, and perhaps for the favor of the King.

"Keep me informed," he said briefly, and I nodded without hesitation. Each time I nodded, I marveled at the pang I felt. How should it be that I felt disloyal no matter what I did? Every night before falling asleep, I practiced saying a version of the day's events that was close enough to the truth to be checked by anyone else Temar might speak to, and yet carefully edited to remove anything pointing to Miriel's own motives or emotions.

Yet even knowing that I was helping Miriel by providing a steady stream of harmless information to Temar—and thus, the Duke—I still felt guilty. Nothing secret was divulged, and still I felt as if I should have asked her permission first. And even as I felt that I was betraying Miriel by telling Temar too much, I felt that I was betraying him by telling too little.

We were walking slowly, stretching our muscles, when we heard the sound of shouting from the Duke's chambers: the Duke's voice, and Miriel's. Temar and I exchanged one anguished glance, and started running.

Chapter 27

Miriel's voice, shrill with anger, and the Duke's snarl, were loud enough to be heard from the main hallway. Temar and I could hear the fight even as we ran through the main room, and as we pushed our way into the study, I froze for a moment at the tableau: the Duke roaring his anger, and Miriel facing into it with a determined scowl.

"—waste an opportunity like that!" The Duke's hand slammed down on his desk, and Miriel jumped slightly. Silently, I took my place at her side. I knew that she had no wish for my companionship, and yet in the face of the Duke's anger, I found that I wanted nothing more than to help her. She swallowed, unsure of herself; I was not certain that she had even noticed my arrival.

"Sir—you had said—"

"Not a word." He cut her off and turned his furious gaze on me, and I tried not to shrink away. "What do you think, shadow? Has she squandered her opportunity with the King? The opening she saw, and took?" He repeated her words mockingly, and I saw Miriel bite her lip.

"My Lord, I believe he is quite taken with her," I said honestly. "I believe he did not speak to her further because of his mother's presence." I saw Miriel's head start to turn, as if she thought to look at me, but she changed her mind and looked back at the floor.

"Huh." The Duke had not expected this; it distracted him from his anger for a moment. "That is the truth?"

"It is, my Lord." Conscious of his scrutiny, and Temar's, I bit my lip on the words that Miriel knew how to play this as only a woman could. She could do by instinct what the Duke tried to do with logic. I could not say that, but I added, "He is afraid of how the girls act towards him, but with Miriel, it is the other way around— he thinks she is afraid of him."

The Duke was intrigued despite himself. "You do not think he will forget her?"

I shook my head, trying to appear confident enough to shield Miriel, but not so confident that he wondered what else there might be to the story. "No, my Lord. He sought her out, and still she retreated. He will be wondering why, I think."

The Duke turned his gaze on Miriel, and she dropped her own eyes. He watched her for a long moment.

"All the maidens are to be presented to the King at the Winter Festival," he said at last. "You will contrive to say something interesting to him when you dance together."

Miriel's head came up at that. "We're to dance?" she asked.

"I expect him to dance with some of the maidens. And as your shadow is so confident of his attraction to you—" he showed his wintry smile "—you will be one of those girls." The threat in his voice was clear, but he continued to speak. He always underestimated her intelligence. "If Catwin is correct, we will know it in a week's time. If she is not...we will need to discuss the behavior used to attract a man, and why you, with a fortune in training, cannot accomplish that one thing.

"Now. Show me your curtsy to a diplomat." The speed of the change was jarring to me, but Miriel swept a curtsy without hesitation. It was deep, as deep a curtsy as she would show to a duke, but not quite so deep as to royalty. As she did everything—save, perhaps, being pleasant to the Duke—she did it perfectly.

"If circumstance brings you close to the envoy, you are to be as bland as possible," the Duke said. "We have all seen how bland you can be, so I shall assume you will have no trouble with this." Miriel said nothing, but her color rose. "If anyone asks, you are desirous of peace and are pleased that the envoy is here.

"One more thing—you will give every appearance of enjoying the banquet, but you will not appear awed by it. We need no reminders of your provincial upbringing.

"*You*," he said to me, "will stay as close to her side as possible. Do not let anyone draw her away from the crowd. You will watch that no one puts food on her plate or wine in her cup without first serving another. You will teach her a signal to warn her of such dangers without alerting others. Take note of those servants who do such things, and find them after the meal. Do not engage them yourself if it can be avoided; bring their names to Temar, and he will do the rest."

"Sir—my Lord—is there another plot I should know about?" My heart was pounding. Every time we spoke of this, I fought my own sense of the ridiculous. It was undeniable that I was here at the palace, being trained to be an assassin and a bodyguard, but it was undeniable, as well, that I had killed a man who was trying to poison Miriel and leave her for dead.

And yet—and yet. Since the assassination attempt, I found myself thinking every day that I might wake up and find that all of this had been a dream. It did not seem possible that the stakes should be so high, not for the rebels and not for the courtiers, whatever the money and power to be played for. Whenever the Duke spoke of Miriel's would-be killers, my heart turned over as if I was hearing of this for the first time.

"None that I know of," the Duke admitted. "It's early yet for the courtiers to see her as a threat. But in the confusion, anything could happen. And it would be clever to kill her before there was a clear motive." His eyes narrowed. "Or Jacces might make another attempt." Miriel swayed slightly, and before I could stop myself, I reach out to steady her. She was as white as snow at this casual discussion of her murder.

"I won't—" I said, and broke off as I saw Temar and the Duke watching us, sharp-eyed. I drew back slightly. "*We* will not let any harm come to you. My Lady." She nodded mechanically, but the look in her eyes said that she doubted our ability to protect her. I looked at her, wanting to ask if she was alright, and yet not wanting to voice the words in front of our audience.

"There will be new dances taught on the night of the banquet," the Duke resumed, as if nothing had occurred. "Your instructor knows them, and he will show them to you tomorrow. You are to know them perfectly."

The irritation was back in Miriel's eyes. I could see her wanting to retort that she knew her duty, and she did it. She always learned her dances perfectly. But she held her tongue, as she always managed to do, and we left. I sighed with relief to be away from the Duke's scrutiny, but Miriel did not relax. She broke into a run as soon as we were out of sight, and I ran after her.

"Miriel!" I did not use her title, but she hardly noticed. "Stop!" I grabbed her arm.

"Let me go!"

"Where are you going?"

"Away!" She tore her arm out of my grasp and ran again, turning down one corridor and then another. I did not think she was looking at where she was going; she just ran, and ran. "He wants me to be a nothing, a cipher. He would be me if he could, but he can't." She was crying, I realized, from the sob at the back of her voice. "And I can't *do* it anymore!"

"Miriel—" At last we were alone, and I grabbed her arm to stop her. This time, she did not pull away.

"I can't!" she finished in a breathless rush. "Do you hear me? I can't do it anymore!"

"Shut up!" Her face went white. She did not even know what to say to my outburst. I lowered my voice so that she had to lean close to hear me. "Do you have any idea what the Duke would do to both of us if he heard you speak that way?"

"I don't care!" She had flared up, looking up at me, her fists clenched. She was as proud as royalty. "He can do anything he wants! I still won't do it. I'm leaving. The longer I stay, the worse it gets. For the love of the Gods, Catwin, someone tried to *kill* me! I have to go now."

If I could have taken her by the shoulders and shaken her, I would have done so. "Listen to me," I said fiercely. "You can't leave—you, he'll hunt down. And you *will* do what he says. You don't know what he can do. You think you would be able to hold out, but I swear to you, you can't. You'd do what he wanted in the end." I leaned a little closer to whisper in her ear. "And you'd hate yourself for that."

"I'd hate myself knowing I didn't even try," she whispered back, passionate.

"You don't know anything," I hissed back. "We can't win against him."

"We could!"

"We could win, if we chose our time." The words were out of my mouth before I even knew what I was saying.

She should have laughed. I should have laughed. It was ridiculous. But, at the same time, it was deathly serious. Miriel had always known that she was a pawn, as any other young noblewoman would be, but she was realizing that the game was more dangerous than she had known. She knew that I meant what I had said when I told her that the Duke could win; if we were to try now, we could not ever triumph against him.

If we waited...

For a moment, she looked hopeful. She was transformed. And then her face slammed back into the mask of nothingness she wore almost always now. She went icy.

"I know where your loyalties lie," she said coldly. I swallowed down my retorts, and my hurt.

"Think what you want," I said, as cold as she. "You still have to do what he says."

Her shoulders slumped for a moment, and then she took a deep breath, drew herself up, and walked back down the hallway towards her rooms, as if nothing had occurred. She was as mechanical as a little doll, and she did not speak to me for the rest of the night. She had her maid take off her gown and brush her hair, and then she slipped into her robe and went to her bed, lying hunched under the covers. I snuck into the room as quietly as I could, and lay on my cot, sure that we were both awake, and wondering what she was thinking.

I was almost surprised to find her still there the next morning. I had expected her to flee, but she was almost her usual self. If her charm was a bit too forced, her smiles a bit too bright, she was nonetheless resolutely cheerful. She was being fitted for gowns when I heard shouts outside and looked out the window. I saw the standards of the Ismiri guard, and my eyes widened; the envoy was here, early, causing a commotion with his procession to the palace.

I looked over at Miriel, and after a moment of thought, I decided that I did not think she was in imminent danger of being stabbed by an assassin posing as a seamstress. I let myself out of the room quietly, then raced down the stairs and into an alleyway, arriving in time to see the envoy's caravan roll through.

He and his guard—small, as befitted the rules of diplomacy—rode white horses, dressed as for a tourney in red and gold, the colors of Ismir's royal house. He himself wore a suit of rich brown velvet, lustrous and expensive, but modest. This man did not set himself as minor royalty, as he might have done. He could have been any age between thirty-five and fifty, even to my practiced eye—strands of grey ran through his long brown hair, but his bearing was proud and strong. He was lean as a whip, with a hooked nose and a thin mouth, and he was watchful, too. I sank down behind a rain barrel as he turned his head to look down the alleyway where I hid.

The next afternoon, Roine sent for me, and when I arrived, I found the serving girl. She gave me a timid smile, and I drew her to the doorway, away from Roine's curious look.

"You said you'd want to know about who came to visit him," she said. I nodded, and she held up one hand, fingers splayed, to count. "A man with a sigil of two crossed spears, one of the Royal Guard and the King's steward, a whore from the city, a man with a sigil of a lion, and one of the priests."

For a moment, I could hardly speak at this windfall of information. Then I found my tongue. "Here." I pressed a piece of silver into her waiting palm. "I want you to mark the whores that come and go—if it's always the same one, try to learn her name and where she works. Anything else?"

"Man with a sigil like yours, asking me to report the same things to him. Wanted t'know who else asked me. I said no one."

"Thank you." I held up two more pieces of silver. "You can keep telling him everything that goes on," I said. "I don't care about that. This is for telling me he asked, and this is for keeping your silence about me." I blinked. "Why did you tell me about him, if you didn't tell him about me?"

"Didn't think to tell me not to, did he?" Her smile was sly. "And I'm guessing he serves the Duke, and *you* serve the girl?" She laughed at my face. "No need to answer. But I'd serve her afore serving him. My thanks for the silver." She laughed as she disappeared down the long hallway, whistling.

"Who was that?" Roine asked me, and I shrugged. She frowned at once. Roine did not approve of me spying.

"You wanted me to help Miriel," I said simply, and I turned and left.

Miriel was being fitted for her banquet gown when I returned. All of the maids were to wear white, a color that did not suit her skin, and so she was having her gown trimmed with sapphire blue and silver to distract the eye. I waited until the seamstresses had taken the gown and withdrawn, and then stopped her before she could leave the room.

"I heard from the woman in the envoy's chambers," I told her. "He's had visits from the Torstenssons and the Conradines, *and* one of the bishops. And I had word earlier from the choir boy: the Head Priest has had a visit from an envoy from Mavlon." She raised her eyebrows at me, unimpressed by the value of my information.

"Your plan won't work," she informed me, as if lecturing the deeply stupid. "You told me there's no fighting my uncle, but you don't seem to know it yourself."

"We aren't fighting him," I protested. "Not now. But we'll never be able to if we only know what he chooses to tell us."

She waited a moment, pondering that, and then she said only one word: "We?" It had all of her mother's malice, all of her uncle's coldness, and in a moment, she was gone. I heard the key turn in her bedchamber door.

Chapter 28

Whatever hatred Miriel nursed for her uncle, whatever she felt for me, or schemed for the King, none of it showed on the night of the Winter Festival. She was radiant: a girl on the cusp of womanhood, beautiful and rich, with the world at her feet. One would never know, to look at her, that she feared a violent death, that she had been bidden to ensnare the King and was doing so with the skill of a woman twice her age, that she felt terribly alone each day. She laughed merrily, exclaimed over the decorations and the other maidens' gowns, and joined her table in a dozen toasts.

The banquet was very fine, with twenty courses, each grander than the last. Each was carried out on golden platters and presented to the King, the Dowager Queen, and the Ismiri envoy. There were great haunches of venison, roasted geese, capons, fish of all kinds, pastries and breads, a wine to go with each dish. Pages carried bowls of rose-scented water for the guests to wash their fingers, and serving girls walked to and fro, handing flowers to the women; the hall was fragrant.

The King neglected his mother, leaning close to the Ismiri envoy and talking in an undertone, prone to gesture emphatically. The older man wore the tolerant smile of those who know the way of the world, but at times I saw a bemused, almost wary look on his face. He was finding that the lion cub was not a weak, sick boy, as they triumphantly reported in Ismir; nor was Garad a coddled baby. He was a young man with a kind smile, but sharp eyes and a quick mind.

I wondered if there would be any way to secure a copy of the envoy's report to his King. This man did not look fool enough to leave drafts of his letters lying about. I wondered, then, if there was any way to find out from Temar, without the assassin realizing that he was telling me. He would only tell me about the envoy unprompted if he thought it relevant to Miriel's entrapment of the King.

After dinner, the maids and young men performed a pretty dance, a masquerade with all of the men dressed in black and the young ladies dressed in white. Never good with the flowery symbolism of masquerades, I tried not to yawn as I scanned the crowd. There was no undercurrent of tension here, no sense that something awful might happen. There was avid interest, of course, divided between the young women on the one hand—I was sure I was seeing bets placed as to which one might become Queen—and the Ismiri envoy, who sat in state at the head table, given a place of honor at the King's left hand.

Having watched the King and the envoy at dinner, I watched the nobles now. The members of the oldest families in Heddred, for whom the rivalries ran deepest and the plans were laid most carefully, rubbed elbows happily enough with the minor nobles, at court to rise a little in the world with wealth and bargaining. The most ruthless of the plotters and spies smiled at each other, kin for a night. The division between plotters and pawns did not seem so wide this evening—the Winter Festival was the happiest night of the year, friends and enemies drank together, laughed together, and ate from the same dishes. Each entertainment was greeted with roars of approval.

The great hall had been transformed. From the vaulted ceiling, down to the walls, hung white silk trimmed with gold. Candles hung above the crowd like little stars, and the great pillars had been circled with pine boughs and ribbons. The servants wore armbands of white and gold over their palace livery, and the Dowager Queen was resplendent in a white gown trimmed with pearls and diamonds.

Gifts were brought out. Each noble gifted the King with something clever from their own land. From the Kleist family, it was a perfect copy of the city, made of a single piece of marble from their quarries. From the Cessors, there was a fountain shaped out of leaping fish, wrought of gold and aquamarines. The house of Orleans, who had the most grain in their land, gave the King their gift baked into a loaf of bread. There were more, pretty carved orbs of ivory, a lump of ambergris, a massive sapphire from the Duke, mined in the mountains of Voltur. Then the King called for gifts for all of us, and pages arrived to shower the tables in sweets.

Indeed, it all seemed to be going very well, until the Queen called the young women forward to be presented. They lined up, Miriel near the back, and a strange hush descended over the tables closest to the throne. There was an edge to the Queen's smile as she surveyed the girls, and the nobles, ever-watchful of their monarchs, could sense Isra's displeasure. Everyone knew that something was about to happen, something beyond pretty curtsies and kind words, but no one knew what it was. They quieted, still as rabbits hiding from a predator, and they watched.

One by one, the young women walked towards the King and the Dowager Queen, and made their curtsies. Some were dressed very fine indeed, with ropes of pearls or golden cuffs set with jewels. The King and Queen greeted each one courteously, and the Queen embraced her niece, Alexandra, and smiled warmly at Marie de la Marque. When it was Miriel's turn, I heard a murmur from the crowd. They had murmured so for Marie, and for poor Cintia Conradine, who had flushed scarlet at the attention.

"Miriel DeVere?" the Dowager Queen asked, as Miriel approached.

Miriel dipped into a curtsy and came up smiling, and the whole court held its breath. The mother lioness was coming face to face with a commoner's daughter, the rival of a favorite. Everyone knew that the King had bowed over Miriel's hand when he went to the maidens' chamber after dinner, everyone knew that he had remembered Miriel's name without ever having been introduced. The King might have picked a favorite, and the court, hungry for scandal, had not seen theater this good in years.

I drew in my own breath, sharply, when the Dowager Queen swept down the stairs, arms open to Miriel, smiling the same welcoming smile as a poisonous adder.

"Oh, my dear, you are exquisite!" she exclaimed. "And the very image of your father. What was his name…no, don't tell me, darling. Let me look at you." She tapped her mouth with her fan, and I was overcome with foreboding. I cast a glance over at the Duke, and saw his face in the impassive expression he could maintain so well.

"Edward!" the Queen exclaimed. "The eldest brother, wasn't it? That's it, yes. Oh, but you have his eyes."

"Your Grace—" The whispers started, and Miriel's color rose. I watched, anguished and—to my surprise—angry. The scandal of Miriel's mother had been forgotten, and now the Queen had found it and dragged it out into the open once more. On the dais, I saw Guy de la Marque smiling, and I knew that he had been complicit; he and Isra, together, had set themselves to find something that would discredit Miriel.

"Oh, how silly of me. I was wrong, wasn't I? Was it Henry, then? Such a charmer, that man. All the ladies of the court were in love with him." Miriel swallowed.

"Roger, Your Grace."

"Roger! Wrong twice, how embarrassing." The Queen fluttered her fan over her cheeks, as if she were blushing. Her eyes bored into Miriel's. "Well, have a lovely banquet, my dear."

"It looks like we were wrong," Temar said softly, at my shoulder. I jumped and looked over at him, and he gave a grim smile. "The boy isn't so subtle as we thought."

"And?" I did not bother to mention that I had never doubted Miriel. I was watching her as she stepped back to take her place with the other women. She was struggling to regain her composure, but her head was up and her spine straight; it would take more than a single slur to make her leave the field of battle. I saw her eyes narrowed slightly; the Queen had made an enemy this night.

"The game changes again," Temar said. "Cheers." He handed me a mug of wine, and took a deep gulp from his own.

"You're drunk," I accused him.

"Not very." He looked over at the Duke, and when I saw his strange, lost expression, I remembered just how young Temar was. "I'm still quicker with my knives than any man here."

"Go look to the Duke," I admonished him, and I took his mug. "They're going to dance now. We have to watch this." Grown ups, I thought, as I watched him make his way back to the Duke's side, were very strange. And Temar looked sad when he was drunk. I tossed the wine out on the floor and gave the cups to a serving girl, then resumed my post at one of the pillars.

The King danced first with Elizabeth Cessor, and I could see further muttered bets from the gentlemen's table. Henry Cessor looked on, well-pleased that his daughter had been singled out; he did not notice how the King's eyes strayed over Elizabeth's shoulder. Elizabeth did not notice, either, she was flushed and laughing by the end of the dance, and she simpered at the King's bow to her.

He managed one more dance—leading out poor, shy Maeve of Orleans, who blushed scarlet at his attention—before he could bear it no longer. I saw the murmurs from the crowd, the craning heads, as he led Miriel out. She held her head high, her fingertips just barely resting on his hand, and he looked at her as if she were an illusion that might fade away at any moment.

It was one of the dances that they were to have learned that day—a sprightly country dance, with kicking and clapping, but they danced it as elegantly as a pavane, Miriel's tiny feet kicking up in graceful arcs, their eyes solemn on each other's faces even when they stopped to clap. They looked as if they were holding their breath, both of them, and the courtiers around them fell silent to watch.

They were a strange pair, her dark curls and his light brown braid, her blue eyes dark and his eyes a warm brown. Despite his illness, he was as tall as any man in the banquet hall, and Miriel did not even reaching his shoulder. But they danced as if they were made for each other. Miriel made a show of looking away from him at the start of the dance, but when she finally looked into his eyes, she did not look away until the music stopped.

I wondered, unbidden, if she wished that she was staring into Wilhelm's eyes. Since she had caught the King's eye, Miriel had not once looked to the young men's table. She did not meet their eyes, she was a girl carved from ice. This act of overwhelming love was too well-done to be without a grain of truth, I thought—and was it the King's kindness that she loved, or was it Wilhelm's quick mind?

As the music drew to a close, courtiers burst into applause, and Miriel looked around at them as if she had quite forgotten they were there. She blushed and turned to curtsy to the King, and he bowed to her, drawing her up to say something I could not make out; his lips barely moved. Without even a pause, he turned and offered his hand to Marie de la Marque, and Miriel once more moved to the edge of the dance floor.

I met Temar's eyes across the crowd, and gave a small, triumphant nod, and he nodded back, one eyebrow raised. *What did he say?* he mouthed at me, and I shrugged. *I'll ask*, I mouthed back, and he nodded. From Miriel's small, self-satisfied smile, however, I was fairly sure that I knew, and I was also sure—my stomach flopped—that there was going to be more sneaking around, and more lies. By the end of the next dance, I had already started practicing protestations of innocence in my head.

For the time being, I settled back to watch Miriel enchant the court. I cast a look, half-worried and half-amused, at Isra, and saw that she was far from enchanted. She had settled back in her throne and was looking about the court as if she would banish every girl who stood between Marie de la Marque and the King.

When I saw a shadow behind Isra's throne, I nearly cried out, thinking that the Duke was correct and there were assassins ready to strike. Then I saw that it was Guy de la Marque, accompanied by the Head Priest. They both bent close to her ear for a whispered conversation, and the three of them looked first to Marie, confident and lovely in her white gown, and then over to Miriel, who was being drawn into the formation for a circle dance. They looked at her coldly, and, with an odd, dizzy feeling, I realized that the Duke had been correct all along: there were people at this court who would not blink at the thought of killing a fourteen-year-old girl.

And all of them, it seemed, were the Duke's enemies.

We returned to bed late that night, and Miriel was too quiet, too smug. I had been given no opening to speak to her about the King's words, for she had not deigned to respond to any of my opening gambits. But, I reasoned, there was only one thing that could have her looking so pleased with herself.

And I was right. Sometime after midnight that night, the bed creaked, and my eyes snapped open. I remained motionless, barely breathing, and then I heard the rustle of blankets from Miriel's bed. Her maidservant was snoring, undisturbed, and I heard the whisper of Miriel's gown on the floor, the faint sound of her palm on the post of the bed, and the creak of floorboards. I gave a silent prayer of thanks that it was not an assassin, and I turned my head very quietly, and saw her silhouetted in the dim light. She was tying a robe over her nightgown.

I did not say anything, I only sat up, and she looked over at me sharply. Just as carefully as she had been, mindful of the maid, I levered myself out of my cot and began to pull on my clothes. Miriel stood watching me, and when I went to the door and opened it for her, she went through without a word. We passed through her privy chamber in silence, and then into the outer room, where the dying fire glowed red.

"What are you doing?" she asked, when I went to the door.

"Going with you," I said steadily.

"You're to stay here," she ordered me. She drew her robe around herself and curled her toes against the cold floor. Her hair gleamed in the dim light.

"You know I can't do that," I said wearily.

"I won't have you telling my uncle where I've been!" she whispered fiercely.

"I won't, and even if I would, me staying here won't help with that," I retorted. "Anyone could guess where you're going." She wavered. "And I know where he stations guards," I added

---

209

persuasively. "But can't we just go back to bed? You've been doing so well without this."

"Fool," she said simply. She slid the deadbolt back and lifted the latch carefully, and I raised my eyebrows. She moved more quietly than she should know how to do. She had been watching me. She peered down the hallway, and then turned back to me. "Tell me where the guards are," she ordered.

"I can't tell you that. I really can't!" I protested, at her glare. "It's patrols. You see the first group, and then you need to time it right."

I could see her warring with herself. "And you can get me past them without them seeing me?"

"If you listen to me," I said warningly. She nodded, then dropped the latch very quietly and beckoned me towards her. When I approached, she grabbed my collar and pulled me close.

"You won't tell my uncle I was ever away from my rooms," she said fiercely. "If you come with me now, you have to promise."

As she needed me to come with her in order to make her way through the palace unseen, she could hardly dictate conditions, and what use was a promise when we were surrounded by people like the Duke? But none of that would help my case, and I could not take the chance of her being caught—or, worse, being attacked. And I had no intention of telling the Duke anything.

"I promise," I said simply. "But you had better think of a good reason, in case he finds out somehow."

"Mmm." She peered down the hallway again. "Alright, show me."

Chapter 29

It was not far; Miriel directed me to take her to the cellars, and so we crept down back stairs to the kitchen, then down from there. To my surprise, she listened to my directions, and used taps on my shoulders to direct me instead of speaking. When I looked over at her, I could see her lips moving; she was practicing her greetings.

He was there already when we arrived, sitting on a barrel in one of the wine cellars to our own building. Over Miriel's whispered protests, I had insisted on going into the cellar first, in case this was some sort of trap. I saw a flash of fear in his eyes before he recognized me, and I bowed deeply. He raised his eyebrows to see me, but gave me a courteous enough nod.

I listened carefully, but heard no one else. He seemed to be alone, and I beckoned Miriel down the stairs. This seemed like a dream, I thought. I was a peasant girl, but I was standing only feet away from the King himself. We were children, but were meeting secretly in the night like spies and mercenaries.

He swallowed when he saw her. I stepped aside to let her pass, and they walked up to each other, her clutching her robe closed at her neck, him watching her like he still feared she was a dream.

"You came," he said brokenly, and my heart twisted. I wanted nothing more than to look away. I should not see this. But my eyes were fixed on their faces.

Miriel smiled. "*You* came," she said, her eyes very bright.

"I had to see you again." He held his hand out and after a moment's hesitation, she reached out and put her hand in his. He bowed over it, and then he drew her over to the barrel where he had been sitting. "I'm afraid there's only one seat," he said. "I could lift you if you wanted."

"I can't sit while you're standing," Miriel protested. "That's not right. You're the King." He grimaced, and then he put his hands on her waist and lifted her onto the barrel. She stared down at him shyly, and he smiled.

There was an awkward silence. It seemed that he could find nothing to say, and so it was Miriel who broke their reverie. She said the words no other girl her age would have thought to speak:

"This can only come to nothing, can't it?" His head jerked up and he stared at her, stricken. Miriel's lips parted, and then she pressed them together and looked away. Her hands were clasped in her lap, and they trembled. She took a deep breath. "You were so kind to me, and I thought...I heard...but I know it could never be."

"What could never be?" He reached out to take her hand. "Please, tell me." He expected tears, and he was clearly unprepared for her to turn on him, eyes blazing.

"Do you know what it is like?" Miriel demanded fiercely. "To see what I wish for most snatched away from my grasp? To know that no matter what I learn, what I think, none of it will ever matter? I see the troubles in Heddred, and I have ideas—I can think of ways to solve things, but no one will listen to me because I am only a child. And when I am a woman, my uncle will choose a marriage for me, and I will become nothing. All I have ever wanted was for someone to see *me*, myself." He stared at her. He had not expected any of this. I stared, too, amazed—amazed at her daring, at her instinct, and also at the ring of truth I heard in her voice. I did not know where the line was, anymore, between true and false.

"I had heard that you...you wanted more than wars and intrigue. I wanted to meet you, and then—I did, and you truly saw me." There was a sob in her voice. "The other men, they speak of nothing but hunting and clothes and titles, and to find a man who might have listened...and then to have him be you, someone I could never hope—" She squeezed her eyes shut.

"My uncle will choose a marriage for me," she repeated. "And your mother will choose one for you. It has been a waking nightmare, to see you always amongst the other women, and know that you must choose one of them. There are a dozen with better connections than I have, and we must both marry to further our families. You must marry for peace. And so this can never be, because any friendship we have must turn into love, and then my heart will break when I must leave you."

I expected him to withdraw, to protest that he had had not thoughts yet of love or marriage between them, but he shook his head and leaned closer to her. Miriel had seen through the glamor of the crown, and she had known what note to strike. She did not seem to play on her beauty—though I knew that every curl was placed just so, that every gesture had been practiced a thousand times or more—and she did not simper and curtsy. She spoke of the future of Heddred, she spoke of dreams for peace; Garad could not help but be drawn in.

"No," he protested. "Please—look at me." She raised a tearstained face. "Do you know, I heard your name spoken by the young men of the court? It's true. My cousin Wilhelm is quite taken with you." She went very still, but he did not notice. He smiled up at her, on her perch. "They spoke of how intelligent you were, how charming, how you were kind to everyone. I knew I must meet you, and it was fate that led us to meet in that hallway. I was captivated from the first moment I saw you." He reached out to take her hand, and she drew it back away from him. I tried to mute my indrawn breath.

"This will ruin both of us," she told him. Her blue eyes were wide, almost luminous against her pale face.

"No, no, it cannot. I would never ask anything dishonorable of you," he promised her. "We are still almost children, aren't we? Although we are both to be married soon." She nodded, her head turned away from him. "But don't you see?" he asked her. "Becoming a wife is like becoming a King."

She looked back at him, her lips parted in genuine confusion, and he looked up at her with pain in his eyes. "I am nothing, my Lady. I am only blood and bone that they will follow, and they do not even follow me. They thought I would die, and before they even thought to grieve for me, they were planning how they would rule the kingdom after my death. To them, I am an inconvenience, a boy who did not die so that they could take my place, a boy who is nearly old enough that they will find their power much diminished.

"I never dared to dream of my future, but when it looked like I might recover, I began to hope. I thought that I could bring the country to a golden age, a peaceful age. I could make this land more prosperous, bind the nations of the earth together. But that is not how it is—to rule is to have a pit of dogs fighting over scraps, and any one of them could turn on me at any moment. I had no allies who could share such a vision—until you.

"No one listens to what I might think about how to solve the problems Heddred faces. When I became King, I became no longer a person. Now, I think all they want of me is for me to let them rule in my stead, and get them an heir. And of course, all of them have daughters that they push forward." He bowed his head for a moment.

"What I lack are those I can trust. My cousin Wilhelm has been my friend since I was small, but now they try to separate us, they do not trust him for his blood. He is almost forbidden to talk to me. I have disappeared, they see only the crown." He clasped her hand in his, and this time Miriel did not pull away. "Please, my Lady," he said. "You were the first one to look at me and see the man under the crown. I have almost no one, I cannot face life without friends, and I have precious few who wish to see me live. Your King asks you—will you be a friend to him?"

Her face fell. "I wish that I could say yes," she whispered. "I do." He stared at her, wide-eyed, as she shook her head. "But I cannot," she said. "It would be to compromise you, and how could I do that to my King?"

"No one need know," he protested.

"They will find out," she warned him.

"We will be discreet," he assured her. "And if they should come upon us, what will they see? Two friends talking, nothing more." He craned to look up into her face. "Would you wall yourself up, my Lady, away from one who understands what you see, and what you fear?"

She shook her head. "I..." I knew that for a moment she was beyond coquetry, truly she longed to tell him what she feared.

As she weighed her words, there was a rustle from the dark, and my dagger was in my hand faster than thought. It was only a young man, sandy-haired and blue-eyed, who emerged from beneath the stairs. I raised my eyebrows as I recognized Wilhelm Conradine.

"The guard is changing soon," he said to the King. "We have to go now. My Lady." He bowed to Miriel, his eyes sliding away from the sight of her sitting, hand-clasped with the King. She stared wide-eyed at him. For a moment, caught by surprise, she forgot herself and I could see the turmoil behind her eyes. It was gone by the time the King turned back from his cousin.

"Wilhelm helped me to come to you tonight," the King told her. "Tell me I can meet you again? We can talk. I would hear your thoughts on the envoy." She managed a smile, and it was not all coquetry. She fairly glowed that he was asking her advice.

"How can I say no?"

"Indeed, I hope you cannot." His eyes were very warm as he lifted her down from the barrel and bowed over her hand. At the door, he looked back, and when he saw me peering into the darkness, he grinned.

"The passageways run all over the palace complex," he said lightly. "Didn't you know?"

"No," I admitted. I wondered if even Temar knew about these. The King smiled again.

"Keep her safe," he told me, and he bowed once more and was gone, leaving us to sneak back to her rooms, where we slipped into bed silently and waited for morning.

I, at least, slept little. I could hardly think of anything save the King's words, and Miriel's clever responses. Her dances, her curtsies to the court, I had seen—but that was a moment only, like glimpsing a play from the edge of the stage. In the cellars the night before, I had seen Miriel's abilities, and I knew now that they exceeded even my expectations. She was masterful.

And she was not such a fool as to appear smug in front of the Duke. He had been well-pleased at Miriel's dance with the King, and had been taken the Dowager Queen's malice as a back-handed compliment. When the Head Priest preached on the sin of adultery and the duty of honoring one's parents at the next service, I saw the Duke's rare, grim smile. The noblemen complimented him, insincerely, on Miriel's good fortune, and he smiled insincerely back. Everyone had seen that although the King danced with every young woman, it had been an empty courtesy, save when he danced with Miriel.

However much Miriel claimed not to have noticed a thing, the girls still asked her. The men spoke of it in the halls, and I heard from Temar that the odds on Miriel were now 2:1, above Marie de la Marque at 3:1 and Maeve of Orleans at 7:2. I laughed, not believing him, until he showed me a scrap of paper with Miriel's name on it. Miriel was the favorite of the moment, the rising star in the court, and her kindness and wit were much remarked upon.

Still, the Duke was not easy in his mind. Royal favor attracted enemies, like flies to carrion, and Miriel had risen in favor even faster than he had dared to hope. Her enemies were massing: the Dowager Queen was reported to be meeting near-constantly with the Head Priest and with Guy de la Marque, and the girls of the maids' chamber were more spiteful than ever. A week after the

Winter Festival, the Duke called us to his study and considered Miriel.

"I would have waited to put ourselves out in the open like this," he said. "We can play it that we've no more plans than any other family, but to have caught Isra's eye already is to attract trouble. If she manages to arrange a marriage before his preference for Miriel is set, we have little way to bring him back." He tapped the desktop with his fingers and looked at the far wall, thinking hard.

"Continue your studies," he ordered Miriel. "I will arrange for the King to have a meeting with you in a few weeks' time, so that he will not forget you, and I will give you instructions on how to behave. You may go."

We left; I had only narrowly avoided saying that Miriel knew how to behave with the King, and that his preference for her was very well set, indeed. There had been no more public encounters, and so there should be no reason for me to think that the King even remembered Miriel's name.

I knew that he did, of course. In the week after their first meeting, they had met twice more, Wilhelm Conradine and myself standing in awkward attendance at the corner of the room and saying nothing to one another. What did a commoner say to the last heir of the former ruling house, when the present King was having a clandestine meeting with an unmarried noblewoman not ten feet from us? Clearly, nothing. I spent a good deal of time staring at my feet and trying not to notice that Wilhelm stared at Miriel as if she were a goddess.

The fact that the King and Miriel only ever spoke of politics only added to the sense of the ridiculous. She had been well taught, and she was the King's match in any of a dozen topics. It was like Miriel to consider a political puzzle and quote philosophy, or cite a historical example, or even mention theology. The King was eager to speak of trade and of the rise of the merchant class, although he frowned when he spoke of the uprising in the south.

What was the strangest to me was not that the King had kept his word that the meetings would be honorable—itself noteworthy—but how much joy they seemed to bring to Miriel. I had been wearily impressed with her seeming fascination during the King's discussions with her, watching her animated gestures and intent expressions with the jaded eye of a courtier, and I had been genuinely surprised to realize that Miriel had spoken the truth when she said that she had ideas on how best to rule Heddred.

Now, with someone listening to her ideas and offering his own for her consideration, Miriel had blossomed. Her eyes might be shadowed from lack of sleep, but when she sank into repose, there was a half-smile on her lips. I often caught her staring off into the distance, and I knew that she was thinking of the King and of good points to make in their next debate.

More and more, I wondered if she might feel something for him beyond ambition, and if so, if it was anything more than the intoxicating feeling of attention after so much neglect. Her appetite for a partner, a match, a mind as quick as her own, had been whetted by her conversations with Wilhelm. Now she believed with all her heart that the King, brilliant in his own right, was the man she sought. There was no denying the leap of genuine pleasure on her face when she first saw him each night.

The King had been delighted to meet a girl who could match him, and Miriel, in turn, was learning the joy of speaking with a man to whom politics and philosophy were intertwined, living subjects. Miriel had been taught to scheme, and her education had been no more than adornment—she had been told to leave her bookish ways behind. Now she was learning that there could be a place at Court for her love of knowledge.

But whenever I caught her in an unguarded moment, openly happy, I felt a twinge of disquiet. There were a thousand dangers in the court, I told myself. I should worry about a sly smile, or a threatening insult. Heddred was poised to slide into war; there were rumors of peasant uprisings in the Norstrung Provinces. But somehow, Miriel's happiness seemed the most precarious of the balances I watched each day. It was going wrong, sliding somehow into darkness.

I told myself that if I suspected that the man she truly wanted was not the King, but instead the King's cousin, well—it was neither my place, nor in the interest of my faction, to tell the King that. And it was better for all of us if Miriel could truly believe it, and be happy—for happy she was, and it was the first time I had seen her so. I could not bring myself to shatter that beautiful illusion. It was too precarious a balance, just too close to the surface for me to mention it.

Certainly, Miriel never looked over to where Wilhelm sat next to me, his head bowed. She did her best to forget his presence in the darkened cellar, and even when they must make their bows as he left with the King, she barely acknowledged him. If one was looking closely, they would notice that she never met his eyes. They would see that when he bowed over her hand, their fingers did not touch—they hovered, barely apart; his lips touched only the air over her hand. But the King did not notice, he had eyes only for the serene beauty of Miriel's face, and her face gave away nothing.

And yet, I knew without a doubt that someday it must come tumbling down. I could only hope that, by the time it did, she had a crown on her head and a son in the cradle.

Chapter 30

Once more, I walked the long road back to gaining Miriel's trust. I had never apologized for my cruel words to her, just as she never apologized for any of the taunts and insults she made. Neither of us spoke of our role in the palace, or of how much resentment we carried for the other, who was our jailor and our companion all in one. I could not look at her but that I saw the reason I was here, in danger, and I assumed that Miriel could not look at me without being reminded of her uncle's plans. We watched each other in wary silence.

The year turned, and, in the dark and cold of the new months, Miriel's fifteenth birthday came with a little feast in her rooms, and gifts of new gowns and jewelry. The maidens feted her with a special dance, those who liked her wishing her well and giving her little gifts, Marie de la Marque and her faction smiling tightly and wishing her a joyous birthday. Marie was much diminished, and she could only try to accept her status with as much grace as Miriel had shown.

A month later, my own birthday came and went with barely an acknowledgement. No one other than Roine even knew when my birthday was—few enough peasants could name the day of their birth—and so I had only a little fruit pie and Roine's whispered, "Happy Birthday." She gave me a little carving of a mountain range, knowing how I missed home, and I came back to Miriel's rooms and put it on my tiny shelf, next to my clothes.

"What's that?" Miriel asked sharply.

"A gift from Roine. For my birthday." I looked over at her, but she had already looked away. I thought that was the end of it, but the next day, I found a new leather belt lying on my bed. Miriel refused to be thanked for it, saying sweetly that of course I needed a new belt—could I not see what a mess I looked? I bit my tongue, but I did not forget the incident. I found myself turning it over and over in my head, quite unable to figure out the constant puzzle that was my mistress. It seemed like, whenever the pieces came close to coming together, they split once more and shifted around.

"Do you trust her?" Roine asked one day, while I was grinding leaves for an ointment. One of the cooks had cut his hand quite badly, and Roine had offered to make him a salve that would keep the wound from festering. Having declared this a learning opportunity, she was overseeing me as I worked.

"No," I admitted.

"But you work to gain her trust."

"Yes."

"And she does nothing to earn yours."

"Yes." I shot her a quizzical look, and then squinted at the ointment.

"Why should she not work to gain your trust?" Roine persisted, and I paused for a moment, considering the question. Such a thought would never have occurred to me. Miriel had insisted on doing any number of dangerous things, and I did not trust her in the slightest not to sneak out in the night, or do something that would lead her uncle to kill both of us in his rage.

"It's different for nobles," I said, after a moment.

"It is not," Roine said sharply. "Nobles are no more than ordinary men. You should not exempt them from common courtesy." I raised my eyebrows and focused on the leaves. All I had meant was that there was always the chance that I might one day run away and be free of this poisonous court, and Miriel did not truly have that choice. If I did not trust her, I could leave—if she did not trust me, she must live in fear that she would die violently. But Roine never seemed to hear anything I said about myself and Miriel, but that she must tell me I was no less a person than my liege. Sometimes, I wondered if Roine was trying to sour me towards Miriel, so that I might take her advice and run away from the court. Between this thought, and trying to concentrate on grinding the herbs, I forgot to guard my tongue.

"So populist. You should talk to Miriel," I joked. "Give her fodder for her next debate with the King." The moment the words were out of my mouth, I froze. Roine was staring at me. "Oh, it's nothing," I said, blushing and cursing myself. "Don't look at me like that."

"A nothing that the Duke would thrash you for?" she asked, keenly, and I nodded. "Has he had her?" she queried, and I stared at her, openmouthed.

"For shame," I said, blushing. "They're children. They only talk."

"Children who might well be married by now," Roine said, shrugging. "I hear one of the maids was just betrothed."

"Evelyn DeVere," I said, naming Miriel's cousin. For all that their fathers had been brothers, and they shared the same curly hair and pointed chins, one would never know that there was the slightest connection between the girls. Evelyn hated Miriel with a passion, and Miriel knew better than to cause a scene with the noble half of her family. Her claim to nobility was slim enough. "To Piter Nilson's son," I added, though I doubted Roine had any interest.

Roine was, indeed, paying no attention to my words. Her eyes were narrowed.

"What did you say about populist sentiments?" she asked, and I felt a twist of fear. Then my urge to tell someone won out, and I leaned close.

"She... sympathizes."

"With the rebellion." Roine's face was a study. "The Duke of Voltur's heir sympathizes with the rebellion."

"Yes," I said, unable to find any other way to say it.

"They tried to kill her," Roine said. I felt the familiar anger, but a touch of vindication.

"That's what I told her."

"And she said?" I sighed. We had spoken of it earlier in the day, Miriel and I, her wanting to share her newfound learning with me, and me wanting nothing to do with it. What was, I saw now, another peace offering, had turned instead into another fight. I swallowed. I still could not believe that Miriel's fascination with the rebellion was anything but folly.

"She spoke nonsense. She said she wanted to know why someone would do that. She wanted to understand what it was that man believed in. And now she's been reading..." I dropped my voice. "I can't tell you what. Forbidden books. And she agrees with them." The disbelief was evident in my voice, and Roine smiled.

"And you do not?"

"I don't agree with killing children, anyway," I snapped back, and her face fell at once.

"No," she agreed. "That is a very great crime. A damnable crime." She looked down into her tea for a moment. "But you're sure?" she asked softly. "About Miriel."

"Yes," I said, still moody. "She's crazy."

"She's not crazy," Roine said. She shook her head. "She's very honorable, that girl."

"Honorable?" Honorable was for knights and Kings, not scheming girls. Or crazy girls, I thought spitefully.

"Think about it." Roine smiled, but the smile was strained. "If you would leave me, Catwin, I need to pray." I nodded, bemused, and then realized that I had seen the sadness in her eyes when I had reminded her of the assassination attempt. She looked so sorrowful that I reached out and squeezed her hand.

"I'm alright," I reminded her. "I'm okay, no one else has come for us." She nodded.

"Yes," she agreed. The sadness did not leave her eyes. "I will see you tomorrow for your lesson, Catwin. Please be safe." I could see the tears in her eyes, and I did not know what to say. She did not get up from the table so that I could hug her, so I squeezed her hand once more and left. As I closed the door behind me, I could see through the crack in it that she was kneeling before her little altar, her head bowed. I felt a strange twisting in my chest, and realized that it was grief. Roine was bearing her worry and her sadness as best she could, and I would not heed her and leave this place.

But for the first time, I knew my own mind. I knew that no matter what it cost me, and what it cost Roine, this was where I must be. I knew that no matter how many times Roine begged me to go, I would stay, and, for the first time in my life, I made my way to the little chapel in the servants' quarters in our building, and I stared up at the
icons of the seven gods for a very long time, the candlelight shifting and sliding as tears welled up in my eyes and rolled down my cheeks.

This is what a prophecy is. The thought was whisper-soft, I could not have known if it was mine, or some wisdom from the gods. *Fate lies heavy on you, and the road you walk will not be easy.*

Not a few days later, I was shocked to hear Roine's sentiments from Miriel's mouth. We were in the wine cellar once more, Wilhelm and I perched on two barrels that had been left by the stairs while Miriel and the King sat a discreet distance away. The King had come directly from a meeting of the Council, and had his head sunk into his hands.

"It's one thing after another," he said miserably. "I managed to undo Guy's error, the tensions with Ismir are finally subsiding. I had thought the rebels had gone away, too, but now a note from Jacces, demanding...insane things. What do these rebels want? I am a fair King, I have never levied high taxes or taken their crops. They can have no complaints. And do you know," he looked incredulous, "the High Priest spoke to me, and bid me to listen to them. Senile old man. I don't know why my mother keeps him around."

"Does your mother support the rebels' cause?" Miriel looked surprised, and I admired the question. It would be quite a strange thing, for the Dowager Queen to support rebels against her son— but the King shook his head.

"No. I don't think so. I can't imagine so. He came to speak to me alone. He said—you'll laugh—he said that the early teachings of the Gods were very populist. Fool."

"They just want to be heard," Miriel said gently. "They are people who are learned, they know what they wish for from their lives, and they wonder why they cannot make it come to pass."

I froze, but she seemed quite unaffected by fear. It did her no good. The King looked at her blankly; he was far from pleased at her words. "Well, then they should speak to their lords. I don't know why Nilson is still here—the marriage, I suppose. But he should be back, calming his people. He should remind them of their duty to the crown. They subsided once, it would be easy enough to calm them if they knew their lord was there, watching them." For the first time, I heard a petulant note in his voice, and from Miriel's faint frown, I gathered that she did as well. But she tried to calm him.

"Perhaps they wonder why Nilson has the power to change their lives, but they do not," she explained.

"That's how the world works," the King said flatly. There are lords, and there are commoners. The lords rule the commoners, and I rule the lords. How else could it be?"

Miriel looked for a moment as if she had been slapped. I saw a dozen thoughts flash behind her eyes, but she only bowed her head and nodded. Only a few moments later, she mimed a yawn and the King, once more solicitous, told her that she must rest. She was trembling as we snuck back to the room, and in the darkness of the public chamber, I paused.

"Did you get that from Roine?" I asked her. "About wanting to be heard, and wanting to change their lives?" She hesitated, then nodded. The light from the hall illuminated the line of her jaw.

"She said that I shouldn't tell the King," she said. "That he wouldn't like it. But I thought, normally he's so thoughtful. I thought he would find it interesting." I gave a silent sigh at Roine, who should have known better than to tell Miriel not to do something.

"I think...it doesn't fit with his plan for a golden age," I said slowly.

"What could be more enlightened than this?" Miriel asked, with the limpid simplicity of the privileged.

"You're joking."

"I'm not," she said. She was utterly serious. "Have you ever thought about it, Catwin? Did you read the book?"

"No. And I knew from the start it was a mistake to get it for you," I muttered, and she pinched me on the arm.

"Don't talk to me like that," she said sharply. "And you think about it. Really think about it."

"*You* think about it," I whispered back, hearing my voice come out strained. "Miriel, that was dangerous, what you did. If he turns on you, you get nothing. If he suspects you of being a sympathizer, he could have you killed."

"He wouldn't do that," she said, but she said it uncertainly. She was very quiet as we snuck back to bed, and for the next few days I saw her mulling over what had happened. She and the King had never disagreed before, and she could not seem to believe what had happened.

It was painful, to watch her. She tried to speak to him of the principles of the rebellion, but he would not listen, he would not be led, he refused even to consider the High Priest's point of theology. At my side, Wilhelm would nod at her points, draw breath as if to speak. He was her partner in this argument; but he could not intervene here, and the King refused to hear her.

"Can you not let it be?" he snapped at her, once. He was apologetic at once, but she had learned her lesson. She did not speak of it again, only looked hurt, like a dog that has been cuffed about the ears and cannot understand why.

She did not speak of her disappointment to me, but I thought I could understand it, a little. I had been thinking on the King's quest for a Golden Age more and more over the past days, as I heard the him expound on his dreams for the future. He had never expected to live, to have any legacy at all except as the Boy King, tragically dead at a young age. His mother had coddled him, she had not told him that he must plan for the future.

Now, he did so with obsessive focus. His grandfather's coup had left the country unstable, and the nobles hungry for power. He was right to call them fighting dogs, for they circled one another and fairly growled, no more dignified than animals. The King was determined that the peace with Ismir, won at such a high cost, should not be thrown away. He had sent for the Ismiri envoy against the advice of all his Council—save the Duke, who had wisely absented himself from that meeting—and he was driven to prove that he had been right to do so.

An uprising in the south, aimed not at him but at the whole of the nobility, was nothing he wanted in his kingdom. It meant that the common people doubted him, they did not long for the golden age he had promised to give them. His pride was hurt, and there was something more to it as well, the siren call of power that had taken his mother's good sense, and de la Marque's.

Miriel no longer smiled in repose. I thought she looked sad all the time, even when dancing. Had she noticed the same thing—that the King seemed to care less about a golden age for the happiness and peace of Heddred now, and more for the fact that he would be remembered as a great king? He spoke of Evan III and his great buildings, Wilhelm IV and the libraries and ports. He wanted to know how he would be remembered.

"Why *can't* you let it be?" I asked her one evening. We had just returned to our rooms, and I put out a hand to keep her in the main room, away from the sleeping maid. I had seen the faint frown on her face as Garad expounded on peace and prosperity, and the folly of rebellion. If only I could unravel that secret, I thought, I could make her stop talking to him about it. I could stop the constant arguments that were so painful to watch. She tilted her head to the side.

"I don't know," she said finally. "Well. I do. I can't find words for it." She stared down at the table, her lips pursed in thought. "It's the first thing I've ever believed in. It's like being drunk. It's..." Her lips curved in an involuntary smile. She was soft, her gaze faraway. For a moment she had forgotten herself. "It's like being in love. With an idea."

I said nothing. I only bit my lip. I did not know how to argue her out of this, and she leaned forward across the table.

"It could be wonderful," she said. "Roine was right, you know. Not all nobles are wise, not all of them take good care of their tenants." I drew back; I did not want this conversation. It was a danger I could have done without. Sudden fear made me speak sharply.

"Well, you had better not let him hear you say that," I said roundly. "You know he doesn't like it."

All at once she remembered whom she was talking to. The wondering girl was gone. Her face closed off, she looked away from me. Before her eyes left mine, I saw something different in her face, something I had never before seen: she was betrayed. She had spoken to him of her ideas and he had brushed them aside, and because he was the King, she must yield.

Miriel had woven such a lovely fantasy that she and the King could be equals together, sharing ideas and ruling Heddred justly, that she had begun to believe the fairy tale herself. She had forgotten, for a few days, that ensnaring the King was her purpose, and she had viewed it as a joy, and half fallen in love with him. Now she saw the man she had idolized for nothing more than a man, and unlike other women, who could turn away when they wished, she was bound to continue on.

I had known that Miriel hated to lose, and now I saw her realize that, in success, she faced a life where she would lose every single day, and be expected to smile throughout. It had not been so bitter to walk past all of the other men, Wilhelm among them, when she thought that she had found the finest of them. Wilhelm had taught her that there were those who might view her as an equal, those she might adore for their own sake alone; then, she had met the King, and she had done her best to believe that he was one of those men.

No matter what I had wished, she had realized her mistake before she had the crown on her head, before she had a son and heir in the cradle. She was not surrounded by the comforts of a Queen—no, she must still devote her time and her skill and her beauty to attaining something that brought her no joy. She had no escape. She was bound to the very man who had disappointed her, and she could not think what to do.

Chapter 31

The news came in the very dead of night by messenger, a man who had been so long in the saddle that he seemed half-dead. He gasped out his message from horseback before collapsing onto the cobblestones, and the moment the news was known, pages were sent flying to wake the members of the Council, to wake even the King himself.

I knew none of this. I knew of his presence almost before any of the great men, but I knew only that a man had ridden hard from my homeland with urgent news. The rider was from Voltur, and the moment the guards had seen his standard, they had sent for the Duke. Temar sent a runner for me, not knowing the nature of the danger, and I was awake and crouched in the darkness by the outer door within minutes.

"What is it?" Miriel asked, sleepily, from the door to her privy chamber. I could hear her companion's snores even from here; I thought briefly that someone should make sure Miriel had a better chaperone, and then realized that it was better for the woman to be a deep sleeper. Best for as few people as possible to notice Miriel's nightly disappearances.

"Nothing," I said. "Go back to sleep for now." To my surprise, she did not nod and disappear back into her bedroom, to nestle under the covers. She wrapped her robe tighter over her nightgown and came to sit near me on the floor, tucking her feet up under her to keep away the cold. As I had told her always to do, she sat with me between her and the door.

"Can I light a candle?" she whispered.

"Best not," I said uncertainly, after a moment. "I don't know what's going on."

In the dim light that filtered under the door, I saw her nod. She did not get up and go to one of the chairs by the fireplace, nor back her bed, but sat quietly beside me on the cold floor instead.

We huddled in the darkness together for a few minutes, listening to the commotion in the halls. The tension made a knot in my belly, and I focused to keep my breathing deep and even. Enough tension to help me move quickly if I needed to, not so much that I would falter. I wished Temar would come to tell us what was happening. We heard more shouts from the courtyards, more footsteps pounding down the hallways, and I grew more and more fearful.

"Roine says there's a prophecy about you," Miriel said unexpectedly, out of the dark.

I looked over at her. She had clasped her hands and sat with her head bowed. I felt my usual flicker of grudging respect for her, sitting quietly in fear instead of crying. I wondered what news she was steeling herself against, as she waited beside me in the dark. What news could there possibly be from Voltur? I reckoned that she was thinking of the same two possibilities that I had come up with: the border had been overrun, or the Lady was dead. Perhaps both.

Then I remembered her question, and I frowned. I did not want to answer her. I felt a twinge of self-consciousness that I should speak of this, so personal, so close to ridiculous, with her. The dreams of it had been growing more frequent; I knew my mother's face perfectly, I could speak every word of my parents' conversation by memory; I did not want to bring the dream into the waking world. But I knew what it would mean to Miriel to be able to talk of something else, think of anything other than the messenger. I hunched my shoulders and tried to find words.

"My mother said when I was born, that I had been born to be betrayed. She said that when I was, there would be an ending, and the balance would tip." Here in the dark, with the shouts of the guards and the clank of weapons, with the terrible fear that something had gone terribly wrong, the words felt less ridiculous than they ever had before. I added defiantly, "Then she gave me away, because she didn't want to raise me." Perhaps if I said it, Miriel could take no joy in mocking me for it. But she did not respond to that at all, and she did not snort in derision at the prophecy, as I had expected.

"Do you believe it?" she asked instead.

I opened my mouth to say what I always said out loud: that no, of course I did not believe it, it was only childbed fever that had caused my mother to speak nonsense, but this time I could not say the words. Close to sleep, close to fear, I admitted the truth to myself.

"I don't know," I said slowly. The strangeness of the conversation loosened my tongue. "Do you know, I used to feel special, like I would wake up in a fairytale and be a great hero. But now..." She just waited, quietly. "I don't know if I want to be in a story anymore," I admitted. "It's like I am already, and I don't think I like it. And what would it mean if it were true? What would it mean for you?"

I asked without thinking, and she bit her lip. "Like driftwood in a river," she said dreamily. "I'd rather be right at your side than in your path." I looked over at her, and she shrugged and pulled her robe tighter around her. Her eyes glittered, and she said, almost a breath it was so soft, "Sometimes I think this is all a dream, and I'll wake up and be back home."

It was so close to my own thoughts, and my own hopes, that I could not find anything to say. I was still puzzling over it when we heard footsteps in the hall, slowing as they approached our door. I motioned her back, and she slipped over to the window, crouching down where she might run and lift the shutters and jump, or duck behind one of the chairs. I nodded to her and slipped into the shadows near the door. As a knock sounded, I tensed, my palm very sweaty against the haft of my dagger.

"Catwin?" Temar's voice. "News from Ismir. Miriel is safe. You should come with me."

I stayed silent for a moment, warring with myself. I always did, now, with Temar. I knew I was playing him, and I might never know if he had figured out the game, too. Was it a trap? Was he trying to lure me away from Miriel? But the messenger had been real enough—

"Open it," Miriel said softly, pushing me towards the door. I drew back the deadbolt and let the door creak open. Temar poked his head around.

"What is it?" Miriel asked, standing up from behind the chair. Temar raised his eyebrows at her as he slid into the room. "Nothing that need concern you," he said, mildly. "You may return to bed, my lady. The Duke has sent men to guard the door."

Miriel did not even glance at me, nor did I flick my gaze sideways at her. We both looked to Temar with the open, biddable faces of youth. "Thank you," Miriel said, with the brilliant smile she directed at male servants, and she yawned as she walked back to her bedchamber, slipping off her robe. It was only when Temar had preceded me into the hall that I saw her look back over her shoulder and shoot me a look under her thick lashes, and I smiled back at her, one conspirator to another.

Temar would play his game, as the Duke bid. And we would play ours.

"What is the news?" I asked Temar, as I trotted down the hallway at his side. He spared a glance at me and held his tongue as we passed a group of servants, chattering excitedly.

"The heir to Ismir has been killed," he said shortly.

I tried to remember, and scraped a name out of my memory. "Vaclav?"

Even now, he took pride in my learning. He gave me a flash of a smile. "Yes. Brother to…"

"He has no brother," I said, frowning at him to show that I knew it was a trick question. "Eight sisters, Marjeta and…I can't remember all of them. But it's his cousin, Kasimir, who will inherit now. Yes?"

"Very good. Now tell me what the Council should advise the King." His voice had dropped to a murmur as we began to navigate the wide corridors that led towards the heart of the palace, to the council chambers.

"I'm going to see the Council?" He looked at me; now was a time for lessons. I sighed, and thought. "Wouldn't it be best simply to send condolences to King Dusan?" Temar said nothing. I thought for a few moments, saying nothing even when Temar stopped outside a side door into the Council chamber. He watched me as I thought. Finally, I said, "They'll be worried that Kasimir wants war."

"Yes," Temar said shortly.

"But why should he want war?" I asked. "Trade is beginning to prosper. The war cost them most of their royal family."

Temar said nothing, and I sighed at him. I was about to say that I did not know the answer, when it popped into my head. "Kasimir's father was killed at the Battle of Voltur."

Temar leaned close. "In Ismir, there are those who call that battle the Battle of Betrayal. Do you know why?" I shook my head. I did not know much of the end of the war. "Duke Dragan, Kasimir's father, was heir to Voltur—they considered it their land. You know that Voltur was the original seat of Ismir, yes? It had always been contested. It looked like Ismir would win the mountains.

"Dragan arranged for his troops to move through a small pass north of the battleground. They would have circled back behind our lines and cut the men down in the dead of night. It was a good plan, but Dragan's advisor, Mihail, betrayed them. Dragan's best warriors were caught in the pass by our archers. Dragan signed the peace treaty in return for his life, and his brother has held to it. But Dragan killed himself nine days later, and there are rumors that Kasimir seeks to avenge his father by taking the land he considers to be his."

There were the shouted cries to make way for the King, and the clamor of his guard, and as the great ceremonial doors opened, Temar and I slipped into the side chamber, taking our places behind the Duke.

I tried not to look around myself, awed, and focus on the people in the room. As always, I was struck by how young the King appeared—until one saw his eyes. He was hale enough now, but Garad's recent illness was slow to leave him, and his rich clothes hung loose on his frame. Even with his height, he seemed young, at best gangly and coltish despite the proud set of his shoulders.

For once, I had the chance to look at him in proper light, not trying to pretend that he and Miriel had privacy in some darkened cellar. I was able to examine his face, and I was struck by what I saw. His eyes were old. They were not handsome, or long-lashed, or particularly expressive: they were a middling blue, set deep in his pale face. But they were old. Those eyes had stared death itself in the face, I thought. And worse things, I thought wryly, thinking of the matters the Council discussed. Those eyes had seen death warrants and torture reports, had heard the accounts of famine and disease in his nation, rebellions against him before he had even had a chance to rule in his own right.

I looked around at the men, each of them puffed up with their own importance. They were ready to give advice, and they expected it to be taken. But this was not a boy for the ordering, I thought. Garad was no longer the sickly boy who must take his medicine, who had no strength for political matters. This was a young man who had seen darkness and trusted nothing. He was a young man who had started to form his own council from the children of those his Council trusted the least. The Council was going to find themselves with a handful of trouble one of these days if they did not have his goodwill, and I wondered how many of them knew it.

Looking around at the faces of the great Lords, I thought that some might be beginning to understand. Arman Dolgurokov, the Dowager Queen's brother, watched Garad with a measuring gaze; he had been intelligent enough neither to ally himself with any of the three generals, nor set himself forward. He would lay low until he knew which way the wind was blowing. The Duke watched

Garad as he watched everyone: as if he would strip away all of the masks and illusions and see his soul naked.

Guy de la Marque scanned the crowd as if he would see where danger waited. He had the look of a man who has found the earth crumbling under his feet. The court, willing to accept his army with only alarmed mutters in dark corners, had turned on him with a vengeance when they heard he had tried to snatch up the King as a son in law. Now, faced with a warlike rival in Ismir, and allegations that he himself had provoked the Ismiri towards battle, his best hope was to escape this meeting unnoticed.

"So, my Lords." The King's voice was light. "It is time to compose a formal message of condolence to King Dusan regarding the regrettable death of his son and heir, Vaclav. My messenger tells me that Vaclav was found dead by his servants, either of illness or of poison." He paused, and scanned the crowd. If he saw me, he gave no sign of it.

"The more pressing matter," he continued, "is that Kasimir, Dusan's new heir, has accused us all—you, my Lords, as well as me—of murder. He is advising Dusan to march for the border."

Whispers rose, and the King held up his hand. The room went silent. "I do not need you to whisper to each other," he said. "I need your advice to me. When I have made a decision, all of us can return to our beds." He gave a glimmer of a smile. "It may be the last good night's sleep we have for some time."

Hours later, I rapped at the door to Miriel's room, then slipped inside. As my eyes adjusted, I could see Miriel sit up from her post in one of the chairs. She drew her robe around her against the cold and looked at me, her face a pale oval in the dark room.

"Duke Vaclav died," I whispered. I came and sat in the other chair and propped my boots on the fender. "He was King Dusan's heir." A terse nod from Miriel showed that she remembered this.

"Murder?" she asked, in a whisper, and I felt a brief pang that a girl of fifteen, woken from sleep, should ask about murder as if it was an expected part of life. But I nodded back.

"Everyone thinks so. Everyone says it would be Kasimir, the new heir, only Kasimir was the first one to say it was murder. He's saying it's us."

"Was it us?" There was no horror, only interest. She asked, knowing full well that she was expected to marry the man who might have ordered such a thing.

"I don't think so."

"What will the King do? What does he *want* to do?" There was a good deal of bitterness in her voice, more than the question warranted, and I frowned at her. She looked down at her lap. "Now that I know I must say what he wants to hear."

I did not respond to the sentiment. She had been a fool to think differently, and she was realizing that now; it did no good to comment on it. "He still wants peace," I said. "His councilors are urging war. Guy de la Marque's forces are still close, they could be on the march with the royal army within a week. The Duke doesn't like that it's not his command and his men, but he doesn't trust Kasimir."

"Garad won't go to war," Miriel predicted. "He didn't want to, and now they've told him to do it, he'll be set against it. He's always hated how the three generals fought on the Council, he says war is the worst thing for a nation."

"We had better rest," I said, reaching out to help her to her feet. "And you be on your guard. The stakes have gone up again, and the Duke will be having you watched. He'll be planning a way for you to play this; he'll be working on a way to keep you in the King's eye so no jumped-up lordling with a talent at war and a pretty heir catches his attention."

"Like he did, himself?" she asked, with a flash of her dark humor. I did not smile.

"Exactly like that," I said.

Chapter 32

Time passed with agonizing slowness. It seemed that the courtiers hardly dared to breathe as they waited, each day, for a messenger riding hard from the west. After so many centuries of war, border skirmishes and misunderstandings that had turned to outright battle and destruction, the courtiers could not help but think that war was inevitable. Garad might stave it off, but he could do no more than that; no one could do more than that

Months turned slowly, and spring came and went. The Dowager Queen, who had first commanded that the Court go to services twice daily to pray for peace, gave way in the face of the muted panic she saw in the nobles. She no longer assured them that their prayers would keep war from Heddred—now she organized parties and banquets where the ladies danced as the spirits of spring, or paid tumblers came to delight us all with their skills. Even she, that most grave and pious woman, was trying to distract everyone from the looming specter of war, and even she could not do so: as soon as the tumblers departed and the last strains of music faded, eyes turned fearfully to the empty throne, to the doors, to the pages waiting in the corners. Nothing could keep the fear at bay for long.

Summer dawned, and still the country teetered on the brink of war. Messengers seemed to come and go daily, but no one knew what news had been brought. No one knew what to do at all. The members of the Council were most often absent from dinner, and when they were not they sat at their places looking drawn. In response to relentless queries, they would say only that the King had everything in hand, and the Court should rejoice and make merry; that they themselves did not believe it was clear, and the Court grew more and more afraid each time they heard the lies.

The most lively portion of the court was the maidens, who continued to dress finely and dance prettily, but even they knew enough to speak quietly at dinner and appear grave for the Dowager Queen. There was little laughter, there were no toasts or cheers. Everyone's eyes flicked up to the royal table, as if they might gauge the mood of the royal family. The maidens were caught, expressly commanded to enchant a King who was most often absent, and who, when he did manage to come to dinner, refused absolutely to speak of the issue at all.

The courtiers petitioned, but Garad refused to comment on the situation publicly, beyond an initial assurance that the peace held. When he came to dinner he sat, perhaps looking grave and drawn, but serene. He would speak to his mother, who, having at first been calm, and then forcedly cheerful, now looked as if she might have been carved from a block of ice.

Garad would also lean to his left, to speak to the envoy. That man looked harried, more afraid even than the courtiers, he looked as if he expected a knife under the ribs or poison in his food, and he ate his dinner each night without looking out at the hall, where every pair of eyes watched him with mistrust and avid interest. The maid I had hired to spy on him told me that a candle was always burning in his study, that even when she came at dawn to take his laundry away, he was working, and that his manservant went everywhere in their chambers with dagger, ready to defend his master. The envoy was worn down with the strain of trying to keep his country at peace, and he was terrified.

Messengers came and went every day, riding hard and being escorted directly to the Council chambers. Messengers set out from Penekket, proclaiming the king's innocence in Vaclav's death and asserting, with stilted formality, that House Warden would be forced to respond decisively to any accusations. Just as often, messengers arrived from Ismir, often escorted by guardsmen from Voltur, and what they said, no one knew. The members of the Council walked about with their faces like thunder, and the rest of the court subsisted on scraps of information and rumors.

Miriel's conversations with the King meant that, for the first time, I had an idea of how much Temar might be filtering the information he gave me. I was chagrined to realize just how much he passed on to me when I thought to ask. I could only conclude that the Duke saw no reason to keep Miriel ignorant, not imagining that she would have any use for such information; with an impending war on his mind, his mistrust of his niece had faded. I would have liked to believe that Temar was passing information on to me of his own accord, feeling guilty for having once told me that I did not need to know such things—I knew, however, that Temar would only tell me, and thus, Miriel, those things that the Duke expressly permitted.

I knew, therefore, from both the King and Temar, that the King was desperately trying to avoid war. It seemed that he alone believed it could be done. Dusan, like the majority of the King's Council, had lived through two wars between the nations, and they believed that enmity and war were the natural state. The envoy was quick to assure Garad that King Dusan was also desirous of peace, but equally quick to murmur that Dusan's Council was as warlike as Garad's. Kasimir daily demanded justice for his cousin: the heads of whoever had been party to the assassination, and, of course, the return of Voltur, to avenge his father. When Garad demanded to know how many of Dusan's Council agreed with Kasimir, he was met only with silence.

"All of them," he whispered to Miriel one night, his head in his hands. "Every one of them thinks I'm a murderer and wants me beheaded, or thinks I am innocent but would stand by and see me killed anyway."

I knew from Temar that Garad did not lose his temper in the Council meetings. Temar could see that the King was not best pleased, but had never seen Garad yell, had never seen him insult his councilors. The Shadow wondered at it, calling it unusual in a young man, and I must work hard to keep my face straight. However much the King might have entered into this crisis with a vision of peace and prosperity, he was now wavering between fear, worry, and frustration. He did not rage at his Councilors to their faces, but he fairly shouted his anger later, as he met with Miriel in the darkened cellar. He pounded on wine barrels and threw up his hands as he ranted of their stubbornness, their relentless warmongering, their belief that he was a naïve child. He had no sympathy, and no love, for those who could not share his vision of the Golden Age.

"And the uprising in the south," he had snarled. "As if now was the time, when we might be overrun by the Ismiri!" Miriel said nothing to this, she had not voiced her thoughts on the uprising since she and I had spoken. She would speak with Garad on any other topic, appearing as light-hearted and earnest as she ever had, but she would not speak of the rebellion. When the topic arose, she sat back and let him speak, and said nothing at all.

"I cannot have such ideas spreading," he said, shaking his head. "If they cannot support me, then I will need to show them that just because I seek peace, I am not weak. This Jacces will need to learn that he cannot understand the way of the world, so far away in Norstrung. His ideas have no place in Heddred. I've told Nilson that there is nothing more important than bringing this man to justice—he will see it done, and then the rebellion will crumble. It would not hurt for the Ismiri to see such a thing, I think."

At my side, Wilhelm Conradine looked down at his feet. I had noticed that when Garad spoke of the uprising, it was not only Miriel who fell silent. Wilhelm would watch the two of them converse when they spoke of theology, or history, or discussed how best to word a statement to King Dusan. He looked at Miriel as if he thought his heart would break, but he watched the two of them with a smile. But when Garad mentioned the uprising, Wilhelm always looked down, as if he, too, disagreed, and he, too, knew better than to say anything. Worse, he looked disappointed; he had hoped that although he was too cowardly to do so himself, Miriel would continue to defend the rebels, and he chafed at her reticence.

Miriel made little meaningless murmurs, stifled a fake yawn, and escaped back to her room as soon as she could. She walked as she always did now, she walked through her whole life as if she were hollow inside. The King no longer seemed to see her, or surely he would have noticed that there was something sad behind her eyes.

Not seeing her pained smile, he joked with her that he would make her a part of the Council, for she was the best of his advisors. He even told her that he should thank her uncle for raising such a wonderful girl, not hearing the note of hysteria in her voice as she protested against it. The King, powerful and precious in his own right, had never feared his guardians as Miriel did hers. It would not have occurred to him to think of it.

Miriel now sparkled as brightly as ever when she was being watched, but the moment the doors to her room closed behind her, all of the life drained away. She no longer pretended to ignore me, or snapped criticisms of the things I did; she knew that I continued to keep the secret of her meetings with the King, and she cared little enough what else I did.

Now that the matter of the King's marriage had been set aside, the Duke had ruled that Miriel was in less danger. No woman was making progress towards marriage with the King, for the King no longer tolerated discussion on the topic in Council meetings. He was devoted, entirely, to the situation with Ismir. He did not visit the maids' chambers, and he barely watched the court as they

237

danced. Most importantly, the Dowager Queen did not watch the women as closely.

"You may return to your lessons," the Duke told me one day, barely looking up from his paperwork. "You are to continue learning from Donnett and Temar especially. They have been told what to teach you."

And so I returned to my lessons with Donnett, who snorted at the idea that I had been busy enough to warrant a halt in my training. He drilled me on the use of a shield and a spear until I could barely lift my arms, and when he finally deemed me proficient in the use of both—after several weeks—we began all over again with the first dagger strikes he had taught me.

"Aye, ye practiced 'em before," he agreed, over my protests. "Will ye never learn, lad? It's better to know fewer things better. What good does some fancy strike do ye, if ye're dead in the first minute of a fight?"

Temar, also, returned to the basics of my training, almost deathly earnest. We sparred every day, until my disused muscles returned to their former strength, and he lectured me on the exercises I must do every day, on my own. Then, he pushed me harder. I trudged down to the laundry every day with a pile of clothes, unwilling to lie all night in sweat-soaked linen, and prayed every night before going to sleep that no assassin would come for Miriel when I was so exhausted.

Roine re-mixed the potions for my lessons, and took me back into her rooms each afternoon without comment. She insisted, however, that I be her assistant. Every day, for the duration of my lessons, I was to deal with any basic injuries that would arise. I set bones, bound cuts, and applied salve to burns. It did not matter how much I spoke of my need to learn more antidotes, Roine was implacable.

"I have to go to my other lessons," I protested.

"People aren't healed just because you have lessons," Roine said, flatly. "When you've brewed tea for the pain and delivered it, you can—" She broke off, and I looked round curiously. Miriel stood framed in the doorway, hovering uncertainly on the threshold. It was the first time I had ever seen her look as if she was not sure where she should be.

She had a new gown, I noticed, a warm brown trimmed with gold. The Duke had insisted that she have new things to wear, that she be dressed finely all the time. He had ordered her a new wardrobe for the fall, warm colors that suited her and set off her eyes. He said he could not take the chance of having an opportunity for her to meet the King, and have her looking dowdy and provincial. I had tried not to laugh at the thought of Miriel meeting the King each midnight in her nightgown and robe, knowing that the Duke would not find it amusing in the slightest.

"Can I hide here?" Miriel asked, without preamble. I noticed that her face was white, her jaws clenched.

"Of course you can," Roine said smoothly. "Catwin, you can make Miriel some tea while you brew Eric his pain medicine." I rolled my eyes and went to comply, ladling water from her urn into a pot that hung over the fire. I cast a curious glance behind me. Roine did not seem the least bit surprised by Miriel's presence, and I remembered that sometimes, while I was learning to fight, Miriel would find her way to Roine's rooms and talk of philosophy and politics. I felt the usual wave of jealousy.

"Do you want to talk?" Roine asked, low-voiced, and Miriel shook her head, then shrugged. Self-consciously, she adjusted the necklace she wore, topaz and citrine set in gold. She was not accustomed to wearing so much jewelry, but the Duke had expressly commanded it.

"It's nothing new," she said helplessly. She took a pomander from a bowl on Roine's table, one of the few luxuries Roine had in her rooms, and rolled it in her fingers, looking at the pattern of the cloves in the orange.

I stood off to the side, watching this strange friendship and trying to shove away my jealousy. I should not complain, I knew, but Roine was the closest thing I had to a mother, and Miriel was the closest I had to an enemy, even if she was probably the closest I had to a friend, too. Even if we had settled into a tenuous peace now, I could still remember the days of her endless cruelties. Our newfound friendship did not make her friendship with Roine any more bearable.

"Has something happened?" Roine asked.

"My uncle wants me to meet the King," Miriel said. "He has plans for it, and what I must do, and what I must say, and what I must wear, and he lectured me on it until I wanted to scream. I wanted to tell him that I had met the King already...but I didn't," she added hastily.

"Have you told the King of this?" Roine sat across the table from Miriel and watched her carefully. Miriel nodded.

"I told him he must seem to be surprised, that he must not let my uncle know we had met before. He laughed and said that he was the King, and nothing bad would happen to me if he commanded it. He said that my uncle would be glad to know that his niece was so clever with advice. I..." I saw tears in her eyes. "I *begged* him not to say anything, and he laughed at me." Her voice was shaking, and I looked away, not enjoying the memory of the last night's meeting; I had wanted to make an excuse and drag her away, but had been unable to bring myself to accost my own monarch. At my side, Wilhelm had looked as if he, too, would hit his cousin and take Miriel away. But neither I nor Wilhelm had done so; it had been Miriel who stood up to Garad, and she had done so alone.

Now, Roine reached out to take her hands, and I saw Miriel grip them so tightly that their skin was white as death.

"I'm so scared," she whispered. "He'll kill me." I thought of her uncle's cold smile and shivered. I had no doubt that she was correct.

"He won't kill you," Roine said carefully. "You mustn't think that. He will be angry, my Lady, but what he wants is for you to have the ear of the King, and when he knows that you have it, he will accept that."

Miriel shook her head. "He'll never forgive me. He'll always suspect me now. And what if the King tells him what I've been advising?"

I placed the tea on the table, in its little earthenware pot, and then went back to the hearth. I would be late for my lesson, I thought, and Donnett would make a fuss, but I needed to hear this.

"What have you been advising?"

"That he be lenient with the uprising in the south." Miriel picked at her nails. "He wants to crush it. So there's only war on one front, he says."

"But?" Roine poured a cup of tea and handed it to Miriel.

"Thank you. But I don't think it's right. And anyway, it's taken hold, he won't crush it with soldiers, especially not quickly. He's planning it all wrong." I felt my mouth quirk, even as Roine's face gave a flicker of distaste. Miriel was very like her uncle sometimes.

"What he doesn't see," Miriel said, her voice rising slightly, "my uncle, I mean—what he doesn't see is that it doesn't matter what I tell Garad, or what anyone tells him. He'll do what he wants to do. He wants to send soldiers, and so he will, and what I say doesn't matter."

"It *does* matter," Roine insisted. "It is up to you to find a way to speak to him that he will listen."

Miriel wrapped her fingers around the mug of tea. It was jarring, to see a woman in exquisite silks and embroidery, sitting in a healer's workroom and holding an earthenware mug, but Miriel seemed to think nothing of it. Her eyes were far away.

"Now that my uncle knows I am giving advice, he will tell me what to say," she said carefully. "He will say that it is my duty to convince the King of one thing or another, and he will expect me to do so."

"My Lady, listen to me." Roine's voice was earnest. "You told me that the King could free you from your uncle, and that was true. If the King loves you, and takes you into his household, then the Duke's anger will be nothing to you. Whatever you may feel for another man..." Miriel looked at her sharply and Roine broke off. "No other man can give you the safety of the King's love."

"What is the point of that?" Miriel demanded, resentfully. "When the King is only another man, who wishes to hear only those who agree with him?" I could hear the disappointment sharp in her voice.

"The King will learn in time to listen to you, even when your thoughts are different from his," Roine assured her. "It is your duty to be a good advisor to him. Else, what will come of your ideas for the future of Heddred?"

"I'm tired of duty," Miriel said flatly. "I have no heart to advise the King anymore. He will do what he wishes. I care not—I only hope to survive." She looked off into the distance. "I know what to do, it has only been foolish fancies that have kept me from doing so until now."

"What is it?" Roine stared at her, worried.

"I'll teach him how to crush the rebellion, if that's what he wants to do." Miriel stared down into her tea. "It's what my uncle would do, and it might just save me if he found out I'd been advising the King.

"And I'm not his heir for nothing, anyway," she added. "I know how to use an army." Her voice was so distant that I had a vision of her as a general, staring out at a battlefield. I almost thought I could see the battle reflected in her eyes, men clashing together, fighting and bleeding and dying while she watched without expression. "It will endear me to both of them," she said thoughtfully, as if she had not a thought for the people she was sending to their deaths.

"At a terrible cost! At the cost of a cause you, yourself believe in!" Roine was stricken. Miriel looked over at her like a beautiful statue.

"Yes," she observed. "But, do you know, I will not lay my life on the line for Garad or my uncle to cut it short. They have taken all my hope from me, and I will be damned if I will let them take my life as well. They have taken everything, and all I have left is ambition—I will live, if only so that one day I can wish them the joy of the woman they have created. And so now, I will choose my time, and when Garad asks, I will teach him how to crush the rebellion and it will be over in a month."

I was reminded of the girl who had looked so haunted as she stood in front of me, covered in bruises. I was reminded of the girl in the cart, wrapped in furs and looking as if she was waiting for something. Had she been waiting for this? I shivered. I no longer knew which of us was the light, and which was the shadow.

Miriel stood and smoothed her gown. "Thank you for the tea," she said courteously, and then she swept from the room.

I ran after her, and at the door, I held up the stoppered bottle of pain medicine Roine had wanted me to brew. I did not want a lecture on my own duty. Roine hardly noticed me; she was staring after Miriel, and she looked sadder than I had ever seen her.

Chapter 33

As winter drew closer, the Duke arranged for Miriel to meet the King. The kings of Heddred had always given audience during the days, even the Conradines had done so when the capital was at Delvard. Garad had never been able, however—as he lay sick in his bed, business took place in the Council chamber in his name, and his mother had been the one who listened to petitions from landowners and religious houses. Now, well once more and keen to prove to his people that the country was as secure as it had ever been, Garad would begin granting audiences, starting with formal presentations of each of his lords, and their families.

I was to accompany them, and so I was given new clothes once more, so fine I could hardly believe they were meant for me. I could have laughed to think that a year ago I was wearing castoff, patched homespun. This fabric was as fine as water, and the clothes were tailored exactly to my growing frame. I would fade into the background, for sure, but I did not care. I would look as if I belonged in Miriel's train, even though she was being fitted for a gown that was a triumph of sophistication. She was to look chaste and queenly, the Duke had said, and he himself had come to the fittings to speak with the seamstresses.

Miriel's coloring was ill-suited to the usual pale colors worn by the maids, the brilliant whites and palest blues and pinks that they wore, fur-trimmed, for the winter. Unlike Marie de la Marque, whose pale skin and golden hair were set off perfectly by yellows and whites and pale blues, Miriel faded, her rich dark hair out of place against the modest color palette. Her skin might glow against a deep red, and her hair might lie beautifully against cloth of gold, but those colors were immodest for a young woman, and cloth of gold was for royalty. The Duke would not be so overt.

In the end, they chose a gown of deep blue, trimmed with silver and cream. The color was passably solemn, not so inappropriate for a young woman.

"Like a winter sky with stars," the seamstress said, and I saw the Duke's grim nod.

"It must be perfect," he said, and the seamstress curtsied and set to work.

Miriel was to wear it modestly, with a muslin shift underneath the beautiful square neckline. For her ears, the Duke had given her beautiful earbobs set with pearls and diamonds, simple enough but lovely against her hair.

On the day of the meeting, we were both called to the Duke's study for a lecture on etiquette. It was strangely reminiscent of my first meeting with him, I thought, my clothes new and finer than any I had worn before, and my hair freshly-washed and braided back tightly from my face.

Now, however, I stood at Miriel's shoulder. I was no longer an unknown, an urchin with dirt under my nails and no thought of the future, or the country. I was a girl who stood at the right hand of the woman who might be Queen. I knew more of the country and its squabbles than did many of the great lords. And the stakes were higher: instead of a girl who might be banished back to the kitchens, I was a girl who could be beaten or killed for disappointing the Duke.

My heart was already pounding as we left the room together, all of us walking silently together, Miriel and the Duke, and behind them me, and Temar. I watched the proud set of Miriel's shoulders, and wondered what she was thinking. Was she still afraid that the King would betray her secret to the Duke? I thought that her fear of her uncle was the one emotion she still felt these days; I doubted that she ever feared the Dowager Queen, or the enmity of Guy de la Marque.

The King's audience chamber was humming with activity. Liveried servants offered refreshments to petitioners, who looked awed to be holding such fine goblets. Nobles packed the room, all dressed in their finest clothing, and the King and Dowager Queen sat in state on their thrones; at his shoulder, Guy de la Marque, and at hers, the High Priest, an ever-present show of Godliness. I had found, from watching, that I feared him. I saw how his eyes could pick out any face in the crowd, how he looked on each of the courtiers with the self-satisfied disdain of the pious. I wondered what he saw in us. I wondered what he advised the queen, and what counsel he kept in his own heart.

Next to Miriel, I watched as each family moved forward to be presented, showing off the elegance of their houses. Minor nobles and members of the old houses alike had adorned themselves with so many jewels that they could barely move without clinking.

I saw the Duke's sneer at this, and thought it amusing. The old families held that displays of wealth were Common, and the Duke, now holding one of the oldest titles, disdained the behavior as a matter of course. He must, for he came from a merchant family; when the other members of the council had sneered at his wealth, he had been too unsure of his new status to be as shrewd as he was now. He had not heard the note of jealousy in their voices.

When the cry went up, "Voltur!" I felt my heart twist. Miriel's chin lifted slightly, and she placed her hand lightly on her uncle's arm as they processed up the length of the room. Temar and I were forbidden to be at their sides; only nobles would be presented, and to have bodyguards would be to doubt the King's peace. Indeed, all were forbidden from carrying weapons in the King's presence, and so the two of us had only the multitude of weapons we could carry unseen. We moved along the side of the room to stay close to our charges. Luckily, no one seemed to notice us. Miriel was still a favorite for the King's hand, and attention was focused on her as she gave a beautiful curtsy. The King and his mother inclined their heads, and I saw Isra watching Miriel with narrowed eyes.

"My Lord Duke." The King's voice was light and warm. "Today, we give you thanks for your service on our Council. Your advice guides us always." The Duke inclined his head, looking pleased.

"Your Grace," he said smoothly. "If I may present my niece, the Lady Miriel DeVere."

"I remember her well. You are to be commended, Voltur. The Lady is both charming and intelligent," the King said, and I saw the Duke's eyebrows raise in surprise. "I had heard her name spoken as one of the most worthy of the ladies, and when we were introduced at the Winter Festival, I knew the words to be true. Indeed, in the past months, I have often sought her advice."

There was a moment of absolute silence, and then the whispers began. Isra was leaning back, the High Priest whispering in her ear, but her eyes were open wide, staring at Miriel in amazement, and the Duke seemed to have frozen in place. Out of the corner of my eye, I saw Temar turn to look at me, accusingly; I kept my eyes, resolutely, ahead, and watched Miriel. She had gone white as snow, but stood with her usual half-smile on her lips.

The King beckoned the Duke closer, and he went, looking bemused. I strained to hear; even the Queen was leaning forward in her chair, the Head Priest inclining his head to hear without looking as if he, too, was listening in. My ears were sharp enough to pick out the flow of the words, at least.

"My Lord, I pray you do not take it amiss that I have sought out her advice," the King said, casting a smile at Miriel. I felt a flash of anger—he truly thought that all would be well. He had no idea the danger he had put her in. "It was I who asked her not to speak of it to others. I see that she has kept my confidence, and I am glad of it."

"She is a good girl, Your Grace." The Duke's grim voice was like ice. "She is loyal to the crown, as are we all, I am sure."

"Of course." The King settled back in his chair and smiled over at his mother. This had been a warning to her, I realized, to her and to de la Marque, who had smiled confidently when Garad danced with Marie. He was warning them that he would not be ordered to marriage, just as he would not be ordered to war.

At that moment, I hated him; my fingers clenched, and I only barely stopped myself from reaching for one of my daggers. Garad was my King, and I would have struck him down if I had dared. He had thought to give his advisors a warning, and he had done so at a terrible cost to the woman he claimed to love. I did not think he had spared a single thought to the enmity and hatred that would follow her now. I did not think he had realized that his mother, thwarted, would not direct her venom at him, but at Miriel.

He could not, perhaps, have known what vengeance the Duke would exact, but he might have taken a moment to wonder why it was that Miriel pleaded with him so desperately not to tell her uncle about their debates. He could not see, even now, the undercurrent of tension that ran between Miriel and the Duke as they walked backwards from the throne. I myself felt a hand close like a vise around my arm.

"The Duke's study," Temar said softly, his mouth right by my ear. "*Now.*"

Miriel and I were nearly thrown into the center of the room by the Duke's guards, where we stood together in shame, trying not to reach out to one another for support. I could not bear to look at Miriel's face; her hurt at the King's betrayal would be too heartbreaking to witness, and her fear too closely echoed my own.

The Duke, cleverly, did not yell. He paced up and down behind his desk and he let the silence grow and stretch. He cast looks over to both of us that were filled with loathing, with disgust.

He gave us time to wonder what he was thinking and what he would dare. He could not kill Miriel, perhaps—I trembled at the thought that I was not even certain of that—but I knew that he could kill me. Who would protest? Roine? I was no one, I could disappear and no one would think to miss me.

What would he do to teach Miriel a lesson? If she would no longer heed him, the most he could do would be to gain from her glory, take whatever scraps she and the King threw to him. He would never accept that. They were the same in that way: Miriel's own furious pride might have come directly from him.

"I told you when you first arrived here that I would tolerate no rumors against your chastity," the Duke said at last. He swung around to face us. I saw Miriel almost sigh with relief. The waiting was over. "I see now that this was inadequate," the Duke continued. "I see that your mother failed to instill in you even the most basic sense of duty and proper behavior, or of family loyalty." Miriel's jaw tightened at the reference to her mother, but she said nothing.

"Do you know what you are, Miriel?" She shook her head. "You are nothing," the Duke stated coldly. "You are the daughter of a second son and a merchant girl. Your mother made a fool of herself at this very court, did you know? I thought perhaps that if I took you from her soon enough, you would not learn her regrettable standard of behavior. I was wrong again. You have no sense of loyalty, and you have no sense of propriety."

Abruptly, his hand slammed down on the desk, and both of us jumped. "You are nothing!" he yelled again. "Nothing!"

"I have the ear of the King!" Miriel yelled back. She had come, abruptly, to life. "Which is what you wanted of me!" There was a moment of silence, while the Duke walked around the table and took her by the chin. He jerked her head up to stare her in the eyes.

"You gained the ear of the King with whore's tricks," he accused her, venomous.

"She *didn't*!" I cried out, before I could stop myself.

It was as if the Duke saw me for the first time. "What?"

"I swear to you, they talked, only. She told him that she could not meet him like that because it would compromise them both, and he told her that he wanted a friend, only that. He insisted, my Lord. And I swear to you, nothing has happened beyond talk."

The Duke released Miriel, and I heard her give a long, shuddering breath in as he walked over to stand in front of me. I stood up and looked him in the face, sure that I saw my death writ there. He was going to kill me now, he was that angry.

The blow, when it came, was almost as hard as any I had received from Donnett, from Temar. My ears rang, my vision clouded. I could taste blood in my mouth and there was a cut from his signet ring on my cheek. I staggered, and just when I had recovered myself came the second blow. This time, I fell, and the next thing I felt was a kick to the gut. I cried out, I could not help myself.

"Do you see, Miriel?" the Duke's voice came from above me. "This is what happens to those who betray me. How did you buy her loyalty? How did you trick her away from her rightful lord? Answer me!"

"I didn't, I never asked it of her," Miriel whispered. "I told her not to come with me to meet the King. I told her she should not know." I could hear fear in her voice. She did not know the right thing to say.

"Liar." He kicked me again, and I doubled up, holding my stomach. I could feel tears starting in my eyes; I did not want to die like this. I waited for the next blow.

"My Lord." Temar's voice was light and clear. "If I may offer an opinion?"

"Yes?" The Duke did not sound pleased to be interrupted, but he knew to listen to Temar's advice. He used the toe of his boot to push me over on my back, and I stared up at him, tears in my eyes, waiting for Temar's words. Useless to attack the Duke, if Temar was not on my side; I must pay attention. I must know what the assassin would say.

"The Lady Miriel made a terrible error in judgment, my Lord, but she did so on the order of the King. I believe Catwin that nothing improper has occurred, and indeed, the King is taken enough with the Lady that he was willing to speak of it publicly. This is not a man who wishes to ruin the girl secretly and marry her off. The Lady Miriel has secured his affections, as you had hoped.

"Miriel has obeyed the King, and Catwin has obeyed Miriel and kept her safe. What Miriel and Catwin require, my Lord, is a reminder of where their first loyalties lie—which is with you, of course. "

"Huh." The Duke looked at me. He studied me for a moment. "Get up," he said, at length.

My head was still ringing, and I was sure that there was blood dripping from my nose. I scrambled up, hunching over my stomach. I caught one glimpse of Miriel's face, anguished, and looked away.

"I am not convinced," the Duke said softly. "I told Catwin to warn you, Miriel, that I had no use for an heir who would not heed me. Did she do so?"

"She did, my Lord Uncle." The title was bitter in Miriel's mouth.

"And did you not understand? Was it too complex a concept for you to grasp?" His voice rose, and he took a deep breath. "I remind you of it now," he said. "I, and I alone, will decide how you are to behave with the King. Your loyalty lies with me, and I will not tolerate disobedience from a girl such as you. I will decide how best to deal with this breach of trust.

"I told you once that if you caused a scandal, I would have you beaten to within an inch of your life. I no longer believe that will be sufficient. Clearly, another approach will be necessary. Go, and do not leave your rooms until I send for you. You," he said to me, "will stay with Roine until I decide what to do with you. It is clear to me that I cannot trust the two of you in the same place."

Miriel curtsied, and I managed a bow. Temar left with us, and at the door to the hallway, he stopped me with a hand on my arm.

"The Duke will not forgive lightly," he said. "And consider this my warning to you, too, Catwin. I could have let you die, but I put myself at risk to speak against it. I will never intervene on your behalf again. Do you understand me?"

I looked up into his black eyes, as pitiless and hard as jet, and so much bitterness rose up to choke me that I could not respond. I left him standing in the doorway and followed Miriel without a word, ignoring the curious stares at my battered face.

Chapter 34

Roine tended to me quickly, passing her hands in front of my face and studying my eyes. There would be no concussion, she said, and there were no loose teeth. My nose had swollen slightly, but was not broken. No ribs had been cracked when the Duke kicked me, although the bruises would last for some time. She pointed to a packet of herbs that I could use for the pain, and told me that I should study, to distract my mind.

I shook my head, listless. I should be with Miriel, I thought. She would feel very alone without anyone except her maidservant. She would be wondering if she would be sent home, or to a nunnery. If she were to stay, her life would be a misery—the Duke would watch her closely now, and she would have the hatred of the most powerful nobles in the kingdom.

"How is Miriel?" Roine asked, guessing the flow of my thoughts.

"Despairing," I said bleakly. "She took a liking to Wilhelm, and she gave him up to pursue Garad, never knowing what might have been. Then she thought she had found a friend, and now it seems he does not care for her at all. She does not see anything anymore, save ambition."

"She would have been a good Queen," Roine observed.

"She might still be Queen," I said, surprised.

"Not a good one." Roine was labeling herbs as she spoke, wrapping up the little packets. She looked up and saw the question in my eyes. "She could have been his match" she explained. "He would have learned to respect her, and she could have guided him to a more enlightened age. But she crumbled."

"What do you expect?" I asked, my own pride pricked on Miriel's behalf. "She has no one to support her if she loses the King's goodwill. She'll never have her uncle's trust again, and he's a hard enemy. Without the King, she has nothing—and he's the King, she has to say what he wants to hear." I rubbed my eyes. "I have to go see her."

Roine only raised her eyebrows and shook her head, evidently deciding that the discussion was beyond resolution.

"Well, you can't go now, the hall's swarming with guards. Go study," she directed me, and I trudged over to my workbench.

"I'll go later," I said. "I'll go check on her when everyone's asleep."

"Then work. I will be back soon, I am going to go pray."

I worked late into the night, jumping every time someone came to the door, but it was never the Duke's men. Very late, when I had drifted into a doze on the bench, one of the palace guards came with food for me, and Roine shook me awake.

"You should go straight to bed. A guardsman brought you a tray, but the food is cold now."

"I can't go to sleep." I shook my head. "I have to see Miriel."

"You don't," Roine said simply.

"I'm going," I said to her, tired of her admonishments. "What time is it? I'll go an hour after midnight."

"Then eat," she said softly. She was pale and her eyes were red-rimmed, and I thought that she must be very tired. "I must go tend to something, but you eat, and go to sleep for a bit."

All I wanted to do was go to sleep now, first, but I knew her advice was sound. As she left, drawing up the hood of her cloak and slipping out the room, I sat down at the big table and ate as much dinner as I could force into my twisting stomach. My eyes felt heavy by the time I gave up, pushing the tray away mostly untouched. I should have gone to sleep at once. Instead, I propped my chin on my arms and considered the day.

I was alive only by luck—by the grace of the Gods, if I were inclined to be religious. I was not. It had only been a twinge of loyalty from Temar that had saved me, and I could never depend on the same in the future. I wondered if it had been worth it to use that now, knowing what might come.

The Duke would be furious right now, I thought. I did not even know if Temar's intervention on our behalf had worked. I should prepare myself to return to the Winter Castle in disgrace, or accompany Miriel to a nunnery. But, on the other hand, Miriel had the ear of the King. If the Duke thought he had any chance of controlling her, he might wish to keep her here, and try to cow her into obedience.

What I feared more was the enmity I had seen in the eyes of the Queen. She had stared at Miriel today as if she would slay the girl where she stood. She had leaned back to whisper in the Head Priest's ear, and he had nodded, his own eyes like chips of stone.

And on the other side had been Guy de la Marque. The Duke had been correct that they would not flinch at killing a child. They saw power slipping out of their fingers, and I did not think they would realize that it was the King's will—they would see Miriel as the threat, and set themselves to destroy her.

I wished I could talk to Temar about this, but I knew better than to send for him. He would not come, he was angry with me, although that would be only part of what he felt. He would be feeling a fool, knowing that I had fooled him, and he would not like that. He would be feeling betrayed, that the girl he had trained had turned away from him. He would be feeling worried, as the Duke felt, that their plans were unraveling.

I sighed, and resolved to talk about it with Roine in the morning. She would yell at me when she came back and found me still awake, I thought, with a wan smile. As I knew she would want me to do, I tried to arrange the things on the food tray, reaching for the fork to place it neatly on the plate.

It fell, clattering away from me, and I stared down at the floor in surprise. I reached for it, but I could not seem to make my hands move properly, and when I bent down my head spun. I barely steadied myself on the bench, and tried to shake my head to clear it. I reached for my goblet, for a gulp of wine, and only managed to knock it over.

I stared, my head starting to spin. Something was very wrong, I thought, but the thought was far away from me. I knew that I should care, but I could not to feel very worried about it. Why should I care? I tried to remember, but my thoughts might have been moving through molasses.

Miriel.

Panic stabbed through me. That was why I should care. Miriel. I shoved myself back from the table and tripped, sprawling. As I lay, my cheek pressed against the cold flagstone, I thought that I should care because this was poison, poison in my food, and anyone who thought to poison me would know how to poison Miriel. And no one would poison me, who did not wish to poison her also. I tried to think, and felt despair rush through me. I could not make my mind work. I could not think of what I should do.

Roine would be coming back, but I did not know when, I did not have time to wait for her. I pushed myself up off the floor, barely making it to the table before my legs gave way. I leaned on the surface and tried to wrap my thoughts around what I must do:

an antidote. I needed an antidote for me, and a dose for Miriel. Quickly.

There must be a part of you that nothing can touch, Temar had told me. I had failed, that time. I could not fail now. I could hear his voice in my head, echoing strangely. *Now you're dead, and Miriel is dead.*

Oh, Gods.

Poor focus. Lost balance. Slow muscles. Tired. I scraped my teeth over my tongue, trying to taste anything unusual from the food: pine, and something warm. A spice?

Roine and Temar had both taught me that a proper antidote was mixed not only to the particular makeup of the poison, but also to the strength of the poison. I had no time to determine any such thing. I made my way over to Roine's shelves, propping myself up as I went. This was a slowing herb, and I knew what to use to counteract that. I could only hope that whatever was in my food had had no special properties to it.

I poured leaves into the mortar, mashing at them desperately. I had no time. I needed this to work. I did not even mix them with water, unsure if I would be able to make it to the bucket and back. I put the leaf mixture in my mouth and chewed, trying not to spit the mixture out at the bitter taste, trying not to choke.

It was the best shot I had, and I did not have time to see if it would work. If I waited any longer, Miriel might be dead; I could not face the thought that she might be dead already. I poured the leaves, shakily, into a scrap of paper on the table and folded it as best I could, then pushed my way out into the hallway.

It was almost deserted, only a few servants and guards to remark on my progress, the guards laughing at me as I staggered.

"Ye need to learn yer limits!" one called after me. "Boys these days," I heard him say to his companions. "Can't hold their liquor." Their laughter rang after me as I ran. I thought that it was getting easier to see. By the time I reached Miriel's rooms, I was sure of it; my fingers closed easily around the latch, and I pushed my way in. Her maid was such a fool that she had not even closed the deadbolt on the door.

"Miriel?" I asked, into the dark. "Miriel?"

Nothing, no sound greeted me. I pushed my way through her privy chamber, still unsteady on my feet, and was met at the door by her maidservant.

"What do you want?" She asked. "You're not to come in. The Duke's orders. And she's not well."

"Let me through."

"No, you—" I managed to get my foot behind hers, and spun her, shoving hard and slamming the door in her face, bolting it. "Miriel!" I hissed. It was pitch black, and I made my way to the bed with my hands stretched out before me.

There was a faint rustle, and a slight moan.

"Miriel?" I climbed onto the bed, reaching out to touch her face, her hair. I shook her shoulder. "Are you alright? Do you feel alright?" I shook her shoulder again, desperate, and her head lolled towards me. She was not waking, although I could see her struggling to get out of the haze.

"Please," I said desperately. "Miriel, wake up. Please wake up. You need to wake up now." Nothing. My heart was going to beat out of my chest. Awkwardly, I hauled her up to lean against me, her head heavy on my shoulder, and I reached around her to pour the herbs into my palm. "Can you eat this? I'll hold you up, but you have to eat it."

"No," she murmured. "I can't..."

"You have to," I pleaded with her. "Or you'll die. Please."

"Die?" The word was a breath.

"Yes. You've been poisoned." Her head dropped towards my hand, and I tipped the herbs into her mouth. "Chew. Don't spit them out. You have to chew them for a long time, Miriel, to make the oils come out."

"Mmf." I put my hand over her mouth.

"You can't spit them out." I kept my hand there for a minute, counting in the darkness, and then I said, "Now swallow them." I felt her throat work, and she made a gagging noise. She was hardly moving.

The wait was agonizing. The serving woman had banged on the door at first, but that had ceased; I assumed she was going for the Duke. I flexed my fingers, and was pleased with their response. The antidote had worked, for me—but what if I had been too late for Miriel?

I tried to steady my breathing. The worst had happened. Someone had tried to kill me, to kill us, and I did not know who. This was no knife fight in a darkened corridor, with the interrogation techniques Temar had taught me, this was a whisper in the dark, death like a kiss. I tried to run through names in my head, and closed my eyes against the sheer number of them.

Gradually, so gradually that I thought I might have been imagining it, Miriel's breathing grew stronger. She shifted against me, rolling her head along my collarbone.

"I don't feel well," she said, finally, and I could have laughed in relief.

"It gets better," I said, my heart fairly pounding out of my chest, and I found that my arms were wrapped tightly around her. "You'll feel better soon."

"Mmf." Miriel pushed away from me and rubbed her face with her hands, clumsily, then looked up and around the darkened room. "Why are you here?" she asked, curiously. She did not remember, she had been deep down, so close to death that I swallowed to think on it.

"Someone tried to poison us," I said. "I was in Roine's rooms, so I was able to make an antidote."

"Who?" Miriel asked, and I swallowed, then held up my hand. I counted off my fingers.

"The Dowager Queen and the High Priest," I suggested. "Guy de la Marque. Perhaps someone else on the council. Jacces, of course." There was a pause. I did not want to say the last name on the list.

"My uncle," Miriel said, unflinching, and I nodded.

There was a long silence, broken by the sound of men shouting in the outer rooms. Miriel reached over, unsteadily, and pulled me close again. Her dark eyes were shining with tears. Her forehead was nearly pressed against mine.

"Say you're on my side," she said, simply. When I opened my mouth, she touched my hand to stop the words. "My side, and no one else's." Her deep blue eyes were pools of black in the darkened room, holding mine. The beautiful fringed lashes, the red lips, the beguiling tilt of her head—all of it disappeared. There was only the dark gleam of her gaze.

"What, now? Now that someone is trying to kill us?" The pounding of feet was in the privy chamber.

"That's why we need each other," Miriel say. "You're the one who came to save me, you're the other one they tried to kill. I need you to be on my side. Not my uncle's side, not anyone else's. Not Roine's." She paused. "Not Temar's."

I paused, and she, this strange fae creature with her soft voice, smelling of bitter herbs and rose perfume, waited. Neither of us paid any heed to the banging on the door.

"I promise," I said, slowly. I tried to form the question, but I did not need to.

"And I am on your side," she said. "I promise. The two of us, we're our own side." I felt dizzy. I had been given one task alone: to be Miriel's shadow, to protect her. I spent more time in her company, watching her, thinking of her, than anyone else in my life, and I did not think that I would ever understand her.

"Should we open the door?" I asked her.

She nodded, and released her grip on my collar. "Yes. You have your daggers?"

"Always." I exchanged one last look with her, then hopped off the bed and straightened my tunic.

"Open up!" It was Temar's voice. I stared for a moment at the door, saying goodbye to a friend, and then I walked over and opened the door.

Epilogue

The two figures stood in the cold, watching the night sky. Their voices were lowered against the bustle around them.

"It was a foolish attempt." Cold, accusing. "You could have guessed that it would go wrong."

"I saw an opening, and I took it."

"Now they know. Now they're on their guard."

"Now we know for sure what they are capable of," the second asserted. More quietly, they added, "We will not fail again."

"No." The first considered the sliver of the moon. "We will not have another chance at them, before it is too late. We must try a different tack now. Watch them carefully. And watch yourself—they're not fools, you should assume they'll suspect you. This time, you will wait for my orders."

"I will."

####

*Thank you for reading Book I of the Light &
Shadow trilogy! If you enjoyed the book, read on for an
excerpt of the sequel, Shadowforged. Whether you
liked the book or not, I encourage you to take a few
moments to leave a review—not only will your
feedback help other readers to make an informed
choice, but it will help me to improve my storytelling!
You can find more information about my books,
including upcoming works, at my website:*

http://moirakatson.com

Read on for a sneak peek of:

Shadowforged
Light & Shadow, Book II

I knew the dream by heart now. I could hear the snow crunching underfoot, and the hungry moan of the wind, but I felt no cold on my skin. I was home and not home, I would have a chance once more to see the mother and father I had never known, who had given me away on the very day of my birth.

As I did every night, I wavered as I stood in front of the door to their hovel. I could go in and see my father pleading with my mother to keep me, and my mother pleading with my father to give me a quick death, and spare me the betrayal that would otherwise follow me all my life. Some nights, I would walk away, through the village, staring up at the Winter Castle through the billowing snow. Tonight, I pushed the door open and went in.

I watched the familiar argument without comment. I was a shadow in the corner of the room, a young woman that my father could never see. He pushed his way past me every night; I had never been brave enough to see if he would walk through me. Tonight, as I did on many nights, I waited for him to leave. My mother would see me, then—what she saw, I did not know. She did not know me for her daughter, but some nights I truly believed that she had seen across the years, and spoken to me, myself. I waited for her to tell me that I would be betrayed, that my betrayal would be the end, that my sorrow would tip the balance.

But tonight, instead of lying shivering in her pallet bed, she levered herself up and stared at me. After a moment, she motioned for me to come closer and hesitantly, I obeyed her. I had seen this dream every night for a year, and never had it changed. My heart, which had been beating slow and strong with sleep, began to race; I knew this was a dream, but I could not wake, I could not flee. I only knew that I did not want to hear what she would tell me.

"So," she said to me. "The betrayal has come." The sound of her voice came across years, like the baying of hounds, like the trumpeting of the warn horns. "You survived. But it is far from finished."

I woke suddenly, the echoes of her unearthly voice ringing in my mind, and saw the early morning sunlight streaming in the windows. For a moment, I hardly recognized where I was, so jarring was the quiet calm of daybreak after the sound of the storm, and the terror of my dream. I was soaked in sweat and breathing hard, and I lay back and tried to concentrate until the gasps slowed. At last, I opened my eyes.

My clothes were rank with sweat, and I sighed at the thought of going to the laundry. I would be late for my lessons, and Donnett would scold me. Then I remembered that I could not go to the laundry. I could not go anywhere at all. I would stay here, in these clothes until the Duke decided to let me leave this room.

This was the sixth day of our captivity here, and every day stretched interminably. We waited, Miriel and I, for the Duke to make his move, not knowing what events had come to pass outside this chamber. We knew that the court must be in an uproar, quite as shocked as the Duke had been to learn that Miriel was the King's confidant, his friend, his mistress in all but deed. What did they think, now that we had not emerged from our rooms in near to a week? We could not know; we knew only that the Duke was furious with us, and we were growing so tired of waiting for his judgment that I felt we would very nearly welcome the fall of the axe when at last it came.

On the big four-poster bed, I heard a rustle, and I looked over to see Miriel crane her head over the side of the mattress to peer down at me. By the look of it, she had been awake for some time, waiting for me to wake up as well. She raised an eyebrow, as if to ask about my harsh breathing and my sweat-soaked brow, but when I shook my head, she shrugged and inclined her head silently towards the door. I nodded and lifted my clothes off the shelf quietly, and she took her robe from the foot of the bed, and we crept out of the room together—not to her privy chamber, but to the receiving room, where her maidservant might not hear us if we spoke.

Each day for a week, Miriel and I had woken early and gone out to the main room together. She would tie her robe closed and then sit in one of her beautiful padded chairs by the hearth, and I would restart the fire from the last night's embers. When it was crackling again, I changed from my sleeping clothes to my usual black, while Miriel averted her eyes courteously.

Then she would gesture to the other chair—it had become a ritual as graceful as a dance between us—and I would curl into it and stare at the fire. In the half an hour or so we had before the maidservant woke and came out to find us, glaring at us accusingly, we would sit silently and stare at the flames in the grate. Our thoughts went round and round together and both of us knew that there was no need to speak them.

Danger was forefront in my mind; danger, and the fact that we were trapped, helpless, at the eye of a target—no way to run, and nowhere to go even if we could have escaped. In this snare, we thought endlessly on our helplessness, as the Duke undoubtedly meant that we should. When he had found us trapped in Miriel's rooms, frozen with shock at the fact of our escape from death, he had hardly wasted words on us. *Think on your allegiances,* he had said curtly, *think on who you wish to offend.* And he had gone, giving orders to the guards that we were not to be let out.

Now we waited. We were singularly quiet in our confinement; it was one of the things that so unnerved the new maidservant. The old maidservant had disappeared, inexplicably replaced by this dour woman. She had been tasked with watching us, to make sure that we sent no messages, and made no attempt to escape. She was outmatched, completely useless as a guard. If I was minded to, I could have killed her in a moment, and even Miriel was well-versed enough to sneak messages out past her. It was the Duke's guards, and Temar, who kept us confined and cut off from the world. But the woman felt obliged to do her duty as the Duke had instructed her, and she resented us for making it clear that she was ill-suited to the task.

Neither Miriel nor I was minded to make it more pleasant for her; I had taken to sharpening my daggers each afternoon, while Anna looked over at me nervously and Miriel tried to hide her smile. Miriel, meanwhile, affected not to notice that she had been kept in the room by her uncle's order, and took to sending for ridiculous things: a specific book from her uncle's library, a new quill to write with, a length of ribbon to decorate a gown, a lute to practice one series of notes over and over again while Anna gritted her teeth.

All of our jokes were wordless; we shared whole conversations with the lift of an eyebrow, a hidden smile. We moved silently, in concert, and this unity unnerved Anna all the more. We took joy in our unity, for there was precious little joy in our lives. We had no true allies beyond each other, and we had a great many enemies. Miriel had said one day, in a rare break into speech:

"It almost doesn't matter, does it?" I knew what she meant, and agreed with a silent nod. With so many enemies who might kill us, who would kill us—what was the difference in singling out the one who had tried? To follow that lead to its end, oblivious of all else, was to ignore the swarm of enemies that surrounded us. And so, instead of spending my time puzzling over it, I recited, every night, the litany of our enemies: the Dowager Queen, the High Priest, Guy de la Marque, Jacces, the Duke. Every time I recited, I wondered how many more names I did not know.

It was one thing to be practical, and be wary of all enemies, but I held out hope that we might yet learn who had done it—and why. I did not need to tell Miriel to watch the faces of her fellow courtiers when she was finally allowed to leave the room, and she did not tell me to make enquiries to find the servant who had brought us the poisoned food. I was already working to determine what type of poison had been used, and Miriel knew as much. Miriel was always watchful, and I knew as much. Together, if we could find our would-be killer, we could find a motive.

Today, Miriel surprised me by asking:

"What do we want?" I considered the question. We wanted our freedom, but that was not enough. Open the doors to this room, and we were still in the palace. We could not leave—where else was there? Miriel had no family, no allies; she could not live as a peasant. I had nowhere to go, either—Roine was my only family, and she was here at the Palace—and in any case, I could not leave Miriel. It would be to leave a girl to her death, without even the comfort of a companion.

"What do you mean?" I asked, unable to determine what she might be asking. My voice was rusty from disuse. She paused, then shrugged her slim shoulders. Even her simplest gesture was elegant. I thought of my own face, plain and nothing, against the dramatic beauty of hers, and thought wryly that it was good that I was the shadow. She would never fade into the background.

"What's our goal?" she clarified. "My uncle hasn't killed us yet, so he probably won't." She was matter-of-fact; if it bothered her to think that her own flesh and blood would have her murdered, the emotion did not show in her eyes. She could be as cold as the Duke at times. "Which means, we should decide what to do when they let us out of here," she continued. "Every faction has a goal, and we're a faction. So, what do we want?"

I closed my eyes for a moment. It still seemed strange that her words had not been on a dream: *We're our own side*, she had told me. I could hardly believe it, just as, if I were to close my eyes, I could pretend that there had been no attempt on our lives. If I concentrated, I might pretend that the Duke had never discovered the secret of Miriel's meetings with the King. And if I closed my eyes tightly and blocked out the world, I could almost think I was home, in the Winter Castle, ignorant of the world and free of its machinations. Then I opened my eyes once more and I was trapped in this little suite of rooms, with too many enemies to count, and a fifteen year old girl as my ally against the world.

"It's whatever you want," I decided after a scant moment of thought. I did not add, *but I wouldn't mind running away*. I had the wild notion that we could do it, run away and survive on our own. But that would never do—they would find us someday, and Miriel could never be happy in a hovel, with homespun. Still, it was amusing to picture her living off the land.

The truth was that I did not know how to decide what we wanted. I always told Roine that I could not leave Miriel, but the truth was that I had nothing else in my life, no place to take refuge. There was only the palace, and that was Miriel's world, not mine. And above all, I had sworn to shape myself to her like a shadow. I hated the man who had made me promise that, and I had betrayed him—but the promise had stuck, somehow. Miriel's fate and my own were intertwined, but my fate was tied to the words of a madwoman, and the thought that Miriel might be dragged into my fate was too strange; she was the light, the glittering one, the girl who might be Queen.

"Do you know, the brightest hope in my life was that I could love the King, and be a good Queen to him," Miriel said softly. "And that cannot be. Now I do not know what I could hope for."

It was jarring to hear those words from the mouth of a fifteen-year-old girl, and it made me want to cry. It was like peering down into Miriel's very heart, and seeing the girlish hope for happiness, the simple desire that her duty and her heart should lead her to the same end. Somewhere, Seven Gods alone knew where—not from her mother, not from her uncle—Miriel had come into a sense of morality. When her life had descended into a living hell, what she had clung to was her streak of idealism. She had cherished the dream that her purpose of catching the King's heart could do good for the country.

She had wanted it so much that she had tried to forget the boy she might truly have loved: Wilhelm Conradine, the King's own cousin. She had tried to turn her heart, and she had seen only a piece of Garad: his dream of a golden age, a peaceful age. She had once believed whole-heartedly in a future where they ruled as equals, her at his right hand and her advice healing the nation from its centuries of war.

Now she knew that her heart had betrayed her. Miriel had not understood that a boy of fifteen, emerging from the certainty of his own death and burdened with the weight of kingship, could not be the man she hoped to love. He could not admit mistakes, and his decisions were too weighty to be undone without strong will and a graceful heart, an ability to name himself as wrong. Garad was not that strong, he was too driven to be loved, too driven to be a storybook King with a perfect kingdom. Above all, he was not Wilhelm, the boy whose smile inspired Miriel's own, the boy who shared her sympathy for the rebellion. Garad had been born to power and death; having eluded death, he would not give up even a piece of his power.

And, with the unbending morality of the young, Miriel would never forget this, and never forgive it. Having thought that Garad shared her vision, she had believed that her life might yet be happy. It had been devastating to see the illusion shattered, and Garad's belief in his own idealism did not make it any easier to bear. She felt that she had been made a fool of, and she knew as well as I did that her attempt to escape and set her own course had set her in the full glare of the court as well, at the mercy of the forces there.

And Garad, of course, was the King. He could command Miriel to be his Queen, he could ruin her if she refused—and how could she refuse, what else was there for her? What other man could be what she had hoped for from Garad? No other man in the world, save perhaps King Dusan of Ismir, could give Miriel the chance to be such a force for good, on such a large scale. Garad would command Miriel to his side, and then force her to watch as he betrayed the sentiments she held so dear. He would never see her pain, and I could not say if that made things better or worse. I did not know how Miriel would bear it, save by stripping away her idealism. And what was left then? Only ambition.

She was my ally, and the other half of myself, in ways I could not have explained. But I feared her sometimes. I wondered if she ever feared me, who already had blood on my hands, who watched the world through the eyes of a spy. Even I feared myself. And, if I was not so foolish as to believe that I could keep my hands clean by riding out the storm in the Duke's shadow, I feared what would come when we chose a path.

"What *can* we do?" I asked, to distract Miriel from her melancholy. "What choices do we even have?"

"We don't have any choices yet," she admitted. "But I've thought about it, and being on our own side means that we're always waiting for our luck to turn—for a chance, something that could set us free."

"Free from the Duke?" I asked, and she tilted her head to the side.

"Free from our enemies," she said. "But I've thought...what does it mean that we can't tell who wanted to kill us? And it means that everyone is our enemy."

"We should trust no one," I agreed. Miriel smiled, satisfied to hear her thoughts from my mouth.

"Exactly." She sobered at once. "We have to stay, there's nowhere to go, and anyway, no way to leave. Which means we stay in a court that hates us."

"Then our goal is to stay alive," I said. It was a poor jest, in part because it was no jest at all. Miriel's mouth only twitched, half-heartedly.

"Garad is our only ally. Him, and Wilhelm." She took a deep breath, and I saw her fighting to tell herself that what she felt for Wilhelm was nothing more than a girlish fancy, and in any case could cause her nothing but pain. "But, Wilhelm is powerless, and that leaves Garad."

"Not a poor ally," I said. *But a fickle one.* She nodded at the unspoken.

"And then our enemies. We know some of them, but not all, and they're powerful. Which means we need Garad's favor, yes?" I nodded, and she nodded back. "Yes. And I said we should wait for a chance, something that would set us free..."

"The throne," I guessed, and she nodded.

"It's the only way to survive at Court. I must make Garad make me Queen. My uncle should help us. And when I am Queen, then we have power in our own right. But until then, nothing is more important. I mean it, Catwin." Her gaze sharpened. "Not

Roine. Not Temar." I swallowed, as I always did when I thought of him; I hesitated when I thought of Roine's steady faith in me. But I nodded.

"Not the rebellion," I rejoined. "Not Wilhelm." After a pause, she nodded.

"You know, I wanted to make Heddred whole," she said. "Above all, I want to help this rebellion. And once, I wanted Wilhelm. But I can never have Wilhelm...and I cannot help the rebellion without first having enough power to do so. I can't see any other way. So I must forsake it for a time, so that one day I can come back and help it..." I had no response, and so we sat in silence, thinking of what we would give up: for Miriel, her dream of happily ever after, and her sense of justice; for me, my loyalty to my family, and my childish love of Temar.

"You know, if we do this, we will be without honor," Miriel said. I frowned, questioning, unable to follow the sideways slant of her thoughts, and she looked back at me, meeting my gaze openly. "We will be liars, every day, to everyone but each other, won't we?" I nodded, uncertainly, and she smiled suddenly, feral and dark. "Then perhaps we should not fear other sins. We will make our enemies live to regret that they ever went against us. And then, when they are gone, we will shape Heddred to what it must be."

I shivered. Was this only the angry words of the scorned and powerless? I could agree if I believed that we would never be able to exact our revenge; what I feared was that we might be able to. I could imagine it only too well. I knew that at this very moment, I could make my way into any noble's rooms and kill them as they slept. Sometimes, I wondered why I did not do so. I shuddered.

"It is not all dark," Miriel said, understanding. "Catwin, this is a dark path, but the end is good. And think—do we have any choice? I've wondered, sometimes, if the Gods mean us to tread this path. That is our fate together—to lose everything we have held dear until now, so that we may heal our Kingdom." I looked at her, and saw a woman whose fierce idealism was warped into ambition; I feared for her, and yet—

She was right. There was no other path. My dream came back to me, and there was the feeling of a net closing around me, fate drawing me into a pattern too big for my eyes to see. I shook my head involuntarily.

"Let's worry about surviving, first," I said softly, to distract myself. "I don't think that part is going to be easy."

"That's your task," Miriel reminded me. "To keep us both alive. And mine is to enchant the King." Unconsciously, she straightened her shoulders, turned her head to show the line of her jaw. Her uncle had bidden her to learn how to stir a man's desire with only the set of her head, and she had learned it well. He might regret that, now that her talents would be set to the task of enchanting the court for her own purposes, and not his. He had always used us for his own ends; now he was our enemy, even if he did not know it.

"What are you thinking?" Miriel asked me.

"Fooling your uncle is the first thing we need to do," I said softly. "There are only two ways to survive having him as an enemy. One, make him think we're friends again. Two, be stronger than he is." I looked over at her, and she nodded.

"Or both," she said promptly, and I thought that the Duke would indeed be sorry that he had forged her into such a woman. He should not have had her taught military history. She was quite good at it.

"Or both," I agreed. "So for now, we have to make him believe we're all friends again, so he can help you become Queen." Miriel nodded decisively.

"You keep us alive, and I will become Queen." It was a poor jest, in part because it was no jest at all.

"You're not afraid he'll lose interest before you can get a treaty signed?" I asked curiously. It was the other question that had been worrying me. Garad had flaunted her to the court, he had taken great joy in defying his guardian. What if that wore thin, and reality intruded, before Miriel got a crown on her head? But she only grinned at my fears, a knowing smile.

"I can do it," she whispered back. "You'll see. I'll do it. One way or another." She smiled. "I'm the best, the very best."

There was the sound of a door opening, and both of us sank back against the chairs without another word. The maidservant came into the room and glared at us. I smiled blandly back, but for once she had the grim smile of a gambler with a trump card.

"The Duke is coming to see you this morning," she announced. "So look sharp."

Miriel rose gracefully from her chair. "Of course we will make his Grace, my uncle, welcome," she said smoothly. "Come help me get dressed, Anna. Catwin, stoke up the fire and send a page for refreshments. Fresh fruit, and chilled wine."

It was indeed a gracious welcome—and an extravagance, of the sort the Duke abhorred. It was the gesture of a Queen, such as the Duke had wished Miriel to become—and a reminder that she had come closer to the goal on her own account than he would like. I quirked my mouth, and hastened to do her bidding.

Made in the USA
San Bernardino, CA
23 July 2016